ECHO ACROSS TIME

BOOK 1 IN THE ECHO SAGA

Skye Genaro

BRIGHID PUBLISHING
PORTLAND OREGON 2016

This book is also available as an ebook.
First edition published December 3, 2014
Second edition published April 6, 2022 v13
Jupiter Neptune Conjunction

Cover designed by: RAVVEN
http://www.ravven.com

Interior designed by: BRIGHID PUBLISHING

Also by Skye Genaro

ECHO INTO DARKNESS, BOOK 2 IN
THE ECHO SAGA

ECHO INTO LIGHT, BOOK 3 IN
THE ECHO SAGA

ECHO RISING, BOOK 4 IN
THE ECHO SAGA

FOUR FIRST KISSES (AN ECHO ACROSS TIME
SHORT STORY)

AFTER THE DANCE (AN ECHO ACROSS TIME
SHORT STORY)

SUPERNATURAL SUMMER

ANYTHING SHE WANTS

For Chuck, my real life prince, who is there to tuck me in every night.

Lovers don't finally meet somewhere.
They're in each other all along.

-Rumi

CHAPTER 1

Mr. King slapped my physics test face down on my desk. I didn't need to flip it over to know that studying had been a waste of time. I sensed, from the surge of disappointment coming off my teacher, that my grade was awful. I kept my head down, letting my long chestnut hair fall around my face, and debated whether it was safe to look at the test result.

All around me, my classmates were having normal reactions to their grades. They winced and slumped or smiled and fist pumped. Others pasted on a fake smile, trying to cover up that they'd failed. I knew all of this without looking because I felt each of their emotions just as surely as if they'd blasted me with a fire hose. Fun fact? I live with this. All. Day. Long.

"What'd you get?" Becca nudged my elbow and stuffed her test into her backpack. She'd done well. I could tell by the warm, bubbly feeling radiating off her.

"I'm afraid to look." My forehead just above my eyebrows started to tingle, and the tips of my fingers prickled. This was not a good sign. "Why do I even need physics? Gravity:

good. Explosions: bad. That's all I'll ever need to know once I graduate."

"I'm sure you did great. You studied so hard," she replied.

"Come on, Echo, don't be shy," a voice taunted from behind. A smooth hand adorned with a diamond ring reached over my shoulder and grabbed my test.

"Back off, Raquelle," I hissed. I tried to swat her away, but I was too slow. Raquelle flipped the pages over. My test had so much red on it, it looked like a victim of a violent crime.

"Oooo, you got a C minus. Aren't you a smarty," Raquelle mocked. Her arrogant laughter rippled through the air and landed, hot and sticky, on my skin.

"How was summer school, Raquelle?" I snapped back. "What was it you had to retake? Intro to Pottery?"

"Hey, Human Compassion studies is pre-AP. It's way harder than it looks," she huffed.

"Only to someone without any," Becca jabbed. Her comment made me feel better, but an all-too-familiar buzzing began coursing through my body.

I lashed my arms across my chest, crossed my legs, and wished that my ability to feel other people's emotions was the worst of my problems. As my irritation rose, the air grew staticky, like the room could spontaneously combust at any moment.

Mr. King pulled down the projector screen and turned off the lights. Raquelle unwrapped a piece of gum and threw the crumpled wrapper at the back of my head.

I clenched my fists, and the tingling on my forehead intensified. If I squeezed my eyes closed and focused on calm thoughts, maybe I could hold back the outburst. Maybe if I just—

The empty desk next to me slid across the floor. The screen at the front of the room rolled up with a loud snap.

The fluorescent lights flickered, and the projector light bulb shattered.

"The ghost returns!" some kid yelled. Another kid hummed a creepy tune.

This wasn't the first time we'd had this kind of disruption in class, and more than one person had suggested the room was haunted. It's not, though. Not only do I feel others' emotions, when mine become too intense, objects around me begin to move.

I took a few deep breaths, and the room returned to normal.

"Everybody calm down," said Mr. King.

He turned on the lights and the kids around me giggled. The contents of my book bag were strewn across the floor. Notebooks, pencils, and some personal items I'd just as soon not mention, had all gotten caught in my energetic outburst.

The bell rang, and Becca helped me clean up the mess. Side by side, we don't look much alike except we're both small and lacking in curves. We used to raid each other's closets before she took to wearing all black, like the midnight Converse and charcoal lace top that she wore today. Becca kept her fawn-colored hair short and spiky. My chestnut hair grew well past my shoulders. Her natural, year-round tan made my fair skin appear washed out by comparison.

"This room is seriously possessed," she said.

"Right? It's like the second time this week." And a third eruption was boiling up. I had to get out of there.

"The weird thing is, this stuff always happens when you and I are in the same place," she said.

"That settles it. *You're* the one who's possessed, not the room," I joked, knowing she'd probably be thrilled to have some ridiculous ability she couldn't control.

"I *have* been trying to express the full potential of my energetic body. Maybe my meditations are finally working." She waved her hands at the lights. "Come on, *flicker.*"

"You don't want that kind of power, Becca. It will mess up your life." I zipped my bag closed. "I've got to pee. I'll meet you in the cafeteria, 'kay?"

I practically ran out of Physics class, then raced past the girls' bathroom and out the nearest exit. I skirted the corner of the building and pressed my back against the cold brick. Out here, under Oregon's stormy October sky, I could relax. Wind whipped through the school courtyard. Gray clouds billowed over Portland's skyline. This was the perfect cover for what I was about to do.

The insistent buzzing that I loathed pulsed in the center of my forehead. A prickly sensation ran up the backs of my legs and spine. I slid the metal bracelets off my wrist. "Just breathe through it and let it go," I coached myself.

I inhaled, and let the air out slowly. Invisible waves of energy exploded off me and unfurled in the courtyard, scattering garbage and leaves. It upended one of the wooden benches and sent it tumbling toward the parking lot. A loud snap punctuated the air. Above me, a fresh crack cut through a window on the second floor.

My buildup had been worse than I thought. Now my muscles felt slack and my near-constant headache was gone.

I heard a tiny squeak. Then another. At the base of one of the trees, a baby squirrel hunched into a ball, squeaking and quivering. High overhead, its mother sat near their damaged nest, screeching at me for causing her kit to fall out.

"Oh no. Ohnononono. I'm so sorry. I didn't mean to do that." I gently scooped up the squirrel, so tiny it barely filled my palm. "I've got you. I'm just going to levitate you back up there. Right back into your nest." I motioned upward, trying to get my telekinesis to kick in and carry the squirrel through the air to its home.

"You'll just float right up there. Right on up." The squirrel did not budge from my hand. "Nothing? Really? Not when I need this stupid ability to work?"

The mother squirrel scurried to the ground and sat on her hind legs, watching. I set her kit down and stepped back. She crept forward, picked up her baby by the scruff of its neck and clambered up the tree. Thank goodness. I felt bad enough about the damage I'd inadvertently caused without accidentally killing wildlife, too.

The next few hours were precious ones, before the next outburst gathered under my skin and threatened to spill over in public. Until then, I'd feel like my normal self, the way I was before the accident, when my life was a boring set of routines set in days that washed into one another. I wanted so badly to be that girl again.

I weaved through the cafeteria, past the jocks and stoners, the math geeks and royalty, to the table where Becca and I usually sat alone. Today, Becca held court with a new customer.

Becca's presence feels light and airy, which is one of the reasons I like her. Although she doesn't know about my telekinetic chaos, she's probably the only person I could tell who wouldn't faint dead away. That's because Becca is hardcore Wiccan.

She practices potion-making whenever she needs to resolve a problem, and believes that every person has an abundance of hidden secret powers. She spends her lunch hour doling out potions and spell recipes to the lovelorn, forlorn and those hungry for power. Most of Becca's customers insist on meeting her in the bathroom between classes. A few are brave enough to cross the invisible lines between cliques and do business openly, in the cafeteria. I suspect that, like Becca, they don't care what anyone thinks. I admire Becca's courage.

I sat next to her and watched her in action.

"This potion can only be used for good intentions, okay?" Becca handed a small glass vial to a girl I recognized from History class. "Telepathic ability is nothing to take lightly," she continued.

"Uh-huh. This'll make me psychic, right?" the girl asked. "I need to find out if my boyfriend is thinking about Hanna Materi while we're making out."

"Follow these instructions exactly and your mystical third eye will open." Becca tapped the center of her forehead. "It's the gateway to all supersensory ability."

My hand floated to my own forehead. The idea that some sort of gateway had recently opened there unsettled me. The girl opened the vial and sniffed. Wrinkled her nose. "I can't wear this in public."

"Put a drop on your wrist before you go to bed. The smell will probably be gone by morning. It's worth the ten bucks." A white lie, but one that would help Becca. Besides, after this transaction, this girl would go back to pretending we didn't exist.

The girl tapped on her cell phone screen and Becca's cell pinged with an incoming payment. A few minutes later, Becca's last clients ambled across the cafeteria with potions secretly tucked in their pockets.

"Does that stuff really work?" I asked with a rawness I hadn't intended.

"Of course. Why do you think all these people come to me for help?"

"That's not what I meant."

Becca sucked in her cheeks. "I know exactly what you meant. That I'm delusional, and none of us really has any power. It's all right, I've heard it all before. I expected better from my best friend, though."

"I mean, do they ever tell you how it turns out?"

"Sometimes," she shrugged.

"And they're happy with the results?"

Becca plunked her elbows on the table. "I know, I know, you think I'm delusional and that superhuman ability is a bunch of B.S."

"Actually…"

"But there's sixty years of research from parapsychology labs like Yale and Princeton…"

"…and a million data points all proving there's latent ability in all of us." She'd said this so often, I recited the last bit along with her.

"I want to know what I'm capable of, so I explore. Psychic healing, telekinesis, telepathy—it's all built into our human potential. Maybe potions aren't the answer but people like them. Besides, I need the money for a car."

"What I meant was, does anyone ever tell you if the potions work? What if someone wanted to get rid of their ability? Like if they could, I dunno, move stuff just by looking at it. Could you mix something to make it stop?"

"You mean telekinesis? Like anyone would want to get rid of that," she snorted.

"They might if they couldn't control it or if it was getting in the way of, you know, normal life."

"I wouldn't, not ever. Just imagine it, Echo: if we could move stuff with our minds, we'd make a ton of money on YouTube! We'd have our own reality show!"

I winced. The psychics on television were regularly blasted as con artists. And a telekinesis show? I may as well paint a target on my back.

"People would call you a liar and always try to prove you were tricking them," I said. "It would be non-stop hate."

Her eyes widened. "Maybe I could mix a potion to give you telekinetic ability. Then you'd see how cool it is."

"No!" I said.

"A potion to make you see auras?"

"Auras?"

"It's the invisible energy field around a person. It radiates their emotions, and a person who can feel auras is called an empath."

I gave her a startled look. So that's why I was able to feel other peoples' happiness and crankiness and everything in between. I was an empath. Oh, happy day. "Uh…"

"Levitation?"

"You know I'm afraid of heights."

"Walk through walls?"

I laughed at the audacity of this. "Thanks, but no."

"Okay, fine," Becca said. "You want to know if I can expel a power. I could probably find a reversal potion."

I finished lunch while Becca talked about the websites she used to search out potion recipes. I silently thunked my knuckles on my forehead. What was I thinking? Becca's belief in magic only existed to fill a gaping hole in her life.

Becca's parents and older siblings treated her like a baby. They didn't allow her to drive and chauffeured her everywhere, even though she'd gotten her learner's permit the same time I did. If Becca had any real power, she'd have telepathically convinced her parents to buy her a sporty little car and take her to the DMV for her driver's test.

The final bell rang, and Becca and I cut across the school parking lot to the secondhand BMW that my dad bought me. I'd asked for a car more my style, like the rusted-out Volkswagen

Beetle we owned in Seattle, but he was trying so hard to make up for uprooting me that I finally gave in to the super cute, light blue convertible with a black roll-down top.

"Ewwww!" Becca said when she saw my car. Someone had dumped a soda cup and its sticky contents onto my hood and windshield. "Raquelle needs to get a life. You should report this to the school."

"I can't prove it was her, so there's nothing they can do. Besides, her dad is a guest speaker for school psychology classes. Everybody loves Raquelle." I threw my book bag onto the back seat.

"She acts like it was your fault she got suspended, but she's the reason you went into a coma. You could have been killed," she said.

Sometimes, I wondered if that would have been better. Ever since I woke up from the coma, I was plagued with these new abilities. And there was more. While I was unconscious, I'd had a vision—or was it a dream?—and it would come back to me in disturbing flashes of light and pictures. I shoved these images out of my mind before they cloaked me in their feeling of impending doom.

"I think there's a towel in the back seat," I said. "Could you get it?"

Becca stuck her head in the car. "Your dad and stepmom should have sued Raquelle's parents."

"I told you, the principal dismissed the whole thing. They decided Raquelle was innocent." I reached for the soda cup but it rolled across the hood and out of reach. Huh, weird. I wasn't feeling all buzzy and I didn't have a headache.

"Are you sure you have a towel?"

"Check under the seats." I chased the cup as it rolled up the windshield. It was moving on its own, I was sure of it.

A crackling sound made me look up. Sparkling lights floated above the sidewalk, forming a vague, human shape, and then scattering again. The mess on the car vibrated and shifted. Gathered into a puddle and poured itself back into the cup. The cup slid across the hood and stopped in front of me. "Whoa. That wasn't me," I whispered.

"Found it." Becca held out the towel.

"Do you see that?"

She followed my gaze. "It's a sidewalk."

"No. The lights. They're right there." And just like that, they fizzled away.

"If you say so. Are you sure you're okay to drive?" she asked.

"There were lights there, a bunch of different colors." I went to the sidewalk and touched the air. Yes, I looked like a crazy person, but the energy was different here. I could feel it coursing through my hands.

"Are you getting one of your bad headaches again? Maybe that's affecting your vision." She glanced at my windshield. "Why isn't your car wet anymore?"

I gave up on the lights and grabbed the cup. Dropped it in the garbage. "I...uh wiped it off with my hand."

The look she gave me, a mix of concern and pity, hit hard. I hated that look. Adults gave me that look ever since the accident.

The sun came out so I rolled down the convertible top for the drive home. I loved Portland. I loved the elaborate murals painted on old brick buildings. Coffee shops, art galleries, and food cart pods were practically on every corner.

West Vista, Portland's richest neighborhood, was perched on a hill overlooking the city. My stepmom, Kimber, won her beautiful, three-story white house in a divorce settlement. When my dad married her over the summer, we'd relocated here from Seattle. My dad traveled the world for his company,

Bennett Global Imports. While I was glad business was booming, I missed him terribly.

As I wound my car up the slope, I couldn't help but be taken in by the view. Portland spread across the valley below and then continued on the other side of the Willamette River. Large pockets of forest dotted the city. White clouds brushed the tops of a handful of skyscrapers. On the far edge of the horizon, glacier-covered Mount Hood jutted eleven thousand feet into the sky.

"You want to come over for homework?" Becca asked.

"Nah, I've got a… research project to do." Truth was, I needed time alone, to unwind from the stress of hiding my ability from the public. I'd nearly reached my tipping point, my nerves wearing thin with the possibility that someone would find out about the tele-chaosing. I called it *tele-chaosing* because I didn't have any control over the things that flew across the room, or the blinking lights, or any of it.

I dropped Becca at her driveway and drove across the street to my house. I let myself in. The front door closed, sending an echo through the broad entryway and into the rest of the enormous house. Nobody stirred inside. No one called out to see if it was me who'd come in or if I'd had a good day at school. My dad was in Asia—or was it Europe? I lost track—and Kimber usually didn't wander home until after dinner.

My head pounded with the need to talk to someone about what was happening in my life. Becca had her mom to talk to, and I was her sounding board when life got really rough. The list of people I could confide in about my paranormal nightmare came to exactly zero. I wanted to tell my best friend but Becca couldn't keep a secret to save her life. Living on the edge, expecting my greatest secret to come screaming out at the worst possible moment, made me want to cry.

I dropped onto the couch, the six magnetic bracelets that I wore rattling on my wrists. I'd read that magnetic fields could disrupt energy fluctuations, so I'd bought the bracelets online. At first, they kept my tele-chaosing in check. But now, either the bracelets were wearing out, or—and this was the part that kept me awake at night—my energy was getting too strong for them.

I scrolled through websites on my phone, bringing up a page I'd found last week:

EXPELLATOR
$49.95
Proprietary blend of ginseng, red perilla, pennywort.
Guaranteed to clear your energy of unwanted abilities.

My finger hovered over the BUY button. Maybe this would fix me. It could, right? But fifty bucks was a lot of money. And it probably wouldn't work. Would it? I set down my phone. Picked it back up. Chewed my lower lip. Decided it was just a scam and turned my phone off.

I tilted my head back and closed my eyes. The vision I'd had while I was unconscious in the hospital shoved into the forefront of my mind.

I stood on a grassy hillside overlooking low buildings made of crystalline rock that reflected the intense sunlight. On the horizon, a mountain soared above foothills. I had an overwhelming sense that this was my home, and yet it didn't look like Portland.

I floated through the air, effortless, watching a futuristic world of glass and chrome pass beneath my feet. I landed on a grassy hillside overlooking a town square. People levitated through the city, going about their business.

I sensed I was not alone.

"Echo," a male voice said.

I squinted into the blinding sun. "Who's there?"

A hand closed around mine. I tried pulling away, but another hand gripped my shoulder. "Who are you? Let go."

"Stay with me," the voice said. Disembodied green eyes drilled into mine.

I tried to squirm out of his grip. "You're hurting me. Please let go."

"I've found you. You're mine now." He leaned close, those green eyes so familiar but so terrifying. A spasm of fear shot up my spine. I tried to pull my hand away, and his grip tightened. Then a bloodcurdling scream—my scream—tore through the silence.

My eyes snapped open and I sat bolt upright. I've heard that the dreams you have when you're knocked unconscious are a window into your soul, into your deepest fears and desires, that they reveal truths about yourself that you refuse to embrace. Based on what I'd felt in that vision, I wanted to keep this part of me tucked far away, deep in the dark chasm of my being. And I sensed it was tied to my new abilities.

CHAPTER 2

"Stare at yourself much?" Raquelle sniped.

Just moments ago, as I walked past the school office window, I caught a glimpse of someone watching me. But when I turned to look, they were gone. I must have stood there a full minute, gaping at my own reflection, when Raquelle walked by.

"Freak," she said and sauntered down the hallway.

The past few days had been so blissful. Ever since the outburst in the school courtyard, I'd hardly gotten any headaches. I'd kept my energy under control so well, I even dared to hope the tele-chaosing was going away.

Now this. Each time I walked past a mirror or a window, I got this eerie feeling I was being spied on. Out of the corner of my eye, I'd see a face staring at me. It always disappeared before I could see it full on. The little hairs rose on the back of my neck, and paranoia was setting in. I hurried to Physics looking like a demented hobbit, my shoulders hunched, my eyes darting at every shadow.

That uneasiness got ten times worse when I walked into the classroom. The air felt heavy and dark, like a storm cloud was about to dump on us, and the short walk to my desk felt like I was slogging through wet sand.

I looked around, wondering at the source. Mr. King shared a joke with a student. Raquelle gossiped, and Becca was an island of calm. The rest of my classmates looked bored. I took out my notebook and tried to ignore my growing discomfort.

"I had that dream again," I said to Becca.

"The one with the green-eyed guy?"

"Yeah, except this time I was in a strange version of Portland. I could see Mount Hood and it kind of looked like our city, except people were flying."

"I love when I fly in my dreams," she said.

"What's weird is, it didn't feel like a dream. It felt like somewhere I've been before."

Becca's eyes lit up. "A place with flying people? Let's go. You figure out where this is and we will road trip."

Half way through class, a glimmer caught my eye. The same lights I'd seen on the sidewalk by my car now swirled by the window. The glass wavered as though it had dissolved into liquid. I elbowed Becca. "Look at the window," I whispered.

She craned her neck, then shrugged.

"You don't see it?" I asked.

"See what?"

Mr. King shot us a look. I focused on my textbook until he turned his back, and then looked at the window again. The watery edges rippled and swam and took shape. A phantom reflection hovered above the sill. I blinked hard, sure this was an illusion, but the image became clearer. I made out sharp facial features, and a pair of piercing green eyes.

Then, as quickly as it appeared, it dissolved.

"You look like you're going to hurl," Becca whispered.

Prickling bristled on my fingers and I made a fist to stave it off. The image could have been caused by a million things, right? Light playing off wet glass. An illusion created by Mr. King's reflection. I was willing to tell myself any number of things to stay calm. None of them worked.

As if on cue, cell phones around the room rang in a chorus of discordant tones. My textbook quivered and flipped open. I smacked my hand down on the riffling pages.

"What is going in here? I want everybody's cell phones turned off or they're mine until the end of the day." Mr. King pointed to the basket on his desk where students had to put their phones if they disobeyed the rule.

"My phone is off. I don't know why it rang," one of the girls said.

"Mine, too," a boy said in the back.

I was still staring at the window. Why didn't anyone else see that it had lost its shape and was dripping down the wall?

"Echo, you seem to know the material so well you don't need to pay attention. So please solve this equation for us."

I snapped to attention. "Um, okay." I hurried to the front of the classroom, more worried about the lights than the fact that I had absolutely no clue how to solve the equation. I grabbed a dry-erase marker. Those lights at the window were swirling fast, now. I ached to stop and watch, but glued my eyes to the whiteboard. "D equals, um, velocity times time? Plus point five? Er, I mean times time, plus…"

The air next to Mr. King began to shimmer. My voice trailed off and I gawked at the form taking shape. First, a pair of jeans. Then, a long-sleeved black t-shirt with the sleeves pushed up. They floated there for a moment, without a body to hold them up. Nobody saw this except me.

Fear is not a polite emotion. All the blood whooshed right out of my brain and icy dread filled my chest. I moved my mouth to speak, but no sound came out. Just when I thought I'd reached the peak of panic, the chilling scream from my dream rang through my head.

"Miss Bennett, is everything all right?"

I managed a nod. Next to my teacher, a fuzzy human image filled the shimmering clothing. Olive skin on hands and arms. Black hair. Green eyes.

It was the guy from my dream.

The translucent phantom scanned my classmates, searching each face with cold intent. Calmly, methodically, his gaze traced up one row and down the other.

"Can you finish the problem?" Mr. King followed my stare to the space next to him, but he saw nothing. My classmates snickered. No one noticed the *thing* next to my teacher.

"Um," I stuttered. At the sound of my voice, the phantom's eyes locked on me. He raised his chin slightly. Drilled me with his glare. Assessing. Scrutinizing.

"Thirty-six. Just say thirty-six," Becca whispered.

"Miss Bennett?"

I glanced between Mr. King and the apparition.

"Thirty-ssssix," I stuttered.

"Is there something else you'd rather be doing, Miss Bennett?"

"Um…"

The bell rang and I slapped my textbook closed. I leaned down to grab my bag, and when I dared to look up again, the phantom was gone.

Becca caught up to me in the hallway. "I hate to crush your vibe, but you're starting to steal my reputation as the school freak. What happened back there?"

"I feel sick. I'm going to the nurse's office." I left Becca outside the cafeteria and hurried down the corridor leading to the office. I cupped my hand next to my eyes to avoid seeing anything that might be reflected in the office window. Or maybe to keep *him* from seeing *me*.

I dropped onto the bench outside the nurse's station next to three other girls. My panic diminished to a dull stomachache. There had to be a rational explanation for what I'd witnessed: high cheekbones forming above a harsh jawline. Veins prominent on forearms. Probing eyes that made me want to flee. This had to be a figment of my imagination. But if he wasn't real, why was my reaction so visceral?

I rested my fingers on my temples. Surely this was a side effect of the coma. Maybe I'd developed a brain tumor from the fall, and that dark mass was cutting off the blood supply and causing hallucinations. This gave me a glimmer of hope. I wasn't going insane. It was just a brain tumor!

While that theory worked to calm me down, I doubted it would hold any sway with the nurse. I tuned into the girls sitting next to me to find out their stories. Right away, I could tell they were faking their illnesses. Their auras were clean and reminded me of diving into a swimming pool. Crisp. Clear. Effortless. The kid who just exited the office was a different story. His aura clogged the hallway with its dense, depressing weight. A cold, I guessed, or maybe the flu.

The girls whispered their strategies for getting sick notes so they could go home early, going with a migraine, a sore throat, and a stomachache. Migraine Faker caught me listening and flashed me a death ray look. "You got a problem?"

I looked away and took out my phone. I tapped a text to my stepmom, Kimber:

I think the coma messed with my head.

Instead of sending, I deleted the message.

When does my dad get back from China?

Delete.

Something is wrong, I think I should see a psychiatrist.

"No. Nononononono." Did I really want to tell my parents I thought I was going crazy? I put my phone back in my bag.

I realized I had another dilemma. If the nurse set me free, one of my parents was supposed to pick me up. Kimber would be at the Rose Club, lunching and getting a massage. If she found out I was sick, she'd break land speed records to get here. Then she'd hover over me with noodle soup and a thermometer and search WebMD until she attributed my symptoms to either schizophrenia or pneumonia.

I dragged myself off the nurse's bench, choosing phantom hallucinations over an overbearing stepmother.

I pulled my coat out of my locker and tried to ignore Becca's look of pity.

"I know what I saw," I said. "He was standing there, right next to Mr. King. He was as solid as you are."

She was quiet for a moment. "Remember when Carter Nash got brain damage during a football game and then one day, he tried to throw his dresser out his second story window?"

"That's not even close to the same thing," I said.

"The point is, his parents got him the help he needed and he's fine now."

I closed my locker. "He's in an institution in Eugene."

"Oh. I thought they just moved."

"I'm telling you, it was the guy from my dream. It was like he was materializing from another world, right there, in class," I said.

"All right, weird things have been happening lately, so I believe you. What do you think he wants?" she asked.

"I don't want to know. He was terrifying."

"Was he naked?" she asked.

"What? Of course not. Why would he be naked?"

"A girl can always hope."

On our way to the parking lot, Becca pulled a glass vial from her backpack and chucked it in the trash can.

"What was that?" I asked.

"Failed potion. Deep Passion Number Two. I've been wearing it all day, and not one guy talked to me. The next batch, though, that'll be the one. Help me out and try it when it's ready?"

Just thinking about going on a date made me feel so… *normal*, but dating wasn't a luxury I could afford as long as my aura broadcasted my every emotion.

I shifted my backpack uneasily and tossed it in my car. "Guys are too much hassle."

"Roger that, but one I can't live without."

Fifteen minutes later, I pulled to the curb in front of my house. Becca took one look at my front porch and her voice rose an octave. "Who is *that*?"

I followed her stare, past the iron fence and the perfect lawn to the guy leaning against the porch column. Black t-shirt. Dark hair. It was the phantom from Physics.

"You can see him?"

My question sounded comical, but Becca just lifted her sunglasses to get a better look. "Can. I. Ever."

He was far enough away that he couldn't hear us, but near enough to spark my instinct to flee. His t-shirt stretched across a sinewy, muscular chest. Aggressive green eyes stood out against olive skin. His stance was guarded. A cowlick of dark hair curled across his forehead, a soft touch that did nothing to ease my anxiety.

Becca summed up his impact pretty well. "He's so gorgeous, he could make a nun give up the convent. Thankfully, I'm not a nun." She climbed out and strode up the walkway to the house.

I parked the car and ran after her. "We don't know anything about this guy," I said in a low voice.

"He seems to know you. Look at the way he's staring."

"Well, he doesn't." But a voice inside my head whispered "yes."

My street smarts, that calculating edge that kept me safe when we lived in dangerous neighborhoods in Seattle, told me to get back in my car and stay at Becca's until Kimber came home. And yet, I was magnetically pulled toward him.

I followed Becca to the porch. "Can we help you?" she asked.

He ignored her and locked eyes with me. A shock wave of déjà vu rippled down my spine and, against my will, my defenses started to peel away. The corners of his mouth curved into a tiny smile.

Becca stepped in close. He took a step back. There was something unsettling in his manner, a rigidity in his expression that made me think he was as wary of us as I was of him.

"My family might be moving in around the corner and my dad's inspecting a house. Do you have a flashlight he can borrow? He wants to take a look at the attic." His voice was deep and disturbingly alluring. I couldn't get an energy read on this stranger, but my B.S. meter was throwing up red flags.

"Oh, really. Which house exactly?" My voice quivered with sarcasm.

Becca nudged in front of me. "Pardon my friend, she's had a really bad day."

He smiled at this. "I'm Connor. Connor McCabe."

"Hellooooo, Connor. I'm Becca. I live across the street. See that house? The blue one with the Mercedes in the driveway?"

We all turned to admire the house overlooking the city.

"I bet you have a great view," he said.

"It's even better from the pool. Come on, I'll show you."

"Maybe some other time." He turned to me. "And you are?"

My energy swirled. The shrub flanking the stairway shook. Next to it, a stem from the potted vine strained to touch my arm.

Great. Here I was shaking with fear and yet my aura was pulsing with attraction.

I stepped away from the plants. Narrowed my eyes and lifted my chin. "Echo Bennett," I said, and I swear, relief crossed his face.

"It's nice to meet you, Echo." Under his piercing gaze, I dropped my eyes and shuffled my feet. How could a guy be so intoxicating and unnerving at the same time?

"Where are you moving from?" Becca asked.

"South of here. Califor… nia," he stumbled over the word.

"L.A.?"

He hesitated. "Yes."

"So, you'll be going to Lincoln High?" she asked.

"As a senior," he said.

While Becca flirted, Connor stole long glances at me, like he was soaking in my every detail. I checked him out, too. He looked familiar, like someone I'd seen in a movie, or a student I passed every day but barely noticed. His tennis shoes were a brand I wasn't familiar with. My chest fluttered at the way his faded jeans skimmed along his strong thighs. My eyes drew upward and my jaw dropped.

Where he'd appeared solid before, parts of him were fading. I gaped at his hand.

I could see right through it.

CHAPTER 3

Connor followed my gaze to his transparent hand. He blinked with momentary alarm and shoved both hands deep into his pockets.

Becca didn't notice. She was rambling on about how great the West Vista neighborhood was and how he should definitely move here.

"I need to be getting back," he said, cutting Becca off.

"What about that flashlight? We've got one," she offered.

Caught in his deception, Connor took a second to recover. "I think we've got one in my dad's trunk. Thanks anyway."

Becca actually batted her lashes. "What's your cell number? I'll show you around school."

Connor's brow scrunched in confusion. "Cell?"

"Your *phone* number," I clarified.

"I…don't have one," he answered.

"Oh really. No cell phone?" I tested him.

"Well, I do have one but it's not compatible with yours," he answered.

"Right." I'd caught him in the lie and he knew it.

Becca didn't seem bothered by any of this. "Then we'll see you around."

"Yes." Connor's eyes lingered on mine before he crossed our lawn in long strides.

"Dontcha just want to sink your teeth into him?" Becca gawked at him all the way to the sidewalk. "I saw the way you were looking at each other. Just admit you want to go out with him and I'll back away."

"Becca, come on. His cell phone isn't compatible with ours? I don't believe any of what he said and you shouldn't either. I bet he's not even moving into the neighborhood. And he's creepy, the way he stares."

"Then why are you blushing?"

My hand went to my cheek. "I'm not." I was. "I've never seen him before but I feel like I know him. Does that make any sense?"

"Maybe you know each other from a past life," she said, as if there was an easy, metaphysical reason for everything.

As his otherworldly presence crossed the street, Becca dove into her backpack for her cell phone, eager to text the world about the new guy in town.

I took my eyes off Connor just long enough to give Becca a weak smile. When I looked for him again, he was gone.

Inside the house, I pressed my back against the door and dug the heels of my hands into my lids. My life was turning into a science fiction novel.

After Becca left, I'd stared at the spot where we'd last seen Connor. In the span of two seconds, he had simply disappeared. Normal human beings didn't just evaporate into nothingness. Nor did their body parts fade in and out. I stretched my shaking hand up to the light, fingers spread wide. The half-moons of my fingernails let the light through, but my fingers, hand, and wrist were solid flesh and bone. Unlike Connor.

What would have happened if I'd tried to touch him? Would I have grasped muscle and tendon? Or a gelatinous, non-human substance? Or would I have passed right through him? No, I decided, Connor was no apparition. Too many things gave him away. The faint sheen of sweat on his cheeks when Becca's questions became too personal. His uncompromising stance. The flicker of relief when I told him my name.

I'd felt it, too. That's what bothered me most about this boy. More than his sudden arrival, more than his obvious lies. The instant I told him my name, I'd felt it. Deep in my chest, in a place left vacant since the accident, a sense of a sense of relief and connection bloomed.

As if I had no self-control whatsoever, my mind shifted to the way his shirt had clung to his biceps.

"No! Absolutely *not* going there! He could be a murderer, he could be a maniac!" I shoved all thoughts of him aside. I had more important issues to deal with than conflicting emotions about Connor McCabe.

My skin prickled, and pent-up stress from the strange encounter intensified, causing the entryway's grand chandelier to swing. I was pretty sure Kimber wasn't home, but I didn't want to take any chances. I ran up the stairs to my third-floor bedroom.

When we moved into Kimber's house, my dad tried to make me feel welcome by loading up my bedroom with anything he thought would make a teenage girl happy: a television, an iPod dock and speakers, a laptop, and a landline telephone that I never used. He called my room the "penthouse suite" because of the attached bathroom and the view of Mount Hood.

I closed the door and yanked off my bracelets. My emotions avalanched into the room, hurling books off their shelves and slamming them into the walls. Pages fluttered and books dropped like downed birds. Dresser drawers opened, and my clothes tumbled onto the floor. My iPod turned on by itself and static blared from the speakers. As quickly as it started, the telekinetic temper tantrum stopped. In less than a minute, my room had become disaster central.

I flopped onto my mattress. In times like these, what I wanted most was to return to my old life. Not just pre-accident, but before that, even. Before my dad's business took off, when the two of us lived in a tiny, two-room apartment. There, I fell asleep to the sound of gunfire and police sirens. My dad drove me to school past graffitied buildings and rundown residences seeping with aggression.

It sounds scary, but I'd learned to understand gunfire: it started as soon as the sun dropped behind the squat buildings in our neighborhood and lasted until well after midnight. I didn't like it, but it was predictable and I knew how to keep myself safe.

Same with the drug dealers: there was the guy with the patchy beard who seemed to live on our corner, and the others I saw on the drive to school. I made sure our paths didn't cross. I was fine. I'd been surrounded by violence and poverty but I had some control over my life. But this? I looked across my mess of a room. I'd never felt so powerless as I did now.

A soft, rhythmic banging from somewhere in the house broke my daydream. For once, I wasn't the source of the erratic noise. I got up and followed it down to the second floor, to Dad and Kimber's bedroom. The door was closed. I knew what was on the other side.

I opened the door, and six pounds of frantic Chihuahua bounded into my arms.

"Tito! You poor thing. She didn't take you with her today?"

Tito answered with a tiny sneeze. He'd spent hours pouting on his elaborate doggie bed, waiting for someone to come to his rescue. I hugged him close and laughed while he slathered kisses across my cheek. Then I scratched his favorite spot, right at the base of his tail. His back leg twitched spastically.

I set Tito on the floor, and he ran to the top of the stairs, panting and dancing to tell me how dangerously full his bladder was.

Down in the kitchen, I let Tito out the back door and he ran into the bushes to do his doggie business. Even though I had no cause to feel unsafe in my own backyard, the little hairs on my arms stood on end. I scanned the area, looking for Connor. My body ran hot and cold with mixed signals. I didn't want to see him again, but also, I kind of did. I wanted to know why his voice sounded so familiar. Why I felt like we had met before. Not in my visions, but in person.

I pulled out my phone and dialed up FaceTime. My dad's face came into view.

"Good morning!" He shouted over traffic noise.

"You mean good afternoon," I said. "You look happy. Selling lots of computer microchip stuff?"

"Yes, lots of microchip stuff. I picked up another meeting in China so I'll be gone a few days longer."

"Again? I miss you."

"And I miss you. You and Kimber getting along okay?" He was outside a hotel, dodging crowds of people.

"We don't see each other much, so that helps." I didn't mean to be rude, but my dad got it. He was the one who fell in love with Kimber. I did my best to blend into a new life that didn't quite fit, with a stepmom who perplexed me to no end. "Hey, Dad, do you remember anyone with the last name McCabe from when we lived in Seattle?"

My dad raised an arm to hail a cab. "Doesn't sound familiar. Why?"

"No reason, I just met this guy. I mean, not a *guy*, guy. Nobody special. Just some dude. He looks familiar." Why was I rambling all of a sudden?

"All right. Well, I hate to cut this short but I finally caught a taxi in this Beijing rat race. Gotta go. Love you."

"Love you, too." I put my phone in my pocket and whistled for Tito. "Come on, boy, time to go in."

Tito gave me a sidelong glance and trotted in the opposite direction. I couldn't help but laugh a little. He and I had a lot in common. He rustled into the hedge that divided the patio from the front yard and disappeared.

"Hey, get back here."

I squeezed through the shrubs in time to see him trot to the middle of the wide front lawn. He pressed his nose into the turf, sniffed, and sneezed. Then he rolled onto his back and twisted his fur into the grass, stubby legs flailing, growling with pleasure. I caught up to him in a few short strides and leaned down to scoop him up. He skirted out of reach.

"That's enough, Tito. Come here."

His whiskers twitched at a shadow near the sidewalk. A black and white blur darted from the corner of our yard, across the street, and onto Becca's porch. My heart nearly jumped into my throat until I recognized that it was only Becca's cat, now curled on their welcome mat and giving Tito the stink eye.

Tito took off across our yard. I yelled for him, but it was no use. He was a Chihuahua with a Napoleon complex, in a longtime battle with Becca's oversized cat. I sprinted to catch him before he got to the street.

As Tito stepped off the curb, the rumble of a car engine stopped my heart. He was in the middle of the road when the SUV rounded the bend and barreled into his path. The little dog skidded to a halt just in time to miss the front wheels, but his momentum pushed him beneath the vehicle. The back wheels crushed Tito's body and flung him to the curb.

"Nooooo! Tito!" I ran to the street. The driver kept going. I doubt he even saw the dog's tiny form intersecting with his vehicle. I fell to my knees next to Tito.

"Oh God, oh no…" His hind legs were crushed and he panted rapidly. Blood seeped onto his fur from a gash in his abdomen.

I broke into sobs. His legs were so mangled, I was sure that moving him would only make things worse. Tito whimpered. His pupils glossed over. He was dying.

I had to get him to an emergency vet. I forced my quaking hands to type *Emergency vet near me* into my phone. I rammed my finger on the 'Call' icon. The phone rang once. Twice. Three times. "Answer the phone!"

From up the street, the slapping of footsteps against pavement grew nearer. I gaped when I saw Connor clearing the last few yards between us.

"Hang up the phone," he said.

"He got hit by a car. I'm taking him to a vet!" I tried to yell, but my voice was hoarse.

"He'll never make it. Echo, please listen to me."

"But I have to take him…" Connor was right, though. It was too late to save him. I reached out to stroke Tito's fur.

"Don't touch him. Move back from the curb." Connor's voice was smooth and insistent.

I shook my head. My tears dripped onto Tito's coat. The vet's office finally answered. "West Vista Emergency Vet. How can we help you?"

"Echo, you have to move away from him."

"Why? This is none of your business! Why are you even here?" My crazed expression would have caused any normal person to back off. It had no impact on Connor. His voice never wavered. His tone never changed. Yet his presence caused more uncertainty and confusion than I could manage.

"Ma'am, do you have an animal emergency?" the vet asked.

"I can help him, but you have to listen to me," Connor said.

"Hello? Ma'am?"

Tito's breathing became shallow. His life was slowly slipping away. Reluctantly, I hung up on the vet.

"What are you going to do?" I asked.

"Go stand on the grass," he instructed. "No matter what happens, do not move from that spot."

"But what…"

"Do it. *Now.*"

I stumbled to the grass. Connor lay his hands a few inches above Tito. The sides of his palms glowed and became encased in white light. Beneath them, Tito's body convulsed. I clamped my hand over my mouth to hold back a scream. What in the world was I doing? First, I let Tito get hit by a car, and now I was allowing a stranger to hurt him.

Tito yelped, and I lunged toward him, but an invisible force hit me in the chest, hard. Air punched out of my lungs. I fell backward onto the sidewalk.

When I looked at Tito again, I went pale with shock. The dog looked at Connor with bright, clear eyes and rolled onto his little paws. He shook himself out and sneezed. Then Tito took one sniff of Connor's hand, growled, and ran onto my lap.

Connor laughed. "That's the thanks I get?"

"Omigod!" I squished the wriggling Chihuahua into me and kissed him wildly on his neck, his ears, his nose. I fingered his paws and hindquarters. Every inch of him was healed. The blood was gone from his fur. I rubbed the heel of my hand across my wet cheeks and rose on shaky legs.

Connor watched me carefully, keeping his distance. "He might be a little sore the rest of the day, but otherwise, he's as good as new."

"Uh-huh." I stared at him, dumbfounded.

Connor ran his tongue across his upper lip and looked away. He seemed to be debating something. I suddenly wished that if I had to have an unnatural skill, it would be the ability to read this boy's mind.

"How did you do that?" Despite my best effort, the question came out like an accusation.

His eyebrows raised and he twisted his lips, as though any explanation he offered would be way over my head. "Can we go somewhere and talk?" he finally asked.

Around us, lights flicked on in houses. Daylight faded and the sinking sun left a bitter chill.

"We can talk right here," I answered.

"I thought maybe we could get something to eat."

There in the dusk, my eyes wide with awe and my weight balanced on the balls of my feet, I must have looked like a gazelle ready to flee. Surely, he didn't expect me to say yes. Just hours ago, he'd vaporized into my classroom, looking as menacing as a serial killer. He'd stood on my porch and lied to me. He'd disappeared into thin air. When I'd tried to stop him from working on Tito, a mysterious force had thrown me to the ground. If that wasn't terrifying enough, at that moment, the bloodcurdling scream from my dream rang through my head.

"This afternoon, you told my best friend that you're moving here. You're not, are you? And you lied about your cell phone."

"Not technically. It really isn't compatible," he said.

"You disappeared right in front of my house."

"You saw that?"

I nodded.

"I know this is a lot to take in, but you'll forgive me once you get to know me," he smiled shyly.

His power was both thrilling and terrifying. Maybe if I'd been able to read his aura, that would have been enough to ease my distrust. As I debated my next move, I was all at once marveling at the perfect curve of his back, the soft blush of his lips. And that cowlick. He brushed it off his forehead, and it swung back over his eyebrow.

Phantom or not, I knew my place on the attraction hierarchy. Guys like this didn't ask girls like me out to dinner. They went after the Tiffanys and Vanessas with their short skirts and push-up bras. All of this compounded my paranoia.

"I don't hang out with guys who lie." I started up the driveway with Tito in my arms.

"Echo, I can help you."

"But you don't know anything about me," I said, not unkindly.

"You spend your days trying to fit in and your nights knowing you never can because you're able to move objects without touching them. You hate your loneliness, but think you don't have any other choice. Am I right?"

I took a step back. How did he know about the telekinesis? Had he been spying on me? And now, he'd listed my most private fears like he was reading my mind, and that disturbed me beyond everything else.

"You've got the wrong girl," I lied and I ran the full length of the driveway and into the house.

CHAPTER 4

I lay awake long past midnight, searching for a rational explanation for what happened that afternoon. Maybe, in my panic, I'd overreacted about Tito. Was it possible that I'd overdramatized his condition? When adrenaline courses through a person's body, they often misjudge what they see. A dozen people will argue about how an event unfolded, even though they were all watching the very same scene.

No matter how hard I tried to convince myself that Tito's legs had not been mangled and that I'd only imagined blood on his fur, there was one simple truth that I couldn't dismiss. Before Connor showed up, I knew Tito was going to die. I could feel his energy waning just as sure as I could feel the panic pounding in my chest.

I tossed my blanket aside and opened the window. The best part about my bedroom was the flat portico roof that doubled as a private deck, held in place by the columns that rose from the front porch three stories below. I swung my legs onto the roof and sat on the window ledge and pulled a pillow to my chest to counter the chill. The cloudless night was still and the cold air cleared my head, providing some much-needed perspective.

What the heck had I been thinking when I turned Connor down? Here was a guy with amazing abilities who offered to help. But help with what? I'd been so out of sorts, I hadn't even been tempted to ask. He'd come to my rescue, performed a miracle, and I reacted by freaking out and running away. I wanted to kick myself.

For all his strength, there was a vulnerability coursing beneath the surface. I'd seen it in the way he looked at me, in his hesitant manner, as though he feared that one misstep, one wrong move, and he'd lose me forever.

I needed to find him. Maybe he'd understand my reluctance and give me another chance. At the very least, I needed to thank him for saving Tito's life.

The next morning, Tito met me in the kitchen, looking like his usual bug-eyed, twitchy self. I shook my head in wonder and gave him an extra hard hug.

As usual, Kimber was at the gym and had probably burned a thousand calories before I rolled out of bed. Kimber was a pharmaceutical-powered force of nature, a society woman with no domestic capacity whatsoever, but who did her darnedest to feed me the way she thought a good mother should. Which is why I found a glass filled with brown viscous liquid waiting for me on the counter. Next to it, a note:

Enjoy breakfast! We need to talk after school.

She'd dotted the *i* in her name with a smiley face. The last time she'd signed her name like that, she'd dragged me to a baby shower for one of her friends. I shuddered to think what she had in store.

The brown stuff smelled awful. I dipped a finger in and held it out to Tito. He took one lick and his eyes bugged in ecstasy. This didn't necessarily mean it tasted good. He'd eat the poop straight out of Becca's cat if we let him. I poured the rest down the drain, grabbed a bagel, and headed out the door.

All morning, I sought out Connor's mystical presence. I studied window reflections. Gazed into the mirror in the girl's bathroom. Looked for sparkling lights trying to gather into a human form. On the upside, I wasn't startled by a pair of disembodied green eyes staring back at me. On the downside, the rest of Connor was nowhere in sight, either.

By afternoon, my heart sinking, I gave up. I made a quick trip to the courtyard after history to release pent up energy—thinking about Connor all day made me feel like a live electric wire—and then hurried to gym class. I stuffed myself into shorts and a baggy t-shirt and ran out of the locker room.

One step onto the outdoor track and I knew something big was happening. Mr. Kipner was by the bleachers, talking to another teacher which meant that most of the students had their phones out.

Effervescent energy rose off my classmates. The crowd around Becca was three girls deep. I figured she was launching a new pheromone potion to attract guys, but the topic of conversation wasn't metaphysical. It was Connor.

Girls passed their cell phones around. Smatterings of conversation, "Check him out," and "hottie," and "I want that photo" jumbled together in a flurry of lustful voices.

I elbowed my way to Becca. "What's going on?" I asked.

"Connor is what." A girl who'd never spoken to me before thrust her cell phone at me. "Check this out," she said.

Connor's face looked back at me in the photo. He had that same look of longing I'd left him with the night before.

"Where did you get that?" I asked.

The girl pointed at Becca.

"Photo credit goes right here." Becca pointed a thumb at herself.

I gave her a quizzical look.

"Dude. Do you ever check your texts?" Becca teased.

I pulled out my phone. I must have switched it off when I hung up on the vet, and I was so caught up in the mystery of Connor, I'd never noticed.

"How'd you get that picture?" I whispered.

"Better question: what the heck happened between you two last night? I saw you carry Tito up your driveway, and Connor looked like you'd just offed his best friend."

"Nothing, he just saw me walking Tito," I fibbed.

"Well, you must have left an impression because he hung outside your house like a sexy stalker. I snapped a picture before he left."

My eyes narrowed. "What do you mean he 'left?'"

Becca snorted. "Walked home. Whaddaya think he'd do, fly?"

The thought had crossed my mind.

Girls peppered Becca with questions and wove their own theories.

"He looks like the son of that movie star, what's-his-name? The one in the action movie."

"If he's moving to West Vista, he's got money."

"Does he drive a Jeep? BMW?"

"That boy's got Jaguar written all over him."

"We need his last name so we can Google him," said Trisha, a girl who used to be one of my best friends.

"McCabe," I said. All heads snapped toward me.

"How would you know?" Trisha smirked, and I remembered how nice she used to be when we were in the same elite clique, the Partychicks. That was before Raquelle kicked me out. Before the so-called 'accident.'

"We met him," Becca cut in.

"He stopped by my house," I said, jockeying for their attention.

The girls looked amused.

"Your house? Why?" Trisha stifled a laugh.

There's an intoxicating power that comes with being super popular, when everyone looks up to you and you can get away with pretty much anything and people are constantly trying to look like you, be with you, talk to you. I missed that power. I wanted that power back.

"He's moving to my neighborhood," I answered. "He wanted to borrow something."

"Was he going to borrow your man-shirt?" Raquelle had joined the group.

I looked down at the gray tee with a picture of a mountain on it. "You gave me this shirt. For my birthday last month."

She and Trisha exchanged a glance. "We didn't think you'd actually wear it."

"Connor asked her out," Becca said.

And just like that, a dozen sunny, gleeful auras drifted into mine. I sucked in a breath, surprised by the buoyant energy. Oh, how I missed the feeling of being part of a group.

The girls dove into their phones to spread the news.

"Why did you say that?" I whispered to Becca.

"Why else would Connor come back? I saw the way he was looking at you this afternoon. That guy could not care less about a flashlight."

Now that they knew his last name, all the girls began the great Connor McCabe investigation. Good luck with that,

I thought. I was pretty sure he didn't have a regular postal address. The girls searched every social network, people-finder, and movie site.

"Are you sure that's his last name?" Trisha asked when they came up empty-handed.

"Unless he was lying, but why would he do that?" It was meant as a joke but my audience stared blankly, so I added, "He said he'd be around, so I'll get all the details for you, 'kay?"

This sent my classmates into a texting frenzy. My phone pinged with incoming invitations to Tiktok and Instagram. This, from the same girls who made a point of ignoring me a hundred times a day. Still, I smiled at the attention.

I scrolled through the invitations, accepting each one.

Suddenly, my phone was snatched out of my hand.

"Hey!" All my classmates had scattered.

Mr. Kipner loomed over me, holding my cell phone and reading the screen. "TikTok? I love those videos! Have you seen the one where the student gets detention for being on her phone when she should be running laps?"

It took a few seconds before I realized he was referring to me, not an actual video.

"But—"

"You can collect your phone after detention in the gym."

"But—"

"Don't even." He pointed to the track where the rest of my classmates were already running. "Two laps," he said.

"Detention's supposed to be in the library," I protested.

"Not today, it's not." Standing next to Mr. Kipner felt like pressing against a brick wall, and not just because he was an ex-football player. He had a mean streak, and if I wasn't careful, one detention would turn into two.

I dragged myself onto the track and caught up with Becca. "I tried to warn you," she said, "but you were too busy clicking on all your invitations." Her aura was unusually dense.

"Me? You're the one who broadcast his picture to the whole school."

"You know they're only talking to us because of Connor."

"You still loved it." I lifted a shoulder, guilty of the same offense.

"Yeah, well, they can kiss my Wiccan butt before I'd ever join one of their cliques."

Becca would never admit it, but she missed being part of a group, too. She reveled in the popularity that her weirdness offered, but at the end of the day, she was still a freaky chick who got left off all the invite lists.

I stood in the doorway of the gymnasium. Confetti covered the floor. Cans and snack wrappers littered the bleachers.

"Freshman pep rally got a little out of hand. We're going to kick some Northside butt!" Mr. Kipner's eyes gleamed with the promise of a football victory.

I gave him the full attitude head roll. "I'm not spending detention cleaning the gym. I'm supposed to be sitting in silence, contemplating my transgressions. This is unfair!"

Mr. Kipner handed me a broom. "I'm here until seven, so take all the time you need." He left, and the metal door slammed shut behind him.

"This. Frigging. Sucks!" I stomped through the gym, shoving the broom through heaps of garbage. With every pass, my anger rose. No matter what I did, I could not catch a break. I hated what I had become. I hated that there was no end to this living nightmare. I shoved a load of litter into a mound.

"I hate my life!" I yelled.

With a loud poof, the pile exploded into the air. It hung there, swaying low and then lifting again, as though deciding whether or not to honor gravity. Apparently, it decided *not,* because the massive, multi-colored cloud of garbage shot toward the ceiling, twenty feet out of reach.

"Aaaagh! This is impossible!" I swung the broom at it, trying to corral the mess. The litter swirled into beautiful patterns far overhead.

"I cannot freaking believe this!"

A loud boom filled the gym, and the mass doubled in size.

"Oh no. Stop!" It doubled again. Mr. Kipner could come back at any second. How was I supposed to explain this?

I dropped the broom. Aimed my hands at the cloud and tried to guide it toward the trash can. "Down. Please. I will do anything. Just please, please come back down."

The cloud of junk quivered and took on a life of its own, swirled into a funnel and dropped neatly into the can. Next, empty bottles and snack wrappers tumbled out of the bleachers and followed suit. The gym was spotless.

"I did it. I actually did it!"

"I'd like to take you up on that offer," a voice said.

I spun, startled. Connor was right behind me.

CHAPTER 5

Heat seeped up the back of my neck and I knew I was about to turn bright red. How long had Connor been standing in the gym? How much had he'd seen?

"Take me up on what offer?" I asked.

He repeated my words. "'I will do anything, just please come down.' Hate to tell you, but that was me."

"Nuh-uh. I had it all under control." Now I wasn't so sure.

"Show me." Connor tilted his head toward the garbage can, sending its contents airborne.

"What'd you do that for?"

"Prove you can do it," he said.

"Fine. I just need to put it in the can."

"Yup."

"I'll do it," I said.

"I'm waiting," he replied.

I waved my hands. Moved my feet and shifted my weight. I looked like I was performing an awkward contemporary dance. Nothing happened. "Crap."

"It would have hit the floor again as soon as you left. Or as soon as your emotion shifted."

This left me momentarily speechless. "How do you know this?"

"Experience." He twirled a finger and the debris dropped back into the can. "It's easier than you think," he said, "making objects move the way you want." He left a generous arm's length between us. Still, I picked out the flecks of blue that dotted his green irises. The overall effect was that of a tropical lagoon.

"How long were you watching me?" I asked.

"Long enough to know you'll never make it as a janitor." The corners of his mouth twitched. "So, about that offer..."

"Wow. You are relentless. You seem like the kind of guy who is used to getting his way." Sadness flit across his features and I caught myself. "I'm sorry. I can't believe I said that. After what you did for me last night—for Tito—I didn't even thank you. So, thank you. Very much." I took a breath. "Okay. I said I would do anything. Within reason. What do you want?"

Connor picked up the broom and focused on the wooden handle with hawk-like intensity. The wood bent in half as though made of thin wire, tied itself into a knot, and straightened again. My lips parted in disbelief.

"Would you like to try?" He held the handle out for me.

After my epic failure with the trash pile? I shook my head.

"I can help you, Echo. With all of your energetic outbursts."

"I doubt that very much."

"Give me a chance? It paid off yesterday." There was a lilt in his words, the hope that I'd say yes.

True, he'd accomplished a miracle with Tito, and he had the ability to pop up in places unexpectedly, so he clearly knew more about paranormal stuff than I did. This sparked an idea.

"Help me get rid of this. Forever."

"Your ability? I can't do that."

"But you have to. If anyone finds out about me…" No way would I tell him he was right about my not fitting in, or how the tele-chaosing was pushing me further to the fringe. I tried the flattery angle. "Look at all the cool things you just did. And you healed Tito. I don't know how you did it, and I don't care. You've got some crazy magicky voodoo thing going, and I know you can show me how to be normal again. *Please.*"

Connor said something under his breath.

"What?"

His expression hardened. "I said this society is a disgrace. You shouldn't have to live like this, hiding your gift."

"Gift. That's a good one. So, can you fix me or not?"

"Your ability isn't something you switch on and off, Echo." His voice was soft, but there was no mistaking his authority on the subject.

Not until he said that did I realize how desperate I was for help, how overwhelmingly powerless I felt. My stomach hit bottom. "I'm really stuck with this."

"Try not to look at it like that."

"I *look* at it the way it *is.* That's why you keep showing up? To tell me…" I began to hyperventilate. "I can't ever… get rid… of it?" I gulped air.

"Breathe, Echo."

What was with this guy? He claimed he'd help me but clearly had no intention of doing so. I didn't appreciate being manipulated. My breathing relaxed, and I pulled myself together.

"Well, then." I lifted my chin and stood. "Connor McCabe, thanks for nothing and goodbye." My fingers pricked like mad. I needed to get out of there before my aura made a fool of me again. I dragged the garbage can to the edge of the gym.

"I didn't come here just to interrupt your... what do you call this? Detention?" he asked.

"Then why did you?"

"To teach you, and I won't be able to do that until you trust me."

I shoved the can against the wall. "How do you even know about me? Or this, this, *thing* that I have to deal with?"

"Your power? You'll have to trust me on that, too. At least for a little while."

"So, just out of the blue, you show up to help?"

"Obviously, you need it," he said. He might not have intended it, but the insult stung. "Didn't you just say you were afraid someone might find out what you can do? I assume you meant your family or friends. At the very least, I can teach you some control. But also, I'd like to teach you how to protect yourself."

I laughed. "From what? The telekinesis police?"

Connor frowned. "There are bigger forces at work, Echo. People who would love nothing more than to use your power for their own gain."

This got my attention. It was hard to believe my situation could get any worse. "Who would ever hurt me?"

Connor shook his head. "We don't have time to get into that. Your teacher will be checking on you soon."

I mulled my options. Spend a few more minutes with this gorgeous stranger and see what he had to offer or... Well, no better choice came to mind.

"Teach me something, then," I said, regretting the curiosity that crept into my voice. I'd been going for defiant.

He reached into his pocket and pulled out what appeared to be an arcade token.

"Hold out your hand," he said, maintaining that same space between us.

I mirrored his outstretched palm. The token rose into the air, one inch, two, going higher until it hovered above my head.

My mouth hung open as the token lowered into my hand. Given the strange things I'd been doing over the past two weeks, you'd think this would have seemed run-of-the-mill. Yet here I was, giddy. I silently admitted that Connor's proximity had something to do with this.

"Now you try," he said. "Focus on where you want it to go." He held his index finger a foot above my palm. "Imagine it's already floating up here."

That should have been easy, right? Every day, I moved objects without even trying. I held the token the way he did and stared at it. I concentrated until I thought steam would come out of my ears. I willed the token to move, even quietly threatened it.

"I can't."

"You're too worried you'll fail," he said.

"What, you're psychic, too?"

"No. You're practically breaking a sweat, you're trying so hard."

I tried again. This time, I focused on where I wanted it to go while trying not to care if I succeeded. It was almost an impossible task, and yet the coin rose.

"It's working!" I said.

"You've got it," Connor encouraged. "Now send it back to me."

I looked at his outstretched hand. Got distracted by his upper body. His lower body.

"Um, my hand is up here?" he said.

My heart did a nervous flip and heat ran up my neck. The token wobbled out of control, zipped across the gym, and ricocheted off the far wall. He grabbed it before it pegged him in the face. I cringed.

"That was good. That was really good." He put the token in his pocket and his green eyes met mine. "I want to show you more. Can you meet me tonight? Downtown?"

"Um, where?"

He thought a moment. "Twenty-Fourth and Vaughn Street, six o'clock. I know a place where we'll have privacy."

"That's not downtown. That's the industrial district." The industrial district was all but vacant after sundown. Endless rows of low, blocky buildings crowded unlit, potholed streets. If you were looking for a setting for a horror movie, you may as well start there.

The gym doors clattered open and Mr. Kipner marched in. He stormed across the basketball court, eyeing Connor. "Did I give you detention?"

"No, sir."

"Then you don't belong here." Mr. Kipner was in a worse mood than when I started.

"Yes, sir." Connor glanced at me as he left, his upper lip pulling into a smile.

"I'm finished, so can I go?" I asked my teacher.

Mr. Kipner scanned the floor. He inspected the bleachers, eyes narrowing. "How'd you clean this up so fast?"

I tamped down the mix of worry and boy-crush rising to the surface. The last thing I needed was for the garbage can to pull a Mount St Helen's and erupt all over the floor.

"I had to. I've got a ton of homework."

"Fine," he finally grunted. He returned my phone. "Get out of here."

I grabbed my backpack. I still hadn't decided what to do with Connor's offer. He wanted me to venture to a spooky part of town after dark. His short lesson had been fun, but who was I kidding? I'd never control this so-called gift. My primary objective remained. I had to get rid of it.

Scratch that. My primary objective was to spend time with Connor. Drop-dead-intoxicating Connor. So what if he wanted to try and teach me a few things? There was no harm in that. Once he realized just how pointless it all was, then maybe he'd expel my supernatural curse. I was certain he knew how.

I raced through the hallway, the cheerleading banners overhead fluttering as I went by, telegraphing my new crush. One of them peeled off the wall and sailed to the floor. I laughed and jumped over it.

Outside, Connor waited next to my car. He wasn't alone.

"Oh, no." I hurried out.

Raquelle had pulled her red convertible behind mine on the street. She vogued in her cheerleading outfit, one hip thrust to the side, her pompons splayed on the trunk of her Mercedes. Connor must have said something amusing because she laughed as though his every word delighted her. And it wasn't just any laugh. This was her predator laugh, the one she used when she tagged a guy for her Hit List.

That list was the reason Raquelle dumped me from the Partychicks. I had gone out with Mason Peters, a guy I met right after we moved to Portland. He'd dated Raquelle for a while until she got bored and broke up with him. Little did I know, she still had him on her Hit List, meaning she intended to sleep with him. I'd stepped between Raquelle and her prey, and I'd paid dearly.

Now, she had her sights on Connor. Raquelle stretched her chin into the air and swung her shoulder at him, imitating a pose from a fast-food commercial, where the actress can't believe her great fortune at finding such a delicious taco salad. She tongued the sharp point of her incisor, practically daring me to interfere.

"Thanks again for saving Tito," I called to Connor.

"It was my pleasure." His head tipped to the side, still waiting for my answer. His eyes tracked my every move, possessively, like we belonged to each other. Like we always had. I met his gaze. In it, I found a reflection of my own hope.

"Six o'clock," I nodded, and his smile nearly crushed me.

CHAPTER 6

Idashed through my homework. Well, sort of. I'd sketched Connor's face in the border of my physics notebook. A few times. I couldn't help it. My mind kept wandering to his astounding abilities and the secrets that he held; the fullness of his lower lip and the peaks that shaped the upper one. I had to redo my physics problems five times just to get them right.

At five-thirty, I slammed my books closed and FaceTimed Becca. I waded through the clothing in my walk-in closet, mounds of designer brands from Kimber that didn't match my holey jeans and washed-out tee shirt style.

"The hottest guy this side of the Cascades wants to take you to a private place and you think this is a non-date?" Becca was holed up in her bathroom, avoiding her family.

"We're just going to talk about school. Nightmare teachers. Stuff like that." I held up a low-cut shirt.

"Yeah, right. That's a date shirt," Becca said.

I held up a loose blouse that probably cost Kimber two hundred dollars. "This?"

A knock sounded on Becca's bathroom door. "I've got to get back to dinner. It's family night. Do not wear that shirt. Burn that shirt. And text me after your date!"

"It's not—"

She hung up. I finally decided on jeans with no holes and squeezed into a cute tee that Raquelle would probably wear. Not that I cared.

I bounded downstairs and nearly ran into Kimber as she came in the front door.

"I'm glad you're home. We need to leave in a few minutes." She scanned my outfit. "Cute! We practically match! But we need something a little more cocktail hour and less skateboard park." She shuffled toward the kitchen. I wrinkled my nose in confusion and jogged to catch up.

"I'm meeting a friend tonight," I said.

"I left you a note? I should have texted but my battery died and the power cord is I don't know where and how did people survive before cell phones? Anyway, Mr. Crane was there for us when you were in that dreadful coma. It would be rude of you not to show up for dinner."

Dinner with the Cranes? No way. "Your note only said we needed to talk. I've got this school project. For physics. I'm kind of almost failing…"

She pulled a bottle of water out of the refrigerator and struggled to open it without damaging her fresh manicure. I twisted off the cap and handed the bottle back to her.

"Raquelle's in your physics class, right? You can talk to her about it while we're there."

I followed her upstairs. "Raquelle's not my lab partner…"

"I'm sorry, hon, they're expecting us soon, and we need to leave now-ish." She flicked her fingers in the air to show her inability to grasp the exact time.

"But…"

"I know, I know. I should have put that in the note. I thought you'd be excited to spend time with Raquelle and her family. Anyway, Mr. Crane keeps asking about you and your recovery. He was the only one of our friends who came to the hospital after your accident."

I wondered with a touch of desperation how to fix this.

"I promised your dad we'd go," she said.

There they were, the magic words that could change the course of my entire evening. This was important to my dad. "Is he in town? Is he coming?"

"It's just you and me tonight and it's very important…"

"I know, I know, important to my dad," I cut in.

Kimber and I battled often. The first few months of living together, we'd had our share of catfights. When my dad confided in me how much this hurt him, I put my inner drama queen in check and pledged to be a peacemaker.

But still.

"About that physics project, I'm getting help from this guy," I began.

Kimber's lashes fluttered. "A boy? A new school and you're already getting the guys. Good for you. Tell you what, come to dinner, tell him you'll meet up a little later, and I'll extend your curfew."

"I don't have a curfew," I said.

"Oh. Well. I assumed that's why you were always in bed early."

Now dressed in Kimber-approved attire, we drove the few blocks to the Cranes'. The dashboard clock ticked closer to six.

I wondered at the likelihood that Connor would wait for me if I was a half-hour late. I spun the magnetic bracelets on my wrist and tapped my foot impatiently.

"Your dad and I are deeply grateful for Mr. Crane's support when you were in the hospital. It wouldn't kill you to show some gratitude toward him," Kimber said.

"It's kind of hard to, when his daughter is the reason I ended up there."

Kimber shook her head. "Raquelle was the one who ran and got help after you fell. You were bleeding all over the place."

We'd been down this road before. I'd hit my head hard and lost my memory for a while after the coma. Now, the doctors, my dad and Kimber—especially Kimber—questioned my side of the story. "She tripped me," I said.

"Honey, this is what Mr. Crane meant about brain trauma affecting memory. You and Raquelle were friends, remember? You were in her group."

"She got suspended, remember?"

"The principal issued an apology. It was clearly an accident." She heard me huff. "If Raquelle did trip you—and I'm not saying she would ever—then why?"

Nobody believed me, but I remembered that afternoon perfectly.

We'd been at my locker—Raquelle, Trisha and the two Brittanys—figuring out where to go to start our weekend. We always went out after school on Friday.

"Noodle Palace tastes like cat. Let's get Mexican," I'd said.

Raquelle was checking her makeup in my mirror. "Echo's right. I got sick the last time we ate there."

"Let's do Chorito's?" Trisha asked.

"I'll meet you there. I've got to hand in a paper for Mr. King." I swung my bookbag over my shoulder.

"I'll ride with Echo," Raquelle said.

Trisha and the two Brittanys split off towards the parking lot and Raquelle and I went back to our physics classroom.

"I heard you went out with Mason Peters the other night," Raquelle said.

"He took me to see Evil Ted at Satyricon. I didn't think you'd care. It's been, like, two months since you dumped him."

"It never occurred to you to ask?"

"Ask what? I thought you didn't like him anymore." This was just like Raquelle, to change her mind about a guy.

"I haven't decided what I want to do with him. I might want to keep him around just for fun. So, you need to stop dating him."

"Excuse me? You broke up with him because he was 'too economically disadvantaged for your image.'"

"What can I say? Sometimes I like to slum."

I slid my paper under the physics classroom door. "He asked me out again. I'm going to go."

"Say that again?"

I headed down the stairs. "Come on, Raquelle. You don't even like him. I'm going to go out with Mason."

I felt, rather than saw, Raquelle's foot hook mine. But I saw the look on her face as I flailed and tried to grab the banister. It was a look of shock and regret at what she had just done.

She would never apologize. Admitting fault would ruin her reputation. The black mark on her record might prevent her from getting accepted at UCLA. It was much easier to pretend it didn't happen, and then ignore me when I returned to school.

I came back to the present as we pulled into the Crane's driveway. A valet took our car and a butler escorted us into an expansive entryway. Everything in the house screamed super-sophistication.

Kimber's aura turned sharp and competitive. She leaned in and whispered, "Please take off those godawful bracelets."

"They go with the dress," I said. They didn't, but they were my insurance policy against a disastrous evening.

She snapped her fingers and held out her hand.

Fine, I thought, *but it's all on you.* I handed the bracelets over. She tucked them in her purse just as Mr. and Mrs. Crane walked in the room.

Mrs. Crane air-kissed us both. Mr. Crane kissed Kimber on the cheek. Then he took my hands and peered into my eyes. His mannerisms were too personal, and in his presence, I always felt like I was doing something wrong.

He'd taken a particular interest in my well-being after my accident. "How are we healing up here?" He tapped my forehead with a clammy index finger.

"Fine," I replied, resisting the urge to swat his hand away. Ever since my accident he always stood a little too close.

"Raquelle is going out for the night," Mrs. Crane said. "So, you're stuck with us adults!"

That was the best news I'd heard so far. I concentrated on an exit strategy and glanced at my phone. Five after six! My anxiety rippled through the entryway and rocked an expensive looking vase on its pedestal. I discreetly steadied it on my way by.

The dining room was even more elaborate. A chandelier with a million crystals reflected in the mirrors that lined the wall behind Mr. Crane. Tall candles flickered down the length of the table. Several sets of silverware and plates sat in front of me. Oh, no.

A woman in a server's uniform set out bowls of soup. "Excuse me," I whispered, "how many courses are there?"

"Six, miss."

I muffled a groan. It would be rude to rush through dinner. But that didn't stop me from spooning bisque into my mouth as quickly and politely as I could.

"Much like what Echo experienced," Mr. Crane said.

"What's that?" I asked. I spooned a mouthful too quickly and bisque spattered on my dress.

"I was referring to your unusual brain activity after your head injury. I'm studying the short-term effects of brain trauma on subjects, but I'm not as far along on the project as I'd like, due to extra work coming in from the police department." Mr. Crane owned a busy psychiatry practice, but on the side, he worked with the Portland police to help them solve criminal cases.

"Don is working on a murder case," Mrs. Crane said.

Kimber got a gleam in her eye. "How exciting! Are they very grisly or your run-of-the-mill murders?"

Mrs. Crane cast an accusing look at her husband. "Don won't tell me a thing. A bloodthirsty maniac could be wandering the city, and we wouldn't have any clue what to watch out for."

"As long as you don't claim to be a psychic, you have nothing to worry about," he said.

"Someone is killing psychics?" Kimber exchanged a giddy look with Mrs. Crane.

"I never said that, did I, ladies? And I'd better not hear any gossip about it at the country club," he said with a self-satisfied smile.

"My lips are sealed," Kimber assured him.

"You too, Echo."

I stopped eating long enough to nod. The server swooped in and replaced the soup bowl with a plate of trout. I swore under my breath. No matter how fish is prepared I think it smells like algae, and I cannot get past the fact that it was recently covered in its own slime.

Another minute ticked into oblivion. I shoved a forkful of translucent white flesh in my mouth and the candelabra centerpiece shifted ever so slightly. I swallowed and grimaced at the taste.

Mr. Crane turned to me. "As I was saying, I need a few more subjects for my brain trauma study. I thought you would be a perfect candidate. Your injury was fairly recent and you've healed well."

"You think so?" I asked, letting the sarcasm drip. When I woke up in the hospital, the EEG was showing strange brain wave patterns, and the doctors feared I'd slip back into a coma. My brain leveled out again, but the wave pattern was different than a normal person's. Nothing to worry about, they'd said.

Shortly after that, the tele-chaosing had started.

"I still get bad headaches," I said.

"It won't interfere with the data. I'll have our receptionist schedule a time for you."

"Wait a minute, I didn't mean I'd volunteer. I've got, like, tons of papers to write."

"It only involves a few cognitive tests, nothing too intense. I do all my testing on Saturdays," he said.

Like I had any interest in wasting my Saturday in a shrink's office.

"As long as it won't interfere with school, why not help out with his project?" Kimber pressed.

I stabbed at the last of the fish. With each bite, the candelabra jerked until one by one, each of the four flames snuffed itself out. My butter knife began sliding away from my plate. I grabbed it. I never should have given my magnetic bracelets to Kimber.

"The tests aren't painful," Mr. Crane said. "I'm just measuring brainwave changes in response to stress."

"I'm really not comfortable being studied," I replied. *Especially* when I was stressed.

The entire table shook. Silverware rattled against plates and wine sloshed onto the pale tablecloth.

Kimber's eyes grew wide. "Are we having an earthquake?"

"Hang on everyone. This feels like a 3.5," Mr. Crane said.

Earthquakes weren't uncommon in the Pacific Northwest but no one noticed that the table was the only thing in the room that was shaking. They were so busy rescuing their wine glasses, they didn't see the crystals in the chandelier stretch like droplets of water. Or the mirrors warping and melting.

Mr. Crane caught a glimpse of the chandelier. His mouth dropped and I abruptly stood up. The room snapped back to normal.

"Thank you for dinner. I need to go. Science project. Late. Partner…um waiting." I stumbled out of the room, and swore I felt Mr. Crane's eyes drilling into my back.

While I searched the hallway closets for my coat, I calculated how long it would take to get to Connor's meeting place at the corner of 24th and Vaughn. It was downhill all the way home, so I could clear the four blocks in no time, even in a dress. Rush hour was over, so all told, I'd catch up with him just forty-five minutes late. If he was still there.

I found my jacket and shrugged into it. Raquelle clipped down the winding staircase in an off-the-shoulder turquoise dress that showed off her tan. "You're bailing on dinner?"

"I'm meeting someone," I replied.

"Anyone I know?"

"No." I patted my pockets and looked around. "I just had my cell phone."

"You seemed awfully interested in that new guy. What's his name?"

"Connor." I peeked into the dining room. My phone wasn't next to my plate. What the heck had I done with it?

"Oh, riiight, Connor. I met him today. He said he was on his way to meet some girl."

I hid a smile. That girl was me. If I ever made it.

"Hand me that clutch, would you?" She nodded at the purse on the side table.

"Get it yourself," I said.

"You've got a mean streak, Echo. Did anyone ever tell you that? Sometimes I can't believe I ever let you join the Partychicks."

"You want to see mean, keep messing with my car," I scowled. "I know you're the one who dumped soda on my windshield."

Raquelle applied lip gloss in the foyer mirror and smacked her lips together. "How do I look?"

The dress clung to her curves, and her silver earrings dipped onto her golden shoulders. Her makeup accentuated her feline eyes. I'd heard rumors that Raquelle gave guys whatever they wanted. The girls called her horrible names behind her back. The guys just kept calling her.

"Like you charge two-hundred dollars an hour," I said.

"Aw. Always so jealous. Your phone's by the vase," she said as someone knocked on the front door. Raquelle answered it.

"Hello again. Would you like to come in?" she asked.

"No thanks," a guy answered.

Even before I heard his voice, I recognized the dark hair curled at the base of his neck and the jeans that hung seductively low on his hips.

Connor.

Raquelle tossed her gleaming hair. "I'm so glad you could come out tonight."

He appraised Raquelle from head to toe. One corner of his mouth arched ever so slightly. Then he saw me. He held my gaze. "My other plans were a no-show."

"Don't wait up." Raquelle said to me. She stepped outside and closed the door.

My heart squashed between my ribs. I waited until I heard Raquelle's convertible leave, and walked home.

So, that was it. My chance at the new guy had glittered in front of me like an exotic jewel, and then slipped through my fingers into Raquelle's claws. I thought about her Hit List, and the way she slunk next to Connor like a greedy cat that begged to be pet, and my stomach fell.

"'There are bigger forces at work, Echo. I want to help you, Echo.' What a bunch of BS." Mocking Connor didn't make me feel any better.

My cell phone pinged. It was Becca. *How's the non-date?*

Non-date never happened, I replied.

Huh???

My answer was one word: *Raquelle.*

Right away, my best friend called on video. "Forget him. There are better things in your future," she said on my screen.

"He's just so different from anyone I've ever met. He's so…"

"Really? Sounds like he's just like any other guy who sees Raquelle. He's not good enough for you," she said. "Where are you, anyway?"

"Walking home from the Crane's. I got sucked into going there for dinner. Mr. Crane wants to do brain scans on me for some lab study he's doing."

"You're not going to, right?" Becca's voice registered concern. "I said no."

"Good. You know he's been doing psyche evaluations at high schools? He got permission to do brain scans on 'troubled kids'. Ellie Taluco's sister was one of them, and now she's in a facility in Seattle."

I shivered, and not from the cold. "A facility?"

"Ellie said her sister saw visions sometimes. It was no big deal until Mr. Crane got in her head. Then she had a total breakdown. I wasn't supposed to say anything so you didn't hear it from me."

I thought back to my little outburst at dinner. How much had Mr. Crane seen?

"Your phone is shaking. Are you okay?" Becca asked.

Aside from the despair creeping in? "Yeah."

"You know you can tell me anything," she offered.

"Clearly I can't."

"I can keep *your* secrets," she said.

I gave her a look.

"You're the only one I told about Ellie's sister," Becca defended.

"It's just been a bad night." I let myself into the house.

"You're still obsessing over Connor? Forget him. He's nothing special."

We signed off and I climbed the stairs to my room.

I kicked off my low heels, sick at what Connor might be doing with Raquelle. Pissed that he wasn't with me, helping me wipe away my telekinetic misery.

I dug a quarter out of my backpack and set it in my palm. "If it floats, I will figure this out myself and don't need Connor and I will forget about him. If it doesn't, then I suck it up and beg for his help."

I collected the fragments of my pride and focused every bit of intent on the coin. It lay there, lifeless. I tried again. I may as well have been trying to lift a semi-truck.

I flopped on the bed. With no idea where Connor came from or where he went when he left, how was I supposed to find him?

"Connor," I called into the air, "if you can hear me, give me a sign." I scrunched my face at how dumb this sounded. "All right, let's just say you're hearing this. I'm sorry I didn't meet you, but I need your help!" My voice rang vacant against the walls.

Of course, the air in front of my closet did not waver and an exotic, dark-haired guy did not materialize like a genie ready to grant my every wish. I shoved a pillow over my head, feeling like a complete dork.

When I woke, a cheery sun blazed into my warm, stuffy bedroom. The alarm had failed to go off. Class started in twenty minutes. My head throbbed. As an extra bonus, my room was a tele-chaotic mess. Apparently, I was now moving objects in my sleep. Lovely. Just lovely.

My eyes landed on the coin I'd tried to levitate last night. Except the quarter was gone and Connor's arcade token from yesterday was in its place. I distinctly remembered him putting it back in his pocket when we were in the gym, and yet here it was. Despite the warmth in the room, goose bumps rose on my forearms. A glance around my bedroom assured me I was alone. My door was closed, and the windows were locked.

I brought the coin to eye level. It looked like a quarter, except it was made of a different metal, brass maybe. The front was imprinted with a man's face. A building was stamped on the back, and below it, the number 2173. I set it on the nightstand and contemplated what to do with my day. I hated to miss more school. I could knock out the headache with a couple of Advil, but the truth was, I just didn't want to go.

I found Kimber in her room and told her I was sick. My stomach still curdled from seeing Connor with Raquelle, and that counted, right? Kimber pressed her wrist against my forehead, testing for fever, and offered to cancel her tee time to stay home with me. "Do you want me to make you a tofu-kale smoothie? It's great for your immune system!"

"Please…don't. Really, I just need to rest," I said.

She gave me back my bracelets, called the school, and left for the country club.

A shower eased the headache a bit. I towel dried my hair and went to my closet. The fall breeze wafting through my bedroom smelled of pine and autumn leaves. I took an invigorating breath, and my spirits lifted. I dropped my robe to the floor.

As the breeze hit my bare skin, a jolt of distress charged up my back. When I'd gone into the shower, my windows had been locked. Now the curtains fluttered from the draft.

I inhaled sharply. There on the portico, Connor reclined on my lounge chair in the morning sun, his long legs crossed at the ankles, his eyes closed. I yanked my robe around me.

"Go ahead and get dressed. I'm not looking," he called.

"Most people use the front door, you know," I scolded. Secretly, I was thrilled to see him.

I dressed and climbed onto the windowsill. Connor was the picture of peace, his lean body in repose, every well-defined muscle relaxed. Watching him made my pulse hum, but I shut down any trace of a possible crush. He had, after all, spent the evening with Raquelle. There was a good chance he made it onto her Hit List.

"You missed our meeting last night," he said without opening his eyes.

"I had a family obligation I couldn't get out of. My stepmom wrangled me into dinner with her friends."

He sighed. "Family obligations. That I understand. How was dinner?"

"Not great. How was Raquelle?" Right away, I wanted to take those words back. They sounded catty, and there was the off chance he might answer the question. "Sorry, that's none of my business."

"She offered to show me the city. Portland is very different from what I expected." Connor opened his eyes. The sunlight played off them, intensifying their color. He gazed at my face for what seemed like an eternity, absorbing every contour, every freckle. I fidgeted under his scrutiny.

His lips parted to speak, but he must have thought better of it. He blinked away his intention, straddled the lounge chair and stood, his six-foot frame towering over me.

"My offer still stands, if you're willing to meet after school."

My heart pressed hard against my chest. "I can't. I called in sick. I'm kind of playing hooky."

"Hooky?"

"Avoiding school."

"Why?"

"I kind of have a headache," I dodged, too embarrassed to admit that I was also running away from my obligations. Mortified that my ability was so out of control. The fir tree growing next to the portico reached for me and I shoved it away.

"Echo," he said, his voice as gentle as the breeze that carried it, "spend the day with me, and I'll show you things you never dreamed possible."

CHAPTER 7

Connor told me to meet him at the same place—the corner of 24th and Vaughn. I offered to give him a ride, but he declined. I figured I'd at least walk him to the front door but when I pulled the curtain aside for him to climb into my room, he was gone. I don't know why I'd expected him to follow. It was obvious he didn't get on the portico roof the same way I did.

He was waiting for me when I parked downtown.

"How did you get here so fast?" I asked. "One minute you're outside my bedroom window, then you're gone. And poof, here you are."

"I use an advanced form of physics," he said.

"Of course, you do."

"Come with me." He turned on his heels and crossed Vaughn Street diagonally, ignoring the traffic bearing down on him. Drivers honked and slammed on their brakes, but Connor continued, unperturbed.

"Sorry! So sorry!" I called to the drivers. I jogged to catch up, each footfall driving a shard of pain into my head. "You can't just walk in front of drivers, you'll get hit."

"I'm safe, Echo, and so are you."

In the middle of the block, he slipped between two buildings. The lack of sunlight submerged the alley in shade. A dumpster hung open at the end. When he reached the dumpster, he followed a dogleg to the right.

I balked at the mouth of the alley. My instincts needled me about how little I knew about him. The sound of traffic drowned out Connor's footsteps; if I followed and had to call for help, nobody would hear me. But if Connor intended to harm me, he'd had ample opportunity to do so. Instead, he'd come to my rescue, twice.

I followed him and around the corner, I found a door propped open.

"Close the door behind you," Connor called from inside.

I stuck my head into the space. It was dark except for the shaft of daylight that crept in with me. A light switch sat just out of reach. I released my grip on the handle, took a tentative step inside, and flicked the switch on. Nothing happened. The door slammed closed, the latch reverberating like I was in a prison cell. I was plunged into blackness.

"Connor?" I squeaked.

"This is your first lesson." Connor's voice came out of nowhere and everywhere.

It didn't matter how smooth and nonthreatening his tone, my chest iced with fear. I reached behind me for the exit. My hand fell on hard concrete. Panic sparked. I scraped against the wall, searching for an escape. Where was the door?

"This isn't funny, Connor. Let me out of here."

The lights flicked on. I was alone. The darkness had so disoriented me that I'd missed the door, only a few feet away. My pulse dropped below stroke level, and I took in my surroundings.

I was in a storage warehouse. Rows of shelves and metal racking towered over a concrete floor. Headless mannequins crowded into a corner, their smooth, wigless heads stacked on a nearby shelf. Something nagged me to look up.

I gaped at the open sky where the ceiling seemed to be peeled back to let the natural light in. The light fixtures that should have been anchored to the ceiling appeared affixed to the clouds. A jet flew overhead, leaving a white contrail across the blue sky.

A blur dropped into my line of vision, and Connor appeared in front of me.

"Where did you… come… from?" I asked.

"Lesson number one. Never assume something is impossible, especially where your gift is concerned. Got it?"

I stared at the sky with awe and confusion and nodded.

"Everything is possible," I said slowly.

"Good. Now take off those ridiculous bracelets."

"I need them."

"They're blocking your body's energy flow. That's why you wear them, isn't it?"

I squared my shoulders. "And they work really well." In reality, they had failed me time and again, but he didn't need to know that.

"The stronger you get, the less effective they'll be. We're not here to suppress your gift. I want to see it grow."

My palms flew up between us. "No way. Absolutely not. You have to help me get rid of this before it destroys my life. You can, right? I know you said you can't, but really, you can," I pressed.

Connor dug his fingers into the back of his neck. "I told you the truth, Echo."

I watched him for a full minute. Looked again at the clouds and the sunlight streaming in from overhead.

"Yes, I can do all that. But as for your gift..." he shook his head.

I read the sincerity in his eyes, and this time, I believed him. The air gushed from my lungs, and along with it, every bit of hope.

"That's the only reason you agreed to meet me?" he asked.

I snuck in a scan of his body. "Mostly," I confessed.

He sighed. "Take the bracelets off."

His manner suggested he knew I was bound to the life of an outcast, and that he alone held the key to my freedom. My days had become a string of painful risks. What was one more?

I set the bracelets on the floor, and then I felt it: a warm glow, reassuring and soft as feather strokes against my skin. So subtle, if I dared flinch, the faint heat would slip away like wisps of smoke. This was Connor's aura.

"Okay. I'm all yours," I said.

Connor flinched at my words and seemed to hide a smile. Then, he was back to business.

"Watch closely." He closed his hand into a fist and rapped firmly on the warehouse's cement block wall. "You think this wall is impenetrable because your whole life, that's what you've been told. You've been taught boundaries that aren't true."

Then he opened his hand and thrust his fingers right. Through. Concrete.

My eyes bulged. Involuntarily, I took a step back. "That's some sort of illusion, right?"

He pulled his fingers out of the wall, and the concrete melted over the open holes.

"Now you," he said.

I muffled a snort. "I can't shove my hand into a wall! Come on, really, how did you do that?"

He swiped his entire arm through the concrete, as easy as a knife through butter.

"I, I don't understand," I said.

"Just give it a try, and I'll give you back your bracelets."

Somehow, I knew they were no longer on the floor next to me but I checked just the same. He pulled the bracelets out of his pocket and taunted me with a crooked smile.

"All I have to do is try?"

"Yep."

"Fine." I pressed my hand against the cold cement. It was solid and unyielding. "See? Nothing. Big surprise there."

"You're not taking this seriously," he said.

"Of course not! What you did is impossible. All of this… this… none of it makes any sense… but even if… I mean… okay, first of all?" I untangled my tongue. "How do I know you're not the only one who can do this? You materialize out of thin air…"

"I materialized out of energy," he corrected.

"Whatever. You're like a ghost and I'm no expert, but I know they can pass through solid objects."

"You think I'm a ghost?"

I wasn't sure what I thought. "All I know is you and I are not the same. So, it's not fair to tell me to do this."

"I'm trying to make your life better." Impatience tensed his voice.

"Then please, can you show me something useful? Like, how do I stop stuff from…" As if on cue, a dummy head flew off the shelf, missed me by inches, and hit the wall. "That," I said, "has to stop."

Connor let out an exasperated sigh. "That's exactly what I'm trying to do. Okay, we need to start easier." His eyes fell on the space next to me. A minute ago, it had been empty. Now, we were surrounded by office furniture, decommissioned arcade games, and a claw machine—the kind where you try to maneuver the claw to grab a prize.

"Where did all this come from?" I asked.

"It was here the entire time but I altered it so it existed at a different level of energetic vibration." One look at my suspicious stare and some of the patience drained from his tone. "Every atom, every particle, vibrates at a certain speed. It's quantum physics."

"I *hate* physics."

"Then think of it like listening to the radio. If you're tuned into a station, you can only hear the music that station plays, right?" Classical music filled the warehouse. "If you want to listen to different music, you need to change the station, tune into a different frequency." Connor turned an invisible dial in the air and upbeat, instrumental music played. "You've been tuned into one frequency your whole life, so before you walked in, I altered all of this and you were blind to it. Wheel one of those chairs over here," he said.

Intrigued, I reached for a chair… and my fingers passed right through it.

I gasped and jerked my hands to my chest. Did that really happen? Cautiously, I reached to touch the seat's fabric. Again, my fingers drifted through it. I leaned in for a closer look. The chair appeared just as solid, just as real as I was, but no matter how hard I tried, I could not grab hold of it. Pleasure surged through me.

"How did I do that?"

"Now try the desk," Connor said. "Think of it as a pool of water and imagine your hand slicing right through it."

I set my palm on the cool oak top. Felt solid wood grain.

"Go slowly," Connor coaxed.

I pressed downward, and my hand disappeared into the wood. Panicked, I pulled out. I pushed into the wood again, this time through the thin part, where a laptop would sit. My hand disappeared up to my wrist. I bent to look under the desk and saw my arm poking out. I wiggled my fingers. It was the creepiest thing I had ever seen and absolutely, positively, the coolest.

I pulled my arm toward me, and the desk surface rippled as it made way for my flesh. At the edge, my arm met slight resistance. I pulled a little harder, and the wood released it with a pop.

My heart did an unexpected flip, and I was filled with a boundless sense of possibility.

"Well?" he asked with an enigmatic smile.

"Teach me everything you know," I breathed.

The next hour was like something out of a crazy dream. I pushed my hand through metal shelves, walked my fingers through a pinball machine, hitting the bumpers and flippers, and watched the scoreboard light up (he did, too, and I beat him by ten thousand points. Just sayin'.) I karate chopped through a mannequin's neck and arms. And legs. And torso.

"You seem to enjoy attacking that mannequin," he noted.

I did a clumsy spin kick and my foot went through its head. "I have a particular person in mind." I wasn't violent by nature, but what could it hurt to imagine Raquelle while I practiced my new skill?

Sweat beaded on my forehead. "That's exhausting."

"It is, and now you're finally ready." He motioned me to follow him into the alley. "Now through that brick wall," he said.

I touched the rough surface of the building next door. "Really?"

"You can do this," he said.

I bolstered my courage and plunged my arm through the brick. From inside the building, a woman let out a bloodcurdling scream. I yanked my arm out and we ran back into the warehouse. Tears of laughter rolled down my cheeks. I looked at Connor through damp eyes. Maybe I was mistaken, but I thought something like pride played on his face.

"Nice work. Now I want you to do it all again." Connor nodded at the office chair, indicating where I had started.

"Can we try something else? This is cool, but what else have you got in your bag of tricks?"

He crossed his arms. "They're not tricks. Do another round, then we can move on."

"Fine." I was easily bored by repetition, even the paranormal type. I pressed my hand against the desk, and then the chair, but now my fingers barely penetrated their surface.

"What's going on?"

"I've returned everything to their natural solid form."

"So, this whole time, you were making it easy for me?"

"It opened your confidence, and that's ninety percent of any challenge, don't you think?"

That totally sucked. Here I thought I was becoming a bona fide wizard. I tried again and failed. My fingers grew tender from jabbing them against solid objects, and my concentration fizzled. I dropped my arms to my side.

"I need a break," I said.

Connor rested his fingers on his chin. "I want to do one more thing." He stepped toward me, closing that cushion of space he always maintained, until we were near enough to touch.

My senses sparked back to life. I watched his chest rise and fall with each breath. My eyes shifted to the tendons on his forearms as they flexed. Then to his bicep, full and round. Any doubts I had about his humanness left in a hurry. This was no ghost. This was a pure flesh-and-blood male, radiant and very much alive.

Even this close, Connor's aura was little more than gentle tendrils against my skin, sweeping lightly through my hair, down my cheek. Was it my imagination, or was his aura exploring me? Soft heat brushed my throat, then my collarbone. Swept light and silky across my lips. My lids closed, and a glow curled up my spine. Then the feeling receded, and I was left with the impression I'd been kissed.

Connor cleared his throat and I opened my eyes. He smiled self-consciously. "We're going to center your energy now, so when we walk out of here, you're less likely to lose control."

The warmth of his closeness overrode my focus. I couldn't find my voice, so I nodded.

"Close your eyes. Feel your heart. Find its soft, rhythmic beat."

I closed my eyes. Finding my heartbeat was simple because my pulse had jumped with each step he came nearer. I didn't know why, but for once, I had control over my rising emotion.

"Put your hand over your heart," he said.

I settled my palm on my breastbone and tried to block out the sound of his breathing.

"Imagine all of your energy, your emotion, settling into that space beneath your hand. Center it there." He paused, and then he whispered, so close, the sultriness of his words left moisture on my ear. "Can you feel it? The heat building in your chest?"

Oh, could I ever. I opened my eyes. His palm rested in the valley between solid pectoral muscles. I had to know, right then, his warmth, his aliveness. I lifted my hand away from my heart and reached for his.

Connor's eyes snapped open. He stepped out of reach and raised a hand to deflect me.

"No, Echo."

His words were as harsh as a slap in the face. Shame flooded my cheeks. "Sorry," I stuttered. "I need a break, 'kay?" I hurried out the door.

CHAPTER 8

I broke into a run outside the warehouse. The control I had while Connor trained me snapped, and my energy whipped wildly. Cardboard boxes tumbled down the alley. Flotsam twirled out of the dumpster and scattered toward the sky.

I left the industrial district behind and slowed to a walk, my head ringing with embarrassment and confusion. I didn't understand what unspoken boundary I'd crossed, only that his sudden retreat left me feeling like a leper.

Being around Connor was overwhelming in so many ways. He made me aware of every sparking nerve, every voluntary and reflexive motion in my body. My awareness of the external world heightened, too. When I'd held my breath just so I wouldn't lose the sensation of his aura, I knew I was hooked.

But hooked on who, exactly? Who was this boy with raven hair that kept flopping over one eye, who bossed me around— who I *let* boss me—and who seemed so close to opening up that my heart cracked a little bit when he didn't? I did not know, and this odd relationship teetered ever more in his favor. He had all the power; I had none. I needed to put distance between us.

But there, at the end of the block, *somehow,* Connor waited.

"Stop doing that!" I shouted and ducked into a café.

I took a table near the rear, with my back to the door. Lifted a menu and pretended to read.

Footsteps padded across the tile and stopped at my table. "Mind if I join you?"

"Do what you like," I said through the menu.

Connor took the seat across from me and slid my bracelets across the table. A truce. I ignored them.

"I'm sorry I reacted like that," he said.

"Nope, my fault. I get it, some people don't like to be touched."

"I think this would be a good time for a few ground rules," he said.

I slapped the menu down and looked at him in disbelief. "You do? Great, I'll start. First, stop popping in and out of places like, like a sci-fi transporter. If you're going to be spending time here from—where are you even *from*? Never mind, rule one: No creepy popping in and out of places. Rule two, if you're so repulsed by me then stop following me. Rule three…"

But I had no other rules, because everything was in his control. When I saw him. Where we met. Whether or not I had the privilege of touching him.

"It's not like that," he said.

I let out a sharp huff. "You turn into Mr. Freeze whenever I cross one of your invisible boundaries."

My aura began playing with the napkin holder, making the paper flutter. Self-consciously, I grabbed the bracelets and put them on. The disruption ceased.

The waitress stopped at our table, a petite girl with fuchsia streaks in her straw-colored hair. "Know what you'd like?" she asked me.

"Yeah, a turkey sandwich and a glass of water."

"And *you*, what can I get *you*?" Her smile broadened and she gave Connor the once over. Make that the twice over.

"I'll have the same, with potato salad. And do you have," he hesitated as if drawing the word from his memory. "Chili?"

"Sure do."

"Can you put some of that on the sandwich?"

"That sounds tasty! What's your name?"

I rolled my eyes while she openly flirted with the guy who could very well be my boyfriend. Except she must have sensed that he was fair game.

"Connor," he answered.

"Turkey sandwich with chili. The Connor Special. Maybe we should start offering it on the menu. I bet it would be a big hit."

She tilted her head and reached out to touch him on the arm. Her hand stopped a few inches from him as though encountering a barrier. Her expression shifted to concern. She withdrew her hand. Blinked a few times. "I'll get this order up."

"Thank you." The smile never wavered from Conner's face. The waitress retreated to the counter.

I sat bolt upright. "Right there. What was that all about? She was going to touch you but it's like she couldn't."

He chose his words carefully, considered how best to answer the complex question coming from the naïve creature across from him. "My energy field is very intense. Protective, is a better way to put it. It keeps me safe while I'm here."

There it was again, the suggestion that he was from another place. But I was more obsessed about why the waitress couldn't touch him. Why *I* wasn't allowed.

"That's why you weren't afraid to walk in front of traffic. You knew the drivers couldn't hit you," I said.

"Yes."

A new perspective dawned. "And it protects you from us." I waved my hand to indicate all the people in the café. The waitress. Me.

"In a way," he said.

If this was true, then maybe Raquelle hadn't gotten very far with him. That was some consolation.

"But when I tried to, you backed away. What's the deal? I'd get hurt if I put my hand on your arm?"

His jawline tightened. "I'd never let that happen."

"Well, that's good to know." I looked for the waitress so I could tell her to bag up my order to go.

"I meant I'd never let you get hurt. I overreacted in the warehouse."

"I'll say," I said, not willing to forgive him an inch.

Connor turned to the small, decorative lamp sitting between the condiment holder and salt and pepper shakers. He turned the lamp on and unplugged it. Then he held the plug's metal prongs between his fingers. With his other hand, he picked up his fork and before I could yell "stop!" he plunged the fork into the outlet.

My chest jolted from near cardiac arrest. I froze, in total shock, as electricity coursed through Connor and into the table lamp. The bulb lit up, and Connor, encompassed by a brilliant light, glowed. He removed the fork and set it on the table. I picked it up. The metal was hot and the prongs were charred and contorted.

"This is what would happen if I touched you?"

Connor looked horrified. "How could you even think such a thing? I did this to make a point. Everyone feels my barrier and without knowing why, they are subconsciously repelled.

Everyone except you. You don't seem to feel it at all, and if you reach through it and catch me off guard, you'll get a pretty harsh shock."

I gave this time to settle. "What if you knew I was going to touch you?"

He held his answer, just long enough for me to wonder if I'd crossed another boundary.

"I can hold back, but you'd still feel a shock."

Like a moth to a flame, I leaned closer. "Can I try?"

He hesitated, then rested his hand on the table in front of me. "Slowly," he said.

Foolishly giddy, I inched my hand toward his. When I was nearly touching him, the tips of my fingers encountered a subtle, staticky resistance. It was Connor's barrier. He was right. Unless he'd told me, I'd have missed it.

I suppressed a giggle. Then I laid my hand over his. I lasted only a second. An electric current snapped, and I yanked my hand away.

"Oh!" I said and pulled my fingertips to my mouth. A few heads turned our way, wondering at the sharp noise.

"Are you okay?"

"I think it's burned." I inspected my finger.

Worry crossed his face. "Let me see."

"No, I'm fine." Just feeling a little silly, was all. His eyes lingered on my hand.

"Would the same thing happen if you touched me?" I asked.

Connor's smile was wistful. "If we spent enough time together, our energies might find some equilibrium. Until then, yes."

That longing expression he'd had outside my house returned, and my mind tripped back to the warehouse, where I was sure he'd explored me with his aura. Something wasn't adding up.

"Are you really here just to teach me how to protect myself?"

"Yes," he said, but I caught uncertainty in those blue-flecked eyes.

The waitress couldn't have picked a worse time to deliver our orders.

"Oh, what happened to your fork?" she asked. "I'll get you another one."

I slid my silverware across the table. "It's okay, he can use mine."

We ate in silence. I stole long stares at Connor, and the questions piled up. When we finished, he pulled out a few bills and left them on the table.

As we walked outside, I noticed Connor's fingers flicker. In the brilliant sunshine, they resembled light bulbs on the verge of burning out.

"Um, you're starting to fade," I said.

"Thank you." He tucked his hands in his pockets. His shoulders drooped and he set the pace at a slow walk, visibly fatigued. He flashed a knowing smile. "Go ahead."

"What?"

"You want to ask me something."

"I do have a question or two." Or ten. Or a thousand.

I blew out a puff of air. Where to start? "When we were in the gym, you said people would try to hurt me. Why?"

"Let me ask you something. Have you noticed the number of psychics—crystal ball readers and Tarot readers—setting up shop lately?"

I thought about this. Before I moved from Seattle, my favorite coffee shop had been turned into a psychic den. Not far away, someone else advertised medium powers, whatever that was. More notable, though, was Becca, who confided her interest in becoming a turban-wearing-psychic if the potion thing didn't work out. Until recently, I hadn't taken any of this seriously.

"I guess," I shrugged. "But they all seem pretty flakey."

"Some of them are scamming, but many of them are very gifted. There are countless numbers of men and women who can see the future, read other people's energy, and heal with their hands."

"Like you did with Tito."

"Yes. This region is safer than most for gifted people. In other parts of the country, they don't fare so well."

We reached a corner, and he proceeded into the intersection without looking. I stopped to let the cars whiz past. "It's kind of rude to walk out in front of drivers," I said.

"We'll do it your way, then." He waited at the curb with me and continued. "A girl wakes up in a small town in Missouri and for reasons she cannot explain, she's suddenly able to see auras—the colorful energy field around people. She tries to tell her family, good people who love their daughter very much, but they fear she's going crazy. The girl is shuttled from one psychiatrist to another. She stands by her claim and eventually she is institutionalized, 'for her own good.' She's put on a strong regimen of drugs to make her easier to deal with. Eventually, her ability fades. Maybe she's released from the hospital or maybe she's stuck there for the rest of her life."

"That's what I'm afraid of," I whispered.

Connor continued. "A man in Iowa survives a car crash and discovers he now has the ability to predict the future of every person he touches. It's an extraordinary gift, but his friends fall away when they learn he can't deliver just good news. He feels obligated to tell them the bad news, too—that they're about to lose their jobs, or their wives will cheat on them, or their child will become terminally ill. After a time, his family refuses to speak to him, and he's rejected by those he loves most. His next car crash is fatal, because he hates himself so deeply that he drives into an oncoming semi."

I let out a gasp. This story touched a nerve, because I could relate to this man's pain.

"These tragedies, they're happening every day. You're all going through a great awakening. So many of you are coming into your power." Anger flared in his eyes. "But instead of thriving, this world crushes you."

"Did you try to help these people?" I asked.

"We're not allowed."

"What do you mean 'we'?"

He shook his head. "One thing at a time."

"Okay. So, there are a lot of people out there going through this, right?"

"Countless individuals."

"And you're not allowed to help them."

Connor was still.

"And yet you're here with me," I continued.

Heat flickered between us. He looked away. "You said yourself that your ability was overtaking your life. I want you to learn how to…"

"Yeah, I know, manage it and protect myself. But why *me*?"

He stopped and turned to face me. "Echo, there are factions that hunt down and enslave gifted ones like you. Their loved ones report them missing, but they're never seen again, alive or dead."

"What happens to them?"

His eyes darkened. "Just promise me you'll keep your auric energy under control, and you'll be okay."

A tremble of alarm crossed my face. Connor reached as though to console me, caught himself, and pulled back. Sadness filled his green eyes. Then his attention pulled inward. He dipped his head to the side like he was listening to a voice only he could hear. A moment later, his focus returned.

He sighed, clearly frustrated. "I have to go."

"Now?"

"My coming here constitutes a serious breach of authority. If I don't leave now, I risk getting caught."

"But, wait, are you coming back?"

"As soon as I can. You'll practice what I taught you, right?" His voice was urgent. His upper body grew transparent.

I was flustered beyond coherency. "Um, sure, but…"

Sparks filled his body, he fizzled, and he was gone. I stared at the empty sidewalk. "That is *so* cool!"

CHAPTER 9

When I got home, I bounded up the stairs to my room and flung the window open to see if, by any chance, Connor had decided to return to the portico roof. An ache filled my chest when I found the lawn chair empty.

The idea that he risked punishment to spend time with me was so romantic, so… sexy. And even though he insisted he came here just to teach me, I detected hints of something else lurking behind his cool façade. Like, maybe he didn't just think of me as a pity project and he actually liked me.

The notion hit that he might never return. If he was caught traveling back, what would happen to him? I couldn't allow myself to think about that.

I was busting to tell someone about my mind-boggling day. How Connor pushed the boundaries of everything I knew to be true, challenged the way I thought about myself. How my headache eased when I'd learned to control the fluctuations in my energy.

I grabbed my cell phone and pecked out a text to Becca. When I finished typing, the words glared back at me:

Supernatural. Quantum physics. Higher vibration.

My thumb hung over the Send button. Becca could take my text one of two ways. Either she'd dismiss it and think I'd gone loony, or be all over it and pressure me to show her what I could do. How much was I willing to share? Once she knew the real me, would our friendship change? It's one thing to say telekinesis is cool, but would she feel the same way if she watched my bed flip upside down when I got mad, or saw books fly into my bedroom window and fall to the floor like downed birds? Spooky as that would be, I decided yes, she could handle it. She would stand by my side, freakshow and all.

But, could she keep my ability a secret? No way.

Reluctantly, I hit *Delete*. Then I rescued Tito from Kimber's room and took him for a walk. I told him about my day and although his ears perked when I mentioned Connor's name, he didn't seem impressed. Who could blame him? After listening to myself, I could hardly believe any of it.

A quick scan around my West Vista neighborhood told me nobody was within eyesight. I pulled Connor's coin out of my pocket and, as we walked, tried to levitate it above my palm. I'd gone only a few steps before it twitched and rose. With a bit of concentration, I got it to flip in the air.

A black BMW cut me off as it pulled into a driveway. The driver's door burst open and I dropped the coin. It rolled and stopped at Mr. Crane's feet. He had his cell phone pressed to his ear. He looked from the coin to me and back again. He'd seen it floating above my hand.

"I'm tired of excuses," Mr. Crane yelled into the phone. "I was promised full access."

Even though I wasn't the subject of his anger, my body keyed up and went on the defensive. My forehead buzzed, and the shrubbery reached toward me.

"Check it now," he sputtered into the phone. "Yes, I'll hold." Mr. Crane covered the mouthpiece and looked fixedly at me, his neck ruddy from aggravation.

"Have you heard from my office?" he asked.

"Um, what?"

"The research appointment. We talked about this at dinner."

Oh, right, the dreaded Saturday research study. "No one's called that I know of."

"Kimber has the number. Call in and set a time. I'll pay you a hundred dollars."

"I thought it was all volunteer."

"Some of our subjects… dropped out. We're on a deadline." The red on his neck deepened. "We're now offering compensation." He picked up Connor's coin. "What's this, a trick coin? Unless my eyes deceive, it was hovering above your hand."

I swallowed. "Oh, that's an illusion. With the light refracting? Against the shiny object and the angle of the sun?" I was making stuff up at this point. "Lab assignment for physics. I love physics!"

Mr. Crane's eyes narrowed at my clumsy lie but he returned the coin.

The person on the phone came back on the line and I hightailed it out of there.

"You'll never get away with this!" Mr. Crane shouted, and though I was pretty sure he wasn't talking to me, his hostility bore a hole into my back.

Tito had to trot to keep pace with me on the way home. I swore I wouldn't do any more tricks in public.

I thought about how I'd get out of Mr. Crane's offer. A hundred dollars for a few hours on a Saturday was tempting—until you factored in the personal questions that were bound to come up, and the scrutiny as he ran me through who-knew-what-kind of tests. There was no guarantee I could hold myself together through all of it. I hadn't even made it through dinner with him.

When Tito and I got in front of Becca's house, she stuck her head out her door. "Didn't I see you driving through town? I thought you were sick."

"I was home, mostly," I said.

"You are such a bad liar. UPS dropped a box here because nobody answered at your house. My mom signed for it."

I lifted a shoulder, guilty.

Becca and I carried the box home and hauled it upstairs. The packing tape was yellowed, and the faded black writing across the top designated the contents for Echo's Room. I unceremoniously dropped it in my closet.

"Aren't you curious what's inside?" she asked.

"It's been in storage for over a year, so whatever it is, I probably don't need it."

"Then dibs on anything black," Becca said and ripped open the flaps. She reached in and pulled out a few outdated shirts. Beneath these, handfuls of blue and red award ribbons. "What have we here?"

My face lit up. "I thought those got thrown out."

"Best in Show," she read on one of them. "Best in Category. Were you one of those dog show people? No judgement, they're not all weirdos."

"Art shows," I said, taking one from her. "I got into oil painting when I was in elementary school. I was pretty good."

"Understatement of the year." Becca unloaded more first and second place ribbons. "Why'd you quit?"

"I dunno. I guess I lost interest."

We dove into the box. Clothing, printouts of report cards from elementary school, and souvenir trinkets emerged like old friends. Lying at the bottom, mottled with dust and lint, a painting. I pulled it out, and my hand flew to my mouth.

"That's Connor!" Becca said.

We looked at each other and then back at the painting.

"I thought you just met him the other day," she said.

"I did." I studied the dark hair that curled above his ears. The cowlick falling across his forehead. Those piercing green eyes. This was definitely him. Except for one thing. My finger traced the jagged mark slanting from his eyebrow to his hairline.

"I don't remember Connor having a scar," Becca said.

Because he doesn't, I wanted to say. Instead, I said, "Me neither."

"What's his picture doing at the bottom of this box?"

I wasn't sure how to answer that. When I'd painted the portrait, I was ten years old, the youngest member of a special art session held at the high school. I'd begged my dad to let me attend. One day, the instructor directed our attention to a fully clothed male model sitting at the front of the room. The lesson was realism, and our task was to paint the subject exactly as he appeared.

The next thing I knew, the timer went off and my instructor was inspecting our canvasses. I took one look at my work and knew I was in trouble. The man at the front of the room, our subject, was old, and had a gray goatee and glasses. I'd painted a young, dark-haired Adonis.

"Why didn't you paint the man up there?" my instructor had demanded.

"I don't know." The past few hours had slipped away. I couldn't remember painting anything at all.

"If we were grading, I'd have to give you a D," she'd scolded. "Your painting is very lifelike, but it's the wrong life."

Seven years later, her words took on a whole new meaning. As much to convince myself as Becca, I said, "You know what? This looks a lot like my old neighbor." If I appraised it from a distance and squinted really hard.

"Yeah?"

"Sure. He had a scar kind of like that. Same place. Sort of." I pressed my lips together and reinforced my conclusion with a firm nod. "What a crazy coincidence, hey?"

"If he wasn't so gorgeous, I'd be spooked out. Even that cowlick is the same. Dude must have a doppelganger," Becca said.

Those blue-flecked eyes stared back with lifelike intensity. My teacher's words rang in my ears. *Your painting is very lifelike, but it's the wrong life.*

They haunted me the rest of the night.

The next morning, as Becca and I hurried between classes, my phone beeped. I read the news flash, and a moan escaped.

"I know that sound," Becca said. "What did Raquelle do now?"

"She went out with Connor the other night."

Becca grabbed my phone to see for herself. "She posted the pics on Instagram."

"Yup." I took the phone back. Raquelle had never dropped me from her friends list. Probably so I could view the horrible things she wrote about me. Which I never did. Much.

I scrolled through the pictures from the night I'd missed my meeting with Connor. Raquelle and Connor were standing on her doorstep, in a restaurant, in a club. One great shot after another. Raquelle had gone on the hunt, gotten the guy, and posted her trophy pictures.

"Sorry," Becca said. "I know you liked him. Even if you said you didn't." She quirked an eyebrow. "Why are you smiling?"

My grin was ear-to-ear as I flipped through the pictures. "She doesn't have a chance with him."

Becca interpreted my scheming look. "You're going after Connor? No offense, but you're really no match for her."

"Offense taken." But I couldn't stop smiling because I spotted the one thing she hadn't: space. No matter how many people were in each photo, everyone kept at least an arm's length away from Connor. Even Raquelle was left posing solo, leaning toward him but never touching. If he'd let his barrier down long enough for her to nestle up to him, she'd have posted that picture front and center.

All day long I looked at my world differently. I wanted to challenge it. Even though Mr. Crane nearly caught me the other day, the temptation to play with my ability won. When the lights dimmed in physics, I levitated a pen out of my book bag and let it hover over my lap. I sliced my fingers through my textbook while Becca looked the other way. Once, in the hallway, when no one was around, I pushed my hand into my closed locker and pulled it out again. Back in. Out. In. Out.

It wasn't like I decided to accept the freakish things I could do, I just didn't hate them at the moment. Part of what fueled this change was the way Connor had looked at me when I did these impossible things, like I was part of a secret tribe, one where he and I were the only members.

I'd never known a single person to take up so much space in my head. When I rolled over in bed to turn off my alarm, the image of his gorgeous face faded, like I'd been dreaming of him. All day, I relived the scene in the café when he let me touch him, holding back his power so he wouldn't hurt me.

I was replaying this in my head for the thousandth time when I found Becca in the lunch line, waiting to pay for her sandwich and apple. I grabbed a yogurt and gave her a gentle hip-check. The apple nearly rolled off her tray. She said something but I was remembering that part in the café where Connor stuck a fork in the outlet, so I didn't hear her.

Raquelle and Trisha shoved in front of us.

"Hey, no cutting," Becca said.

"Who are you, the line police?" Raquelle stuck her butt out, forcing us to read her signature moniker, Partychick, emblazoned across the seat of her sweatpants. Trisha wore the exact same sweats. If I were still in their clique, I probably would be, too.

"When he's in town again, I'm taking him to the Rose Club," Raquelle said to Trisha.

"Omigod, you have to get the VIP Room. It's private, and you can lock the door from the inside."

"Done and done," Raquelle said.

"I've been fantasizing about those lips since the day we met him," Trisha swooned.

"That's all you'll be doing, bee-otch. When I'm finished with Connor, no other girl will ever measure up."

Hearing this from Raquelle infuriated me. "You're not even Connor's type," I snapped.

"Tall, blonde, hot, and rich? Baby, I'm every guy's type." She and Trisha snickered. Then Raquelle casually reached back with her elbow and brought it down on my yogurt, sending it to the floor.

"Oops." They sauntered to their table.

"God, I hate her," Becca said.

I picked up my yogurt. A harsh buzz danced above the bridge of my nose. The fact that I was powerless to fight back the way I wanted made my blood boil. Nix that. It was the way she talked about Connor, the assumption that he was putty in her dirty hands that sent hateful, black energy into my aura.

Ultimately, it was none of my business what he did. I thought he liked me, but he'd practically said he was training me out of a sense of obligation. For all I knew, the two of them hung out on days that I didn't see him. There it was, the awful truth.

Becca's apple shot off her tray and hit Raquelle in the back. She spun and gave us the finger. I bit my lip to keep from laughing. Whoops.

"What the—" Becca gaped at the apple, now rolling under a table. She shot me an accusing glance, like I'd picked it up and thrown it.

"Don't look at me, I never touched it," I said.

"That must have been me." Becca's face lit up like she'd won the lottery.

CHAPTER 10

Coin levitation. Centering. School. Centering. Centering. Centering.

Every day after school, I locked myself in my room, using homework as my excuse. I devoted every spare minute to practicing what Connor taught me.

Coin levitation seemed to be my thing, and I navigated Connor's token around my bedroom with ease. I turned it into a game, jiggling the token in front of Tito until he snapped at it, and then zipping it out of his reach. None of this was easy. Sometimes, I concentrated so hard, my teeth ground together.

After each little victory, I rewarded myself with a full on, Connor-infused fantasy. If I kept the token afloat for a full minute, I imagined brushing that cowlick from his forehead. If the token circled the entire room without bumping into anything, I closed my eyes and drifted into his kiss.

Days passed without any sign of him. I worried my cuticles down to the last layer, consumed with the possibility that he'd disappeared for good.

At the end of the week, I flopped onto my bed, too disheartened to practice and convinced it didn't matter one iota. My control was dwindling and little annoyances at school were triggering outbursts again.

I gazed at Connor's portrait leaning against the cardboard box. I wished I'd asked more questions when I had the chance. Like where he went when he faded into the ether, and what his family was like and whether they accepted his ability.

I wondered who supported him and his gifts. He'd talked about people here, like the girl who saw auras, and the man who could tell the future after enduring brain trauma in a car accident. Did this sort of thing occur where he lived? Were gifted people a part of his life?

More to the point, why weren't they a part of mine? If Connor was right, thousands of us struggled in this unaccepting world. I had to find them. They understood what I was going through. They were my tribe.

I grabbed my phone and sat cross-legged on my bed. A few web searches told me what I already knew. Portland was home to psychics galore. I found clairvoyants by the dozen, and people who could speak to the dead. These were cool abilities, but compared to what I was experiencing, they were relatively commonplace. I wanted to find the weirdest of the weird, the true freaks. Those people whose abilities had turned their lives upside down.

I sifted through countless websites. The most interesting one listed people who claimed to have gained abilities after accidents, illnesses, or even being hit by lightning. There was the guy who survived a brain tumor and found that he could sketch intricate scenes from memory; the woman who woke from a coma and lost her ability to speak but had become a math genius; the woman who survived a fall and claimed to be able to set things on fire with her mind.

The last one got my hopes up, but she turned out to be a fraud. She'd invited paranormal investigators to her house so they could test her claim. She started fires, all right. The flames got so out of control, the house burned down. When the fire marshal sifted through the rubble, he found well-placed combustible chemicals. Apparently, she'd planted these throughout her house and set them off during the interview.

I tossed my phone aside. Finding my tribe wasn't going to be easy. Further, with so many fakes in the world, who would take me seriously? According to Connor, the ones with a real interest in me were dangerous. His warning rang through my head:

"There are factions that hunt down and enslave gifted ones like you. Their loved ones report them missing, but they're never seen again."

I dropped my head into my hands, unable to see a future where I was embraced by my own kind, a future where I wasn't constantly on guard.

A knock sounded on my door.

"It's open," I said weakly.

The door cracked open and a familiar voice spoke. "Can I come in, honey?"

"Dad!" I jumped off the bed and into his arms. He dropped his briefcase and lifted me off the floor. This was a compromise after so many years of being swung in a circle. I was too big and too old for that now, but age and size didn't diminish the joy that rolled off his aura and into mine. Quick as flicking a switch, my pain lifted.

"Meetings ended early, and I caught the next flight home." He ran a hand through his dark blond hair. If we shared any features, it was the way our eyes turned up at the corners. Cat eyes, he called them.

He pulled up a chair, and we caught up. I grumbled when he told me his company was growing faster than expected and he'd be on the road more. I didn't see enough of him as it was. Lately, he'd been importing some sort of computer part from Asia to sell in the States, and his new clients were sucking up a lot of his time.

We settled into a comfortable routine.

"School?" he asked.

"Hanging in there."

"Grades?"

"Physics is killing me."

"Staying out of jail?"

"As far as you know," I smirked.

"No drugs, pregnancies, or cult activities?"

I rolled my eyes at the pregnancy reference. "Way to sneak that in there, Dad."

"Just feeling like a neglectful parent lately. Where's Kimber tonight? You haven't kicked her out, have you?"

"She keeps the fridge full and we don't fight much anymore, so I thought I'd keep her."

"Very thoughtful of you."

"Yeah, well, you went and married her, so it's the least I could do." I exhaled a dramatic sigh.

He patted my knee. "My girl, ever the diplomat."

I wanted to tell him about my tele-chaosing, but that was one of the few secrets I kept from him. I didn't want to give him a heart attack.

Dad spotted the painting of Connor. His face lit, and he picked it up.

"I remember the day you brought this home. You were so mad at the teacher, you threw it out. I fished it from the garbage when you weren't looking. Are you thinking of starting again?"

"Nah. I'm trying to remember who it is." I had to have seen someone that looked like Connor, right? I mean, I didn't just make him up. "Does it look like anyone we knew from Seattle?"

"No one comes to mind." My dad gave the painting all his attention. "You sure had a thing for green eyes," he finally said.

"What makes you say that?"

"Everything you drew in elementary school had big green eyes. Dogs, cats, made-up animals, trees, houses. It got kind of weird, there, for a while."

I had no memory of this. "Where are these drawings? Did you keep any of them?"

He shook his head. "Sorry, honey, I tossed them in the garbage. I never thought you'd want them."

"It's okay. That was a whole different lifetime ago." I startled myself with the phrase.

While I drove us to school, Becca surfed social media, catching up on news we'd missed overnight.

"Oooo, Trisha and Raquelle's Homecoming party is officially on our calendar."

"We're invited?"

"Not exactly, but we're aware and that's, like, practically invited, right?"

"Unless they block us at the door."

"That was one time," Becca said. "I want to go. I've been eyeing this guy in Civics class and overheard that he might be going. The party is the perfect environment to cast my spell over him."

"*Becca*," I warned.

"Not literally. I was referring to my feminine charm, but while we're on the topic of magical influence, I gotta ask you something. You know the weird things that happened in

Physics class, and then the other day, the way my apple just flew off my tray?"

Uh-oh, I thought.

Becca bit the inside of her cheek and gave me an odd look. "You have to promise not to laugh."

Easy enough. I knew what was coming, and my sense of humor went into duck-and-cover mode. "I promise."

"Here goes. I'm just going to come right out and say it. I think I'm getting telekinesis."

A sharp laugh punctuated the air. A second passed before I realized it was mine. Becca looked at me, appalled.

"Oh, no, Becca, I didn't mean that. I'm just so *relieved*. I thought you were going to say you had bad news or something."

"Yeah, right. You don't believe me. You think I'm an idiot for even suggesting it." She crossed her legs and her foot bounced in irritation.

"It's not that. Seriously, if anyone believes in telekinesis, it's me."

"Oh, now you're a big believer. I never should have said anything, but I'm beginning to see a pattern. I'm writing it all down in my Wiccan diary, for posterity. If I can figure out how to move things with my mind whenever I want, maybe I can cash in on it."

"That's really exciting," I forced myself to say. "I can't wait to hear how it turns out."

Unconvinced, her foot took on a sharper rhythm.

"So, about that party, I think we should go," I said, but only to make amends.

"You don't. You're just saying that because I'm mad at you."

"Not at all. I'm in. We're going."

"Last time you said that, we missed the party of the century."

"I got sick that day." In truth, my tele-chaosing had just started and I was terrified to step outside my bedroom. Becca couldn't find a last-minute ride and was mad at me for days.

"And the time before that…"

"I know, I made us late for the full moon party at the beach and bailed on the camping trip." I leaned in and dropped my voice. "I happen to know that Trisha's bedroom door opens to the patio. We'll sneak in and mix into the crowd before anyone sees us."

Becca gave me a hard look. "Yeah. All right, but you better not back out this time."

"You can count on me."

CHAPTER II

Maybe it was the conversation on the way to school, maybe it was the practice quiz in History, but my aura was out of whack all day long. In Physics, I gripped my bracelets, willing the lights to stop flickering. Next to me, Becca watched the odd activity around us and held back a hopeful smile. I just shook my head. *Be careful what you wish for,* I wanted to say. But of course, I couldn't.

It was pouring outside so I snuck into the auditorium before lunch and let loose. Stage lighting swung dangerously overhead, and the tall velvet stage curtains whipped like they were caught in a wind storm. This release helped, but even with all the training my tele-chaosing was getting more and more out of control. Panic was starting to set in. I did not know what to do or who to turn to, and I wasn't going to be able to hold onto this secret for much longer.

After final bell, Becca and I headed to the parking lot.

"What's that all about?" She nodded at the cluster of upper-clique girls milling by my car. We hung on the fringe of the crowd, unable to move beyond them.

"With these elbows, you will flee. Nasty girls, away from me!" Becca called out the hex and jabbed a girl in the ribs. Nobody budged. Someone pushed back.

"Mooove iiit!" Becca yelled, and the girls parted just enough for us to get through.

As I inched toward my car, my eyes landed on a pair of worn tennis shoes sporting an odd logo. My gaze moved to the jeans hanging on masculine hips, hips that leaned against the hood of my car. A dark t-shirt filled out well-muscled arms. I lifted my chin and met Connor's gaze. A thrill pulsed through every nerve ending in my body.

"Hey," I said and tossed him a cool nod. My legs wobbled.

"There you are. It's good to see you." He flashed a smile.

A tingle rushed to my belly and lust threatened to bubble into my aura. "It's good to see you, too." The crazy intensity I felt was enough to flip my car on its side. I clenched my fist in an effort to keep control.

All around me, the cloud of girls' auras vibrated with astonishment. I didn't have to turn to see the jaws hanging open or the eyes narrowing in disdain. Then the crowd shifted and Raquelle swayed to the front. She placed her body directly in front of mine like I didn't exist, and locked her attention on Connor.

"There you are. You've been gone too long. I've been thinking about you constantly," she cooed.

"You don't say," he responded indifferently.

Raquelle sashayed closer to him. Then her weight shifted to her heels and she stopped. Her lashes fluttered in brief confusion. I muffled a laugh. She'd just bumped into Connor's barrier.

Undaunted, Raquelle angled her elbow, inviting him to link arms. "Why don't you walk me to my car?" she offered.

"Echo and I have plans."

"Huh?" her voice cracked.

I stepped around her. "You heard him."

A collective gasp came from the other girls. I could practically hear Raquelle's claws come out, ready to rip me to shreds. But she'd never lose her cool in front of a guy she wanted on her Hit List.

Raquelle recovered with a sultry smile. "Call me tonight. I made rezzies for us at the Rose Club. The VIP room. Guaranteed privacy." She mouthed the last words and strutted to her car. The rest of the girls scattered, gossiping and texting the latest drama. Becca waved from across the parking lot, signaling that she'd find her way home.

Connor turned his attention to me. "Rezzies?"

"Reservations. She wants to get you drunk and take advantage of you. It's her usual modus operandi."

"Why would I go with her?"

"Well, you went out with her last week." I sounded jealous and wished I could take it back.

He looked at me, quizzically. "I'm not interested in Raquelle. I came here to steal you away," he smiled. "That is, if you're up for another lesson. I don't want to bring on more than you can handle."

My heart pressed against my chest, and warmth shot into my energy field. He lifted an eyebrow. Shoot, he'd felt that. The best I could do was run with it.

"Is that a challenge? Oh, bring it on," I said.

"Let's go, then. Would you like me to drive?"

"Do they even have cars where you're from?" I teased.

I dangled the keys in front of him. In response, he rapped his knuckle on the passenger side door, and the interior locks popped up. He opened the door and motioned that I get in.

Connor climbed into the driver's seat. He pressed two fingers onto the ignition switch, and the engine turned over. The car reversed out of the parking spot, then rolled onto the street and into traffic. He never touched the steering wheel. I shook my head in awe.

"I did a bit of research and taught myself how to drive," he said.

"Don't they teach you this in school?" I baited him so he'd have to either tell me about himself or shut me out again.

His jaw worked and he bit his lower lip, as though wrestling with an internal debate.

"West Region, where I live, doesn't have vehicles like this anymore," he finally said. "East Region still uses them, but of course, no one in their right mind lives in East Region voluntarily. I researched old books to learn how to drive."

West Region? East Region?

"And where exactly is West Region?"

"Right here. Portland is the capitol of West Region. In the year 2173."

My eyebrows hit my hairline. *Are you freaking kidding me?*

"I was afraid you'd react like that," he said.

"What did you expect? You just told me you've traveled…" I tried to do a quick mental calculation. I stunk at math, so I subtracted what I could and rounded down. "You came from 150 years in the future?"

"Closer to 160 years."

"How did you expect me to react?"

He considered this. "If I'm honest, this is about right."

In my state of shock, I hadn't realized that Connor's full attention had been on me. He had yet to look out the windshield. A car cut in front of us.

"Watch where we're going!" I yelled.

He glimpsed at the other vehicle, unperturbed.

"You said back in, wherever, you learned how to drive."

"West Region. Yes, but I didn't say I liked it. You've got all these panels and pedals and buttons."

I couldn't tell you what expression was on my face, but it made Connor laugh.

"It's much more natural to use my mind to control devices. I promise, you are perfectly safe."

My car stopped at a red light and idled, all on its own. I crossed my arms, unable to accept this transition. "Please? At least make it look like you're in control?"

"Really, Echo. You pushed your hand through a brick wall last week, and *this* bothers you?"

"Old habits die hard?" I gave him a sheepish smile.

He took the wheel and faced forward.

"Where are we going?"

"Back to the warehouse. Unless you know of a better place?"

I shook my head. There might have been, but I couldn't think *at all*. "What's it like? A hundred and sixty years from now?"

"Depends on where you live. A lot of horrible things happen between your lifetime and mine." He dismissed an entire century and a half with a shrug, but I caught the hint of sadness in his voice.

"You're holding back again. You start telling me something and then stop. I don't want partial answers anymore."

He assessed me tenderly. "All right. A series of natural disasters destabilize the world economy. Civil war breaks out in many countries, including the U.S. Millions of people die and eventually, the country is split in two. Each side rebuilds into their ideal version of a functioning statehood. My family is lucky. We live in West Region and have done very well there. East Region, the eastern half of the country, struggles under a dictatorship.

"The rest of the world is spotty. Some of it has evolved like West Region, some remains like the East. Much of it is still decimated from the Collapse. So many records were destroyed, we don't know when this started but by the time I was born, most of the world you know is gone."

My mind reeled. Outside the car, my city flashed by. Though I'd driven this route countless times, I was suddenly aware of its unique beauty. I couldn't take my eyes off the bridges, the fountains, the people bustling across the red paver bricks at Pioneer Square. I don't know what I expected to happen in the future. Certainly not total devastation.

"It's all gone?" I whispered.

"That's how events have played out," Connor said carefully. "I know it's a lot to take in. I didn't want to upset you."

We drove in silence while I tried to absorb this. I couldn't. The idea that my beloved world would one day fall to destruction horrified me, but I couldn't let it consume me. Not now, after I'd waited so long for Connor to come back.

"So, West Region. Does everyone wear silver spandex and drive a flying saucer?" I asked.

"Spandex?"

"It's stretchy fabric that always shows up in futuristic movies. Along with laser guns and robots."

A sideways glance at me.

"What?" I asked.

"I just told you I transported across time and you want to know about our current fashion?"

"Well, pardon me, but I'm kind of in shock, here."

"No to the spandex and the flying saucers. Laser guns and robots? Maybe before the Collapse. We do have a portal, though. That's how I move back and forth between my time and yours. Travel is strictly monitored and limited. And it's dangerous. Not everyone makes it through safely."

The quiver in his voice caught my attention. "Was it scary? The traveling part?"

He stayed focused on the road, but he swallowed hard. "Yes. The first couple of times I tried to come here didn't work out the way I planned."

"Like when Becca and I met you at my house and your skin got transparent?"

Connor's eyebrows arched. "So, you did see that."

"Just in your hands."

"What about Becca?"

"I think she was too bowled over by your looks to notice."

His hands tightened on the wheel. Tiny muscles in his jaw flexed. "If I'm going to continue to move back and forth, there can't be any question about my humanness. My first day here, I was hesitant to approach you at all. I could feel parts of me flickering in and out."

"It wasn't as bad as when you showed up in my classroom."

His eyes went wide. "You weren't supposed to see me. Not yet."

"You were pretty hard to ignore. I thought I was losing my mind."

"What about the other students?"

I shook my head. "I was the only one." I thought about how I knew this. The change in emotion would have been unmistakable. Disbelief. Awe. Primal fear. None of which were that common in Physics class outside of midterms and finals week. "I would have felt their reaction," I said.

Connor relaxed. "So, your friend thinks I'm attractive?" He tilted his head back. "Come to think of it, she is kind of cute. Is she single?"

A tiny huff escaped.

"Are you jealous?" It was Connor's turn to tease.

I jerked a casual shrug. "It's none of my business what you do here. For all I know, this could be like spring break for you. All fun and chasing girls."

"I promise, I have more important things to do," he said.

Connor parked my car at the entrance to the alley. Our doors popped open. We slid out, and the doors magically closed. I dug in my bag for my keys.

"Hang on, I want to lock up," I said.

He was already deep into the alley. "Nobody will touch your car, Echo."

I hesitated. Car thefts were a daily reality. If mine was stolen, I'd be in huge trouble. I twirled the keys, anxious, and dropped them back into my bag.

CHAPTER 12

At the end of the alley, I slipped inside the open warehouse door. Today, the roof was in place, with no sign of the open sky. Dust motes drifted lazily through shafts of sunlight coming in through high windows. Connor waited in the sun, his fingers tapping a nervous rhythm on his leg. When the door closed behind me, he relaxed.

"You thought I wasn't coming?" I asked.

"When a guy tells a girl he jumps time through portals, it's hard to know how she'll react. I keep waiting for you to run screaming in the opposite direction."

"I guess one of your talents isn't predicting the future."

"Sadly, no. We have oracles who do that."

Oracles. Portals. The Collapse. I pressed my fingers into my eyelids. "Okay, I gotta ask. This whole time-jumping thing. Aren't you messing up the future by traveling here?"

"The portal won't deliver me to a place where I could cause a negative impact on time. We don't know how or why this works but the fact that I've arrived means it's okay for me to be here," Connor replied.

"Or maybe that you're *supposed* to be here?"

"That I don't know."

"I have another question," I said.

"Only one?"

"Thinking beyond that makes me dizzy."

"One more. Then we get to work."

"You live more than a century into the future. How did you even know about me?"

"Something must have changed in your nervous system recently, and that affected your entire energy field. You might have felt it around your third eye." He pointed to the center of his forehead.

I nodded. "I was in an accident. I had a pretty bad head injury and the doctors said my brainwaves changed."

Connor thought about this. "That must have affected your aura. I'd guess that your aura became so powerful, it acted like a beacon across time. The impact hit me like an explosion. I didn't know why, exactly, but I knew I needed to find you, so I went to the portal and begged them to let me travel."

"And you hopped in the portal and voila, you showed up here." I snapped my fingers, still not believing he'd so easily come to the aid of a complete stranger.

"No. Twice I ended up... I don't know where. Other dimensions, other realities, places that seemed overtaken by Hell. Philip and Jaxon, the portal workers, were barely able to pull me back. They tried to talk me out of leaving again, but your energy, I couldn't shake it. I didn't *want* to. I... *required* them to let me try again. I finally understood that all I had to do was focus my full attention on you, no matter where you were. If I could hold that focus, the portal would deliver me there. After doing this a few times, I've left a sort of a trail, so now it's easier to move between worlds."

As I watched the uncertainty, fear, and determination cross his beautiful face, I finally understood. I wasn't an obligation. Connor had felt me, felt for me, and found me.

Inside, I was staggering. I sensed my aura melting around him. Instead of stepping toward me, as I craved for him to do, sadness flitted across his face and he turned his back.

"Let's get to work," he said.

What was with this guy? His sudden aloofness only made me want to probe more.

"There's something you're not telling me," I said.

"Now you're psychic?"

If only. Then maybe I'd know why his portrait was sitting in my bedroom. Asking about this directly would only sound weird.

"Have we met before?" I asked.

"The only way you'll know is if you master the next task."

"Say what?"

"When you learn it, I'll answer your question. Where's your communication device?"

"It's called a cell phone." I dug it from my bag and set it on the floor in front of Connor. He picked it up. "Take a minute to center your energy the way I taught you last time."

I did, and my aura condensed around my body in a powerful cocoon. Confidence flowed into me, and my chest flared with heat.

"Now take all that energy and focus it into your left palm."

I set my jaw in concentration. My hand became warm and prickly.

"Point your palm at the phone and move it out of my hand and straight at that chair, as though the phone is a laser beam and the chair is your worst enemy."

"Oh, no problem there." I conjured up Raquelle's face and *zing*, the phone shot across the warehouse, tapped the back of the chair, and landed on the seat. I was so intent on getting answers, I didn't even worry about breaking my phone.

"You've been practicing." Darned if he didn't sound impressed.

"Yep. Now, have we met before?"

"Nope. This time, take the phone and…"

"Wait a minute, that's it? 'Nope?'"

"You want me to lie?"

"You've never been to Seattle or Portland, not ever before?"

"No, no, and no. Now I want you to repeat the exercise a few more times."

"No, no, and no." I propped my hands on my hips. Connor's eyebrow arched. "This is too easy," I said. "The phone thing is just a mock exercise. What is it you really want me to learn?"

"To use your energy to blast a hole through that chair."

"Oh." Not what I expected. "Why?"

"So you can defend yourself against the faction, should you ever be attacked by one of their soldiers. You gather every bit of your energy, focus it into a singular beam and impale your enemy with it." His eyes blazed.

"Wait a second, back up. You're saying I'll have to kill someone?"

"Echo, I don't know what the future holds for you. The best I can do is make sure you're prepared for the very worst."

This struck me as odd. "But you live in the future. Can't you go look up what happens to me?"

"If those records ever existed, they were probably lost in the Collapse."

Some of my excitement washed away. I didn't want to hurt anyone. Except Raquelle, and impalement was just wishful thinking where she was concerned. "Isn't there another way to protect myself? I'm not crazy about shooting anyone with a laser beamy thing."

"You need to know this."

I took a deep breath. Connor hadn't let me down so far. I pointed my palm at the chair and imagined a hot, sharp laser beaming from it until the skin turned an angry red.

"This can't be normal," I said.

"Does it hurt?"

It was starting to, but I shook my head.

"Keep going."

I did. The redness traveled into my wrist and up to my elbow. Heat consumed my arm. I squeezed my eyes closed.

"Open your eyes. Never lose sight of your target."

I wrenched my lids open, let out a yelp, and a blue-white light flashed from my palm and hit the back of the chair. The chair bucked and tipped over.

I threw my fist in the air and shook out my burning hand. "Yeah! That totally sucked, but I did it! Now I get to ask another question."

"Go ahead."

The whole enemy faction thing probably should have weighed heavy on my mind, but I was relentless where Connor's personal life was concerned. "You said if you're caught using the portal, you'll get in trouble. What will happen to you?"

"I'll be cut off from coming here."

My stomach flipped. "You mean we'd never see each other again?"

"I can almost guarantee it." His expression turned sardonic.

"The portal workers would stop you?"

He shook his head. "My father. He'd shut down the portal in a second if he had any clue what I was doing."

A kindred bond filled my chest. "He doesn't know you're gifted, does he?"

"Of course he does. It runs in our family. West Region is a haven for gifteds, but he has no idea I come here because I'm not allowed to travel. Philip, Jaxon, drop them in the portal, sure, but not me. Portal travel is too dangerous, conflicts with my responsibilities." From the way he deepened his voice, I figured he was mimicking his father. His cheeks flushed faintly. "I'm ranting."

"It's okay. Families can be a gigantic hassle. Can I ask why your dad is so protective?"

"Sure. Just as soon as you put a hole through those." He pointed to two heavy oak desks, his tone telling me I was capable of doing what he asked. I was certain I could, too, but my moral pendulum swung wildly. Yes, I wanted to protect myself, but what he was proposing represented the kind of violence I abhorred. No way could I do this to another person, no matter how dangerous they were.

Also, my arm ached as if all the tendons had been over-stretched. I shook it out.

"What's wrong?" he asked.

I showed him the enormous blister forming on my palm. He grimaced. "Ew, that looks painful."

"Game over? How about we get something to eat? Or go for a walk?" I was tired from a full day of school, and learning to punch holes in imaginary people didn't exactly top my wish list.

"Okay, but one more thing, first," he said.

"Ungh."

"Arms out to the side."

"What are we going to do?"

"You'll find out. Arms out." The corner of his mouth lifted, like he was about to pull a rabbit out of a hat, except it wouldn't be a rabbit; it would be a two-headed talking fairy or some other supernatural oddity that would rock my world. Fun as that sounded, I had slipped out of order-taking mode and wasn't going back.

"Like this?" I raised my hands and bent my wrists, jazz dance style. Thrust my hip out. Smirked.

Connor tapped an impatient rhythm on his leg.

"Or this?" I linked my fingers above my head and spun like a ballerina. "Hmm. Something's missing. Oh, *I* know."

I began to hum. I pirouetted in circles around him. Then I leapt across the warehouse, ballet style. "I get that I need to be on the defensive, but if I can hide this annoying telekinetic ability, then I'm not in danger, right? I'm pretty good at that already, so let's go do something fun. All we do is hang out in this dusty building."

I danced my way back. Tossed my head and spun on one leg. My hair twirled into my face. I lost my balance and dropped my foot, but it didn't find the floor.

I looked left, then right. Then down. I was floating above Connor's head.

"What's happening? Get me down from here!" Blood pulsed behind my eardrums.

With a graceful rotation of his hand, Connor eased me down.

"You made me float?" I panted from a mix of phobia and exhilaration.

"It improved your dancing," he jabbed.

A big grin swept across my cheeks. "Do it again! Please? But not so high."

"Not going to do it."

"Because you only reward bad behavior?"

"Because the next one's on you."

The next one? "You're going to teach me how to levitate?"

"Then we can quit and we'll do whatever you want. Deal?"

I snapped to attention in front of him. Stretched my arms out to the side. Couldn't help but flick my wrists, just a little bit. "Now what?"

"Come on, you need to take this seriously."

"Are we going to do this or not?"

"Arms out," he sighed.

"They *are*."

"Further. Really reach. Palms down."

"Checkity-check."

"Now think back to what you did to the chair. The way you concentrated your energy and directed it into the hard surface."

"Like a laser."

"This time, direct that laser toward the ground."

I closed my eyes. I pushed every ounce of concentration into the concrete beneath my feet. I opened one eye. I hadn't moved.

"You can do it. Really push the floor away from you."

I stayed in that position for what seemed like an eternity, eyes closed, intently focused, shooting imaginary laser beams into the floor. My arms ached, my hands had fallen asleep and my brain was fried.

Then it happened.

First my heels, then my toes lifted, until I was suspended on a cushion of air. Slowly, so as not to break my concentration, I propped open one lid. A thrill sparked through my entire body. I'd done it! I was airborne! And I was *way, way* too high off the floor. Panic hit. A *boom* echoed through the building, and I lost my buoyancy. I dropped and hit the floor hard, twisting my foot underneath me.

"Ow!" I winced and grabbed my ankle, but I was laughing, too. I couldn't help it. I'd risen at most five feet in the air. Still, I was so exhilarated, it made up for the sharp spasms running through my foot.

"Did you see me? I did it! I got up there!" No answer. "Connor?" I looked around the warehouse. "Um, hello?" My voice bounced off the walls and disappeared down the cavernous rows. He'd left me here. "Are you freaking kidding me?"

I pulled myself to my feet and limped to the chair. Clenched my teeth while I rolled my foot side to side, then in circles. My ankle was sore, but not broken. I swept away the impulse to panic at being left behind and redirected it into burgeoning irritation. I'd followed Connor onto private property, and he'd left me, alone, with my eyes closed for who knows how long. What if the owner had walked in? Or one of those so-called faction people?

Next to me, my phone levitated off the desk. I made a grab for it, but it rose out of reach. I hopped on one leg and lunged, but the phone spiraled upward.

"Get back here!" I commanded. Of course, the anger rippling off me just carried it higher, like a seagull riding the crest of an ocean wave.

Then my phone shot toward the ceiling, clanked against a metal fixture, and clattered to the concrete, shattering to pieces. An eerie hiss came from above. I grabbed my bag and limp-jogged to the door before whatever was hissing could catch up with me. I made it a few yards before the water hit. A squeal lodged in my throat and I realized my phone had activated the warehouse sprinkler system.

Crap. My phone. I limped back, scooped up the evidence that I'd been trespassing, and got out just as the fire alarm sounded.

A door to the adjacent building opened and a worker stuck his head out to check on the noise. I slipped into a dusky shadow and waited until he went back inside. Then I squished to the street and into the front seat of my car, ill-tempered as a flea-dipped cat. A heat blister covered my left palm, forcing me to drive home with one hand.

Girls have done some pretty ridiculous things for their crushes—pretended to like video games, acted ditzy so the guy could be the smart one, used gasoline to spell out his name on the school lawn. Clearly, I'd crossed into lunacy where Connor was concerned. Not in the gasoline-scripting way; more along the intergalactic, ain't gonna happen in a-hundred-sixty-years kind of way.

Entranced by the mystery that was Connor McCabe, I'd flung reality, not to mention all common sense, to the side. We lived in different worlds. He had a bizarre barrier that kept anyone from getting close to him. He came and went as he pleased without even the common courtesy of finding out what I wanted or needed.

I'd be hard-pressed to find a guy more emotionally unavailable. So of course, I had practically flung myself at him. What was wrong with me?

"No more," I said to the windshield wipers, their blades swinging back and forth like a pair of shaming fingers. "From here on out, it's all business." I spent the rest of the drive detangling myself from the notion that Connor was anything more than a short-lived mentor.

Once home, I went straight to my room, changed into dry clothes and dried my hair. When I came out, the doorbell was ringing and Tito was barking manically.

I opened the door and slapped my arms across my chest at who I saw.

CHAPTER 13

Connor stood on the porch, his nonchalant posture provoking my already short fuse. "What happened? I got back to the warehouse and it was overrun with people in uniforms," he said.

"How could you just leave me there? I was, like, all Zenned out, with my eyes closed, and you decide to take off?" Tito stiffened at my raised voice and growled.

"Sic 'em, Tito," I egged.

Tito nipped at Connor's heels. I teetered on my sore ankle.

"You're hurt," he said.

"I can manage just fine, thank you."

I limped back upstairs and plopped on my bed. Pulled my legs to my chest and whistled. Tito hopped up and curled at my feet.

Connor waited in my doorway. He might have walked there, he might have leaped to the third floor in a single bound. I didn't know, and I didn't care.

"You could have given me some warning," I scowled.

His eyes never left mine. "It was completely out of my control. Jaxon pulled me back when he found out my father was looking for me." He held his thumb and forefinger an inch apart. "I was this close to getting caught. What happened at the warehouse?"

"I dunno. Something set the sprinklers off. It doesn't matter what. I'm done."

Anxiety creased his face. "You mean you're done with me?"

"No. I don't know." I shrugged, not sure what I expected from him. I swallowed the lump forming in my throat. "You appear and disappear unexpectedly. One day, you'll leave and not come back. I've had enough of that in my life to know I don't need any more."

Connor paced to the window and stared out at the night-lit city. He was quiet for a long time. Finally, he turned to me, his expression open, defenseless.

"When I'm not here, I'm thinking about you, hoping that the next time I slip through the portal, you haven't changed your mind about seeing me. I'm always afraid it will be my last time with you."

I wasn't prepared for the softer side of Connor, and his declaration took my breath away. I wanted to say "Me, too," but I dug my fingers into Tito's fur to blunt the desire. I couldn't let myself fall for someone who could so easily disappear forever.

"Yeah, well, that really sucks for both of us." A sliver of yearning dulled the edge in my words.

"I wish I could give you more," he said.

My grand decision to keep him at arm's length melted. He was as afraid of losing me as I was of losing him. I longed to touch him, put my hand in his jet-black hair, stroke his cheek, anything. My aura rippled this message across the room.

Connor ran his hand through his hair and closed his eyes for a heartbeat, like he was taking in my unspoken desire for us to connect physically. He looked at me, the cheek I wanted to touch dipped half in shadow. The ache in his eyes mirrored my longing, and my heart nearly cracked in two.

I swallowed, hard. It was time to shift gears. "Do you like it there? In West Region?"

His face brightened a little. "It's magnificent. The main city is beautiful. The people are gifted and always wanting to learn more."

"And nobody thinks they're freaks."

"Times are changing in your world, Echo. In a few decades, your ability will be admired."

"A few decades?" I'd be an old lady by then. I'd have to hide this ability most of my life, and then what? The president would pin a medal on me and declare my birthday a national holiday? Right.

I looked Connor square in the eye. "Take me to West Region. I want to see this place where people like me live."

"The portal is too dangerous. I won't risk it."

"More dangerous than here? I can't even be honest with my dad about who I am, and from the sound of it, society won't be embracing me any time soon. And the best part? Some psychotic faction might want to kidnap me, all because of this despicable…"

"Gift. You have to remember that you are incredibly gifted, and that your place is here, with your family."

Two floors below, the front door slammed. Tito dove off the bed and raced to meet my dad and Kimber. I jumped up and closed my bedroom door.

"I don't know how my dad would feel about me having a guy in my room while he was gone."

"I feel terrible about what happened this afternoon. Let me make it up to you," Connor said.

"Would this involve more physics?" I let the sarcasm flow.

"Maybe, but I'll do all the work."

I studied an errant cuticle. The word *yes* clung to my lips, held back by the slow burn of reality. No matter how much he wanted to be with me, once he left, he might never come back.

"Please, Echo. Spend Saturday with me. You won't regret it." He smiled when he said my name, making his cheek dimple in an oh-so-kissable way.

Mentally, I groaned at my weakening resolve. "Okay. You win. But you have to go!"

I heard Tito race up the stairs, followed by heavier footsteps.

"I'll see myself out." He shared a devilish grin, and then his image fizzled into sparks.

The air in my room still crackled with electricity when my dad came in to tell me he and Kimber were home from the cabin and that he'd caught a string of fish. Then he said he had to leave for Japan first thing in the morning.

We stayed up late, talking. After he went to bed, I pulled out Connor's painting and tried to reconcile the portrait with the guy who I'd just promised to spend more time with. I hardly knew him, but the painting provoked a longing I couldn't explain, like I'd already possessed, and then lost, a soulmate. Like I'd never fully recovered from it.

Some day in the near future he would leave for good—how could he not, for Godsakes?—and the rope of tiny hopes knotted together in my heart would unravel and I would come crashing down. The century's worth of stars stretched between us meant I was forbidden to fall for him. This was a battle I was slowly losing.

The next morning, my dad left for a conference in Tokyo, I drove me and Becca to school, and my life droned back to its grey, Connorless void. Life wasn't a complete mess, though.

For the first time since the accident, I could walk through my world with a peace of mind. Thanks to Connor's training, the headaches were gone and the tele-chaosing was mostly under control.

Passing through the halls between classes, I noticed my classmates were watching me. Not just one or two, but the whole lot of them gave me a sly glance or an odd smile. Half the school had seen me leave with Connor and apparently, speculation was churning about what we'd done together. I liked being the subject of hot gossip. It was a nice change from being ignored.

By lunchtime, I was forced to reconsider my theory. A cluster of girls nudged each other and pointed at me. Smiles changed from friendly to pitiful. When I set my lunch down across from Becca, her clients scattered.

"Why is everyone acting so weird? Have I been walking through school with dirty toilet paper hanging off my shoe?" I checked the bottoms of my tennies.

Becca pulled out her phone. "Oh, boy. Before I show you, I just want you to know I would have stopped this if I could."

She held up her screen showing Raquelle's Instagram page.

I read the last entry: *Guess who spent time in a mental hospital. Can't say who but her initials are…*

Instead of initials, Raquelle had inserted a photo of me, obviously altered to look like I'd spent a month snorting prescription drugs.

I gaped at the screen. "She's telling everyone I'm crazy?"

"If by 'everyone' you mean all of Lincoln High plus every other school in Portland, then yes."

"She's just getting revenge because I left with Connor." Becca had grilled me about Connor all morning. I'd told her what I could, which wasn't much.

"We know it's not true but what if he sees this? This could be part of her master plan to get in his pants," Becca said.

Becca had a point. What if he… wait a minute. Connor and Raquelle didn't surf the same social networks, but I couldn't explain this to her. "He's not into Raquelle. It'll be easy to clear up."

"Wow, you must have really cast a spell over him. Figuratively speaking, of course."

Across the room, Raquelle ate lunch with her clique. Trisha glanced up from her diet soda and saw me watching them. She said something to Raquelle, who turned and waved at me with her manicured pinky. When she turned back, the entire table broke into laughter.

Right then and there, I wanted to take off my bracelets, draw my aura into a tight fist, and whack Raquelle's perky little ponytail into the next dimension. Sadly, that wasn't an option. My ability grew with each training session, but my control? I may as well try juggling blindfolded.

"She's mad enough about you and Connor, it could kill our chance of getting into the party," Becca said.

"Don't worry. I'll get us in."

Rumors blew through the school like wildfire. I had to explain to a few caring teachers that I wasn't on the verge of a breakdown, nor was I suicidal. Even the substitute physics teacher managed to hint that I might need special attention.

Just outside the physics classroom, Becca and I stopped short. A new teacher stood in the entryway with his arms crossed. Vacant eyes followed each student as he or she entered the room. He whistled an odd, unfamiliar tune, harsh and discordant. Every so often, while watching a student, his whistling tapered off. Then it picked up again.

"What a perv," Becca said.

We walked into class, Becca eyeballing the man as she stepped across the threshold. The teacher's tune never altered. In a protective gesture that had become second nature, I blocked his aura and tucked mine in tight.

After the bell, he introduced himself as Mr. Solomon and told us Mr. King was out sick for at least a week. Right away, some of the girls in the back started talking loudly. Another boy threw a wad of paper across the room.

A lot of substitute teachers would have yelled to get control of their class. Not Mr. Solomon. He stood at the front, patiently rubbing his thumb and index finger together. Waiting. Watching.

In less than a minute, everyone quieted down. They looked to the front of the room, uneasy, as though our substitute had, in fact, raised his voice. Next to me, Becca squirmed in her seat.

We'd all felt Mr. Solomon's itchy, impatient aura as it whisked through the room, but this was the first time I'd ever seen my classmates react so decisively to someone's energy. I smiled and flipped open my book, wondering if our new teacher had any idea how much his aura had affected a rambunctious bunch of high schoolers.

"Thank you," Mr. Solomon said when he had everyone's attention. "I know your midterms are coming up and I'd hate for anyone to fall behind just because Mr. King is absent. Please work on the questions at the end of chapter eight while I meet with you individually."

Becca pretended to gag herself with her ballpoint pen. Substitutes who took their job too seriously were such a pain.

One by one, Mr. Solomon called us to the front of the room to review our grades. Then it was my turn. Solomon was what Becca called an *uggo*. His complexion was blotchy and pitted and tinged with pink in places. Permanently raised eyebrows gave him a constant look of astonishment, like he couldn't believe he was stuck teaching physics to a bunch of disinterested delinquents.

I anchored my aura and dove in. "I already know I'm getting a C-. I'm studying harder," I said.

"Have you considered getting a tutor?" Mr. Solomon looked me up and down. Ugh.

I suppressed a smile as I thought about Connor. "I just started with one."

Solomon nodded curtly. "Good. Let me know if I can help in any way."

I turned on my heels and he added, "Any support at all," in a tone that told me he'd heard about the asylum rumors.

"I'm all good," I said, and rolled my pupils so far back that Becca snorted.

CHAPTER 14

In my dream I stood with my feet planted, struggling to maintain balance. Maybe I was in the school cafeteria or outside during gym class, I didn't know, because everything around me was spinning at a dizzying speed, faster and faster until my stomach pitched. My eyes found and settled on two dots of green, the only stationary objects amid the nauseating rush of color. I knew I was looking into Connor's eyes, though the rest of him blurred beyond recognition. I lost myself in them, transfixed, and the world slowed to a stop.

A noise stirred me out of a deep sleep. My eyelids slit open. A silhouette shifted next to my bed in the nearly pitch-black room. I stuffed my face into my pillow. It was too early to get up. Too early for guests.

Guests?

"Don't fall back to sleep," a smooth voice beckoned. My eyes snapped open. Connor looked down at me from the edge of my bed.

"What are you doing here?" I mumbled and peered at the clock. "It's not even six o'clock."

"We're starting our day. It's Saturday, remember?" He sounded wide-awake.

I groaned and pulled my pillow over my head. Of course I remembered, but who in their right mind started a date before sunrise? Not that this was a date. Whatever this was, he'd just have to come back later.

"We have to hurry." He jiggled the bed, probably to prove he could be bossy at any hour of the day.

I was drifting back to sleep when he lifted the side of the mattress, sending me rolling toward the floor.

"All right, all right." I threw the covers off and rubbed my eyes. The dim light turned everything into gray and black blots. "I gotta…" I pointed to the bathroom and stumbled toward it. I splashed water on my face and brushed my teeth. Shoved my hair into a ponytail. There was a knock on the door.

"We're going to be late," he called.

I opened the door. "Not. A morning. Person," I warned.

"Good. Then you'll really want to see this." His smile was a set of white teeth glowing in the gray light. Connor waited on the portico roof while I changed into jeans and a t-shirt. Then he said he'd meet me at my car, so I grabbed my keys and crept out the front door. My car idled in the driveway with Connor in the front seat. I wondered why I carried keys at all anymore.

We wove through the city, toward the industrial district.

"Are we going back to the warehouse? 'Cause I'm going to go all mutiny on you if you try to make me work this early."

"I wouldn't think of it. This is the fastest way to where we're going." My car slowed. "Or was."

One block ahead, red and blue lights pierced the soft gray dawn. Yellow crime tape cordoned off the street and stretched across a wide perimeter. A squad of police cars blocked our progress, and a cop directed us around the mayhem. Connor slowed to let a group of officers cross in front of us. One of the men was out of uniform. Connor recognized him before I did.

"Isn't that Raquelle's dad?"

"Yeah, it is," I answered.

"I thought he was a psychiatrist," he said dryly. His finger tapped on the steering wheel. The motion was aggressive and picked up speed as he glared at Mr. Crane.

Mr. Crane must have felt us watching because his head snapped around to us. I gave him a small wave. He did not wave back. He slid beneath the crime tape and disappeared into a crowd of blue uniforms.

"He works with the police sometimes. I think he profiles criminals for them," I said, and unexpectedly shuddered.

Connor eyed the rearview mirror until the scene was well behind us, then turned back toward my house.

"I thought we were going into the industrial area," I said.

"Change of plan." He drove to the waterfront, where the Willamette River chugged through town and parked next to a trio of condo towers.

The streets were empty except for a guy getting his morning coffee. When he rounded the corner out of sight, Connor stepped up to one of the skyscrapers. He stood so close to the glass exterior, I thought he was checking out his reflection.

"Ready for an adventure?" The peaks of his upper lip twitched in a smile.

I stifled a yawn. "Sure."

He held out a black metal rod about two feet long. "Stand next to me and grab hold of this insulator."

"You mean this stick thingy?" I grabbed the opposite end and an intense, uncomfortable current surged into my arm. I tried to let go. I couldn't. I was more than a little freaked out by this. "Um, Connor—"

"No matter what happens, try not to scream," he said.

"Why would I want to… omigod!" My feet lifted off the ground. Connor and I soared upward, inches from the skyscraper, as though we were in our own personal elevator. I clenched my jaw and squealed. Connor flashed a maverick grin.

We zipped past individual condo units, and I snatched glimpses of their sleepy inhabitants. Residents wandered through kitchens in their bathrobes. Some read the newspaper. One woman was applying lipstick in her bedroom mirror. She caught sight of me in the reflection, but by the time she did a double-take, we were gone.

We landed on the roof. The strange black rod released my grip. I sat down, light-headed from the ascent.

"Um, wow, that was interesting," I said, trying to sound grateful for the experience.

"Come on, the good part's about to start." He walked to the eastern corner and sat with his legs dangling over the ledge. Tentatively, I gathered my legs beneath me. When I called on my feet to move, they stayed glued in place.

"Are you coming?" he asked.

"Is it just me, or is the building swaying?" My internal organs bottomed out.

Connor ran to my side.

"I just need a few minutes to adjust." My empty stomach churned.

"Echo, are you afraid of heights?"

In response, all the blood drained from my face. "Oh boy…"

"What about the rooftop outside your window? You like to go out there," he said.

"I sit on the windowsill. Becca uses the lounger. How far up are we?"

"Maybe three hundred feet?"

"Oh man." My legs gave out and I plopped onto my butt. I gulped air, but it only pitched between the back of my throat and the top of my lungs. Lightheadedness set in.

"Breath slowly. You're hyperventilating."

I sucked a deep breath. A few more, and my color warmed.

"You know I'd never let you fall," he said.

"I hear you say that, but my brain's too busy freaking out for it to register. All I can think about is the time I was eight and I fell out of a third-story window. I nearly died." I lay back and did that staccato labor breathing I'd seen in movies.

Connor jumped to his feet. "Echo, watch this."

I turned my head so I could see him without sitting up. The air next to him shimmered like heat waves coming off pavement.

"Portland," he said, and then he sidestepped into the shimmery mirage and disappeared. "West Region!" I heard him shout from somewhere in the portal.

He stepped back into view. "Your crazy world." Disappeared into the portal again. "The super awesome future!"

Here. "Spandex." Gone. "Levitation!"

He made a bug-eyed face. "Clueless population." He disappeared again. "Schools for the gifted!"

I laughed so hard, I clutched my stomach. "That's not fair, you just made me want to move to West Region. Please take me away from this insanity!"

Connor cleared the portal connection and sat next to me. "It's far from perfect here, but I'm glad I came. You're nothing like I imagined. Sailing through the portal that first time, I had no idea what to expect."

"Disappointed?" I said with a half-smile. I sat up, feeling much better.

"Far from it."

"What *were* you expecting?"

"I'm not really sure." His eyes flicked away. "You're more beautiful than I imagined."

My cheeks went pink. If I tried to sum up how gorgeous I thought he was, I would make a fool of myself. In any case, if he was as good at reading auras as he was at everything else, he knew exactly how he affected me. "The first time I saw you, I had this feeling we'd already known each other for a long time."

"We haven't. No past lives or any of that, if that's what you're thinking." A firmness in his answer shut down further questioning. No way was I going to ask him about the painting now. "No past lives," he repeated, almost to himself.

"Well, I guess the only way to go is forward." I don't know why I said it. The future didn't look good for us.

Indecision flickered in his eyes. Then his gaze landed on a point beyond me. "Turn around."

On the eastern horizon, the gray silhouette of Mount Hood basked against a backdrop of pink and orange. Puffy clouds hung next to the peak, their underbellies chalky yellow from the rising sun. A brilliant orb finally spilled over the horizon, softening everything to watercolors.

The scene was ripe with newness, and I wondered if that was why Connor brought me up here. I stole a glance at him, curious to see what his expression held. He wasn't watching the sunrise. He was watching me.

Pink blossomed on my cheeks again. "What?"

"I came all this way and hardly know you at all. You asked a lot of questions but I never got the chance to ask any."

"You seemed to know a lot the day we met."

"Just what I picked up off your aura."

I cringed. I'd been such a wreck that day. Talk about bad first impressions.

"So, in the spirit of equality, today I get to ask all the questions."

"Go right ahead," I mumbled, my words drowned by a yawn. The bright sunlight made it hard to keep my eyes open.

"Maybe this afternoon." He stood and held the rod out to me again, signaling it was time for us to leave.

The ride down to the ground was no party. I clenched my teeth, squished my eyes closed, and focused on not dry heaving. When my feet touched the sidewalk, I actually hugged the side of the building.

A short drive later—for me, a catnap—Connor walked us to my front porch.

"You get some sleep. I've got a meeting scheduled with my dad, but I'll come back after," he said.

"That sounds very formal."

"It always is. The man never takes a day off, and he doesn't think anyone else needs one either." A small eye roll. Dimples dented his cheeks, and he fizzled into the ether.

I passed out before I hit the pillow. Hours later, I was jerked half-awake by the sensation that I was flying. Sweat dampened my cheeks and my fists twisted handfuls of covers; my pulse whooshed in my ears. Choppy memories of early morning escapades filled my cottony head, and in a snap, I was fully awake.

I rolled out of bed and looked for Connor on the portico roof. The lounge chair sat empty. My heart sank. Then my nose picked up the scent of bacon. Eggs. And… pancakes? Kimber couldn't boil an egg if her life depended on it. My dad was in Tokyo. Who, then, was creating the heavenly smells?

I threw on my clothes and padded into the kitchen. Connor looked up from a celebrity magazine. "You're not going to believe this, but we're still listening to this Bieber guy's music."

"Justin Bieber survived the Collapse? Who'd a thunk it? Is that bacon I smell?"

"Kimber left hours ago, so I took over your kitchen. I wasn't sure what you like, so I took a chance on a few things." He moved to the pans on the stovetop and scooped pancakes, eggs, and bacon onto a plate. He set this in front of me.

"You cook," I said, unable to keep the surprise out of my voice. I took a bite of eggs. A strange, smoky flavor assaulted my tongue. "Interesting." I moved to the pancakes. They were heavy and undercooked. I held my breath in an effort not to laugh.

Connor winced. "That bad? Our servants prepare most of the meals, so I don't get much practice."

I nibbled a piece of bacon. Hard to ruin bacon. "Mmm, yummy. It must be nice to have servants. Tell me more, Connor McCabe."

"Well, I live on the family compound."

"Brothers or sisters?"

"I've got one brother who's three years older. He's at the university, where I'll go when I graduate." He stuck a fork into the pan of eggs and took a bite. His eyes widened and he spit them in the sink. "I am so sorry about that."

I laughed. "It's nice you tried. What about your mom? Does she know you come here?"

"She died when I was six." He raised his palm, anticipating my reaction. "It was an accident, and it happened a long time ago."

"Sorry," I said, anyway.

"You should be. You're cutting into *my* question time."

Reflexively, I glanced at the clock. "Holy cow. How'd it get to be so late?"

"You needed the sleep. I think your body overloaded from the charge running through the insulator when we flew up to the roof this morning."

"You mean the black stick thingy?"

Connor sighed, ever patient. "Yes, the black stick thingy."

I grabbed more bacon and headed for the door. "I'm good to go. Where to next?"

CHAPTER 15

Connor drove us down the winding hill and into downtown. It was one of those glorious fall days that prompted every Portland resident to get outside and soak up the sun before rain clouds overtook the valley until spring. The leaves were turning red-yellow on the trees, and white clouds wisped across a sapphire sky.

He quizzed me relentlessly, wanting to know where I was born, what kind of music I liked, what I did for fun, what my dad did for a living. Being in the hot seat wasn't all it was cracked up to be.

"Did you have telekinesis before the accident?" he asked.

"Nope, I wasn't *blessed* with any gifts until…"

My thoughts dropped away, and went back to the months before Raquelle tripped me. There *had* been a couple of odd incidents after we moved into Kimber's house. A table shifted on its legs as soon as Kimber walked in the room. A book was in one place and then suddenly in another.

Picturing these incidents now, they didn't feel like a part of my own history. The images were too distant and dreamlike. They were definitely my memories, though. The doctor said I might have trouble recalling some things from my past, but eventually everything would come back. How much more had I forgotten?

I told Connor this. "I used to joke to the Partychicks that Kimber was a witch. Do you think that was really me?"

"I never picked up any other special energy at your house. So, yeah, you probably had some telekinetic ability before the accident."

I felt a little sick knowing this had been festering inside me like some sort of pox. Clubbing with the Partychicks, making new friends at Lincoln High, I'd reveled in being part of the popular crowd. I'd been a freak then, too, and didn't even know it.

"What about your biological mom? These things are genetic a lot of the time," he said.

"It's not like I'll ever know. And I don't care, either." My arms lashed across my chest. He'd opened up an ugly, squirming can of worms that was about to spill into our nice day.

"Sorry. I didn't mean to pry."

I considered leaving it at that, or flippantly changing the subject, but Connor risked so much to be here, it seemed rude to brush him off.

I puffed out a lungful of air. "I was born on a Tuesday morning. On Tuesday night, my birth mother snuck out of the hospital. Without me."

"She left you there." It was a gentle clarification, devoid of accusation.

"Yup." I'd never met the woman, and by every indication, I was better off with my dad, but I had to force the vitriol out of my tone before I continued. "She left while I slept in the bassinet next to her hospital bed. At least she had the decency to pin a phone number to my blanket. When nobody came to collect me, the nurses called the number on the note. That's how my dad learned he had a daughter. So, if this woman has telekinesis or an extra arm or snakes for hair, I would not know."

She'd never even tried to contact me, and I rarely gave her any thought. For all I knew, she could be remarried with a soccer van full of snot-nosed rugrats. Or she could be dead. I was pretty sure I didn't care either way.

Connor picked up the jagged edges in my energy field and abandoned the subject. "How about hobbies or hidden talents?" he asked.

"Hmm. I used to be a really good painter." I let that hang between us. When it didn't attract a reply, one that I could tie back to the portrait in my bedroom, I continued, "Never played an instrument, avoided sports at all cost, and can't carry a tune. I'm really not that talented."

Connor broke into a laugh. "You know how ludicrous that sounds."

"This ability still causes more trouble than it's worth."

He pulled into a parking place along the curb. "But without it, I never would have found you." His eyes traced their way from my eyes to my lips. There was no mistaking the desire in that look.

Involuntarily, I pressed my back against the door and stiffened against conflicting feelings.

"Where do you see this going? Us, I mean. We really don't have a future together, do we? So…" I turned my palms up and shrugged, letting my body language communicate what I wasn't strong enough to say: *Stop looking at me like that because I'm trying not to fall for you.*

Connor's expression didn't cool this time. "The future is the big question, isn't it?" He climbed out of the car.

I met him on the sidewalk. "What's that supposed to mean?"

"I don't know what's going to happen, do you?"

"Not a clue."

"Then let's just live for today."

Connor had never been to a mall before. Apparently, they were one of the many casualties of The Collapse and were never rebuilt. So, I didn't feel bad when I dragged him into the behemoth downtown extravaganza, Pioneer Mall. I needed to replace my cell phone, and what better way for him to get a taste of current-day Portland?

We dodged the city train as it screeched to a stop in front of the mall, and pushed open the glass doors to the building. One step into the stew of strangers' auras and I decided I'd made a huge mistake. I winced at the sensation of a hundred tiny fists pummeling me, and the intensity grew when the crowd thickened.

My head swirled. "Whoa. Phenomenally bad idea." I backed toward the exit. Held onto the door handle for balance.

"Echo, you have to learn how to handle these situations."

He had a point. I couldn't go the rest of my life without stepping foot in a mall. God forbid.

"Walk next to me and I'll ease you into it," he said.

A group of kids swished through my aura. My stomach swam. "This is way worse than being in school," I said.

"That's because you've acclimated to your classmates. There might be a thousand people in your school, but you walk the same pattern and pass all the same people every day. You've gotten used to them."

With practice, I'd learned to sense Connor's barrier. Now I closed in on him until his barrier pressed back, a couple feet from his body. I leaned into it. It gave a little, the way firm muscle yields when you squeeze it. A soothing calm flowed over me.

My attention turned to the task at hand. Pioneer Mall was a circular, three-story mall, capped by an enormous skylight. We stood in the middle of the mall atrium. I pointed to the escalators rising up the center.

"First stop, the AT&T store on the third floor," I said.

He led the way, with me tight next to him. The crowd thinned on the top floor, and only a few people were in the store. I took a few cautious steps away from Connor, didn't feel overwhelmed, and took off on my own.

He studied the displays, picked up a phone and turned it on. "So simplistic," he said with derision.

"What do you guys do, just talk to each other telepathically?"

He smiled. "Maybe in another hundred years. We have a telecom system, just different devices. Far more advanced."

"Can I see yours?"

"I left it behind. Wouldn't do me any good here and I didn't want to lose it."

He picked up a slick, high-end phone loaded with the latest software. "This is the one for you."

I'd seen ads for this phone. It was the most expensive one on the market. "I don't need anything that sophisticated. The one I broke is over here."

"If you're going to be stuck in this backward place in time, you should at least have the best technology." Leave it to Connor to remind me how much I was missing out on. I checked out the phone's features. It was very cool, but just not my style.

"I'm just going to replace my old one," I said and grabbed a cheaper model from the display.

Connor got to the counter one step ahead of me and pulled out his wallet to pay.

"What are you doing?" I asked.

"Buying you a phone."

"I was the one who broke it." I glanced at the salesgirl who patiently waited out our debate. I dropped my voice. "That's what set the sprinklers off in the warehouse."

A tiny smile. "This mysterious out-of-control-phone, it didn't have anything to do with my leaving you alone in the warehouse, did it?"

"Everything, actually."

Connor slid cash across the counter to the sales girl. Put his wallet back in his jeans. Then he handed me the plastic shopping bag.

"Thank you," I said. All the while, something nagged at me. He'd bought me a phone, like a boyfriend might. That wasn't what bothered me. I was enjoying his company, certainly more than I should. That wasn't it, either.

And then my internal alarm bells went off. "You didn't just give her money from 2173, did you? 'Cause if you did, we need to run before she calls security."

"Of course not," he laughed. "It's perfectly legal tender."

My eyes widened. "Don't tell me you can magically create money. I bet you can. Teach me how to do that!"

"Oh, now you love your ability. Is that what I'm hearing?"

"I tolerate it, but this would definitely push me to full-on *like*."

"Hate to disappoint you, but I'm not gifted that way. You know that night you and I were supposed to meet, but you had to go to dinner at the Crane's?"

That was the night he went out with Raquelle. "What about it?"

"Raquelle took me to a club and some of the guys there were playing… darts? It was easy to learn and easier to win. After she went home, I stayed at the club and played for money. The guys kept betting they could beat me."

I knew the club he was talking about. Teens from the wealthiest part of West Vista hung out there. They thought nothing of gambling a few hundred bucks, especially if they thought they could take advantage of the new guy in town. Connor probably had fun, making the darts go exactly where he wanted to and collecting their money, game after game.

As we strolled, I marveled at the way people skirted Connor's barrier, even when they looked like they might want to cross into his space. And unless it was my imagination, that barrier was getting thinner. A woman nearly bumped into him as she passed. Out of curiosity, I inched closer to Connor. The two-foot pressure between us never relented.

If I didn't know any better, I'd think he was making a concerted effort to keep me at arm's length.

Before the accident, I could spend an entire day at the mall. Now, exhaustion set in after a short visit. "Let's get out of here. It's too crowded," I said.

Connor steered us toward an exit, but before he pushed through the doors, he skidded to a stop at a store entrance. Behind the glass, a jewelry display glittered. He peered at the necklaces shimmering like pirate's booty.

"Come with me." He went inside. By the time I caught up, a saleslady was holding out a necklace for Connor's inspection. A beautiful twist of sapphires dripped from a silver chain.

"Would the young lady like to try it on?" the saleslady asked.

"She would," Connor said before I realized they were referring to me.

The rich blue stones reflected light in every direction. The silver chain glistened. The tiny price tag read four hundred dollars. I opened my mouth to decline.

"Don't you like it?" Connor asked.

"It's stunning. It's just too much."

"I want to get you something. What about these plain gold chains?"

"You already got me the phone."

"I mean something that lasts longer…" His eyes dropped to the shopping bag I carried, but it didn't take a leap of logic to know he wasn't referring to the phone. He, too, wrestled with the fact that one day, he would have to stop using the portal. He wanted me to remember him then.

Like I'd ever forget.

As his green eyes found mine, we both knew there wasn't a necklace on the planet that equaled the connection pulsing between us. At that moment, my energy crossed onto his, and a full body tingle robbed my power to speak.

There was only one object so infused with meaning that I'd kept it close since the day it mysteriously appeared on my bed stand. I reached in my pocket and pulled out the coin he'd given to me, the one from 2173. I handed this to the saleslady.

"Could you put this on a chain for me?"

The breath that escaped from Connor told me he was touched by my choice. He nodded at the saleslady and ushered me toward the door. "I'll be out in a few minutes. I'm going to pick out a chain."

"What, are you afraid I'll veto your choice?" I joked.

"You're the queen of vetoing today, and I'm trying to do something nice for you."

"Pick out something simple, okay? You already bought me the phone." I'd never had a guy spend so much money on me, and it made me uncomfortable.

Connor motioned me toward the mall exit and went back to the counter.

CHAPTER 16

I waited just outside the mall entrance while Connor finished in the jewelry store. I was happy to leave because I seriously needed some fresh air. Forget my clogged aura, it was Connor who had me reeling now.

At the very beginning, I'd doubted his feelings for me, then dared to think there was something between us, and then raised my defenses and swore resistance to them. That was a fine plan, up until a minute ago, when our energies merged and for a fleeting second, I'd been unable to tell us apart. The tingle rushed down the full length of my body again. I savored it.

Without warning, someone shoulder-slammed me from behind, and I stumbled face-first into a group of guys from my school. My aura crackled and ran loose.

"Way to go, mental case," the she-devil sang.

I spun to face Raquelle. Trisha and a couple other Partychick disciples snickered.

"Knock it off with the psycho rumors," I said between clenched teeth.

"Why so hostile, Echo? Has Connor moved on already?"

"Connor's inside. Buying me a gift."

The shock coming off her made me laugh. Raquelle's full lips smiled, but her eyes were switchblades. "Obviously, it's a farewell gift. It's just a matter of time before he comes to his senses." The four of them swished into a store across the street.

Raquelle's comment hit me where it really hurt. Maybe this was Connor's idea of a parting gift. Just then, he joined me on the sidewalk. One look at my face and he knew.

"Ah, Raquelle," he said. "I saw her leave."

"It was nothing. Let's just go." I hated that Raquelle had such an obvious effect on me.

"The necklace won't be ready for a few minutes."

"Then let's walk." I stormed down the sidewalk, weaving through passengers as they exited the latest train.

"What did she say this time?" he asked.

I waved my hand dramatically. "It's hardly worth repeating." But my hatred boiled to the surface.

"I can't stand her! It's like, she's got this ability to show up at the perfect moment and make my life unbearable. No matter where I go, she finds a way to get in my face!" I rounded the corner and my eyes landed on the car parked at the curb: a hot red convertible, the logo "Partychick" hand painted next to the license plate. Raquelle's car.

"Aaack!" I screeched.

Connor laughed.

"This is so not funny," I said.

"I think the gods of revenge are trying to tell us something." His brows rose in a conspiratorial way. He stepped into an alcove and motioned me to join him.

"What are you going to do?" I asked, but he only smiled and scanned the sidewalk running up and down the quiet side street. He waited while a truck cruised by and a couple of shoppers ambled past. Then the street was empty, except for us.

Connor raised his hands about waist-high. He pointed his fingers at Raquelle's car and latched onto it with his gaze. Ever so slightly, the convertible began to move, first rising a few inches off the pavement and then drifting up and over the curb. He spun the car so that it faced the opposite direction. The convertible creaked under its own weight as it settled into its new location, smack in the middle of the sidewalk.

I covered my mouth in astonishment. "I can't believe you used your superpower on a Muggle."

"Muggle?"

"Never mind. That was the coolest. Thing. Ever."

"It's worth seeing you smile again, even if I did break a few rules. Technically, I'm not supposed to use my power for evil." He wiggled his eyebrows and laughed.

We walked back to the jewelry store. The jeweler had soldered a bail loop to the coin and attached the simple silver chain that Connor picked out. The saleslady held it out to Connor so that he could put it on me, but I knew better. I took it from her and clasped it around my neck. I fingered the coin and looked in the mirror on the counter. It was perfect.

Actually, the whole day was turning out to be perfect. We stepped outside just as Raquelle and her entourage streamed out of the store across the street. Connor and I exchanged a look and followed them. From a hidden spot on the corner, we watched Raquelle walk toward her car, so busy yammering to Trisha that she remained oblivious until she nearly walked into its bumper.

"Three, two, one," Connor said and, right on cue, Raquelle shrieked.

"What the…" She took a cautious sidestep and checked the license plate. Her neck jutted and her eyes bulged. Yep, it was her convertible.

"Who did this to my car?" she screamed. She shot looks in every direction, looking for the prankster.

That alone was priceless, but it got even better. A police officer was jotting down her license plate, in the process of giving her a ticket. Raquelle cursed up a storm. She waved her arms and yelled, trying to convince the officer that she hadn't parked her car backward, in the middle of the sidewalk. Maybe it was Raquelle's offensive tirade, maybe it was her aggressive posture, but the officer never stopped writing. He ripped the ticket off his pad and shoved it at her.

By now, I was laughing so hard, tears rolled down my cheeks. Through wet lashes, I saw Connor's wide smile. He was enjoying this as much as I was.

"We should probably go before she sees us," I said.

I wiped my sleeve across my face and stepped off the curb.

The next few seconds were a catastrophe of sensations. The loud blast of the train horn screamed in my ears. Metal screeched against metal as the grooved wheels locked and skidded on their tracks. The train's conductor gaped at me through his windshield, horror-stricken, willing the train to stop. And my body, hit from behind, was thrown beyond the tracks and away from the oncoming train.

I crashed onto the pavement, hard, and all the oxygen was punched out of my lungs. Slowly, so slowly, I became aware of an arm wrapped tightly around my waist. A hand cupped my head, protecting it from the asphalt; a gentle, electric sensation ran along my skin where another body pressed against mine; and a voice, quaking with fear, called my name.

"Echo. Oh, no. Echo. Are you all right?"

I nodded stiffly. The arms slowly released me. I pushed myself onto my knees and turned to the person who had saved my life. It was Connor.

His gaze dropped to his hand resting on my arm. Slowly and deliberately, he pulled away. His eyes, raw with an emotion I could not read, avoided mine.

A crowd hovered over us. Train passengers circled and asked if we were hurt. The conductor stood on the sidewalk, ghostly pale and trembling. The policeman who gave Raquelle a ticket pushed through the onlookers and came to my aid.

"I'm all right. Everything's fine." I was unhurt, but my voice shook because everything was definitely not fine.

Nobody was convinced that I was okay, so I straggled to my feet. I made a brave gesture of brushing the dirt from my pants. "See? There's nothing wrong with me. There's not a scratch on me."

The officer found this as hard to believe as I did. My elbow and hip should have been bruised from crashing onto the street. My face should have been scraped because it had slid about a foot across the pavement. But it wasn't, because when Connor knocked me out of the train's path, he'd also cushioned every bit of me. The only evidence of the near disaster was scorch marks that arced across his jeans above his knees.

The officer helped Connor to his feet and praised him for his fast thinking. Someone led the conductor to the curb and insisted that he sit down. Out of all of us, he was taking this near-collision the worst.

Soon, everyone dispersed. Shadows shrouded the city as the sun dropped behind the hills. I drifted away from the crowd, stunned by my proximity to death and a new, startling truth. I walked without any destination in mind, vaguely aware of Connor following a short distance behind. He called my name once or twice. When his footsteps grew close, I picked up my pace.

A tempest whirled in the space behind my eyes. Questions, always the wrong ones, danced there. I was so tired of the pile-up of questions, always having to draw out the answers from Connor, speck by speck. I wished he would just take all his secrets and leave.

Connor's sole scuffed the sidewalk, and I stopped and faced him.

"How long have you known?" I accused in a hoarse whisper.

He leaned in to brush a strand of hair out of my eyes. I jerked beyond his reach.

"How. Long?"

"It's been a few days."

"Were you ever going to tell me that you could touch me?"

He glanced into the cold city. Seemed to sink into a place deep inside himself. Away from me.

"I'll take that as a no." My chin quivered and I pressed my fingernails into my palm. No way would I allow one tear to drop. Wind swelled off the river and tore down the street. I shivered.

"Echo, you're freezing." He opened his arms toward me. I lashed my arms across my chest and shook my head. Connor took one step closer, unsure what to do. When I didn't turn away, he took another. This time, I let him close the gap between us. He wrapped me in his arms.

CHAPTER 17

It was pointless trying to hold on to my anger because resting against Connor was the most remarkable sensation I had ever experienced. His hand swept beneath my hair and found the back of my neck, and I felt a faint electric tingle where his skin met mine. His warmth permeated me, recharged my energy, like the effect of a sugar rush. His scent was infatuating, all spice and heat.

"I didn't know if I should tell you that the barrier was gone. I wanted to, but everything is so uncertain. I figured it would be best if I didn't. Best for both of us," he said.

"I understand." That barrier not only prevented us from touching, it had served to keep us safe from unrealistic expectations. Now, our new closeness sprung with tenuous hope, bringing with it the illusion of a future together. One that, any way I colored it, was doomed.

I retreated, allowing my lips to brush across his throat as I leaned away. They buzzed with an exquisite electric sensation where our flesh touched. It took every ounce of discipline to press my hands against his chest and push myself away. I needed distance because the moment I discovered he'd been holding himself back was the very same moment I gave in to him. Utterly, totally, deeply.

"I need to go home. I need time to think," I said.

His expression was fierce. He slid his fingers down my arm, enveloping my hand in his. "No. I can't let you leave like this. I promised myself I wouldn't let this happen. The plan was to come here, train you and go, and I've completely failed us. I was honest with you about the barrier. It protected me physically, the first few times I came here. Eventually, I didn't need it."

"I'm not mad at you."

"I never wanted to hurt you."

"I know." I pooled strength I didn't know I had. "I think we should end this. Now, before it's too late."

He laughed, deep and aching. "It was too late the moment I saw you." The angle of his jawline cast shadows onto his throat, like a private place where his secrets dared to surface. One of them revealed itself, then, coming straight from the dark hollow that rose and fell when he spoke. It was as clear as if he'd held my face in his hands and whispered it in my ear.

"You love me," I said.

He lifted my hand to his lips and kissed the inside of my wrist. "Yes."

"I love you, too." It was the first time I'd ever said that to a guy. My entire body felt wide-awake and weightless, like I could defy gravity and float above the city. Connor held my hand, grounding both of us. The thrill was nearly unbearable, in the best possible way—and the worst. I exhaled, deep and heavy.

The portal. His father. The time difference.

Now what?

Connor put his finger to my lips in an effort to silence my thoughts. He traced my cheekbone with his thumb.

"Everything is possible," he said.

The night drew colder, and Connor flagged a horse-drawn carriage. We curled into the seat, and he snaked his arm around me. It was one thing to lust after Connor McCabe from a distance. Everything changed when we touched. There was something addicting about the electric tingle that remained after his fingers left my skin. An unfamiliar craving bloomed as he caressed my back, leaving me to wonder where his fingers would go next.

I brought his hand to my cheek so I could feel the electricity coursing just beneath his skin. When I laid my hand on his chest, the feeling was nearly lost beneath the fabric of his t-shirt. I palmed his chin and found the sensation running strong. He took my face in his hands, then dropped his cheek to mine. I jumped at the slight shock.

"Sorry about that," he said. "It must be left over from all the portal travel."

"I like it. A lot."

His lips glided onto mine. The gentle sensation of electricity tickled my lips, then my tongue. Every nerve ending in my body lit up.

The carriage swayed gently down the quiet city streets. A cool breeze swept through the valley of skyscrapers, and goose bumps dotted my arms. Connor pulled my legs across his lap, and I nuzzled my face into his chest. We were so tightly nested together I could feel a pulse beating where our bodies touched. Could have been his, might have been mine.

"When did you know?" I asked.

"That I was crazy about you? Probably the time you showed me you could be a stubborn, independent… what's the phrase you guys use? Pain in the butt?"

I laughed. "That covers a lot of time."

"All right, then, I knew from the very beginning."

I turned to look at him. "The first time you saw me? Are you serious? You didn't even know me." Connor was quiet, and I decided to let well enough alone. Love at first sight happened to people. None that I knew personally, until now. It was a dizzying thought, that I had that much power over someone.

"What about you?" he asked.

"The first time or the tenth? Because I've talked myself out of falling for you about that many times."

"Sounds familiar."

I settled back into him. "I've never been in a long-distance relationship before." I cast my eyes at the carriage driver, thinking I should keep my voice low, but who was I kidding? Nobody would believe that my boyfriend had to commute 160 years just to go on a date.

"Me neither." Connor ran his hand down my hair in even strokes. "I'm so glad this is one promise I couldn't keep."

"I made the same promise, but you were hard enough to resist when your barrier was up. Then you had to go and save me."

"You'd rather get crushed by the train?"

I pretended to consider this alternative. "Nah."

My mind jumped back to that instant after Connor had saved me, and the burn marks I'd seen on his jeans. Now I ran my fingers over the scorched fabric, and over the solid muscle beneath. He flinched.

"The train really did hit you! Why didn't you say something?"

"It didn't. Remember how I taught you to push your hand through solid objects? I allowed the train wheels to pass through me. There wasn't time to worry about my jeans."

"What about your legs?"

"The one is a little sore, but there isn't a mark on me. I can show you if you want." He made like he was going to roll up his jeans to prove it.

"Okay, I get it. You're invincible."

The driver dropped us at my car, and Connor drove me home. We stood under the soft porch light, and I swam in his emerald eyes for a couple of heartbeats. I looked down at our hands, where mine was cocooned inside his.

"I can see right through your fingers," I said, not even trying to cover the panic in my voice.

He let out a heavy sigh. "It's been a long day and I need to get back." He dropped his mouth onto mine and pressed his tongue between my lips. My tongue slid beneath his, tasting salt and sweet, and a spark went off deep in my belly. He released me and kissed me on the forehead.

"Sleep well," he said. As his image faded, warmth lingered where his fingers had caressed my face.

I went inside and leaned against the door. In a long, luxurious exhale, I released my energy into the entryway. It swept into the adjacent room and up the stairs. Caught the chandelier overhead and sent it swinging. Then it curled back and settled around me, delicate as gossamer, soft as a silken cape.

Becca had been out of town all weekend, so on the way to school, she grilled me about my day with Connor. By the time I told her about how he'd saved me, she was bouncing in her seat like her butt was on fire.

"No way! No freaking way!" She slapped the dashboard and fanned herself with her hands.

I fixed my stare on the windshield.

"There's more," she said. "There's something you're not telling me."

"Nope, that's everything." I wanted to keep the intimate details to myself, partly because I preferred privacy but also because I didn't want to diminish the memory by talking about it.

"Omigod, you did the dirty deed."

"Geez, Becca. No."

"You kissed him!"

"Did I ever." There was nothing chaste about my grin.

"What was it like? Spill it. Now. You must tell me everything."

"You've kissed guys before."

"'Course I have but he's, like, superhumanly hot." Becca would hound me to the ends of the earth if I didn't feed her some little tidbit.

"He's good," I said.

"That's it? Good?"

"More like really, really, *really*…" I dragged out each word.

"Oh come *on*!" She hit a high note.

I shook my head in wonder. "He is absolutely surreal."

Turns out, that was a perfect description for the entire day. On the way to our first class, we saw a pair of policemen entering the principal's office. Leading them was none other than Mr. Crane.

"What's that all about?" Becca asked.

A kid who had his locker near mine overheard her. "Ryan Hoffman's disappeared."

"You mean like kidnapped?"

The kid lifted a shoulder. "Who knows? He was at the mall on Saturday night and never went home."

"Wait, which mall?" I asked.

"Pioneer."

"Hey, you were there. Did you see Ryan?" Becca asked me.

I shook my head. "He's a sophomore, right?"

"Walks around talking to himself. It's probably why Crane is here."

"Why is that?"

"Crane was his shrink. Don't look so surprised. Ryan and I went to middle school together and he wasn't exactly shy about sharing his private life," Becca said.

I thought back to the group of boys Raquelle had shoved me into. "Is he the guy who always wears an Army jacket?"

"Since eighth grade."

Then I *had* slammed into Ryan at the mall. He was one of those kids who was easy to forget. Always quiet. Always looked like he carried the burden of the world on his shoulders. I couldn't tell you if he was in any of my classes.

In Physics, Solomon handed me the result of my latest pop quiz. I'd gotten a B! Mr. Solomon said something, but I was doing a mental happy dance. "I'm sorry, what?" I asked him.

"I said I heard you had an exciting weekend."

"Me? Not really. I fell in front of a train and someone pulled me out of the way." It didn't seem appropriate to go on about it considering all of the concern about Ryan.

"That sounds like a heroic feat. Was this someone from Lincoln?" Solomon hovered.

"You wouldn't know him." My flippant response had the intended effect. Solomon continued down the row, handing out graded quizzes.

At lunch, I took a seat at our usual spot and scanned the room for Becca, expecting to see her leaning over a table, writing out a curse or delivering a potion. I spotted her, and my jaw dropped. My Wiccan friend with her spiky hair was nestled between Raquelle and Trisha as though they'd been best friends since birth. Becca waved for me to join them.

I crinkled my nose and shook my head. Becca said something to Raquelle, got up, and hurried to our table. "You have to come over," she said. "Raquelle wants to apologize for all the rumors."

"Right. And then she's going to join the Peace Corps and devote her life to saving war-torn orphans."

"Come on," she begged. "Raquelle's trying to be nice. It's like watching a snake try to swallow an entire pig."

Reluctantly, I followed her to the Partychick's table. I plopped down and stared at Raquelle, waiting.

"Yes. Well. All of that stuff about you being psycho? *Joking*," she sang.

Trisha stifled a giggle. Raquelle nudged her.

Becca spoke up. "I was just telling them about how Connor saved you, but everyone wants to know what it was like."

"Yes, Echo, why don't you tell us your side of the story?" There it was, the real reason we were invited to sit with the Partychicks. Raquelle rested her elbows on the table and smiled. She was all bleached teeth and glamor, but tense energy vibrated off her. Tendons showed on her elegant neck.

I was used to Raquelle's placating tone and outright arrogance but today, her essence felt completely foreign. Then I pegged it. She was wary of me.

"Whatever Becca said, that's how it played out," I answered.

"We can't wait to hear Connor tell it. He'll be here this weekend, won't he?" Trisha asked. "Because he's totally invited to the party. You, too, of course."

She gave me and Becca a perfunctory nod and voila, the two of us rose from the muck pile of outcasts and into the warm embrace of Raquelle's clique. Except it felt anything but warm.

"If you won't tell us about the heroic rescue, I'll ask Connor myself. Just make sure you bring him," Raquelle purred.

"Oh, we will," said Becca. She grinned at me and sipped her soda. I didn't have the heart to point out that they were only using me to get to Connor. Becca looked so content, I let it go.

CHAPTER 18

$\mathbf{B}$ack at my locker, I dug out books for my last classes when an intense throb banged against my back. I turned to find Raquelle glaring at me. She probably thought she was smiling. Her mouth was curved upward, showing a sliver of white teeth, but her eyes were cold and grey.

"Oh, Echo, there you are." She studied a fingernail and leaned against the neighboring locker, trying hard to look casual. "So, Connor. He's a pretty amazing guy, huh?"

"Um, yeah." I grabbed my books and slammed my locker.

"He's got this, I dunno, almost *magical* quality about him. Don't you think?"

I stiffened. Her tongue poked at the gum in her mouth. She blew a bubble and popped it.

"So, you are going to think I am, like, out of my mind," she continued, "but I have to ask because if anyone would know, you would. When Connor and I went out, he did something with his hand. Like, made it disappear. At first, I thought it was a magic trick or something? But he did it again. I never told anyone because nobody would ever believe me, right? But you understand. You know what I'm talking about."

This stopped me cold. Instinct told me to deny what she said and make a rude comment about *her* needing to be institutionalized. There was another possibility. If she knew about his transparency, she might know about his other gifts. She seemed genuinely intrigued. Raquelle would have kept this information to herself because, let's face it, talking about transparent guys could seriously damage a girl's popularity. That required a lot of restraint, especially for a gossip queen like Raquelle.

For a fleeting second, the weight of my secret lifted. Maybe I should tell her what I saw and experienced. Maybe this was her way of asking to be friends again.

A rush of satisfaction swirled off Raquelle, mixed with a sense of need, helplessness, and—wait a minute. Wait one bleeping minute. What was that I was picking up?

Deceit. That bee-otch was lying.

"Nice try, Raquelle." I sidestepped her and hurried down the hall. Her long, delicate legs strode once for every two of mine.

"I saw the train run over Connor's legs," Raquelle hissed.

I screeched to a halt. "What?"

"Don't play dumb with me. I saw it happen. And the marks on his jeans where the train hit him."

My shoulders knotted. I thought, fast. "And you called *me* psycho?" I twirled my index finger in circles next to my temple.

"You know exactly what happened. There's something seriously weird about him and you know exactly what I'm talking about."

"I was busy getting rescued. It's all a blur to me," I said.

"Bull. I saw the look on your face after he tackled you. You knew he got hit. I saw the sparks when the train ran over his legs. He should have been killed but he wasn't, and you know why."

"Give it up, Raquelle. Nobody else saw anything." As I said this, my world spun. What if I was wrong?

"Don't screw with me, Echo. Whatever you're hiding, I will find out."

There it was. Not *we* will find out, just *I*, and she didn't contradict me when I said she was the only witness. The knots in my shoulders relaxed.

Students filed into class just seconds before the bell. Raquelle blocked the doorway with her arm.

"Tell me now or when I figure it out, I'll drag you so far to the bottom, they'll never find you, you freak."

I lifted my chin. Waited a beat. "You're right, Raquelle, there is something you don't know." I licked my lips, leaned into her ear, and whispered, "Connor is a *magnificent* kisser." I ducked under her arm and went to class.

After school, Becca met me at my car, phone in hand, on the verge of exploding with news.

"You'll never guess who's going to the party on Friday! Go on, guess!"

"Taylor Lautner!" I teased.

"Oooo, funny." She gave me a sideways glance. "Not for real, right?"

I shook my head. She bounced into the passenger seat. "Lucas from the basketball team! We talked in Civics. The topic, naturally, was Ryan at first, but then I found out he's definitely going to Trisha's party."

On the drive home, Becca told me how she'd always thought Lucas was hot but they never talked even though they sat next to each other in three classes, how she was going to casually bump into him at the party, and the various possible ways this could all work out for her.

"I've got this incantation called Sexy Moon Spell. You recite a special chant under the full moon, right? And it practically guarantees a steamy hook-up. I'm doing one for me and Lucas. Want me to do one for you and Connor?"

"We're good," I said, remembering our intense chemistry on the carriage ride.

"Oooo, we're going to have so much fun Friday night."

I grimaced. "They might not let us in, now. Raquelle and I got into it after lunch again."

"We can do anything, as long as you bring Connor. Which you will do, right?"

It bothered me she was so willing to use Connor like that, but I let it slide. "What ever happened to 'they can kiss my Wiccan butt before I'd join their clique?'"

Becca shrugged and set her phone on her lap. Then she held her hands over it and hummed a single, dreary note.

"What in the world are you doing?" I asked.

"Practicing my telekinesis."

"Oh. How's it working out?"

"Nothing's happened since the apple went flying," she grumbled.

I glued my hands to the steering wheel so I wouldn't be tempted to thunk some sense into her. Wishing for telekinesis was like wishing for a pet unicorn. It sounds like fun until it poops on your favorite shoes and someone gets their eye poked out by the horn.

I dropped Becca off and drove to my house. When I walked in the front door a wave of heat and expectation prickled down my back.

"Surprise," I heard, and Connor appeared from the ether.

I threw my arms around his neck and kissed him. I marveled at how solid he felt, even though just seconds ago, his body had been little more than a shimmery vapor. I took his hand and led him up to my room.

Connor sat on my bed with his back against the headboard and his legs stretched in front of him. I sat on his lap and coiled an arm around his neck, enjoying the odd sensation where our skin touched. I rested my head in that space between his collarbone and chin and listened to the soft rush of his heartbeat.

"I'm so glad you came," I said.

"I got out of class early and wanted to see you." In the time I'd known Connor, I'd never pictured him in school. It struck me as odd that this incredibly gifted person was shackled to the same routine I was.

"Don't you have homework?"

He gave me a puzzled look. "What's that?"

"A huge time suck that teachers load on students to make sure we don't have a social life outside of school. You know, endless studying."

He laughed. "Of course we do. Tons of it. Never seems to end. I'll do it tonight."

"For what classes?"

"Physics—though I suspect it's way different from what you're learning. Calculus. Literature."

"I love lit class. What are you reading?" I asked.

"Pioneering writers of the twenty-second century. I don't think any of them have been born here yet."

I shook my head. "Every once in a while, our relationship feels so normal, and then you go and say something like that."

I wanted to hear more about Connor's life, but other issues pressed. I told him about Raquelle. When I finished, he was the picture of calm.

"She's the only one who saw," he said.

"You knew about this?"

"I did an energy scan after it happened. I would have picked up on anyone else."

"How did I miss that? She wasn't that far from us," I said.

"You hit the ground hard. I'm just glad you got up in one piece."

"How many people do you think she'll tell?" Was I imagining things, or was Connor trying not to laugh? Then I got his unspoken joke. "She's the alpha of her herd. She'd sound crazy if she told anyone and won't do anything that would threaten her reign over her clique," I said.

"Not exactly how I'd put it, but yes." He turned somber. "Moving her car was a bad idea, and I shouldn't have done it. No more tricks in public, from either of us."

"Until you go home. You can do anything you want there." I was imagining Connor's world, where he and his friends probably flew everywhere instead of walking and showed off their skills out in the open, just because they could.

"You're jealous," he said.

"Yeah, so?"

"You've finally come around. You like your gift. Admit it. You're glad I didn't take it away from you."

"All right, yeah, it's kinda cool. It's just that I can't have any fun with it. People respect you for your gift. You have no idea how lucky you are."

He gave me a squeeze and rolled off my bed. "I have to get back. I've got a metaphysics lab to practice for tomorrow. I'm supposed to be able to read a page out of a book with my eyes closed, and I haven't even started the lesson."

"See? Even your homework is way cooler."

He planted small kisses along my jawline and made his way to my lips and stayed there.

"Mmm, are you sure you have to go?" My fingers played with the belt loop at his hip.

"I'll stay longer next time, okay?" A peck on the cheek and he took a couple of steps back. A faint glow washed over his skin. The air around him shimmered.

To this day, I don't know what possessed me to do it, but in the split second before Connor flashed out of sight, I grabbed his hand.

CHAPTER 19

"Aaaaaaaaaaaaaaaaaaaaaaaaa!"

A scream ripped through a great cavernous void, hit something deep in the dark unknown, bounced back, and banged into my eardrums. I recognized it as my own voice. I was encased in blackness, hanging motionless, and in severe pain. I clung to consciousness despite the inexplicable horrors happening to my body.

A million razors scraped at my skin, tore at my hair and eyelids. My insides felt like they were being stretched in opposite directions by a medieval torture machine. My lungs expanded far beyond their capacity and just when I thought I would pass out from pain, the agony eased.

Warmth surged into the top of my head, through the length of my body and into the bottoms of my feet. The heat morphed into a bright spectrum of color that I sensed rather than saw. The soothing cool of blue washed my throat; healing green light filled my chest cavity; tangy yellow suffused my stomach. I was vaguely aware of panic around me. Hurried footsteps. Hostile voices.

I willed my eyes to open, but they wouldn't respond. My mouth was wrenched open and an object was shoved down my throat. I tried to bat this away, but my arm lay dead at my side. I knew, then, that I had stopped breathing.

Connor's voice, plagued with anguish, cut through the chaos. His exact words were lost, but I knew if I didn't inhale in the next few seconds, I'd never hear that voice again.

All at once, my eyes snapped open and I took an enormous breath. My heart jackhammered and blood flooded my brain. Sharp light penetrated the ashen fog shrouding my vision.

I was lying on a cold, hard floor. Some of the grittiness cleared and I made out blurry shapes staring down at me. Handheld devices scanned my limbs. When I reached to remove the object from my throat, I found nothing there. A pair of gentle hands slid beneath my shoulder blades and lifted me to a seated position. Someone handed me a cup with a straw and indicated I should drink. The liquid was syrupy sweet to the point of being offensive, but it soothed my throat and revitalized me. In two blinks, my vision cleared.

Connor knelt next to me, pale as a ghost. He took my hands in both of his and pressed them to his lips.

"I almost lost you out there. I almost lost hold of your hand." The terror in his eyes told me everything he was unable to say, that his touch had been my lifeline between worlds. I sensed that even in my deepest agony, I had only experienced the knife tip of the force that would have ripped me to shreds.

The person who had handed me the drink had a full head of gray hair, thin lips and patient blue eyes. The sleeves on his white smock cuffed neatly above his elbows. The name 'Philip' was sewn onto his chest pocket in elegant script. He surveyed my joints—elbows, wrists, vertebrae—and nodded, satisfied.

He turned to Connor. "Is this what she should look like?"

Connor's eyes never left mine. "Yes." His voice shook.

Philip regarded me with calm intelligence, like a country doctor shuttling a frightened newborn into the world. "Well, young lady, you got very, very lucky. Welcome to West Region City, the city you know as Portland, year 2173."

He addressed a scowling young guy standing in front of a black and chrome control panel. "Run her through the CKS to make sure her organs are intact and get the incident in the transport log."

The guy answered with a single nod. He wore the same white smock and pants as his older co-worker. He was good-looking, chocolate brown hair cut short, dark eyes a shade off black. He was shorter than Connor by a few inches and looked to be my age.

Philip put a wrinkled hand on Connor's shoulder. "We will talk about this later." He exited through a set of double doors that swished open and closed.

The young guy stepped forward and hooked a rough arm beneath mine. Connor took my other side, and I staggered to my feet.

"Thanks, Jaxon, I've got her from here," Connor said. I caught the unmistakable curl of disdain on Jaxon's mouth as he walked back to his station.

Connor slinked his arm around my waist, practically carrying me across the lab. We bypassed three control panels with clear glass monitors in front of them and machines that looked like they belonged in a futuristic hospital room. He set me at the entrance of a vertical glass cylinder the size of my bathroom shower.

"This won't hurt a bit," he said.

I guided my shaky legs onto a set of footprints on the center of the floor.

"Like this?" I asked.

"Isn't she a smart one," Jaxon sniped.

"Knock it off, Jaxon" Connor said. "Just run the test so we can get out of here."

A door sealed the entrance, locking me inside the tube. They watched me through the glass, as though I were a science experiment. The full impact of what I'd done was starting to set in. A knot of anxiety and embarrassment swelled in the pit of my stomach, and the space between my eyebrows buzzed to the point of burning. The glass enclosure quivered.

Jaxon made no effort to hide his disgust. "Collect yourself, or we can't run the test."

"Echo," Connor said softly from just outside the glass, "take a moment to center yourself."

I nodded and forced deep breaths. The tube stopped quivering. Jaxon tapped on the keypad, his attention shifting between me and the glass screen in front of him. Looking at the back of his glass screen, I watched numbers and graphs scroll from the top, turn into holographs, and disappear.

He navigated the control panel with a confidence I found intimidating. Okay, everything about him intimidated me, from his short tone to his obvious contempt for my presence. I couldn't fault him for that. I'm sure I was the last thing he expected to see beaming into his workspace.

The machine whirred and changed pitch. Then the door whooshed open. I went to Connor's side, and he and Jaxon assessed the data output.

"No internal damage," Connor said and kissed me on the cheek.

Jaxon's eyes narrowed at Connor's affection. There was a question behind his hard gaze that he kept to himself. "I recommend assimilating her for a max of one hour. You should probably keep her in the Northwest sector, seeing as this is *way* outside of protocol. And I'd advise you to take her out the back entrance."

"I don't want my dad to find out about this, alright, Jaxon?"

"Yessir," Jaxon growled.

Sir?

Jaxon left through the swishing doors, and Connor and I were the only ones in the lab. His hand was so firm on my shoulder it could have been permanently fused there. I couldn't force myself to look at him.

The potential consequences of my impulsive action were hitting hard. Without permission—and against Connor's warnings—I'd traveled 160 years into the future. I had secretly harbored dreams of coming here ever since he told me about West Region. Now I was terrified I'd never see my dad again.

My chin trembled. "Can I ever go back?"

"Of course you can, but we need to give your body time to recover. We also don't want to keep you here longer than your body can handle." He tapped his finger on his thigh, thinking. "We don't want to wander too far from the Harden Center, so, hmmm. I know where to take you."

He took my hand and moved toward the door. My feet refused to budge. The glass CKS tube vibrated.

"Connor, wait. I am so, so sorry I did this to you. It wasn't something I planned, I swear. I, I don't know what I was thinking."

"Echo, it's okay."

"I heard people arguing when I was waking up. I know I screwed up royally. If your dad finds out that's it for us, isn't it?"

Connor pulled me to him. His t-shirt drew the salty dampness from my lashes. My aura mellowed and stopped wreaking havoc with the machinery.

"Jaxon threatened to report you when you materialized. The things he said about you made me want to thrash him. But he knows better than to tell anyone outside the lab. He'd have to answer to me." From his easy expression, you'd think we were in the middle of an afternoon stroll back in Portland.

I was sure I looked quite the opposite. "Philip was intrigued by your arrival. I'll have a lot of questions to answer, and he'll probably make me do a write-up on the trip for his research, but that will be the worst of it."

"He's not going to tell your dad?"

"No." I picked up an unspoken agreement between him and Philip.

Connor led me out of the lab and down a corridor. The walls on either side of us weren't solid. Instead, sheets of water flowed from openings in the ceiling and disappeared into stone-covered grates in the floor. The overall effect was that of walking between a set of waterfalls.

The rooms on the other side appeared warped by the water, but I could make out offices and more laboratories. I reeled in the impulse to reach into the water, to see if it felt any different from home. As though reading my mind, Conner dipped his fingers in, and let them trail as we walked. I did the same. It was surprisingly warm.

We passed what appeared to be a meeting room and then a lunchroom where about a dozen people sat at a handful of tables. The gentle sound of trickling water muffled our footsteps, yet everyone in the lunchroom snapped to attention when we walked by.

When I glanced over my shoulder, curious heads watched us from a doorway that had parted in the liquid. A tall girl with short brown hair offered a cautious wave. I waved back, and Connor led me outside.

Post-Collapse Portland was nothing like I'd expected. Even though Connor's descriptions made it sound nice, I'd envisioned a dreary, concrete city littered with rubble, but as soon as we stepped outside, we were surrounded by fir trees. Red stone paths wound through the forest, some of them leading to clusters of brick buildings obscured behind thick brush. On one side of the path, the foliage was so dense, I couldn't see beyond a few feet.

Thick clouds hung overhead, fat with the threat of rain. Connor cloaked me beneath his arm to ward off the light drizzle. We continued down a path a while and stopped.

"Want to guess where we are?" The playful glint in his eye let slip this was a trick question.

I lifted a shoulder. "Some kind of park?"

"We're about a mile from your house, at the bottom of the hill. You know the warehouse where we practiced? Well, we're standing about where it used to be."

My eyes narrowed in confusion. This part of the city should be crosscut with streets and parking lots. Art galleries and restaurants had started to open in some of the unused warehouses along the edge of the industrial district. There should have been sidewalks, and patio tables, and people, and music.

"It's all gone? The art galleries? And that café we went to?" The café where I'd tried to escape from Connor held special meaning.

"Remember, factions and an earthquake destroyed much of the city. Everyone had to start from scratch. Some of it was never rebuilt but there are parts you'd recognize. That condo tower where we watched the sun rise? Somehow, that survived."

"Can we go there?" I was having a hard time believing that I was standing in my city. I needed a familiar sight to anchor me, to help me make sense of this place that wasn't Portland, but still *was*.

"Taking you through town would cause too much of a scene. You saw what happened when we left the lab. They know you're not from here."

"How would they know? Does everyone wear a uniform or something?"

Connor laughed. "Your aura gives you away."

Hearing him talk so pointedly about my weakness made my cheeks flush. My aura thinned and waned like it was determined to make a bigger fool out of me, and I was overcome with dizziness. I slumped onto a bench. Connor rested his fingers along the side of my neck, checking my pulse. He rolled one of my fingers in his, presumably testing to see if I was losing solidness, becoming transparent.

"You're feeling side effects from the trip. Maybe this isn't a good idea. We should go back to the lab."

"No! I want to keep going." I rose off the bench and started down the path. I'd never admit it, but each time Connor talked about West Region, I pictured myself living here—going to school, making friends—all within a community that embraced my freakishness, free from the threat of factions and social banishment. This was my chance, possibly my *only* chance, to find out what West Region was really like.

Connor watched me, concerned.

"I feel better already. If I start to fade out, then we'll go back. Are you sure we can't go into town?"

"I'm going to have a hard enough time getting all the lab employees to keep quiet about this. I'll make up some story about you visiting from another part of the region, and how my dad doesn't approve. They might not believe me, but they'll keep quiet."

He steered us down the path into the densest part of the forest, brushing foliage away as the trail narrowed. It ended at an iridescent gate. Like the coin I wore around my neck, the gate appeared made of metal, but not any kind I'd ever seen. It melted into the foliage on either side, giving the impression that we could walk around it. Unfamiliar symbols covered the top half of its surface.

Connor waved his hand in a half circle, and the gate swung open. The scene on the other side took my breath away.

CHAPTER 20

Connor and I stepped through the open gate. Palm trees dotted a sandy landscape. Trunks supported tropical vines, their enormous leaves shading the orchids growing beneath them. A trail dipped into a valley and ran along the base of soaring, green undulating cliffs. There, a turquoise lagoon sparkled.

Humidity leached away my chill. The sweet scent of exotic life perfumed the air. I looked back at the cool pathway lined with fir trees, at the cloudy sky and rain hitting the brick path.

I puckered my brow, wondering how the heck a city in the northwestern part of the United States could look like a picture postcard of Hawaii. A pair of toucans landed on a low branch. Their brilliant orange and green heads twitched side to side, and they studied me with flat black eyes. They seemed to say, "You aren't from around here." Which is exactly what I was thinking about them.

I shook my head in astonishment. "This is *definitely* not Portland."

"You're sure?"

"I give up. Is this, like, a side effect of global warming?"

Connor gave me a wide grin. "Hardly. We're in The Reserve. It's a simulated geography, or simulography for short. It's the future of physics as you know it. In your time, you have holographs, and those are the building blocks for this technology."

A shocking possibility gripped me. "Do I end up inventing this?" A long shot, no doubt, but my physics grades *were* improving.

Connor laughed. "No, you're meant to do bigger things."

"I am, am I?" I raised an eyebrow, waiting to hear why he sounded so certain.

"Well, you've got a gift, right? You've got the opportunity to do great things, if you wanted."

I huffed air. If I lived in West Region? Sure. In my time? Doubtful. "If anyone is destined for greatness, it'd be you. You're the one who's crazy talented." My statement was heartfelt, but Connor's eyebrows rose and he shook his head.

"What? Did I say something wrong?" I asked.

"No. Thanks for the compliment. This," he motioned to the strange world around us, "is what I want to learn to do. I want to be a master physicist so I can build simulographies all over West Region. Ones with mountains and deserts and more beaches."

"Why don't you?"

His lips tightened. "If I have my way, I will. Here, take my hand."

Connor followed a shallow stream that sloped into the valley. He hopped from one smooth rock to the next. I teetered, nearly falling into the water.

"This is why I avoid sports," I said, not wanting him to know that time jumping through the portal had affected my coordination. The dizziness was back, just a little, and my legs felt like they did when I ran track for gym class, heavy and loose all at the same time.

The bird chatter grew louder, and somewhere up ahead was the sound of water gushing into a pool.

"Tell me about the people here, like who gets which gift. Does everyone get the same abilities as their parents? What if you can only do certain things? Does anyone care?"

On the fringe of those questions were the ones that I couldn't speak. *Is anyone considered a freak? An outcast? Are they shunned?*

"I'd say about eighty percent of West Regioners have at least one gift. Some are rare, like the telepaths, so it's not like everyone runs around reading everybody's thoughts. Manifestors are *really* rare. I only know of one."

Connor helped me down a steep incline. At the bottom, a waterfall cascaded into a shallow pool. We sat on warm, flat rocks. I shook my head, in awe of the blue-green water tumbling over the cliff, the foreign birdcalls that trilled from the treetops.

"What's a manifestor?"

"Someone who can harness the power of quantum energy to create, well, anything, as long as he has a sample of it or can picture it in his mind. The way it's explained to me is everything already exists in the metaphysical sense. A manifestor can bring it to life, so to speak. Create something out of thin air."

"And you've seen someone do this?"

"Lots of times. As for the people without any gift, they seem happy enough. Some of them get tutored and find they have a hidden talent. Others just don't care."

I marveled at this sense of inclusion. It was cruel, really, to be saddled with a gift and *not* live in West Region. My head wagged in disbelief. "I feel like I was born in the wrong time."

Connor took my hand, and his current trailed into my fingers. "It's a time of evolution, the hundred years that exist between us." He swept a lock of my hair behind my ear and kissed me on the forehead.

Then he lay back on the smooth rocks and closed his eyes. I rested my hand along his breastbone, watched his chest rise and fall. His heart beat soft and steady. It was the one thing that seemed true and real in this outrageous world, and I anchored myself to its rhythm. If it weren't for that beat, I surely would have thought I was dreaming.

My breathing slowed until each inhale, each exhale, was on pace with his heart. I pressed against the firm muscle of his chest. My breath quickened, and so did his heartbeat, until they meshed again. The synchronicity sent a rush into my belly. Connor opened his eyes and took my hand. He kissed the inside of my palm and then my wrist. He sat up, and his lips reached for mine.

My whole body heated, sending a flush of warmth racing down my spine. I was full into the kiss when Connor stopped and pulled back. His lids rose half-mast, and then his eyes widened at something just over my shoulder.

"Don't. Move."

His low tone froze me in place. I felt a dainty pressure testing the top of my shoulder. Something was crawling on me. A faint flutter against my hair nearly sent me into convulsions. All I could think was *spider*, and it felt huge. I tensed, waiting for Connor to smack it off me. Instead, he gently scooped the thing in his hand and brought it around for me to see.

I stared in awe at the largest butterfly I had ever seen. Each wing was as big as my hand and colored in iridescent blues and greens. No, wait, the wings were amber and blue. My brain tripped over itself until it registered what I was looking at.

"It's got two sets of wings!"

"Nobody knows where they originated from, but the Hecate butterfly has been around since the end of our civil war with East Region. That's when we were finally free to use our paranormal ability without persecution. The Hecate became our Region's symbol. The first set of wings reminds us of the losses we endured seeking freedom to use our gifts. The second set reminds us to use our ability to preserve and spread peace."

He coaxed the creature onto my forearm. It flexed its wings, fearless.

"That's it, I'm never going back," I said. "I'm going to live right here, in this simul-thingy place forever. Care to join me?"

Connor frowned. Not the sort of reaction a girl's looking for when she asks a guy to live with her, even if she is half-joking.

"Wouldn't that be nice, to live here free of worry, blissfully ever after? Nothing would make me happier," he said. The butterfly took flight and rode the air current across the lagoon. Connor picked up a handful of small stones and tossed them at the waterfall, one by one.

"You'll think I'm crazy, but the truth is, I envy your life," he said.

"You've got to be kidding."

"West Region is amazing, don't get me wrong. But my role in it?" His gaze drifted deep into the pool and stayed there. When he continued, he sounded far away, like he was trying to detach himself from the truth. "The civil war ended decades ago, but West Region is locked in constant tension with East Region. They'll do anything to take us over, oppress our citizens and use our abilities against us. We're forever on guard against attack."

"That's terrible." I couldn't imagine living under that kind of pressure.

"And I'm expected to lead West Region in a few years."

I didn't think I'd heard right. "Wait a minute. You mean, like, be the president?"

Connor nodded, lost in that infinite pool.

"But you're so young. And what ever happened to elections? Don't people get to choose who's in charge?"

"They do, but our family is one of the most…" He searched for the right word. "Powerful is what people like to say, but really, we're just very gifted. We're trusted and respected for our gifts. My grandfather made the region what it is today, a haven for those with paranormal abilities. Not long after, my father was voted into office. There have been a few other leaders, but my family has a history of stewardship, and my father was eventually voted in again. The citizens trust us because we have the most to lose if, for instance, East Region were to invade. Energetically, we're able to do things that nobody else can, no matter how hard they train."

With this, he directed his palm toward the waterfall and the water stopped flowing. He flipped his wrist and water ran backward out of the pool and up the cliff. He snapped his fingers again, and the water plunged back down as nature intended.

To say I was blown away was an understatement, but the pain on Connor's face overshadowed my astonishment.

"What is it?" I asked.

"Technically, I have the choice whether or not to lead the region. Realistically, I don't. It's part of our family honor, to use our ability and our knowledge to serve. I was born into the position."

"What about your brother?"

"He could do the job, but he's one of the twenty percent. No gift whatsoever. The region wants *me*." He whipped a stone against a far boulder with such force it ricocheted toward my head. He redirected it with a flick of his hand.

"Leading the region means I forfeit any chance at having a normal life. I can count on one hand the number of times I've met with my father outside the boardroom." Off my look, he added. "That's an exaggeration, but not by much."

Something like a freight train slammed me out of my Utopian stupor. Here I was, innocently dreaming about living with Connor in West Region, like I was gallivanting off to Disneyland during summer vacation. I was so deep into this fantasy that my head practically danced with pixies.

But West Region was a real country with dangerous enemies and complex problems, and the guy I'd fallen for had some serious decisions to make about his future. Decisions that I might be clouding.

In the lab, I'd noticed I was unable to read Jaxon's or Philip's auras. My aura, however, wasted no time throwing a public tantrum. These small details added to the stack of reasons why I shouldn't be here. Color it any way I wanted, I really had no business in this world. Even if Connor chose not to follow in his father's footsteps, West Region was still his life. He belonged here. I did not.

The unspoken truth lay splayed between us, raw as a fresh scrape. There was no solution to our little problem. No matter what he had said, everything most certainly was *not* possible.

I sat back on my heels and pushed the pain down deep. There was no way I'd let this show, not while we were side-by-side in this island of paradise. I linked my arm through Connor's while he tossed the remaining pebbles into the stream. One by one, they hit the water, sent shock waves rippling toward the bank, and sank to the bottom.

The sun was low on the horizon when Connor led me back up the trail and toward the Harden Center, where the portal awaited. The temperature had dropped, and Connor held me close. We walked in the greyness, in silence.

The trip was taking a toll on me, more emotional than physical. I felt like I'd been gone a very, very long time and worried that Kimber would notice I wasn't in my bedroom.

My bedroom. One hundred and sixty years in the past.

"How much time has gone by… back home?" I asked.

"The same amount as here. Time runs parallel for us, but we just live in a different year." He nudged me, trying to lighten the mood. "If you were going to ask me to go back to the mall and do something worse to Raquelle's car, I couldn't. That moment has already passed."

When we reached the Harden Center, I stopped. My fresh heartache was now layered with dread. I'd nearly died on the trip here. If something went wrong on the way back, I'd be without Philip or Jaxon or their advanced medical tools. I swallowed hard. "Is the portal trip going to be like last time?"

"Echo, do you think I'd let you go if I thought anything would happen to you? I'm taking you back myself."

My shoulders dropped with relief. When we got to the lab, the girl who had waved to me on the way out was standing at the control panel with Jaxon. She was tall, with a narrow face and big, soft eyes. Thin wrists poked out of her white smock. She took one look at me and smiled.

"See? She looks great. Like she's recovered completely," she said to Jaxon.

Jaxon scowled and busied himself at the panel. The girl came forward and held out her hand.

"I'm Carina. I help run the portal and keep Jaxon in line."

He grumbled while I shook Carina's hand. In one long look, she took me in. Then she smiled and arched a knowing brow at Connor. "Now I understand why you're making so many trips back." If someone had that reaction back home, they would have been commenting on my looks, because that's what everyone's preoccupied with. But in West Region?

Maybe Carina was talking about my aura or some other non-visible feature.

Carina removed a device from her pocket and held it to the side of my neck. I held still through the series of toned beeps, and she studied the device's readout. "I heard you arrived barely intact, but everything looks fine now. Did you have fun while you were here?"

I smiled. "This place is amazing."

"I took her to The Reserve," Connor said.

"Good. You rested. Well, you are approved for departure." Carina retreated to her spot next to Jaxon and nodded at Connor. "Any time you're ready."

My pulse raced. Little black dots danced in front of my eyes.

Connor squeezed my hand. "Everything will be all right. You'll be wrapped in my field the entire time."

I forced a nod. A metal door slid open, and we stepped into a well-lit space the size of a walk-in closet. The walls were metallic and vibrated in a high-pitched hum. The floor, though, was solid rock. In the center, a roundish pit about five feet in diameter gaped, black and ominous. It throbbed with an energy all its own.

He nodded at the hole. "This is the portal."

"That's it?" I was expecting some sort of time machine chamber complete with cushioned seats and rotating lights.

"It's a natural portal, so it's been here for probably thousands of years." He led me to the edge. I averted my eyes from the opening and forced myself to breathe normally.

"Wrap your arms around me," he said. I embraced Connor in a death grip. He didn't seem to mind. "Now, all you have to do is relax."

"Piece of cake." My voice wavered. "Then what?"

"Enjoy the ride!" With that, Connor lifted me off my feet and stepped into the void.

I shoved my face into his chest. "Omigod, omigod, omigod, omigod!" I screamed into his t-shirt until his voice broke through.

"Echo. Sshhh. Keep your voice down." He gently shook my shoulder. Tentatively, I opened one eye, then the other. We were in my room.

"We're back?" I asked. "So fast?"

"I told you it would be easy."

I swayed. Connor grabbed my elbow and sat me down. My arms and legs went noodly, like I'd just stepped off a roller coaster, and I was light-headed, without a care in the world. A part of me longed to stay there, in that groggy, dreamlike state where I floated between worlds. Intuitively, I knew I was safe there, far away from a dilemma, a problem that cursed me. The bliss trickled away and just like that, I was mired in predicament.

What would I do about this boy who had outrageous life decisions ahead of him, who was so kind and giving, and seemed determined to overlook our little time-jumping problem? What could I say to this boy who I loved like I had known him for a thousand years?

My wiser self said it was time to set him free. It wasn't fair to string him along, ignoring the inevitable separation coming at us like a freight train. I had to cut him loose. Now.

I opened my mouth to speak, but Connor cut me off. "I hate to reward bad behavior so I probably shouldn't say this, but I loved that you came with me today."

The current running from his fingers into my bare neck bumped up a notch. My wiser self warned of unbearable heartbreak if I didn't release him. He was expected to lead an entire nation, for crying out loud.

"I loved it, too," I said, and a vice-like anxiety gripped my chest.

"I think I can come back at the end of the week," he said.

I searched for an excuse as to why that wouldn't work. "Echo?"

My wiser self was still yelling out warnings, rallying forces against my heart. Attacked it with logic, assailed it with rationale. Threatened it with full-on destruction. But it was no use. The heart knows what it wants.

"I can't wait to see you again," I said. I laced my fingers into his hair and kissed him.

CHAPTER 21

Before he fizzled back to the twenty-second century, Connor asked me to look for a new place for us to train. Since I already had a stash of skills that I had to keep hidden, I balked. What was the point of learning more? But he insisted. I only had four days; he was coming back on Friday when my school was out for teacher inservice.

The new place had to be spacious, he'd said, somewhere we could make noise. Most important, we needed privacy. He wouldn't tell me what he had planned but promised it was a big step and that we'd have fun.

A private place where we could make noise? My heart flipped and my imagination ran wild with presumption. Did this next step involve nudity? Was I ready to go there?

The next morning, while I got ready for school, I racked my brains for such a place. The school property was huge, with outbuildings and little-used back rooms, but it was public and anybody could walk in on us at any time. An unused warehouse was the best choice, but how would I find one? We couldn't return to the old one. If someone saw us trespassing, they'd know for sure we were responsible for the damage caused by the sprinkler system.

I clasped the coin necklace around my neck and centered my energy. Slid the bracelets onto my wrists and swung through the kitchen for something to eat before picking up Becca.

Kimber's phone lay on the counter, charging. She wasn't up yet, so I flipped through her calendar to Friday. Her day was packed. Extra bonus, she planned to be out of town. That settled it. Connor and I would spend the day upstairs, in my bedroom. If Kimber came home unexpectedly, he'd have time to disappear before she climbed to the third floor.

Thus began the long countdown to the end of the week. All the internal conflict I'd felt in The Reserve was quashed beneath my eagerness to see my supernaturally sexy boyfriend. He hadn't been gone more than twelve hours and already, I was distracted beyond sensibility. I nearly ran a stoplight on the way to school; I slammed my sleeve in my locker and had to open it again to set myself free. And that wise voice that had tried to steer me in a different direction? She was missing Connor as much as the rest of me.

I buried myself in homework to make the days pass faster. By mid-week, I was three chapters ahead in Literature, and I'd made a real friend in Solomon by asking for a bunch of extra credit.

Thursday classes came and went, and when I looked at the hours stretching until Friday morning, I thought I'd crack. Becca was busy with her family, Tito was with Kimber, and when I tried to watch television, I nibbled my cuticles raw during any scenes that were remotely romantic. Finally, I grabbed my book bag and headed out. I had a research paper due in Social Sciences and figured I may as well get a start on it. Talk about desperate for distraction.

I drove to the downtown library and, once inside, dropped my bag on a table in the most remote spot I could find. If I was going to spend a non-school night surrounded by twelve-foot stacks of books, I darned well better get some work done. No noise, no other students, just a wall against my back and a long row of bookshelves on either side of me.

I searched for the texts I needed for my research—material my teacher had suggested that I couldn't just look up on the Internet—and dropped them on my table.

Deep into my research, I absentmindedly swiped at a stray hair tickling my forehead. The feeling came back, more of an annoying scratch this time. I swept my hair away from my face and kept reading. But like a loose lash that you just can't seem to fish out of your eye, the annoyance persisted. It was more of a friction now, right on the skin between my brows. I rubbed the spot, expecting to feel the start of a big zit. Just my luck, with Connor coming the next day.

That's when my aura picked up another presence. Malignant and dark. Close. I looked down the row. I was alone, but as I scanned past the shelves, I caught a pair of eyes peering at me from between two books. The atmosphere swelled with harshness. Thoroughly unnerved, I slammed my book shut.

"Hey. You. Get lost or I'm going to report you," I said. The downtown library occasionally attracted weirdos. Security did a good job of keeping the place safe and trespassers were usually harmless, but even after the face retreated, the dark energy didn't. This bothered me enough to want to find this person and report him, or her, to the front desk.

I jogged to the end of the row, each step echoing intrusively against the silence. There wasn't anyone at the next set of tables, nor did I see anyone racing out of there. Whoever it was had gotten out fast and, come to think of it, they'd done so without making a sound. It was like they were there, and then they weren't.

I went back to my table and picked up where I'd left off, but my concentration was gone. I checked the books out and lugged them home.

When I pulled into my driveway, a black BMW sat in front of our garage. Inside the house, voices murmured in conversation.

"Echo, is that you?" Kimber called.

I found her on the couch with her legs curled beneath her. Her arm wrapped tightly around Tito, and her other fingers clutched the hem of her skirt, twisting and pulling the fabric into wrinkles. Her face was splotchy, like she'd been crying.

Next to Kimber, Mr. Crane sat in an armchair, still in his coat, his keys dangling from his hand.

"I just got back from the library. Hi, Mr. Crane." He smiled at me, just barely.

The air was dense and oily. I did not want to spend another second there, so I turned to leave.

"Echo, Don tells me he saw you in the industrial area last weekend before dawn. What were you doing up that early?" Kimber's voice was croaky.

"Oh, Connor and I got up to see the sunrise," I said.

"Connor?"

"The boy that Raquelle's been dating," Mr. Crane answered.

Little darts of irritation threatened to pierce through my aura. "Connor is *my* boyfriend."

Mr. Crane's eyebrow piqued with interest.

"I didn't know you were dating anyone," Kimber said.

"For a few weeks. He's really nice." I waited a beat, then, "I'm going to my room."

"The industrial area is a strange place to watch the sunrise," Mr. Crane said.

"We went to the waterfront. Connor drove and he took a shortcut, I guess. What happened down there?" I asked, remembering the squad cars and crime tape.

Kimber clenched her skirt. Tito writhed out of her arms and trotted to me. I scooped him up.

Mr. Crane cleared his throat. "A young woman was killed early that morning."

"Two of them," Kimber whispered.

"There, there," Mr. Crane said, and he patted Kimber's knee. "Kimber knew one of the women."

"She was so talented. She's the one who advised me to marry Echo's father."

"Both the women claimed they were psychic," Mr. Crane explained.

My first reaction was *you needed a psychic to tell you to marry my dad?* But I let it go.

"And there was another girl, from two weeks ago," Kimber added.

"Three deaths in as many weeks. Though the first woman claimed to be a medium, and not a psychic." Mr. Crane nodded. Kimber sniffled. I reeled in shock.

"Do you think they were being targeted?" I heard myself ask.

"For what?" Mr. Crane asked.

"Idunno. Maybe because of their gifts?"

He looked at me, long and hard. "That's an interesting theory, Echo."

I involuntarily took a step back because for a split second, I thought I caught a smidgeon of dark energy coming off him. It reminded me of the loser who had been spying on me at the library. It receded as quickly as it came.

"Those poor, poor girls." Kimber wiped a tear from her cheek. "I don't want you in that area anymore, Echo. Especially when it's dark."

I forced a shaky nod. Mr. Crane, the ever-vigilant head shrink, picked up on my unease.

"Is something the matter?" There was something I'd learned about Mr. Crane—maybe all shrinks were like this, I didn't know—but he would never let you know how much he really knew. He would ask questions he already had the answers to, stuff like that. It was hard to like a man who made me feel like a lab animal under scrutiny.

"I'm just shocked by the news," I answered. "I won't go down there."

Satisfied, they let me go. I took the stairs two at a time. On my bed, I pulled Tito close, trying to sort out what I'd felt in Mr. Crane's presence.

Auric energy is like a fingerprint, and though I wasn't a good enough reader to identify people with my eyes closed, I was starting to notice subtle differences between auras. Becca's might condense when she's feeling insecure, for instance, but it still feels bubbly. Kimber's scrapes at me no matter what kind of mood she's in. And until that night, I had never felt anything as repulsive as the presence in the library. Now, I'd felt it again, coming off Mr. Crane. Or thought I had.

The conclusion that my mind raced toward was absurd. Ridiculous. Mr. Crane, in the downtown library, spying on me? That was too sick for words. Besides, he was here consoling Kimber.

But how long had he been here? He hadn't taken off his jacket and his keys were still in his hand. On a quiet night, the drive from the library to my house was just a few minutes.

Tito yelped, and I realized I'd been tugging at his ear.

"Sorry, boy." I let him go, along with my ludicrous accusation.

Curiosity about the murders drove me to do a search on my phone. I surfed to a Portland news website that blared the headline *New Deaths Haunt Warehouse District*. The names of the victims had been released. I was relieved that I didn't know any of them. The article said all three were in their early twenties, but it didn't provide any details about the crimes.

The fact that all the victims claimed to have a paranormal gift shook me. I wanted to know how they died or a theory as to why, but all the websites repeated the information that Mr. Crane had shared.

That was enough bad news for one night. I turned off the light. Tito curled up next to me on my pillow. I didn't fall asleep until I heard Mr. Crane leave.

CHAPTER 22

In the light of morning, shock from the recent deaths wore off. The warehouse district wasn't exactly crime central, but I'd gladly avoid it. As for all the victims having some paranormal gift or another, I had to chalk it up to coincidence. If I allowed myself to jump to conclusions about the deaths being connected—that people with paranormal gifts were being targeted—I would have stayed hunkered under my comforter.

There was no telling when Connor would show, so I grabbed a quick shower and pulled my hair into a ponytail. I ate breakfast in front of the television, and numbed my brain with game shows.

A couple of hours passed, and still no sign of him. My phone rang and I answered it in record speed, forgetting for a moment that he wouldn't be calling me. Sometimes, the odd barriers in our relationship were beyond my grasp.

"Want to watch the Wiccan Warrior trilogy with me?" Becca asked.

Thank goodness I had plans because if I had to watch the Wiccan Warrior movies again, I was going to hurl in my mouth.

"Connor and I are hanging out today. Did you forget?"

She *squeeeeed* so loud, I pulled the phone away from my ear. "Totally forgot. Come help me decide what to wear to the party before you go."

I headed to Becca's house, secure in knowing that Connor's innate ability to track me across time would lead him to her room. Not so long ago, I'd found this ability disturbing. Now, I took comfort in it.

Becca had eight different outfits draped across her bed, combinations of jeans paired with a variety of black tops. She sported new ear jewelry, too. The girl had a penchant for do-it-yourself piercings and a pain tolerance that I envied. An ornate pewter dragon slithered along the rim of her ear, anchored in place by two new holes that she'd punched into the cartilage.

When I was ten, I begged my dad to get my ears pierced. I passed out when the gun punched a single tiny hole in my lobe. I didn't have the guts to do the other one and eventually let the one close up.

"Is this too much?" Becca held up a dark shirt dotted with pink and yellow skulls.

"You're going back to Goth?"

"I don't want to hit Lucas with the Wiccan stuff just yet. I'm not even sure he knows."

I rolled my eyes just a little. "The word is out, Becca. Everyone knows."

She agonized over the decision. You'd think the future of mankind depended on what she wore. I looked out her window at my house for a sign of Connor. She held up another outfit. I shook my head. She debated the next one, her index finger lodged between her teeth.

"Do you ever get the feeling you and Connor are soulmates?" she asked.

"Yeah, kind of." Or at least I used to, before our talk in The Reserve. Now, I didn't know what I thought.

"Lucas and I are, I just know it." She turned to me, her face ruddy with happiness. "We just figured out we used to go to the same elementary school, and his parents used to hang out with mine. *And*, we both went to the same speech therapist in kindergarten. We both had lisps. It's like the universe has been trying to bring us together."

"I know exactly what you mean," I said, thinking back to the familiar feeling that tugged at me since the first day I'd met Connor, and the way his portrait called to me. "Except I don't know where I know him from."

"Did you ask him about the painting?"

I gave her a blank look.

"Pul-ease. That story you made up about it being a picture of your old neighbor? I so never believed you. On some deep soul level, you knew about Connor when you painted it. Aren't you dying to find out if he knew about you?"

"But what if he didn't? And the guy in the painting has a scar. Connor doesn't. I'll look like a fool if I ask him."

"Not if you set things up right." Becca went to her dresser. She held her palms in front of the top drawer and stayed there, frozen in place.

"Um, Becca?" I asked, wondering what she was doing.

She huffed out a sigh. "Forget it." She pulled the drawer open.

Oh, right, she still thought she had telekinesis. She pulled out a tiny glass vial. "Boiled rosemary and juniper berries, with a pinch of my hair. It's like a pheromone. It'll draw our guys to us like flies."

I squinched my face.

"Flies that we're hot for," she corrected. "You can ask Connor anything, and he'll be so into you that he won't care. Not that he isn't already, but if you're nervous about asking him…"

Hmmm. Connor and I didn't need any help heating up our relationship, but if a simple potion could block out the absurdity of my question… I *was* dying to know the answer.

"It smells good, too." Becca waved the vial under my nose.

My gag reflex kicked in.

"Too much hair?" she asked.

I fanned the stink away from my face. "You can't wear that. Lucas won't get within ten feet of you." I stole another glance out the window.

"Why don't you just text Connor and tell him you're at my house?"

"Um, his phone is broken?" Becca was right. I was a bad liar.

Becca signaled *whatever* with her palm. "Just go."

I jumped up and hugged her. "Wear the black and blue shirt with jeans. I'll pick you up at eight," I said.

"*Eight*," she repeated.

"I'll be here."

She arched her eyebrows.

"I know, it's your big chance with Lucas. I won't be late."

"We're, like, soulmates."

"I promise," I assured her.

"You're sure it's a *no* on the potion?"

"Uh, yeah." I ran out the door.

On the way up the driveway, I saw the air shimmering on the porch. By the time I cleared the last step, Connor had sparked into full form. I leaped into his familiar, electric embrace. He took the full impact of my weight without budging. After a moment, he broke our hug.

"Is anything the matter?" he asked.

"I'm just relieved Philip let you come back."

"He was more concerned than angry. I convinced him the data they collected from you was worth breaking protocol."

"I'm a lab rat," I shrugged. "Fine with me. What about your dad?"

"He still doesn't know."

I swept the cowlick off his forehead with my fingertips. It flopped to its natural spot again.

"Did you find a place for us?" he asked.

"I have great news. Kimber's gone all day, so we can practice here." I opened the door. Remnants of my stepmother's piercing energy tumbled into us. Connor jerked back, like he'd been slapped in the face.

"It's always like that in here," I said, apologizing for Kimber's auric presence. "It'll be nicer in my room."

He glanced at the neighboring houses and up and down the street. "Who else is inside?" he whispered.

"Nobody. The house is empty."

He grabbed my arm, hard, and pulled me next to him. "Are you absolutely sure?" he whispered. He eased into the entryway, scanning, listening, and blocking my body with his.

"Connor, you're scaring me."

"Sshhh." He pulled me inside and crept down the hall, blocking me protectively the entire way. When he reached the living room, his green eyes grew fierce.

"Someone was here earlier. Who?"

"Um, just me. Mr. Crane came over last night to talk to Kimber."

"Anyone else?"

"No."

His tone dropped to near primal. "Let's go." With his hand on my lower back, he ushered me toward the door.

I skidded to a halt. "I'm not going anywhere until you tell me what's going on."

A faint violet light effused his silhouette. "What did Crane want?"

"He had some bad news for Kimber. Maybe that's what you're picking up."

Connor tilted his head at me, waiting not-so-patiently. I told him about the night's conversation. About the murders.

Connor's jaw tensed as his molars ground together. The violet light intensified. "We're getting out of here. Now."

His tone scared me enough that I let him drag me out of there. I snagged my car keys and a jacket on the way out the door.

We sat at a traffic light on a main boulevard in the heart of the city. The eerie violet light around Connor had faded. I nibbled a cuticle and sat with my legs crossed, my top foot jiggling an anxious rhythm.

"I picked up faction energy in your house," he said.

"What?"

"I've felt it before on terrorists from East Region. It was disgusting, and I'll never forget it. When I sensed that same vileness in your living room…" Violet tinted his aura again. "You didn't sense anything strange when you talked to Mr. Crane?"

"I'm not sure." My foot took on a new, guilty bounce. "Something happened at the library last night." I told him about the auric blast I'd felt, and how maybe, just maybe, I'd gotten a whiff of the same from Mr. Crane.

Connor dropped his head to the steering wheel. "Echo."

"Well, how should I know it was this bad? The guy at the library was probably just some gross loser stalking girls. I was freaked out enough that maybe I misread Mr. Crane when I got home."

"Maybe." He didn't sound convinced. The light changed to green and he continued down the boulevard.

"Wait a minute. Why would Mr. Crane have the same energy as someone from East Region?" I asked.

"The factions in your time are just a precursor to the ones that run East Region a hundred sixty years from now. Same psychopathic profile, same vicious methods, except more advanced. The people in the factions all have similar energetic profiles."

"And you know this why?"

He gave me a deadpan look. "I'm the next leader of West Region. It's my job."

"Right."

"By the time I was born, factions ran East Region. But here, in your time, they work behind the scenes, fighting for power, trying to overtake the government."

"These are the ones who cause The Collapse?" I asked.

"Yes. As best we can tell it doesn't happen for almost a hundred years from now."

"You keep saying *as best we can tell.*"

"Most historical information was lost in The Collapse. We don't know the exact date it happened, or what exactly triggered it. We do know some facts about your time, though. Like, faction members here appear to lead very normal lives. They blend into society, hold regular jobs, drive their kids to school. There's even a hierarchy. The leaders are usually executives for private companies where they funnel huge amounts of money into the cause.

"Members at lower levels could be anybody you know or anyone you meet as you go about your life. You'd never suspect their one goal in life is to rise up the faction hierarchy. They're the ones who hunt down gifted people. Hand over enough gifteds to faction leaders, you get promoted."

We stopped at another intersection.

"We're going in circles," I said. "Go left and take the onramp."

He tapped a finger on the steering wheel as he drove, lost in thought. "Crane's got the perfect cover," he finally said.

"He's a psychologist."

"Who works with the police. Again, the perfect cover."

Connor let the accusation hang. I latched on and yanked it back into believable territory. "Listen, I don't like Mr. Crane, either. He's annoying and presumptuous and his daughter is my own personal nightmare, but no way did he kill those girls. Maybe his aura feels weird because, Idunno, maybe he's got a big secret or something. Like maybe he's having an affair with the pool boy."

"Why aren't you taking this seriously?" he asked.

"You're asking me to make a gargantuan leap."

Connor was completely out of patience. "Whoever owns the energy I picked up in your house has the capacity to hurt you."

"I get that, but you're suggesting Mr. Crane would murder me."

"If it came down to it, Echo, I would prefer he murdered you."

I spun on Connor. "*What?*"

"You heard me."

My mouth went dry. I glared at him, caught between demanding he take me home and waiting for an explanation. My forehead stung and my fingertips numbed. I peppered him with pellets of outrage.

He winced and swiped at the air between us. "Stop doing that. Do you want me to explain or not?"

I crossed my arms. "This better be good."

CHAPTER 23

Connor waited until we were on the highway headed east before he spoke again. "The factions were first formed by governments looking for ways to win the World Wars. You know, the ones that happened before you were born. Tanks and bombs didn't always give the world leaders the advantage they wanted. They needed a weapon that was so different, so unexpected, their success would be guaranteed. The leaders started looking closely at military personnel because all of them go through psychiatric evaluation. Someone—I think his name was Englemen—realized that some of the personnel had psychic abilities. He then set out to see if these soldiers could develop their ability even further. Englemen succeeded, but it wasn't easy. Sometimes a soldier was reluctant. Sometimes he wasn't interested. So Englemen found ways to make him cooperate.

"Englemen discovered that the more he tortured a gifted person, the further the soldier would push his gift. Threaten a supernaturally talented soldier with shock treatment and he would develop his ability until he could move objects."

"Telekinesis."

"Yes. Threaten to kill him, and the soldier would force himself to learn how to move his hand through concrete. Threaten to kill his family, and he would do anything you told him to, even develop his psychic gift to stop another man's heart. Imagine the power you'd have if your soldiers could kill the leader of another country with their minds. Or set off a nuclear bomb by sending an energy trail halfway around the world. You'd have an army of psychic assassins. The perfect weapon."

I stared at Connor with my mouth open.

"Eventually, Englemen ran out of gifted military people to experiment on, so he searched for them elsewhere. Orphanages. Psychiatric wards. As the factions expanded, the leaders kidnapped gifted ones off the streets."

"Why didn't someone go to the police or something?"

"You've learned how to keep secrets, haven't you? And nobody's even threatened to hurt your family. Terror is a powerful tool."

My stomach did a slow roll.

"You are a goldmine of supernatural gifts, Echo. The things they would do to you…"

"Okay, okay, I get it." My hands flew to my ears. This was too much to wrap my head around. The notion of danger had seemed vague up to this point and vague worked just fine where torture was concerned. I didn't care to hear any of the details.

No matter what Connor said about Mr. Crane, though, I just could not picture him doing any of these things. He treated Raquelle like a queen. His wife was nice. He'd gotten some award last month for his contribution to the police department.

These rational thoughts steadied me. The only way I could ever assign such a horrible profile to someone I knew was if he was arrested for it, or if I felt the dark energy myself. I was shaken enough when I left the library that my flustered reading of Mr. Crane could hardly be called evidence.

I turned to the changing landscape outside my window. We'd left the city far behind, and traffic thinned. Now, rolling, tree-covered foothills surrounded us and Mount Hood towered ahead.

"You need to take this exit and turn right," I said. "Then go to the end of the road and take another right."

"Where are we going?"

"Kimber's cabin."

The turn signal clicked into action even though Connor never touched it. The rapid clicking struck a discordant beat against the quick pace of my heart.

"I want you to stay clear of Raquelle and her father. The less they know about you, the better," he said.

"If it were up to me, I'd avoid them both for the rest of my life. But Raquelle is in most of my classes and I promised Becca I'd meet her at Trisha's party tonight, where of course, Raquelle will be. Dodging Mr. Crane should be easy, though."

Connor couldn't talk me out of the party, so he agreed to go long enough to drop off Becca and make sure she met up with Lucas. Then he got very quiet. I slumped in my seat and watched the forest grow thicker around us. The fir trees towered a hundred feet and the one-lane, potholed road seemed narrower than ever. The car felt claustrophobic. I rolled down the window. The scent of pine needles, usually so sweet, left an acrid taste at the back of my throat.

"How much further?" he asked.

I spotted the driveway as we sped past it. "Oh, go back. It's this house right here."

Connor hit the brakes. He peered through the trees at the shuttered, two-story house that filled two spacious lots. "I thought cabins were small versions of houses."

"Kimber doesn't do anything small."

He surveyed the cabin, or more precisely, the plot of land in front of it. His mouth curled into a mischievous grin. "Time to lighten things up," he said, and cranked the steering wheel sharply to the right and hit the accelerator. The car lurched off the road and across a shallow culvert into the woody grove that separated the house from the street. Even with my seatbelt in place, I tossed wildly in my seat.

"Hey, watch out for those trees." I pointed at a small grove right in our path.

"Echo, remember what I taught you?" He steered us directly toward the thicket of saplings.

I braced my hands against the dashboard. "What are you doing? You're going to crash us!"

"Think back to the warehouse."

"What? Which thing?" All the lessons came back in a jumble.

"Everything…" Connor prompted.

"Everything is possi– aaagh!"

Connor aimed my car at a six-foot pine tree and hit the gas. I threw myself to the side as the center of the car's grill slid right through the tree. Its branches swept right between us. I screamed and laughed and squeezed myself into the door.

"Take this next one!" he said, just as a low shrub disappeared into the front quarter panel. I only had a moment to prepare before it passed through my body. Each branch and twig entered my skin and burrowed a path through my organs on its way out the other side.

"Aaagh! That was so gross! That was so cool! Do it again!"

Connor veered left, and the low branches on another sapling whipped through my ribcage and out my back, knocking the wind out of me. When I recovered, I was grinning ear to ear.

As we passed an ancient fir tree, Connor stuck his arm out the window. His hand sliced right through the trunk. "Yeah!" he yelled. And then, "Whoa!" He jerked the steering wheel to strategically position me away from the next tree. It was huge, nearly as wide as the car. As we pushed through it, I heard a soft *whoosh*. Connor disappeared into the hardwood and emerged out the other side.

We bumped our way over exposed roots and divots and came to a halt on the driveway.

"Oh man, that was more fun than a roller-coaster," I said.

"Roller-coaster?"

I laughed. "Never mind. Thanks for taking that big one. I don't think I could have handled it."

He bowed slightly. "Any time, m'lady."

/ # CHAPTER 24

The first floor of Kimber's cabin was one big wide-open space, with no walls between the kitchen, dining area, or living room. The vaulted ceiling made the room look even bigger and reminded me of the warehouse we'd practiced in. The back wall was all windows and looked out over a small lake.

"This is the place. What was it you wanted to show me?" I asked.

Connor reached for my wrist. "Is your hand healed?"

I figured he was talking about the burn I'd gotten from our last training session. The redness was gone, but the blister formed by the intense heat hadn't fully healed. He ran his fingers across my palm, and I winced.

"Too much too fast," he said, half to himself.

I took this to mean I was off the hook where lasers were concerned. That was fine by me. Based on our conversation in the car, the next logical step would be Connor telling me to blast a hole in Mr. Crane. Like I was even capable of such a thing. Sure, if he tried to hurt me *and* that dark, malignant energy came off him, then maybe I'd consider such a drastic measure, but not before.

"If you're ever attacked, I want you to disable your assailant. We can't work on that until your hand is fully healed. So if you can't fight, you'll need to flee," Connor said.

"That's my usual response, but I'm not much of a runner."

"Remember the day I taught you how to levitate?"

Did I ever. That was the day I was concentrating so hard, I swear I heard smoke coming out of my ears. The day I'd twisted my ankle when I slammed back to the cement. The day Connor left without so much as a goodbye.

"Vaguely," I said.

He smiled. Arched one brow.

"I do not like what I think you're thinking. Are you going to teach me to fly? Because I'll pass, thanks."

The look on Connor's face said pretty much what any other rational human being would be thinking: *Did you not hear what I said about the factions?*

"I'm terrified of heights, remember? As in, if I had to choose between floating ten feet off the ground or facing a charging lion, I'd take my chances with the cat."

Connor dug his fingers into the back of his neck, probably wondering why I had to be such a pain.

"What about reading minds? If I can do that, I'll be one step ahead of everyone," I said.

"I can't teach you to read minds. You'll either develop it or you won't. Besides, you can already tap into auras, which is just as valuable if you use it right. For now, I'm teaching you how to fly. If you master it, you'll be able to get out of most dangerous situations, and learning to fly can be a gateway to much greater power."

The last bit sounded intriguing, but the part about my feet leaving the ground? I squeezed my eyes closed and gritted my teeth.

"You're going to be all right, Echo. I haven't lost a student yet."

I let out a long sigh. I knew when I was beat.

With a wave of his hand, the couch skidded across the floor until it rested against the far wall. The tables, floor lamps, and large potted palm magically did the same, leaving the center of the room empty.

"Same drill as last time," he said. "Arms out—"

"Yeah, yeah, I remember." I extended my arms out to the side. Pushed my fingertips toward the cabin's walls and imagined all my auric energy surging into the floor.

To my shock, I rose a few inches. "Connor! Look!" I whisper-shouted, as though any loud sound would send me crashing to the tile.

"That's it. Keep going. Just a little more," he coaxed. Out the corner of my eye, I saw him, arms stretched, ready to catch me.

I held my concentration and pushed higher. My feet rose level with Connor's head. I didn't feel light and airy, like I expected. My limbs coursed with raw energy. My neck tendons strained from tension.

"How are you doing? Can you go higher?"

I answered with a single nod. As long as he was acting as my safety net, I was willing to try. I aimed my intention at the thick beams bolted to the ceiling, rose another foot or so, and looked down. For a minute, all I saw was Connor smiling at me, his tongue wetting his lips before it slipped out of sight. Then I thought *wow, he is really,* really, *far down there.* The floor seemed to move in undulating waves and everything went fuzzy. An electric snap echoed off the walls and I dropped like a lead pigeon.

"Aaack!" Next thing I knew, I was sprawled in Connor's arms. He'd never admit it, but he looked as startled as I did. One quick kiss on my forehead, and he set me on the floor.

"That was kind of fun." I was thrilled at what I'd accomplished.

"Before we leave today, I want you to be comfortable doing somersaults at ceiling level."

"Oh no. I could never go that high. I just tried and came crashing down. Do you have any idea how exhausting this is? I feel like I just ran a marathon."

He responded by holding his arms out in front of him, palms up. "Lay on my hands, on your stomach."

I tilted my head. "Are you sure you can hold me?" I lacked even an ounce of faith that he could. I don't know why. I had yet to find his weakness.

"Starting this way will be easier for you."

I leaned onto his outstretched hands. Cautiously, I lifted one foot off the floor, testing his ability to hold my weight. His strength held, so I lifted my other foot. I had to stretch my arms straight out in front to hold the position. My t-shirt slid up a few inches, and my bare stomach pressed against one of Connor's hands. His finger rested under my waistband. The warm, tingling sensation was almost more than I could stand. I held my breath to keep my mind from wandering.

Connor got the wrong impression. "Breathe, Echo. This is no time to be nervous. Fear only cuts off your power."

Your touch is too distracting, I wanted to say. *We should be on the couch making out.*

"Now, try again." His electric touch trailed below my waistband, traveled south of my belly button. This was not exactly an incentive to fly—why would I want to push myself away from this feeling?

"Echo?"

"Huh? Oh, right." I trained my eyes on the floor and gave it everything I had, hoping I'd fail and be stuck there.

"It's not working," I said when I hadn't moved an inch.

"You don't think so?" Connor had stepped to the side. His hands were no longer under me, but the delicious tingling lingered on my skin. He was right about one thing. Levitating in that position was a lot easier. Moving? Not so much. I tried to rise, and my body tilted sharply.

"Whoa, this way is way harder," I said.

He took a step toward me.

"No, I can do it." My energy field had created a dense cushion between me and the tile floor. I pushed into it, and this time, when it tilted unexpectedly, I leaned and righted myself. *Yes, I've got this.* I rose a few inches and stopped. This position required more concentration than anything I'd ever done. Everything went fuzzy again. I knew I needed to put my feet down before I lost control, but my limbs froze.

My elbows hit the tile first, and then my knees. Pain shot through my funny and not-at-all-funny bones. I moaned and rolled to a sitting position.

Connor knelt next to me. "Are you all right?"

I pushed up my sleeves to see if I'd started to bruise. I might have dark hair and eyes, but my fair skin was about as sturdy as porcelain. Red welts rose off my elbows. My lips formed an *o* when I tried to rub the sting out of my skin.

"I'll try again," I said. "I just need a minute." A minute passed. Then five. Finally, I clenched my jaw and straightened my aching knees. "All right, let's do this."

Connor registered the hesitation on my face and came to a silent conclusion. He marched to the French doors and threw them open, taking in the expanse of lawn leading to the narrow strip of beach.

"What's that red thing down by the lake?"

I followed his gaze. "That would be a canoe." I drew the words out, mocking his question, just a little.

"Show me how it works."

"Really?"

"Unless you'd rather practice?"

I was out the door in an instant. My red canoe rested upside down on cement blocks. I flipped it over and handed him a paddle.

He studied it a moment before he asked, "The wide end goes into the water, right?"

"Oh, this is going to be fun." Now I got to be boss for a while.

Paddling a canoe is easy work, though, and he picked it up before we reached deep water. We paddled past the only other house—empty this time of the year—and then to the far side, where the lake gave over to marshland and the water was shallow and murky and dotted with cattails gone to seed. Ever the scientist, Connor touched and studied everything. I let my brain click out of learning mode, content to listen to the water lap against the side of the boat.

We steered the canoe along the shore toward a small lagoon and disrupted a pair of great blue herons. Connor watched them fly out of sight, and then we paddled to the middle of the lake.

There, we let the canoe drift. I tilted my face to the sky. Inhaled deeply. The day was crisp, the sunlight was warm, and the only sound came from a hawk screeching far overhead.

The boat shifted side to side, and when I looked to the front, my eyebrows hit my hairline. A tiny smile crept to the corners of my mouth. Connor had taken off his shirt. His upper body was a chiseled work of art. Though I couldn't imagine him spending time at a gym, his arms and chest were as defined as any weightlifter. His abdomen rippled with muscle. His skin glowed with a hint of tan.

I uttered a small whimper. He heard this and smiled without looking at me. He began pulling off his jeans. I tried not to gawk, tried to act like it was perfectly normal for a gorgeous, magical guy to be stripping down, right there in my canoe.

And just for the record, I can say for sure because I've seen it myself, guys still wear boxers in the year 2173.

"What are you doing?" I asked.

"Going for a swim."

"But the water's freezing."

Connor leaned over the side of the canoe and stuck his hand in the water. Stroked the surface so that the water rippled between his fingers. "Warm enough for you?"

I dipped my fingers in. It was the same temperature as our heated pool. And then I bit my lip, hard, not because of the cool trick, but because I hoped he would decide to go skinny-dipping.

No such luck. He dove in wearing boxers. He resurfaced and shook the water from his hair. "Coming in?"

I pulled off my jeans, left my t-shirt on, and jumped in. The temperature was perfect, as soothing as the Mediterranean Sea. I glided underwater, dove deep, and then kicked my way to the surface.

"You're a good swimmer," he said.

"I love the water. I'd live in the ocean if I could." I breast-stroked to him, and he set his hands around my waist so I didn't have to tread water. He didn't seem to be exerting any energy. I had no idea how he was staying afloat.

Water glistened on his face, and his dark cowlick dripped down his forehead. I put my hands on his shoulders and flutter kicked until I was high enough to plant a kiss on his lips.

"I have an idea," he wiggled his eyebrows.

"Mmm. Do tell." The water intensified the current running from his skin onto mine. My imagination conjured up new fantasies. Uncharted territories. But then, Connor released my waist and stretched his arms in front of him, the way he had in the living room.

"Ungh. Really?" I asked.

"You have to admit, it's the perfect place. We're the only ones on the lake and if you fall, well, you love water, right?"

He left me without reason to argue, so I floated onto his hands. A familiar calm settled over me, as though my body had been primed for this exercise, which, in a way, it had.

Within seconds, I rose off the surface. When I got too high, and that panicky feeling hit, I tucked into a cannonball and splashed into the lake. I came up laughing.

"Oh, that was so fun! Put your hands out again."

The rest of the afternoon whizzed by while I played my new favorite sport: fly diving. At first, the breeze blowing across the lake made it hard to keep my body in the right position, but I figured out how to steer into it. I never got more than a few feet off the water's surface, but every inch I crept upward sent a thrill to the marrow of my bones.

"Now try a somersault," Connor called as I hung above him.

I curled forward and tucked my head to my knees, rolled and regained my balance.

"Wahoo!" I shouted. I did a series of them until dizziness set in. When I stopped, he flew to my side. In one easy swoop, he soared over my head, into the water, and back out again. Then he did a bigger loop, flying upside down like a daredevil airplane pilot, bending backwards and soaring into the water as gracefully as anything I'd ever seen. When he came up, I was clapping wildly.

With his index finger, Connor beckoned me to come closer. I flew to him, but when I tried to wrap my arms around his waist, he slipped out of reach.

"Hey!"

"Think you can catch me?" he taunted.

I slapped my hands on my hips. "Guys are supposed to do the chasing," I said, and I took off across the lake. I flew as fast as I could, skimming just above the surface. My heart was slamming in my chest, partly from the speed, partly because I knew I was no match for him. The rush of knowing he was going to catch up, grab me, made my breath come short.

Connor blew past me in a tan blur and cut me off. I squealed and veered sharply to keep from hitting him. Before I could escape, he snagged the back of my t-shirt and reeled me in. He pressed our wet bodies together.

"I made it too easy for you," I said.

Connor laughed. "Easy is *not* a word I'd use to describe you."

I gave him a look of mock irritation.

"Okay, okay, you win. You made it easy for me," he said.

"Really? What do I win?"

"What do you want?"

A blush warmed my cheeks. Connor took my face in his hands and kissed me so deeply, I felt it right down to my toes. My concentration broke, but the moment it looked like I'd fall, he wrapped his arm tight around my waist.

"I've got you," he said.

Yeah, you do.

CHAPTER 25

The sun had disappeared behind the trees when Connor and I got back to the cabin. We dropped our wet clothes in the dryer and wrapped ourselves in thick robes that Kimber kept in the guest rooms. A fire blazed in the fireplace, and we raided the cupboards. It wasn't long before the food and exercise took their toll and we fell sound asleep.

I woke up shivering. The fire was out and the room was pitch dark. I wrapped the robe around me and padded to the laundry room. My shirt lay folded on the dryer. Connor's clothes were gone. I groaned. He must have gotten yanked back to West Region.

I jumped when a moth banged against the screen door, trying to reach the laundry room light. I turned on every light in the cabin, remembering Connor's story about the factions. No wonder I was twitching at every little sound. His story stuck in my head like a haunting fairy tale that parents read to kids when they're too young process myths and their monsters. I wished what he'd told me was one of those fabricated tales. I trusted him enough to know it was not.

I tugged my shirt over my head. My hair swept into my face and I took in the lingering scent of lake water. Visions of racing—flying—over the lake filled my head. I'd never gotten very high, but I'd done things I'd never dreamed possible. The fear of heights still rattled inside me like a pile of loose bricks, but I had to admit, I was in a better position to take care of myself.

My jeans lay in a pile next to the dryer. When I pulled them on, I reached for my phone in the back pocket. The clock showed it was after eleven. I had four texts from Becca:

You're coming, right?

Dude. My soulmate is waiting!

Where are you??!!

And finally:

Found a ride. You. Suck.

"Oh, nooooo." I dialed Becca's number, but my call went straight to voicemail. I texted her an apology and waited. Nothing, not a word from her.

I snagged my jacket and went out the front door. Thank goodness I'd brought keys because Connor wasn't around to magically start my car.

Behind me, a twig snapped. My chest jolted from a near coronary. I spun with my fists raised and strained to see into the dark. A deer, no less startled than me, froze and then bounded from the shadows and into the woods.

I dropped into the driver's seat, shaking. In the safety of my vehicle, I wondered how I would have responded if that deer had been a person from the faction, someone who wanted to hurt me. I wondered whether I would have frozen up or flown away.

My dashboard clock read midnight when I pulled up to Trisha's house. Chances were that Becca had gone home already, but I felt so bad about bailing on her for the fourth time in our friendship that I was on a mission to find her and apologize as soon as possible.

The front door hung open. Inside, the lights were low, and the floor and couches were covered with teenagers who were passed out, zombied out, or making out. I followed voices to the kitchen.

"Heeyyyy," a bulky form trudged down the dark hallway toward me. Definitely drunk. Definitely not Becca.

"Heeeeeyyy," it said when it got closer. One of the football players, soaking wet and reeking of beer, slapped a soggy hand on my arm.

"Ewww. Get off." No telling if he understood English at this point, but he teetered into the wall and stumbled away.

I stepped into the kitchen, which was actually two large rooms. The seating area off the eating bar was sunk in darkness, probably packed full of more drunken couples. A keg of beer sat in the middle of the kitchen floor. A few kids clustered around it and though they were very drunk, I deemed them alert enough to answer one simple question.

"Has anyone seen Becca?"

Bloodshot eyes turned in my direction.

"What are you, her mom?" Trisha wobbled from the dark seating area and steadied herself against the keg.

"Is she here or not?" I repeated.

This bought me vacant stares. I may as well have been talking to a herd of cows. I turned to leave, figuring I'd be better off searching the house myself.

"I don't want you in my house. You stole Raquelle's boyfriend." Trisha clutched another girl's sleeve and swayed. "Raquelle and Connor were like this," Trisha told her and tried to cross her two fingers, "and then *she* promised him psycho sex. And then he broke Raquelle's heart."

"You know how completely moronic you sound, right?" I asked.

Two of Trisha's friends laughed so hard, their legs gave out. They fell onto their butts behind the keg. The girl attached to Trisha directed her glassy eyes at me.

"Slut." She slurred so heavily, it came out as "schlut."

"For your information, Connor was never into Raquelle," I hissed. "And he's way too good for her. You can tell her I said so."

A flash went off. Trisha had taken my picture with her cell phone, right in the middle of my rant. "Hey Lincolnites," she slurred as she texted, "the rabid mental girl crashed my party."

My temper rose. "Knock it off, Trisha."

"*Knock it off, Trisha,*" someone mocked.

"If U R awake, please text me how 2 make it leave," Trisha thumbed her message.

The girls' voices squealed. I knew I needed to be the bigger person, and that it was a total waste of time to argue with a bunch of drunks, but the disgust on their faces stung.

"It's mad," someone said.

"It's frothing at the mouth," Trisha texted.

"I said stop it!" I yelled and swept my arm in a wide arc at the counter behind me. My fury seized the wooden knife block and hurled it across the room. It smashed into the cupboard, and knives clattered to the floor.

Everybody froze.

Trisha and her friend stared at me, jaws dangling, horror in their eyes. The friend's face went white and she passed out. Trisha knelt to revive her. I ran for my car.

I was quaking from head to toe by the time I got home. It had been a long time since I'd lost control but even at my worst, I'd never done anything like that. Since Connor came into my life, my auric outbursts were practically non-existent. Now I'd let my guard down and opened myself to disaster. My only hope was that Trisha and her friends were too drunk to believe what they had seen.

For hours afterward, I monitored all my classmates' social media sites. No news was the best news of my life. I fell asleep with my phone in my hand.

On Saturday, I texted Becca a few times, but she never replied. From my window, I saw a lamp flicker to life in her bedroom. I ran across the street and knocked on the door. Nobody answered.

Fine. I deserved the silent treatment. I gave Becca the rest of the weekend to cool off and continued to obsessively check the Internet for signs of my mistake. Instagram was lit up with pictures of Raquelle and her latest conquest-turned-boyfriend, but nobody was talking about the psychotic girl at Trisha's party. It was as though my careless flare-up never happened.

Monday morning, I waited outside Becca's house, reciting ways to apologize. None of my tries came out right, sounding either defensive or lame. My efforts were moot, though, because Becca never came ambling out her front door like she did every other school day.

She didn't meet me at my locker after Chemistry, either, so I went to Physics without her. When I walked in, Solomon waved me to his desk. I waited while he dug into a stack of papers. He handed me the extra credit I'd turned in. I'd gotten an A.

"Yes!" I said. My bracelets, once again a permanent part of my outfit, clattered when I shook my fist in victory.

"You've taken a liking to physics?" Solomon asked.

"It's not so bad." *Especially when your boyfriend teaches you how to defy all the laws of physics.* I smirked at my private joke.

"If you really want to boost your grade, you should come in for extra lab time." Solomon's jagged smile revealed a set of yellow teeth.

"Thanks, I'll think about it." I lifted an indecisive shoulder, even though I had no intention of spending one-on-one time with him. He was nice, but he was always offering his help, and he just plain creeped me out. Not because of anything he'd done; he just gave off this sense of neediness. I was starting to think the guy was looking for a friend.

Raquelle was absent, so the air was fresher than usual. At the last second, Becca flounced in. Yes, my typically low-key BFF practically tap-danced across the floor. She saw me sitting in my usual spot, crossed the room, and took an open seat three rows away.

Well. How about that.

When class ended, she avoided eye contact and hurried out before I even closed my textbook. Now I was really hurt. All I wanted to do was apologize for Friday night, and she was cutting me out. I went to our table in the lunchroom. There was no sight of her, but Raquelle was back, and she and Trisha were in heightened, snotty form. Their glare carried an uncharacteristic viciousness. Even from my spot at the far end of the room, their burning malice was unmistakable.

The rest of the Partychicks swung their heads to see who had Raquelle's undivided attention. When they saw me, they turned away with bored expressions—except McKyla, the girl who had passed out next to Trisha Friday night. I remembered her name while I was obsessing over the weekend.

McKyla watched me with hard, cold fear and hunkered out of view behind Trisha. Then Raquelle said something to Trisha, and whatever it was caused a flurry of conversation between the three of them. Trisha kept her jaw set and her eyes down. Every few seconds, Raquelle shot black glances at me.

"I said no!" Trisha's voice rose above the lunchtime clamor. Raquelle jerked upright. Mere groupies did not speak to Raquelle like that. Something big was going down.

It wasn't hard to figure out. Alcohol had not blurred their memories, as I'd so desperately hoped. The girls knew what they saw, had compared notes, and were spreading the word. I was, to put it lightly, screwed.

CHAPTER 26

"What kind of energy depends on mass and speed?" I asked Connor. I lounged on my couch and worked on my physics assignment. Connor looked up from his super-advanced physics textbook. He sat at the other end of the couch, legs stretched across the cushions and resting against mine.

"Kinetic." His eyes dropped back to his book.

"Oh, yeah, right." I jotted down the answer.

In the days since the cabin, Connor and I had gotten into a routine where he'd meet me in the parking lot after school and we'd do homework at my house until dinner.

I never told him about the incident at the party, partly because after the argument in the cafeteria, the issue never came up again. All week, I'd braced myself for Raquelle's backlash, but the expected confrontation never happened. Instead, she and Trisha took to ignoring me completely, and I started to relax. I must have jumped to the wrong conclusion about their argument in the cafeteria because if Raquelle had gotten word about my late-night magic act, she would have been in my face.

But the overriding reason I kept this to myself was the reaction I knew I'd get from Connor. He'd likely be angry, what with the warnings he'd dished out and instructions to not use my ability in public. That, I could handle, but with it would come disappointment in me that he may or may not be able to hide.

"When is a bosonic string theory most unstable?" Connor asked.

"Um, X minus Y divided by the square root of how-the-heck-should-I-know?"

He laughed. "Just kidding. I have no idea, either."

I closed my book and leaned into the couch, sick of homework. My attention drifted to the room's high ceilings. I imagined the two of us floating up, up to the crossbeams, twenty feet above, and flipping somersaults. How we'd try to outdo each other's acrobatics. He guessed what I was thinking.

"Go ahead, fly around for a while. I'll watch for Kimber."

"Nah." I still didn't trust myself more than a few feet off the ground, so it wasn't much fun unless we did it together and Connor wasn't exactly Mr. Fun lately.

Ever since he warned me about Mr. Crane, he was more watchful than ever. When he met me at school, he scrutinized anyone who came within a few feet of us. On the drive home, vigilant eyes circled from me to the rearview mirror, to the vehicles around us, and back again.

Hard intent seemed permanently stationed behind his eyes. I recognized that look. I'd seen it the day he materialized in my physics classroom. He was searching for somebody. When I asked him about it, he just said he was only being cautious. I felt safe when he was around, but when he went home at night, I couldn't shake the edginess that set in.

Kimber bustled into the house smelling of expensive lotion and hair spray. She set Tito on the floor, and the dog leaped into Connor's lap.

"Why is he wearing a bow?" Connor poked at the oversized, glittery pink ribbon tied around Tito's neck.

"Probably to match Kimber's nails. I think she took him to her spa."

Sure enough, Kimber and her glittery pink fingernails paraded into the living room. When she first met Connor, she'd giggled like a high school girl when he shook her hand. Then she'd mouthed "Wow" to me when he wasn't looking.

"Would you like to stay for dinner?" she asked him. He said he would, and we ordered a pizza.

A little while later and still on the couch, Connor and I munched a Thick Crust Special. Kimber brought in her microwaved diet dinner and turned on the television. The volume was low.

"How are you settling into your new school?" she asked Connor.

"School's fine," he said.

"It's too bad the sale fell through on the house in our neighborhood. How do your parents like the east side of town?"

"It's all working out, I guess," he said casually. He hated these conversations where he had to pretend he had a life here. His answers were always closer to half-truths than lies.

"We'll have to have your parents over for dinner when Echo's dad is home."

Connor smiled politely and said nothing. An image on television stole Kimber's attention.

"Shh! Shh!" Kimber turned up the television volume. The local newscast filled the screen and a picture of crime scene tape slashed across the upper corner.

The news anchor's voice blared into the living room.

"…making no headway into the murder investigation of three Portland women. Though the police won't reveal details of the deaths, they have confirmed that all three victims died from head trauma. Police have ruled out theft, saying that no money or personal belongings appeared to have been stolen. Anyone having information about these crimes is asked to contact Portland police."

Kimber clicked the television off. She let out a strangled whimper.

"Kimber, are you okay?" I asked.

She nodded, quick and hard. Her jaw was slack, the color draining from her cheeks. Connor and I exchanged a look.

"Mrs. Bennett, can I get you anything?"

Kimber shook her head and set down her dinner.

"She knew one of the victims," I whispered to Connor.

"How terrible for you," he said to her.

"They have to find out who did this atrocious thing. Jenifer was so beautiful. How could anyone do that kind of damage to a person?"

Again, Connor and I exchanged a look.

"Do what, Mrs. Bennett?"

Kimber plucked at her lower lip. "It's not public information yet. Don—Mr. Crane—thought they'd announce it today. He wanted me to hear it from him first."

Kimber's thick, viscous energy poured into the room, as though warding off an incoming blow. That was enough to tell me I didn't want to know more, but since it involved Mr. Crane, I had to ask. "Announce what?"

"About the case. It's so horrible."

Kimber waved us off, but she was desperate to unload whatever he had told her. Her eyes flicked frantically around the room, as though searching for someone who could speak for her, or some way she could tell what she knew without betraying Mr. Crane's trust.

Connor leaned in, feet on the floor, elbows on his knees. "Whatever Mr. Crane told you, it must have been hard to hear."

Kimber focused on Connor. "It's *awful.*"

"I'm sure you'll want to talk to him about it, but until then, we're here to listen."

Relief softened her downturned lips. "You know, Connor, you're very wise for someone your age." She wrung her hands and I suppressed the urge to shake the story out of her.

"He didn't just hurt them. He *maimed* them. Right here." Kimber touched her index finger to the space just above and between her eyebrows. "It was like he hit them with a big hammer. Just *crushed* the girls, right in the…" Kimber broke into tears.

I hurried to Kimber's side and put my arm around her. She bawled into her hands. I muttered soothing things in a voice that seemed detached from the rest of me. What she'd said imprinted grotesque images in my mind.

Connor didn't take the news well. The muscles in his jaw flexed in and out. A magenta halo surrounded his body.

"Connor," I whispered and nodded toward his hand. His face piqued. He centered himself and the halo dissolved.

Kimber sniffled and excused herself from the room. Connor still sat with his arms on his knees, motionless.

"It's them," he finally said.

"The faction?"

He nodded.

"How do you know? Is it the way they…" I couldn't finish the sentence with the hard lump forming in my throat. Kimber's description was so graphic, the same spot between my brows began to pulse.

"The third eye sits at the center of the forehead," Connor said.

I nodded. "The seat of paranormal ability."

"They crushed the victims' third eye. It's the mark of the faction. They're rounding up gifted ones, but these women fought back."

"Are you sure that's what happened?" My own third eye buzzed madly. My fingers flew to my forehead, as though I could stop its mystical energy from flowing into my aura.

"If the women hadn't fought back, they would have been kidnapped. They might have sensed they were in danger, but faction soldiers work fast. Those women never had a chance."

I held my arms tight across my chest so he couldn't see me shaking.

"Do you think Kimber would let me stay here tonight?" he asked.

This caught me completely off guard. "Maybe in the guest room. Wouldn't your dad come looking for you, though?" I was sure that would be the end of us. This wasn't a trade-off I was willing to make.

He dug his fingers into the back of his neck, torn. "The faction is on the hunt. If they pick up the energy coming off your aura, they could track you to here," he argued.

A shiver ripped up my spine. "They won't. I'll recenter while I'm at school. I won't give myself away, not even a little bit."

"Wear the bracelets, that will help."

"I already do whenever you're not around."

I hated that he was so worked up about Kimber's news. It brought my fears into the light, fears that I'd been able to sweep into that place where I locked away unreasonable worries: my dad dying in a plane crash, failing a grade and not graduating, things like that. Since the night at the cabin, I'd been able to pretend the whole faction thing was too far off to affect me. It was easy, when the so-called enemy didn't have a face or a name. And no, Mr. Crane wasn't on my list of bad guys. Now, Connor was freaking me out.

"I'll meet you after school tomorrow. Don't leave without me, okay?" he said.

"I thought you had to do stuff with your dad."

He groaned. "I completely forgot. I might not be able to come back for a few days."

I forced a smile. I didn't want him to sense how scared I was.

"Practice," he said.

"I will."

"Don't go anywhere by yourself. Mix in with the regular auras, like your classmates. You'll be harder to pick out."

"I'm on it."

He kissed me, and then he was gone. The walls seemed to close in. I wanted to go outside and let the night air clear my head but unspeakable dangers lurked beyond the safety of my house. I went upstairs, grabbed my comforter, and opened the window leading to the portico. I sat on the sill and filled my lungs. Blew a long stream of white air into the cold night.

In the valley below, countless shimmering lights glowed across the city. Headlights. Bedroom lights. Store lights. All brightening the way for millions of people going about their lives. Sometimes, looking out over the skyline cheered me, made me feel like I was a part of something bigger. Not tonight.

Just a few weeks ago, I was sure all I needed to be happy was to find and befriend other paranormal freaks like me. My tribe would be fun, special, and we'd keep each other safe. They'd be there to fill the agonizing chasm created when Connor left, which he eventually would. But I could no longer find strength in numbers. Alone, my energy was like a bullhorn calling to the faction. The more of us who got together, the louder our energy would broadcast.

Wind shook pine cones from the nearby tree, and they peppered the portico roof like buckshot. My skin felt papery thin, hanging loose over my bones and barely strong enough to protect me from the icy breeze. I pulled the comforter over my head and peered through a gap in the fabric. It was no defense against the loneliness chilling me from the inside.

CHAPTER 27

The next morning, I went to school at the peak time, making sure to park in the busiest part of the lot and blend in with kids as we made our way inside. I clung to the crowd between classes. In physics, I plopped into my chair, already worn by the effort of not standing out.

The one person I did want in my personal space was still doing her best to avoid me. I'd known Becca to hold a grudge but never for this long. I got it—I'd been an awful friend when she was depending on me—but if she'd just drop her anger long enough to hear why I missed the party, I was sure she'd understand. But, our paths hardly crossed anymore, and when I saw her getting a ride home with Lucas, my heart panged with loneliness.

Raquelle sauntered in, so focused on her phone that she smacked into the desk at the end of our row. It tipped over and slammed to the floor. I laughed, loud and sharp.

She shot a hateful look in the direction of my laugh. When she saw it was me, her pinched expression slackened and her mouth parted slightly. Slowly, she looked back at her phone, and then quickly dropped it into her bag.

Her eyes never left the back wall as she took her seat behind me. Metal legs scraped against the floor. From the diminished stink of her aura, I guessed she'd moved her chair back a few feet.

Raquelle had been acting very unqueenly as of late. She'd cooled her bullying in favor of ignoring me all together. Where Trisha and McKyla were openly frightened of me, Raquelle had become strangely reserved.

"Echo," Solomon said, "show your work for yesterday's assignment on the board."

"Again?" I protested. This was the third time in a week. Mr. King had always asked for volunteers before he made people go to the whiteboard.

"Did you finish it?"

"Yes."

"I'm sure you got it right, so go on up," he said.

I jotted the problem on the board. When I finished, I took a step back to check my work. A warm channel pushed into my aura and I had the sensation that Solomon's hand rested on my back. The feeling continued, like he was probing me with his fingers, checking me from head to toe, all without laying a hand on me. I resisted the urge to shoot him a dirty look and hurried back to my seat.

There was something about Solomon lately that made him weirder than usual. A sense that he was restraining himself. Like the way someone with body odor keeps their armpits clamped shut because they know they smell bad and don't want anyone to else know. It was like that. He was hiding something, and by the way he gawked at the students I was beginning to think he really was a pervert.

"Nice work, Echo," Solomon said with too much warmth.

I mouthed "Thanks" and pretended to write in my notebook.

When I pulled into our driveway after school, I slammed my brakes at the sight of Mr. Crane's BMW parked in front of our garage.

I sat there, debating what to do next. Mr. Crane was about the last person I wanted to talk to and sometimes he stayed for hours. I slipped through the side door and dashed up the stairs, two at a time. On the second floor, I nearly smacked into him and Kimber.

"You're home early," Kimber smiled.

"I always get home now," I replied.

Mr. Crane carried an armload of books that I assumed were from my dad's library. Prickles danced on my neck. I reminded myself that, despite Connor's accusations, Mr. Crane wasn't guilty of anything until I had solid evidence to link him to the peeper in the library. So that's what I needed. Evidence.

"Hi, Mr. Crane." I homed in on his aura. Smooth and cool as ice.

"We were just talking about you," he said. "The research study is coming to a close and I very much want to include you in it."

Kimber opened her mouth to speak, but I cut her off.

"What kinds of tests do you do, exactly?" I adopted a snotty tone to see if I could agitate him into showing me the truth behind his mask.

"A variety, but cognitive, mostly."

"Like what? I mean, you expect me to come in on a Saturday. Is this going to be fun or like sitting in detention all day?"

"Echo," Kimber scolded.

Mr. Crane gave me a thin smile. "Tests that measure decision making. Judgment." He waited a beat. "Controlling impulses."

My pulse skipped at this last item.

"Activities that most teenagers struggle with. Who knows, you might learn something about yourself," he answered evenly.

I couldn't tell if he was gaming me or being patient. The tingling in my fingers grew. I wasn't getting what I wanted, but my own paranormal impulses were starting to peak. I had to hurry.

"I heard Ryan Hoffman was part of the study," I said. I'd heard no such thing. "But he's gone missing, so I'm not sure I'm comfortable getting involved."

Kimber drew a sharp breath at my audacity. I felt bad for being rude, but the air had changed. Cancerous energy punctured the façade behind Mr. Crane's smile. Like a hypodermic needle, it was so fine in its structure it almost went unnoticed. He recovered too quickly. Maybe he was the one in the library, but I couldn't get a match.

Mr. Crane searched my face, impassive. "I can't share any information about clients or cases I'm working on. You should know that."

"Right, confidentiality. Well, I'm going to pass. Too many tests coming up."

Kimber touched Mr. Crane's arm in apology. Then she said, "I've already made an appointment for us, Echo. I'm helping with the study, too."

Um, *what*??

"Oh, I see." I was out of snappy comebacks and on the verge of letting my anxiety clatter uncontrolled into the hallway. I pushed past Kimber and ran up the last flight. I locked the door behind me and went to the window. My third eye burned. I shoved the heel of my hand over it and held it there. If Mr. Crane was one of them, one of those faction people, would he feel my energy building in the house? Feel the walls tremor, ready to purge themselves of pictures and books?

For the next hour, I stared down at the BMW in our driveway. My fingers grew numb and a killer headache set in, but I kept it together until he finally got in his car and disappeared up the hill.

Then I slumped in a chair while the resulting outburst turned my room into shambles.

In the school parking lot, me and a handful of stragglers pounded the pavement to beat the bell. Someone stood behind the door and held it open for my classmates. When I got to the entrance, though, the door practically slammed shut in my face.

"Hey, watch it!" I scowled.

"And good morning to you," Connor said. He stepped out from behind the door.

I grabbed him in a rib-busting hug. "I hate when you stay away so long," I said into his t-shirt. I inhaled his spicy, exotic scent.

"Me, too."

The bell rang, and I was officially late for class. Great. If I hurried, I might be able to talk my History teacher out of handing me detention. Then I remembered why I was running late in the first place.

"Mr. Crane was at my house yesterday." I raised a defensive hand before Connor bit off a reply. To his credit, he listened quietly while I filled him in on my sleuthing. When I finished, he looked at me like my brains were leaking out of my ears.

"I told you to stay away from him and this is what you do?"

"Connor, you need to level with me. Is it possible that you're wrong about Mr. Crane? I mean, isn't there the tiniest possibility that you overreacted when you picked up that bad vibe at my house?"

"No."

I waited for him to explain. Just when I thought that was the end of it, he said, "I know what I sensed. If Crane and Kimber were the only ones in your house that night, then you tell me your conclusion."

"It's not Kimber," I said.

"Definitely not."

"All right. I don't know, but I can't talk about this anymore. I've got to get to class."

"No. We're getting out of town today."

I looped my fingers into the waistband of his jeans. "I can't leave. I've got a quiz in Chemistry and a paper due in English. Can you meet me here after?" I reached for the door, expecting he'd say yes.

"Absolutely not." The sternness in his voice caused me to do a double-take. This protective role was getting to be a bit much. If I skipped school every time he thought I was in danger, I'd never graduate. But he held down a smile that showed off his dimples. His eyes glimmered. He looked... playful. "I've got a big day planned."

I groaned. "Really, I don't have time to train. And school's perfectly safe."

"Call in sick."

"But my quiz..."

"Voluntarily or involuntarily, you're coming with me."

"So, you're kidnapping me?" I laughed.

"You'll thank me for it later."

I fidgeted, truly torn. That mischievous grin practically guaranteed a fun-filled day. "Aaagh, I shouldn't. I can't." I bobbed my head in weak protest.

Connor shrugged. "All right. You had your chance." He stretched his arms out for a hug.

"Great, then I'll see you after school." I wrapped my arms around his neck and kissed him on the cheek. He clasped my waist and kissed my forehead at my hairline. I moved to pull away, but he tightened his embrace. His skin felt unusually hot, and the gentle electric current coursing through him grew stronger.

Connor's body had felt like this once before, not so long ago, when he promised I'd be safe as long as I held him tight. My subconscious mind began arranging puzzle pieces from the past, trying to grasp what was happening. Then it came back to me.

"Hey!" I pushed against him, but his grip was firm.

"Involuntarily it is," he said, and we fizzled into the ether.

CHAPTER 28

I was so startled to find myself hurling through the portal that I didn't have the chance to be frightened. My eyes stayed open, and I was glad they did. Gold and white clusters of stars streaked past us. The pinks and blues of celestial nebulae hung in the distance: stunning, real-life versions of the Hubble telescope pictures hanging on the walls in physics class. Red stars exploded in a beautiful arc across the black background.

Our bodies zipped and turned at an unthinkable speed. My stomach flipped, and everything went dark. Suddenly, we were bathed in light. My feet found a solid surface, the air changed, and I recognized a high-pitched hum. We were in the Harden Center lab in West Region, standing next to the portal hole.

The metal doors swished open. Jaxon stood at the panel with his arms crossed. He wore a black sateen tunic that fell to just below the waist. It was tailored to his swimmer's build and brought out the deep chocolate color of his eyes. It seemed kind of dressy for working in a lab, but what did I know? He held the same disdainful scowl from my previous visit.

"You're late." Jaxon cast an accusing glance at me.

"I'll take it from here," Connor said, and Jaxon breezed out of the lab.

"What a treat to see him in such a good mood," I muttered.

"Be nice. Today's a holiday, and I asked him to come in as a special favor." Connor ushered me into the CKS tube.

"Is that why you made me come here today? For the holiday?" I asked while the tube checked me over.

"Made you? I thought you liked it here."

"I do. It's just, the timing's not great." Already, in my head, I was testing out various excuses I'd use to explain my absence from school. The CKS finished its scan. Connor studied the results with an impassive expression. Then he took out a pen-like device.

"Hold still," he said. He touched the pen to different points down the center of my body. His jaw tightened while he read the digital display. I leaned in to look.

"Is something wrong?"

The device beeped, and he relaxed. "All your vitals look great. How do you feel?"

"I feel great," I said. I bounced on my toes. "Are we going back to the Reserve?"

Connor tossed the pen thingy on a desk and took my hand. "Nope. Today is the Region's biggest celebration of the year. I want you to see why I love West Region so much, and what better time to show it off?"

"I get to see the city? Finally!"

We ran down the empty hallway to the front doors. When we stepped outside the Harden Center, my jaw dropped and my eyes got ridiculously huge. The building's domed roof and pillars sparkled like diamonds in the sunlight. Statues lined a glimmering walkway. If the Greek temples had been carved out of crystal, they probably would have looked like the Harden Center.

The fountain in front of the building completely mystified me. Instead of water coming up out of the ground, it plunged downward from an invisible source two stories above us, and spilled into a crystalline bowl that levitated overhead.

And people, dozens of them, flew in organized patterns in the sky as if following invisible sidewalks to their destinations.

Ahead, a plaza bustled with more people. Like Jaxon, the guys were dressed in sateen tunics. The women wore brightly colored flowing gowns. Even the kids were dressed up. Classical music filled the air. Everyone was in a festive mood.

Connor and I swung into the crowd. Faces lit up at the sight of him, and they nodded in a sort of reverence. When they saw my fingers linked through his, their expressions turned to puzzlement. After they passed, I sensed their eyes were still fixed on me. I squirmed, but Connor stood tall, and the exuberant smile never left his face.

"Still doing okay?" he asked.

"Fantastic." Truth was, I felt deathly out of place. "Where are we going?"

"To my house."

Finally, I thought.

"And to introduce you to my father."

I flinched. "Now? Today?"

He squeezed my hand. "No time like the present. Isn't that a saying you use?"

"Yeah, but without the irony." I pulled my hand away and wiped my sweaty palm on my jeans.

"I told my father about my trips back to your time, and about you." Connor dismissed the shock on my face. "He knew I was up to something, the way I kept disappearing every chance

I got. He found out I wasn't with my friends, and nobody knew where I went all the time. He finally asked me. So I told him."

"What… did… he… say?" I asked.

"Well, at first, he was furious. He told me I had to stop. Forbid me to visit you anymore, and all that. He was going to demand that Philip shut the portal to all non-scientific travel. Then we argued about *that* for a while and he threatened to ship me to the university early so I'd have no way to get to you."

Something the size of a boulder dropped into my stomach.

"When he cooled down, I told him how talented you are, and how dangerous it is for you." Connor smirked. "And you know what? He actually confessed that he'd time-jumped to Portland, long ago. Back before you were born. He knows what your world is like."

This was all good news, but there was only one answer I cared about. "He's still letting you use the portal?"

His brow wrinkled. "Yes."

"But?"

He dug his fingers into the back of his neck. "I asked for two more weeks."

"Two weeks!"

"I was afraid he'd ban me altogether if I didn't at least start negotiating. But he'll meet you today. He'll see why I want to be with you. I'll come up with some sort of plan, some way to get his permission to make this work long-term. Then everything will be easier for us."

"How can you be so sure?" I did a fair job of hiding the dread in my voice.

"Even if he said 'no,' I'd find a way to get to you." He sounded so confident, but the pressure was on. I had to shine in this introduction. Connor led me deeper into the city. "How do you like West Region City so far?"

"It's got wow factor, I'll say that much."

We'd crossed the plaza and continued down a wide stone walkway between rows of buildings. Overall, it still looked like the Portland I knew, but only if we were to let fruiting vines grow up the sides of the buildings and plant vegetable gardens where there used to be roads. People levitated alongside the buildings and harvested ripe fruit. Others filled overflowing baskets with late season tomatoes, squash, and some vegetables I didn't recognize.

"No cars?" I asked.

"We're in the old city. Everyone walks. Or flies." As he said this, a group of elementary grade kids floated by, pushing and prodding like any kids would, except they were flying ten feet overhead. "Across the river, in the new city, most people ride trains or community vehicles."

Connor motioned to a series of low buildings with glass fronts. "This is one of the metaphysical schools my dad built. Kids learn the same things I'm teaching you. If you were here, this is probably where you'd go to school. Pretty cool, huh?"

"If I were here?"

"Well, you know, if you lived here."

My heart rate tripled. Where had that come from? I squashed the urge to speculate. It would be foolish to read into such a casual statement.

We turned onto a residential street where modest houses sat tucked between more trees and stopped in front of an expansive park.

"Well, this is it," he said.

"What?"

"My family compound."

"You live *here*?"

Far back from the walkway, beyond sculpted gardens and a line of fountains, sat a cross between a mansion and a castle. It was four or five times bigger than Kimber's house, and regal right down to the stone turrets rising at each corner. When Connor used the word *compound* to describe where he lived, I'd pictured a fortress-like structure surrounded by razor wire.

"My father keeps building on to accommodate the refugees escaping from East Region. They stay with us for a while and work here before finding their own place to live."

I stared at Connor. So that's what he meant when he talked about the "servants" who worked for his family. His father was starting to sound like a saint, instead of the frightening, portal banning despot I'd imagined. We rounded the mansion to the back of the property. Red, orange, and blue banners filled the sky, creating a colorful, fluttery awning. Gold trimmed the quartz stone walkways. The grounds were ornately decorated and teeming with people busy setting up for an event.

The refugee-servants directed lines of chairs into place with a simple wave of their hands. They arranged a stage the same way, magically and effortlessly. Connor addressed each servant by name, and even though they were rushing to set up, each one watched me for a moment longer than necessary.

"Is there going to be some kind of party?" I asked.

"Yesterday was the anniversary of my father's rule and today, a few hundred of his closest friends are coming here to celebrate." Connor turned to face me and braced himself. "And you are my guest."

"This holiday is for your *dad*?" What had Connor gotten me into? I glanced at my faded sweater and holey jeans. Worried at my windblown hair. Even the refugee workers were dressed better. "Can't I at least go home and change?" I sounded shallow but there was a lot riding on this introduction, not to mention that, as Connor's guest, I'd be the center of attention.

"Sorry, there's no time." He linked his arm through mine and shuttled me inside. We walked into a massive entryway and beneath the largest chandelier I'd ever seen. Then he whisked me through the mansion, past a ballroom, and past two rooms that must have been kitchens, based on the heavenly smells coming from them. The rooms took up more space than my school's gymnasium and looked more like the portal lab than a kitchen, except for the endless platters of food stretched across every surface.

Our footsteps echoed on stone tile as we made our way down a long hallway. At the base of a staircase that spiraled four stories, we doglegged right into another wing. Just outside an open doorway, Connor pulled up short. He thrust his shoulders back and nodded at me, his green eyes bright with certainty.

This was it, our big moment, my one and only chance at making the perfect first impression. My adrenaline spiked.

"Wait. What do I call your dad? President McCabe? Mr. President?"

"He's not your president. Just call him Mr. McCabe. Or Unrelenting Dictator of My Life." Connor rolled his eyes and smiled at his sort-of joke.

We stepped into a large office lined with dark wood shelves. Sunlight glinted off plaques and awards that covered an entire wall. At the center of the room, a man stood with his back to us, studying a 3D hologram of a city. As we crossed toward him, I stumbled on the plush carpeting. Connor cleared his throat.

"Yes, Connor?"

"Sir, I'd like you to meet—"

Without turning around, the man interrupted. "It's obvious who she is."

Mr. McCabe turned and fixed Connor with a stony glare. He didn't resemble his son at all. He had lighter hair and complexion, a longer face, and deep-set, guarded eyes. He loomed over us with military poise.

"This is what you've been doing this morning? You might have told me your plans." He examined me with the same interest he might give a hand grenade. "I take it you're my son's guest today."

"It's nice to finally meet you," I stuttered. My neck heated and I prayed that my bracelets were strong enough to hold back the insecurity rolling off me.

Mr. McCabe let out a short huff of distaste. Then he turned to Connor. "I assume your next stop is Manny's studio. Drop her with him and return to my office at once."

And that was it. No handshake. No "Welcome to West Region."

Connor led me out of the office and down the hall. Electricity raced through his palm and he looked straight ahead.

"He had no idea I was coming," I said to myself.

"It was better this way."

I shot him a look of disbelief. We'd ambushed his dad on the man's own personal holiday. How could this be a good thing?

"Trust me, this is the best time to introduce you. All of us will be together during the entire celebration, and by the end of the night, things will be different."

"I should go home," I said. "I'm intruding, and your dad is really pissed."

Connor pulled me to him. "Please, don't go. Having you here means so much to me."

I shifted uncomfortably. "Your dad hates me."

"He doesn't. He hates how much I care about you."

The furrow between my brows grew deep. He cupped my face.

"He knew I wanted to introduce you eventually. When I told him how much you've been able to achieve with your gift, he was impressed."

"He said that?" I asked.

Connor tilted his head and squinted. "He'd never admit it. That would only encourage me. But he recognizes that you're very special. Please stay."

I couldn't undo what had already happened, and I didn't really want to go home, not yet.

"Okay, I'll stay. So, who's this Manny guy?"

CHAPTER 29

I stood on a pedestal in a bright room while Connor leaned against the door frame, smiling and twirling my coin necklace on his finger. Moments ago, he had introduced me to Manny, "the most extraordinary manifestor in the Regions," and instructed him to fit me for a dress. Manny's face had lit up when he helped me onto the pedestal. Now he scrutinized me from every angle.

Manny was all of five feet tall and nearly as round. His face pouched at the jowls and his left lid drooped. He held his hands in front of him, palms touching, tapping the pads of his fingers together.

"Step down, please," Manny directed me. He latched a hand under my elbow as I clomped down the few steps to the floor. He circled me again, this time periodically swiping his fingers across my body. He ran his index finger across my back from shoulder to shoulder, and then circled my waist with his pinkie. He did the same thing ankle to hip, shoulder to wrist, and around my rib cage.

Connor read the confusion on my face. "Measurements," was all he said.

"Did you have anything specific in mind?" Manny asked Connor.

"Surprise me."

"Do you prefer floor length or a skirt that ends at the knee? And what do you think about a jewel color to contrast her skin?" Manny asked him.

Connor's eyes found mine. "She looks beautiful in anything."

I propped a hand on my hip and cocked my head in mock offense. "Um, hello, do I have a say in this?"

"If you specialize in the celebratory couture for the year 2173, then yes, share your ideas freely," Manny answered.

"She did mention something about spandex," Connor offered.

"Is that the name of a designer?" Manny asked.

I fired Connor a look. "No," I said, "I'm sure whatever you have will be fine."

"We'll get started then. And you, dear boy, need to return to your father's office before he paces a hole in the floor. And while it is none of my business, you got what you deserved by springing this visit on your father. However, you should have had more consideration for your lovely guest."

Connor grumbled, apparently accustomed to Manny's scolding.

"News travels fast here," I said. Connor hadn't said a word about his father since our discussion in the hallway, in the far wing of the mansion. I imagined the servants catching wind of the argument and the chain of gossip reaching Manny before we did.

"Sure does," Connor said with sarcasm, and he disappeared into the hallway.

Manny swung open a set of double doors and entered a walk-in closet. The shelves were empty except for four white dress boxes stacked on top of each other. Manny tapped his fingertips together and seemed to deliberate over his choices.

In the room where I waited, there wasn't a sewing machine or dress mannequin in sight. No bolts of cloth or unfinished sewing projects, either. The room was sparsely decorated with a sofa along one wall, a low table, and the pedestal. There wasn't nearly enough time to design and sew a dress from scratch, so whatever I was going to wear must be in that closet.

Manny finally settled on a box and placed it on the pedestal. "Open it." He pulled his hands to his chest like an eager child.

His excitement was contagious. Full of anticipation, I lifted the lid. "This one's empty," I said, feeling a little foolish.

Manny nodded emphatically. "Back on, please."

I replaced the lid. He laid his hands on the box for a few seconds and then stepped away.

"Again," he said.

Perplexed, I lifted the lid. I gasped. Inside lay the most beautiful gown I had ever seen. It was a rich shade of red and had silky, delicate straps. I looked from the dress to Manny, unable to decide if I was more amazed at his trick or the stunning creation that awaited me.

"Yes, yes. Try it on." He pointed behind me, where a privacy screen had appeared. I changed into the dress. It fit perfectly, as did the shoes that came with it. I came out from behind the screen, feeling like a princess. I curtsied, and he clapped his hands.

"Oh yes! Exceptional! Bellisima!"

Manny examined every inch of fabric. He smoothed the silk around my hips.

"I wonder," he said, tapping his fingertips together. He placed his hands on the box and repeated his quick meditation. "Again!" He grinned ear to ear.

I bit my tongue to keep from giggling and lifted the lid. This time, I found a stunning black sheath with a jeweled neckline.

"Oh, Manny!" The shoes were no less spectacular, with thin, jeweled straps that crisscrossed their way up my calf, from ankle to knee.

Manny liked the black dress on me the best, but I'd fallen in love with the red one. When I told him this, he tsked at me.

"Don't pick favorites yet, Butterfly, we've only just started." He pointed to the box and this time, I pulled out a purple ball gown with a flowing tulle skirt.

And so it went, until I had pulled out, and tried on, over a dozen gowns, each worthy of a spot on a Hollywood Red Carpet. Then Manny attacked the rest of me, using normal everyday spritzers and combs plus a bit of magic. When he presented me with a full-length mirror, I hardly recognized myself. My dark hair was brushed to a silky sheen and fell in soft waves over the dress's straps. My fair skin glowed. I was drop-dead gorgeous.

"What do you think, Butterfly?"

"Wow. And wow. Thank you for all of this." I was still taking in the transformation when I asked, "Why do you keep calling me Butterfly?"

"It's the symbol of metamorphosis, is it not?"

"It sure is." I collapsed on the couch, wearing the first red gown, exhausted and bewildered by the whole experience. Connor hadn't returned yet. I was debating whether to ask about his whereabouts when Manny said, "He's helping prepare for the event. He'll be back soon enough."

Early in my dress-up adventure, I'd realized that Manny was one of those rare and special individuals in West Region who could read people's thoughts. This hadn't bothered me while I was trying on clothes. I'd loved every one of his creations. Now, though, my mind kept flitting to Connor and how angry his dad had been when I showed up. I was dying to know what they were talking about while I was with Manny. If Manny would just give me a hint…

"You'll know soon enough how their discussion affects you," Manny said.

I slumped. "I have a pretty good idea. You should have seen the look on Mr. McCabe's face when I showed up in his office. My aura was all over the place. I came off like a total rookie. Which I guess I am, compared to everyone here."

Manny patted my hand. He'd convinced me to stuff my bracelets in my backpack, claiming they didn't compliment any of the gowns, but he knew I was using them to hide a part of myself. Trying to hide behind them was silly, really. The people here were so astute, they knew I was different even when the bracelets mellowed my energy. If anything, wearing them highlighted my weaknesses, and if I truly wanted a chance with Mr. McCabe, I had to show him my authentic self, flaws and all.

"But can you at least tell me if I have a chance?" I pressed.

"What President McCabe has to say about you and Connor's future together means less than you think."

"How is that possible? He could shut down the portal or send Connor away."

"There are many, many factors at play, dear. One man's opinion cannot change the course of fate. He may redirect it, he may delay it, but your relationship with Connor will happen the way it was meant to. That much I know."

That was another oddity about Manny. He had suggested more than once that he knew about events before they happened.

The door to the studio opened and a young, blond woman brought us a lunch tray. She set it on the table in front of us, handed me a plate, and poured me a cup of golden liquid from a gilded pot. She studied me out of the corner of her eye.

My stomach growled, so I picked up a sandwich. I nibbled at the bread crust and told myself to be brave so I could ask the one question that had haunted me since I'd met Connor. At the same time, I stuffed the question below my conscious mind, wanting to keep it from Manny until I was ready to hear the answer. I washed down the sandwich with the golden tea, trying to loosen the lump that had formed in my throat.

"You can see the future, can't you?" I asked.

"A person's aura carries hints about his past and future. Not everything is revealed to me, but yes, I know many things that haven't happened yet."

I spit the next words out. "Then you know if Connor and I are meant to be together."

Manny gave me a curious look, like I should know the answer to this already. "Why do you think he went through all the trouble to find you? He's been searching for you his entire life, even before he was old enough to understand why he felt incomplete. I saw this the day he came into the world. He was born looking for you."

My heart raced. Manny continued. "His innate sense told him you didn't exist in this time, but he wasn't satisfied with that. He was just ten years old when he asked me for guidance. I told him that one day you would find each other."

Once Manny said this, I knew: Connor had always been there, within me, around me, of me. He was my twin soul, entangled and inseparable, until we were ripped apart and flung in different directions on a timeline that stretched for eons. Time had acted like a thick membrane, our sense of connection passing through like fluid, but never allowing us to meet. Until he had come crashing into my world.

"It's true, then. We are meant to be together." Joy flooded me and I laughed softly before I realized I'd cut Manny off. I was expecting him to share in my happiness, but found his troubled gaze.

"Yes. And no," he answered.

Distress wasted no time crushing the joy right out of me. "Well, which is it? Are we supposed to be together or not?"

"You are." Manny's expression was dark, and his tone pushed me to find the right conclusion.

Suddenly, I understood. I'd probably known it all along but, until that moment, I hadn't been willing to listen to my inner voice as it wove the tapestry of dissatisfying truths. I wasn't prepared for the answer I encountered.

"But not now," I said. "We weren't supposed to find each other now."

Manny leaned in and fiddled with the strap on my dress, then smoothed a nonexistent wrinkle from my lap. "Connor didn't know how to tell you, so I will. The time-space continuum has been very cruel to you. If the workings of the universe were fair, you and Connor would have been born during the same time, in the same city, and been allowed to live out your destiny together. But it wasn't meant to happen in this lifetime, you see? Perhaps the next one."

My sandwich dropped to the plate. "But you just said…"

"Please understand that your and Connor's auras are so entwined, it's nearly impossible for me to tell when and how you will be together. I only know that you will share a life and that your bond will be inseparable."

I grabbed Manny's arm. "But we found each other *now*. There are a hundred and sixty years between us, and that couldn't keep us apart. That has to count for something."

"True, you've already done the impossible. I've never seen such a strong connection between two people."

"But what else do you see? Do we get to live in Portland together? Or West Region? Can you see us getting old together? Do I lose him? Does he fall in love with someone else? What do you *see*?"

Manny gently removed my grip and pressed my hand between both of his. "I see all of that and more. Echo, the two of you have so defied the odds that not even I can see the true outcome. In all reality, it is unlikely that your relationship will survive much longer. You were never meant to be in West Region. We were never meant to have this conversation."

My heart was dangerously close to crashing. I grasped at the one remaining thread of possibility.

"There's still a chance," I said, "that it could work out in this lifetime."

"Chances are slim, but yes, it may happen."

I wanted to scream with frustration, or cry, or both. Manny would have none of it. He tilted my chin with his knuckle until we were eye to eye. "In the absence of our dream, we must live for today."

"Connor said that, too. Live for today." Now I understood the pain I'd seen on his face when he'd said it.

CHAPTER 30

With the pads of my fingers, I dabbed the dampness from the corners of my eyes.

Manny slapped the crumbs off his lap. "Now, Butterfly, we still haven't decided on a dress."He took one look at me and said, "Yes, I know *you* have decided, but I can't very well send you to the ceremony wearing red. That means we must find a way to make everyone happy. Stand, please."

I took Manny's hand and rose to my feet. Red fabric cascaded around my ankles.

"You will wear deep green for the ceremony, black for dinner, and red for dancing."

I brightened. "I get to wear three dresses?"

"You will use your power to change the color and style of your dress between events."

"Me? I don't know how to do that."

"It's quite simple."

He ran me through the exercise, with my eyes closed and my focus drawing to a single point. When that pinpoint of light filled my vision, I pictured my dress as it was and then pictured it as the one I wanted it to be. I opened my eyes, looked down, and saw myself sheathed in the black, jeweled dress. I threw my fists in the air.

"Yes! This is the kind of trick a girl can use. If Connor would have taught me this up front, I would have listened to him better."

The blonde-haired servant slinked in and picked up the tray, again avoiding my eyes. As she headed for the door, she snuck a glance at me. I wanted to ask Manny what this was about, but he had a faraway look, like he was in mid-conversation with someone only he could see.

"I'm needed on the first floor," he said. "Connor will be up shortly to collect you, but first, a few final instructions. You can change your dress in the privacy of the lady's lounge, or make a fabulous entrance and do it as you step into the Grand Hall. Wherever you're most comfortable. Just please remember to alter the shoes, too, yes? We don't want any fashion disasters."

My palms dampened at the thought of showing off my ability among a crowd of onlookers. "Nobody's going to look at me weird if my dress suddenly changes color?"

Manny looked at me with adoration. "This is West Region, Echo. Enjoy your power. You are so very gifted."

Manny's words were like gold. My power wasn't a detriment here, it was an expectation. Darn right I was going to use it in public. While I waited for Connor, I practiced shifting the dress from one color and style to another until I could make the change in a matter of a few strides. The shoes were harder for some reason, but I eventually got the hang of it.

Now I waited, alone. I thought about what Manny said about Connor and me, and was fully obsessing over what "a slim chance" really meant. I caught myself chewing on a cuticle and laced my hands in my lap. Waiting was driving me crazy.

I decided to look for a bathroom. Manny's studio didn't have one, so I trekked down the hall in the direction Connor brought me. I searched the long corridor, but no luck. Cut down another hallway, and then another, doubling back and forth until I finally found what I was looking for.

When I came out, I stopped at the threshold, uncertain how to get back to the studio. All the hallways looked the same. I took a left and hoped for the best. In the quiet of the mansion, my worries crept up again. I fixated on the circumstances that acted for and against our "slim chance." I wished I had some inkling of what Mr. McCabe had said to Connor. I wished for a sign to tell me what direction Connor and I were headed. *Very funny*, I thought, *I can't even figure out which direction will take me back to Manny's studio.*

I'd ended up in an unused section of the mansion. Tall doorways on either side of the corridor opened to one empty room after another. Where the hallway dead-ended, I peered into the very last room, expecting it to be vacant. Instead, I found an unmade bed and guy's shoes scattered on the floor. Clothing, familiar in their color and style, was tossed over the back of a chair. Textbooks teetered in a messy stack on a crumpled comforter. I made out one of the titles, "Pioneering Writers of the 22nd Century."

This was Connor's room, and I'd discovered one of his secrets: my polished, precise, super-talented boyfriend was a slob. I thought back to our first training sessions, when I'd been so intimidated by his sternness. He wasn't so perfect after all and boy, would I have fun teasing him about it.

My eyes landed on the far wall. "What the—"

Hanging above his desk was a painting of a ten-year-old girl with wild brown hair and sad brown eyes. It was a portrait of me.

I high-stepped over the pile of shoes and took a closer look at the picture. Whoever had painted it had captured every detail accurately, right down to the purple hoodie I'd gotten for Christmas and the three freckles on each cheek. I'd worn that hoodie nearly every day, including to the advanced painting class at the high school that winter. There, I'd painted Connor's portrait without ever knowing about him.

Or had I? Did I, like Connor, struggle with a longing for someone I'd never met and transfer that pain onto the canvas? The girl in the picture was so foreign to me now that it was impossible to connect with her, to remember what she thought or cared about. I only recognized the distant look she carried, the one I still wore when my classmates ignored me. Which was often.

"How did you get all the way down here?" Connor said from behind me.

"Went to the bathroom. Got lost." My eyes never left the portrait. Connor put his hands on my bare arms.

"I used to paint a lot," he said by way of explanation. "One night, I had a dream that was so vivid, when I woke up, I couldn't believe it wasn't real. I painted the only thing I remembered clearly."

"It's me."

"I know. I should have told you about it."

"It's okay. I've got one of you, too. When I was that age, I painted you as you are now, except I added a scar on your forehead."

"I've never had a scar there."

My mind reeled back in time, to the class, to the vision that prompted the painting. Had I made that part up? I shook my head in confusion.

"I don't get any of this. It's like somehow I knew you were part of my future." I paused and said carefully, "The way you've known about me since you were born."

Connor breathed into my hair. "Manny told you everything."

"I wish *you* would have told me."

"It didn't seem fair to, when I didn't know how it would all work out. Why didn't you tell me about your painting?"

"I thought it would sound crazy."

Connor rested his forearm across my collarbone so that his current ran across my bare throat. He pressed his chest against my back. "I was wondering something," he said.

"Yeah?"

"What do you think about…" he paused. "Would you like to spend more time in West Region?"

My heart simultaneously swelled and pinched. When I'd found the painting on his wall, I'd taken it as the positive sign I'd been looking for. But this unexpected invitation felt burdened with a condition.

"Your dad is letting me come back?" I asked, cautious. Maybe Connor had talked him into extending the two-week limit.

"No, he got pulled into a meeting before we could talk. This whole time, I was busy helping the crew set up the pavilion."

Oh great. His dad was going to flip if I began showing up without his permission.

When I didn't answer, Connor asked, "Don't you like it here?"

"Of course I do."

"I thought some days after school, we'd hang out at your house and some days, we'd come here."

"But what about your dad?" I asked. "And the two-week time frame?"

Connor's body tensed. "You know what? If I'm going to be the next leader of this region, then I should get to choose who I spend time with. So, what do you say?"

"I say yes!" I spun to face him and green silk rustled around my ankles.

He took a step back to get the full effect of me in the dress. Connor's lips curled in a wicked smile.

"You like?" I asked.

"It'll do," he teased, and sunk his lips into mine.

The noise in the back garden was deafening. Hundreds of people were already seated and more were filing in. I craned my neck to look down the front row because surely, we'd have the best seats in the house, right? Then, as Connor coaxed me toward a short set of stairs, I realized that our seats were *on* the stage.

"Seriously?" It was all I could utter.

"Everyone will be watching my father speak. They'll hardly even notice us." Which was the biggest fib I'd ever heard because as soon as we mounted those steps, we became the center of attention. From the pointing and stares coming from the crowd, you'd think we were royalty. Connor was, in a way.

I set my shoulders and carefully placed one high heel in front of the other until we got to a table where two empty chairs awaited us. Mr. McCabe was already seated next to a glass podium. He watched our arrival with hard eyes. I nodded to him. It was the only act of deference I could think of aside from curtsying. Mr. McCabe did not nod back.

When the crowd's reaction to Connor and I didn't wane, Mr. McCabe hastily signaled for the host to proceed with the event.

Connor clasped my hand under the table, and I relaxed enough to take in the setting. Earlier in the day, the garden had been thick with shrubs and flowers. Now, stadium seating replaced them and people sat on thick cushions that hovered overhead without support. I had no doubt that once the people cleared out, the seating would disappear and the garden would be restored back to its natural state, probably with the snap of a finger.

The host stepped to the podium. He talked about how it was a great honor to celebrate the anniversary of their leader's command, how the McCabe family had devoted themselves to providing the region with decades of security and integrity, and how, if it pleased the people, the region would continue to thrive under the watch of President McCabe and his successor.

At this, the host motioned to Connor and the crowd cheered. Mr. McCabe smiled at his son with deep warmth. Pride thrummed through my chest as Connor rose and waved to his people.

Mr. McCabe took his place at the podium. He thanked the crowd and joked with them. I didn't understand most of what he was talking about, but he had everyone laughing so hard, tears streamed down their cheeks. Then his tone sobered and he spoke about the challenges they faced with East Region. How it was his life's mission to bring peace to the people of the East and re-unify the country. When Mr. McCabe finished, the crowd jumped to their feet and applauded with such fervor, the vibration rattled my bones. I was clapping as hard as anyone, beaming with hope and pride as though I'd lived in West Region all my life.

With that, everyone pooled toward the Great Hall. Every few steps, Connor had to stop to shake someone's hand. His other hand rested firmly on my waist. The women smiled warmly and the men lightly kissed my fingers. More than once, I caught them glance at one another when we parted.

We were about to cross the threshold into the Hall when I pulled Connor out of the flow.

"What's going on?" he asked.

I inhaled deeply. Took a moment to prepare. Then I tugged my perplexed boyfriend back toward the entrance. "All right, let's do this," I said.

"What exactly are we–"

I hopped over the threshold. Quick as a spark, my gown transformed into the elegant black sheath. Guests who caught my magic act clapped and smiled. Connor's cheeks dimpled.

"Remind me to thank Manny," he whispered in my ear. "You look even more stunning in this dress."

CHAPTER 31

Connor continued to be the center of attention long after we took our seat in the Great Hall. I was so mesmerized by the way he interacted with the citizens of his region that I hardly noticed my dinner. Everything about him captivated me, as if it were the first time we'd met: the way his mouth moved when he spoke to the guests; how his eyes flitted from my face to my plate, a gentle signal that I was to eat and enjoy; the feather-light kiss on my earlobe. Connor's affection won me a toxic gaze from Mr. McCabe, but not even this could stamp out my happiness.

During dinner, everyone's attention turned upward to watch a troupe of airborne acrobats. This being West Region, the performers flipped and spun overhead without a trapeze or net. One particularly daring acrobat dove in and stole the wineglass right out of Mr. McCabe's hand. Mr. McCabe's deep laugh formed crinkles in the corners of his eyes, and I got a glimpse of a man who didn't terrify me. I tried to keep that man in mind because I needed to talk to him, to convince him how much I cared about Connor and charm him into giving us more than just two weeks together.

Getting a private moment wouldn't be easy. Mr. McCabe was constantly surrounded by guests or distracted by the entertainment. Now, one of the acrobats was performing on our table. The man, hardly bigger than a twelve-year-old boy, did a series of handsprings and twisting somersaults across the surface. I clapped ridiculously loudly.

Then he bowed to me and kissed my hand. "And who is this lovely creature with the face of a princess? Are you from the East?"

The table went quiet and all eyes were on me. Now my stomach was doing handsprings.

"Oh, um, no. I, uh…"

Connor rose swiftly from his seat. "May I have this dance?"

"Allow me," Mr. McCabe said, and he strode to my side.

Connor stiffened.

"That would be lovely," I said.

Mr. McCabe grasped my elbow and steered me toward the ballroom floor. When we found a place among the other dancers, my confidence took a turn. I would have been out of my element in a regular ballroom, but here, couples floated across the floor—literally. They levitated elegantly, their feet moving on a cushion of air. Why hadn't Manny prepared me for this? Panic skittered along my spine and I wondered if I should just wing it and try to levitate under pressure.

But Mr. McCabe didn't question my limitations, he assumed them. He placed one hand firmly on my waist, took my hand in his, and we shuffled across the floor. I moved rigidly to the orchestra music.

"Loosen your arms and follow my lead," he said, picking up on my obvious lack of ballroom training.

I tried to relax and keep pace with him. I lifted my chin and smiled. "I think it's wonderful how you take care of the refugees," I said in my most adult voice. "Connor told me you let them live on the compound until they're ready to start over on their own."

"We take care of people here in a way your culture can't even conceive. The citizens are well aware of their good fortune and nothing is taken for granted."

"It really shows. I've never seen anything like West Region." I cringed at how naïve this sounded. "Of course, I wouldn't. It doesn't exist yet. It's just that we don't have any place where people can use their power. West Region is like an oasis. I'm so honored to be here."

I tried to maintain eye contact, but Mr. McCabe nodded and smiled at the other dancers. I was beginning to wonder if he'd even heard me. I took his aloofness as a challenge.

"Mr. McCabe, sir. I want to apologize for intruding on your celebration. If I had any say, I would have asked Connor to introduce us on a quieter day."

His knuckles pressed into my back. "Connor does have a way of pushing people. Too often, his willfulness works against him. Take you, for instance. He violated lab protocol just for the sake of giving you a few training sessions, or so he claims. He could have finished without my ever knowing about it and resumed his life in West Region. Instead, he makes excuses as to why he must continue to travel through the portal."

Static built in my fingers. "Well, he's still showing me how to use my ability. I would have been lost without him. We also care for each other a lot."

"Yes, he's told me how he rescued you from certain self-destruction. It's a very enchanting story, but Connor is not a fairytale prince; he is the next leader of a very complex region. He seems to have you convinced that you have a future together."

My composure shriveled and my errant energy swirled around us. Couples threw an odd look our way and gave us space. Mr. McCabe faked a chuckle, like my wacky energy was our private joke. I didn't join in.

"Your son means everything to me. Nothing will change that," I said with more nerve than I had.

"Now, there is something we have in common. What do your parents think about your relationship with my son?"

"Um, well, they don't know about us."

"Ah. Why doesn't that surprise me? And if you and Connor were to become serious," he hissed the last word, "how do you think your parents would react to this unusual arrangement?"

"We're pretty serious already," I said. "And I don't know how my parents would take it, but I'd do anything to be with Connor."

"So, you're the kind of girl who would abandon your family and, let's say for the sake of example, move to another city or country for someone you hardly know?"

"Well, no, but…"

"But you expect Connor to do that for you?"

"I, I guess we haven't really…"

"No, I'm sure you haven't," Mr. McCabe said sharper than he must have intended because he eased his grip on me and cleared his throat. "I do understand your dilemma. You've found a place where you can use your ability without repercussion. You've fallen for my son. I can't blame you for wanting to be here. West Region must seem like utopia."

Mr. McCabe danced us to the middle of the floor. I stumbled to catch up and stepped not-so-lightly on his foot. He winced. I opened my mouth to apologize, but he broke in.

"Did you enjoy your time with Manny?"

I nodded as Manny twirled by with his dance partner. They floated across the floor, as delicate as rose petals on water.

"Manny was one of the first to escape from East Region. He's been with our family for more than a generation. After the Imperators took over East Region's Statehouse, we saw a huge influx of refugees. Conditions in the East were always abominable, but the Imperators caused mass atrocities. They starved and executed their paranormally gifted citizens in an effort to eliminate any possible attempts at rebellion."

I didn't understand why Mr. McCabe wanted to talk about Manny or the Imperators, but I desperately needed to steer the conversation back to Connor. Just as I was about to, a man floated past, staring at me with curiosity. Mr. McCabe felt the defensiveness in my aura.

"The citizens are trying to figure out where you're from," he explained. "Nobody can quite pin down the odd sensation they get from the girl who is wandering the compound with my son. You're clearly not from West Region, everyone can sense that. Only a select few of us are aware of Connor's escapades through time." His tone was clipped now. "Fewer know that he has fallen for a girl from another world, and who would ever guess that he would disobey his father's directive and bring her here? Adding to the confusion, they sense your deeply repressed power. It's astonishingly similar to refugees from the East."

"Would it be a problem if I were?" I asked, confused.

My reaction tripped Mr. McCabe's fuse. "Of course not. The citizens in the East are respected here. You would know that if you had any idea what they endured. The Imperators enslave an individual's power and use it for their own purposes. They slaughter and terrorize their citizens to keep them under control."

"Why are you telling me this?"

"The Imperators want nothing more than to do the same thing in West Region. We devote ourselves to protecting our beloved territory. This is the world we live in, Echo, the world that Connor wakes up to every morning, and the challenges he will face as our next leader. He doesn't need any distractions. I've made my feelings clear to Connor. It's best if your relationship is severed immediately."

My body went numb. "Connor would never agree to that. If he's going to be in charge, doesn't he have some say in who he gets to be with?"

"You underestimate how persuasive I can be." His mouth bent into a confident smile and his eyes settled on a couple dancing at the end of the ballroom. It was Connor and a girl who'd been sitting at our table. She'd been seated two down from Mr. McCabe and had graced Connor with an occasional flirtatious smile. She'd also taken my seat as soon as Mr. McCabe whisked me to the dance floor. Now they leaned into one another, their levitated steps in sync, laughing easily.

"They make a striking couple, don't you think? Both born and raised in West Region. They dated for a while, before he went on his wild trek to find you."

With that, Mr. McCabe delivered me back to my chair. I sat, motionless. The Great Hall seemed to spin around me, like I was caught in the center of an out-of-control merry-go-round. Light and color ran together, and noises warped. I closed my eyes to ward off the rising nausea.

Someone touched my elbow and I vaguely heard, "Are you all right?"

It wasn't Connor's voice, so I only nodded.

CHAPTER 32

I stayed in my chair at the dinner table and tried to forget the horrible picture Mr. McCabe had imprinted in my mind. I watched the acrobats flying overhead and pretended to be enthralled by their tumbling act.

Warm, electric fingers trailed along my neck.

"Any chance I can still get that dance?" Connor asked.

It's funny how the sound of one voice can melt away the turmoil writhing inside a person. While nothing could make me forget Mr. McCabe's ugly words, Connor's voice was something of an anti-venom. In that moment, I could almost have asked him to blindly jump through the portal with me and land in some unknown destination, light years away from both our worlds. We'd start over, together, and defy the 'slim chance' imposed on us by a heartless universe.

I took Connor's hand, and he led me to the dance floor. I wrapped my arms around his neck and we swayed in unison, my feet finding purchase on the solid floor. I pressed my ear against his chest. Let the steady beating of his heart carry me away from my growing fear.

As we swayed gently side to side, my feet left the floor. We were floating. Probably through Connor's power because I felt sapped of mine.

"No transparency," he said as he studied my hand. "You're adapting better than I ever imagined." I felt his breath pause. "Do you want to come back this weekend?"

"Maybe it's better if we stay in Portland." Away from his father, who would never warm up to me, no matter how hard I tried. Away from that girl.

"But it's safer here, at least until they find out who killed those women in Portland. And West Region is a lot more fun." By the lilt in his voice, I got the impression he was trying to cheer me. "It's my father, isn't it? What did he say to you?"

If I told him the truth, I risked saying something horrible about his dad. If I mentioned the girl, I'd lose it for sure.

"Not now, okay? Let's just dance."

I peered up from my sanctuary against his chest. Connor scowled across the crowd. Up until Mr. McCabe's assault on my plans, this had been the best night of my life. I didn't want it to end on a downturn. Then I remembered the one last trick I had saved up.

"Twirl me," I said.

Connor released my waist and circled my arm over my head. As I spun, my black dress swirled into a brilliant red. The skirt cascaded around my hips in a crimson wave. The sensation of twirling without touching the floor was breathtaking.

"You are amazing." Connor held me tight against him.

The party was still going strong when we decided I should head back. When we stepped outside the Great Hall, I expected to see a pitch-black sky. It wasn't as late as I thought, though. The sun was just about to disappear on the horizon.

Carina, the girl who worked with Jaxon at the lab, met us on the walkway, sweat shining on her cheeks, busting a few dance moves. The party had been so big, I never even saw her in the Hall.

She smiled, all gap-toothed, when she saw me. "How are you holding up? Are you experiencing any molecular instability?"

I gave my body a quick once over. "Everything seems to be in place."

"Great," she nodded earnestly. "I love your dress!" She turned to Connor. "I'll take Echo to the lab and get set up. Your dad wants to see you in his office."

"Now? Did he say why?"

She shook her head. "Just that he needed you right away."

"I'll try to be quick." He jogged toward the mansion.

Carina and I walked to the Harden Center in the fading light. It seemed everyone who wasn't at the party was celebrating in the plaza. Torches burning colored flames lined the walkways, and lanterns decorated the sky. People sang, danced, flew, shape-shifted and challenged each other in friendly contests to show off their talents.

When we reached the quiet path to the Harden Center, I took a long look behind me, sad to be leaving such a cool place and wondering if I'd ever be back. Connor and his dad were probably arguing about that right now. The very idea made my blood boil. I was so sick of feeling caught in the middle.

Then why didn't I take a firmer stand? Until Mr. McCabe forbade it, I should spend every possible moment in West Region, proving to him that I was worthy of his son and showing him just how gifted I was. Also, digging up dirt on that girl Connor had danced with. But first things first.

"Carina, how long do you think I could stay here before my body…" I didn't know how to finish the sentence because I couldn't fathom the consequences.

"Before your molecular integrity begins to fail and your structure disintegrates?"

"Uh, yeah, that."

"Hmm. That's a good question. As far as I know, the longest anyone's successfully traveled through the portal is a little over forty-eight hours. I hear one time, a guy was gone for a few days and his DNA was so scrambled when he came back that Philip could hardly identify him. Why do you ask?"

"Just curious. Has Connor been affected at all?"

"Not after those first few trips. We always test him when he gets back, and his system just keeps getting stronger and stronger. I'm beginning to think he could last for weeks out there."

The Harden Center was quiet except for our footsteps. In the lab, I waited patiently while Carina turned on and adjusted the equipment.

"What kinds of tests do you do on Connor?" I asked.

"Oh, the usual. The CKS and the stratifier." She held up the pen thingy that Connor had used on me that morning. "The vortifuge, multiphotometer. Sometimes we run more, depending on how long he's been gone."

I crinkled my brow. "Do they take long to do?"

"Not really, why?" She blinked a realization. "Are you coming back? I knew it! You're dating in both worlds now, huh?"

"Well, that depends on a few things." *Understatement of the century*, I thought.

"Let's full-scan you. Oo-oo! We'll run a gamut test, too. Then we'll know better how long you can stay." She waved me into a leather chair.

I slipped off my heels—omigod it felt good to be out of them—and nestled into the chair. Carina clipped monitors to my fingertips. She pointed a light into my eyes and a robotic arm scanned me from head to toe. Then we moved on to the next test, and the next, and the entirety of our conversation was summed up as:

"Wow," she would say.

"*What*?" I'd repeat.

When we finished, I hung over her shoulder and looked, clueless, at the monitor full of charts and numbers.

"Was that 'wow' as in 'very cool' or 'wow, I'm going to die a slow painful death'?" I asked.

Carina pointed to lines and dots on the screen. "The functionality ratings are extraordinarily high and assimilation results fall within point zero eight on the solar scale."

"English, please?" I begged.

She paused, wondering how to best dumb it down. "Well, your results are really close to the locals. We haven't full-scanned many visitors, but over the decades, a few people have dropped in. They always rate very different from us, but you…" Her voiced trailed. "It's almost like you belong here."

My heart burned in my chest. Until one second ago, so much of my life had felt like one wrong event after another, a series of glitches that played out in a displaced world and began long before tele-chaosing disrupted my life.

But now, it all made sense. I was one of those mistakes that happened in nature, like a two-headed snake or a human baby born with a tail, except I wasn't plagued with a deformity. It was the timing of my existence that was in error.

Why did my mother walk out just hours after I was born?

I was a mistake.

Why didn't my dad know I existed until he got a phone call from the hospital?

Mistake.

Why were Connor and I born more than a century apart?

Mistake.

Why was I born at a point in history when my ability could get me killed?

Mistake.

Maybe I belonged in West Region. Maybe the universe was trying to correct this error. This explanation probably wouldn't get me far with Mr. McCabe, but when I came back, I'd definitely tell him about the lab results. In the meantime, Connor and I would find a way to make this work, even if it meant traveling back and forth daily.

"Carina, how long do you think I could stay here without getting sick?"

"Hmm. I'd have to take a closer look, but—"

Carina was cut off when the lab doors swooshed open and Jaxon strode in.

"Party's over," he said. He tossed me my backpack. It hit me square in the chest and I coughed air.

"We're still waiting for Connor," Carina said.

"Looks like he's changed his mind. You have orders to escort her back." Something in Jaxon's knowing smirk made my stomach fall.

Carina and I exchanged a look.

"Is everything okay?" I asked.

"It's not really any of my business. You're done here and His Highness won't be coming." He stepped to the control panel and jerked his head toward the portal. I glowered at Jaxon, hating that he had the power to dismiss me like this. Hating that he showed so much disdain for Connor.

"Should I change?" I didn't want to cause any more trouble by leaving with Manny's dress.

"Keep it. Consider it a consolation gift."

My body heated. "Consolation for what?"

But Carina pulled me through the metallic doors, and the portal's hum made it impossible for Jaxon to hear me. I looped my backpack over my shoulders and Carina wrapped her arms around me.

We stepped into the gaping hole. There was a burst of light, and we arrived in my bedroom. I swayed from the familiar sensations of disorientation and noodly legs. This time, I shook off the fog and stared at Carina until I could make out the black lines around her irises.

She gave me a head-to-toe glance. "Anything feel out of place?"

I ignored the question. "What did Jaxon mean when he said 'consolation prize?'"

"Don't take Jaxon seriously. He's a jerk. I don't know why Philip puts up with him."

"Do you think Connor changed his mind about coming to the lab?" I asked.

"I'm sure it's nothing." But she found a place to look, and it wasn't at me.

"Carina?"

"I'm sure Connor's mad that he didn't get to bring you back himself. It's still early. Maybe he'll come by later."

I tried to cling to her reasoning. She made sense, except she didn't know what Mr. McCabe wanted to do to me and Connor. *Sever* was what he'd said.

"Connor was dancing with his ex-girlfriend tonight." I hadn't wanted to sound like a jealous spy, but I had to know. "They looked pretty happy out there."

"They did?" Carina's brows arched. "Don't worry about her. The breakup was bad. Her dad and President McCabe work together on the Council, so she and Connor get stuck going to a lot of the same events. They have to be decent to each other." She added this last bit like it should be enough to erase my worries.

"Let Connor know I'll stay up late in case he wants to come by." I forced a cheery voice.

"Will do."

After Carina fizzled back to West Region, I lay on my bed and closed my eyes. It took some discipline to shut out the image of Connor holding the other girl on the dance floor.

Weariness set in and my limbs became dreamy and light. I imagined I was back in his arms, floating across the ballroom, my ear pressed to his chest, and I fell asleep to the sound of his heartbeat.

CHAPTER 33

Tick. Tick. Tick.
Tick.   Tick.

Tick.

Tick.

I lay on the living room couch, listening to the wall clock count away the seconds. The space between ticks grew longer and longer until the lengthening silence screamed volumes.

That's what it was like while I waited for Connor to beam back into my world. Months, years went by without any sign of him. At least that's how the past couple of weeks felt.

The red dress hung in my closet next to my hoodies and tees, a frustrating reminder of the life that I dared to look forward to. Every day, I held the dress to my face and inhaled Connor's scent, that otherworldly fragrance that had embedded itself in the fabric when we held each other on the dance floor.

To keep myself occupied, I created a game where I searched for him everywhere—in the lunch line, among the crowds as I drove to and from school, in every window reflection. It was much the same as when we'd first met. I'd catch a glimpse of movement out of the corner of my eye and hope would bubble up like a mountain spring before I realized I was looking at my own reflection.

For the first couple of weeks, I fully expected Connor to show up 'any time now.' When he didn't, I had to find ways to keep the anticipation from busting me in two.

I laid out all the shirts I never wore, and had me some Manny-style fun. Just like he'd taught, I put on a fuzzy pink sweater Kimber had bought me and pictured it the way I wanted it, black and off the shoulder. After a few tries, it looked just like the one I'd wanted in an online catalog. I took a pink blouse – Kimber had a thing for that color – and turned it blue and cropped it above my waist. A plain white tee now had cutouts beneath the collarbone and on the sides.

Soon, I'd turned the boring clothing in my closet into tops worthy of a Rodeo Drive boutique. What I didn't have was a way to explain where I'd gotten them, so I had to pretend to go shopping.

"Kimber, can I have some money for some new clothes?" I asked.

"Why don't we just get you a credit card?"

"Um, sure, but I want to go this week, and a card will take a while to get here."

I wasn't really heading to the mall, but I had to make up an excuse for all the awesome new shirts I'd created.

"Check my wallet. You can have whatever's there," she said.

I removed the generous bunch of twenty-dollar bills and thanked her profusely. Then I tucked the money in my dresser and promised myself I'd remember to get Kimber something really nice for her birthday this year.

School days blurred together, and about the time I was desperate for a new diversion, Mr. Solomon called me to his desk during physics.

"You still haven't made up the lab you missed last month. Mid-term grades are going out at the end of this week and you are currently sitting at a C+," he said.

Missed lab? "Oh, right. I was out…" *with Connor, in West Region, having the time of my life…* "sick that day. I completely forgot. Can't you just give me extra homework?"

"Afraid not. You'll need to come in after school and do the lab, otherwise you will drop a full grade."

"You're going to give me a *D* because I missed one lab?" What was with this teacher? His skin condition had gotten worse. Skin on his cheek was flaking. Maybe this was putting him in a mood but I didn't like that he was taking it out on me.

His energy shifted and I felt the need to take a step back. "I could fail you for not making any effort to complete it. Come in after the final bell today and get this taken care of."

I dropped into my chair next to Becca. She hadn't forgiven me for the party incident, and we were still barely talking, but she'd at least moved back to our lab table.

"I hate this stupid class," I said.

She dropped her voice. "He's still looking at you."

"I don't care," I said, and when I glared back, he busied himself at his laptop. Like he'd been caught doing something he shouldn't have.

"I don't like this, Echo. He's weird around everyone but especially you. And now you're going to be alone with him? If he tries anything, kick him in his man-parts."

This brought a smile, mostly because that was the most Becca had said to me since I bombed our friendship. "I will, thanks."

The last bell rang and I dragged myself back to the physics classroom. Solomon looked up from his laptop. "Your table is set up and instructions are on page forty-six." His smile was meant to be welcoming but instead, he reminded me of Mr. Crane, with his intense stare and 'I care about you!' attitude.

I opened the lab book and started reading about the bouncing ball experiment. One person would hold a yard stick and the other would time the bounces and write down height measurements. Uh-oh. "Um, Mr. Solomon? This is a two-person project."

"Oh, so it is. I guess I'll have to lend a hand." He let out an impatient breath as if this were an imposition. "I'll hold the…" he seemed to search his mind for the word… "measuring stick and you track bounces."

I knelt at Solomon's feet, picked a red rubber ball out of the full box, and dropped it, watching where it reached its crest and turned downward. I logged the height and seconds in my lab book. The whole time, I felt my teacher's eyes on me. I didn't usually feel Solomon's aura at all, but today, it felt dense. Pushy.

I wished I could feel his intent, but unlike my classmates, his aura didn't give away his emotion. Or maybe he was always like this, cold and flat and pushy and unfeeling.

"Are you still working with a tutor?" he asked.

"Who? Uh, yeah, he's still helping me." I'd all but forgotten I'd told him about having a physics tutor. Connor was teaching me a ton, but none of what I learned transferred to the boring tests I had to take in class. Where was he, anyway? Connor had never been gone for so long.

"I have another student who could use help outside of class. What is your tutor's name? I'd like to provide a referral."

There it was again, that shift in Solomon's energy. Where there used to be empty space, greyness flowed. "One second," I stalled, and dropped the ball from a higher point. My eyes followed it, up, down, up, down, but mentally I was considering how to answer. My fingers had begun to prickle and my heart was racing. The air felt wrong.

"Myles," I said, and the dishonesty quivered through my aura. I made the ball bounce hard and fumbled the catch on purpose. It skittered to the back of the room. "Oh, whoops. I'll go get that." I needed to get away from Solomon, needed to think. He was asking about my tutor but lying about the reason. That much I could tell.

"I don't have anyone by that name in my classes. What school does he go to?"

My mouth opened to give him another misdirection but stopped. A flap of skin was peeling off my teacher's cheek. Fresh pink skin lay where the old layer was sloughing off.

"Eww." Okay, not the most compassionate thing to say to someone with an obvious health disorder, but *my* skin was beginning to crawl. He was standing too close, and when he leaned in to talk—completely unnecessary considering he was right there—his hot, stale breath seemed to suck away all the oxygen.

Solomon's fingers went to his cheek and his face colored. "Excuse me." He stepped into the hallway.

I let out a deep breath and all the rubber balls lifted out of the teacher's lab kit and careened around the room, pinging against the whiteboard and lights. "No! Nonono!"

As quickly as I could, I centered my energy, and they dropped to the floor. I grabbed my book bag and left. I didn't care if I got a bad grade.

The next day, I found the word psycho written on my locker in permanent ink. I could have made a complaint at the school office, and even flat-out accused Raquelle, but that would have taken all of ten minutes. I needed an activity that commanded my free time for at least a few days. An activity that would also take the edge off that make-up lab with Solomon. Not only was it awkward-bordering-on-creepy, but he had the nerve to give me partial credit for my work. *Partial credit.* Even though he was the one who left in the middle of the experiment.

I wanted to blast something.

I went online to Raquelle's Pinterest account, where she'd posted dozens of photos of herself with her latest boy toy. I printed one out, using the best quality setting. I wanted her blonde hair to gleam and her brilliant white teeth to dazzle on the paper. I scissored the guy out of the picture and dropped him into the garbage can.

I jammed a thumbtack through the top of the fresh print and into my wall. Stood back a few feet. Aimed my palm at the picture of Raquelle and thought back to the way she'd flirted with Connor on that first day. With all my energy focused, I blasted an electric bolt straight into her head. Well, sort of. I'd only done this once before, and that was with Connor to coach me, so the energy came out like a sad fizzle and barely shifted the paper.

I didn't have him guiding me so I did my best to imagine his voice. *Center your energy and focus it into your palm. Imagine a beam of light shooting from it and hitting Raquelle right in her conceited smirk.*

I might have added that last bit about her judgy smile.

That day he'd taught me, I'd felt squeamish about hurting another person. I set that fear aside. This was just practice, just a picture.

Center. Focus. Aim.

My palm burst with a flash of light and I zapped the photo dead center.

"Yow!" I jumped. My hand burned as though a hot spike had been jammed into it. I hopped around the room, shaking out the pain, and laughing at the coin-sized mark that now blackened Raquelle's cheek.

I did it. On my own. I couldn't wait to show Connor. He'd be impressed and that meant his kisses would be intense.

If the factions were still a danger, then I should be practicing anyway. But the truth was, I'd never felt safer. Mr. Crane had gone out of town unexpectedly and rescheduled our appointment. The murders had stopped. Ryan Hoffman was still missing, but rumor had it he'd run away from home.

Each night, I stared into the darkness, watching for that spark that would flare into human form. And each morning, before I opened my eyes, I imagined he was there, his face hovering above mine, ready to wake me with his alluring kiss.

In a quiet place far, far back in my mind, I rationalized why he hadn't shown up yet. It was his father, of course. By now, his dad would have told him we couldn't see each other. Mr. McCabe might even have banned his son from the portal, but Connor had assured me he would come back. *I'll find a way to get to you.*

One afternoon, I gathered the dress against my cheek. I inhaled. I smelled nothing. I moved my nose to another spot, and then another. There was no trace of Connor left in the silk. Slowly, like a sound wave from a far-off explosion, shock rippled down my body.

All the signs I'd ignored since my return began to pile up. I didn't need a calendar to tell me what I'd refused to see before. Up until the dance, we hadn't spent more than a week apart. Now, the two-week reprieve that Mr. McCabe had granted us was long past. Connor said he'd come for me, no matter what, and I was certain he would have done so by now. Even if he was unable to travel, at the very least, he would have sent Carina, or even Jaxon, to tell me what was happening. I was sure of it.

Something had changed. There was only one possible explanation.

I clutched the dress and scanned through the harsh events of that final night. Mr. McCabe's grip, solid as a steel plate against my back. His smile as he watched his son dance with his ex-girlfriend. What was it Mr. McCabe had said? *You underestimate how persuasive I can be.*

And then, as if following a script, Carina met us outside the Great Hall. Connor ran to meet his father. Jaxon arrived and quickly shuffled me through the portal with the dress, the consolation gift.

The grand prize was Connor. The loser went home with a dress. Looking back, it all seemed sickeningly well planned.

I sunk my face into the fabric one last time. Connor's scent was gone. The illusion I'd been clinging to evaporated like a fine mist in desert air. Mr. McCabe had severed us. Clean. Fast. He had convinced Connor to move on with his life.

Mine came to a screeching halt.

"Echo, you have to eat." Kimber sat across the counter, a pizza box flipped open between us. Becca was there too. She'd completely forgiven me the moment she found me slumped at my locker, my eyes red and puffy from crying. She'd been trying to cheer me up ever since, splitting her time between me and Lucas.

Becca tried to tempt me by twisting a long string of cheese onto her finger and into her mouth. The smell of hot pepperoni, sausage, and spicy red sauce filled the kitchen. The very sight of food made me gag. My clothes were hanging off my already slight frame and my skin was ashen.

"I mean it this time, or I'm taking you to a doctor," Kimber said. A tiny pucker formed above the Botoxed bridge of her nose. She was serious.

I picked at the sausage and stuffed a piece in my mouth. It chewed like rubber. Tasted like glue. I forced myself to swallow.

"Happy?" I asked.

Kimber shifted back on her stool. Her pained expression jolted me.

"I'm sorry, Kimber." I pulled a slice onto my plate and ate bits of the crust. Then I sank back into the numbness that had consumed my mind and body. I wanted to descend into the vast gray nothingness I felt every day since I'd shoved the red dress into the back corner of my closet.

"No guy is worth this," Becca said. "Just give me the word and I'll shrink his winkie to the size of a raisin."

Kimber gave her a strange look. "You know, whenever I broke up with a guy, I always went out with another one right away. Watching a new guy try to win you over is such an ego boost. My masseuse has a son your age. Why don't I have him give you a call?"

The crust gathered in a glutinous clump on my tongue. "No, thank you."

Kimber tsked. She seemed bound by some maternal code to come to my rescue, even though I'd brushed away all her advice.

"I once caught a guy cheating on me, and the only thing that made me feel better was to burn all his clothes," she said, a little too chipper.

"Oooo, that sounds like fun. Let's burn something of his," Becca said.

I looked at them through bleary eyes. "Connor didn't cheat on me." Saying his name out loud drove a spike through my soul.

"I didn't mean that he did, only that sometimes it helps to do something really radical after a breakup, like tear up his picture, or throw away his CD collection." Kimber leaned in. "Or slash his tires. I've always wondered how that would feel."

I barely heard any of this. "Do you think he's with someone now?" I descended a little lower.

"No, honey. He's probably hurting just as much as you are."

"Oh great, he's gone back to his ex-girlfriend, hasn't he? Oh, I bet his dad just loves that. That perfect little West Region priss!" I stuffed my face into my hands.

Kimber grabbed me in a hug and uttered soothing words into my ear. I rocked into her embrace until a familiar pressure clawed its way up my back.

"I gotta go." I scrambled off the stool and ran to my bedroom. This probably distressed Kimber and Becca even more, but if I didn't go, and fast, they'd see me contort with agony and would rush me to the hospital, because the day the illusion broke, I'd pledged I would never use my power again. I swore I'd never even let a sliver of it escape. Any trace of my ability—the tiniest flicker of a lamp, the wave of a curtain—reminded me of what we had, drove a dagger into my heart.

So I locked it down.

As it turned out, the one promise Connor made that stuck was that the more I used my gift, the stronger it would get. Now, it fought for release like a caged animal. I held it in no matter how much it hurt.

And hurt it did. Times like these, when I reeled from Kimber's comments, a volcanic pressure filled my spinal cord and burned into the back of my head. It built up until I thought my skull would split. Waves of pain seared my stomach. I doubled over and panted, clutched by dry heaves. An excruciating hour passed before it let up, and when it did, I lay crumpled in a corner.

The nights that followed these episodes were bad, too. My muscles clenched all night long against the torrent of hateful, bitter energy that threatened to roll off me. Mornings, I awoke drenched in sweat.

Kimber's advice only made me realize just how little I had to remind me of Connor. I didn't have any pictures to tear up. Not even a phone number to delete. I didn't know where the coin necklace was and I didn't care. But the phone had been a gift. The dress, too, in a way.

CHAPTER 34

That Saturday, I drove through the pounding rain to a quiet spot near the river and parked in an empty lot in the industrial district. I wadded the dress under my arm and climbed out of the car. The rain came down with such force, I was momentarily blinded by the drops hitting my face. In three steps, I was soaked. In six steps, I stood at the railing overlooking the Willamette River.

Swollen from a solid week of rain, the river had broken its banks and swept trees, car tires, lumber, and the bloated carcass of a small animal into its current. The debris flowed like a watery trash heap through the middle of the city.

I fished my phone from my pocket and threw it in a long arc. I lost sight of it before it hit the water.

The dress was rain-soaked when I shoved it over the railing. It fell, a dead red mass, toward the slate gray water. The wind seized it and flung it toward the far shore until it was no more than a bloody splotch against the flat, lifeless sky. A crosscurrent whipped the fabric into a red streak and plunged it into the cold river.

I climbed into my car, sopping wet and shivering. The windows fogged from the scant heat coming off my body. I turned the defrosters on high and cleared a spot on my windshield with my sleeve. Through the rear glass, I made out the shape of a vehicle blocking me in. I smacked my fist on the console. Who was so stupid to park directly behind me?

There was a tap on my window. Outside, a man hovered under an umbrella. I figured it was a security guard, about to tell me to get off private property, which I obviously was trying to do.

I jammed my finger on the button and dropped the window a few inches. Mr. Crane peered in through the crack.

"Are you having car trouble?" His fingers curled over the top of my window.

"Why would I be having car trouble?" I snapped. I made no effort to hide my foul mood. Mr. Crane's aura was steel.

"It's an odd place to park. What are you doing down here?"

"Nothing. What are *you* doing?"

"I'm on my way home from the office and spotted you. I'm also wondering why you missed our appointment this morning. Kimber and I waited and I eventually ran the tests without you."

"I completely forgot." Yeah, right. Nobody asked me if I wanted to go. They just signed me up.

"Luckily, I have the afternoon free. Why don't you follow me back to the office and we can do it now?"

"Because I'm not interested. I never wanted to be a part of your study, and Kimber made the appointment without even asking."

Mr. Crane's jaw tightened. "Why didn't you tell me?"

"I *did* tell you. You're not going to find anything interesting anyway." I didn't like being rude to people but Mr. Crane kind of deserved it. He acted like I owed him. I ramped up to tell him what I really thought about his stupid experiment when I realized he'd stopped listening.

Mr. Crane took a long, slow look at the river, his eyes narrowing like he noticed for the first time how cold and fast and dirty it had become. He swung his gaze across the empty lot, past the buildings that were closed for the weekend. We were the only two people around for blocks. His aura darkened. His eyes dropped onto me. Wisps of hair from his nearly bare scalp plastered to his forehead. Rain that had blown under the umbrella dripped down his face, and dark thoughts seemed to form behind his eyes. I pressed into my seat.

Just then, a couple of joggers splashed along the road behind us, snapping Mr. Crane out of his trance.

"Lies have a way of catching up with us, don't you think?" Threat was thick in his tone. "You know, this isn't a safe place for a girl to be alone. Ryan Hoffman's body was pulled from the river not far from here."

"Ryan is *dead*?"

"It's a tragedy, a young boy losing his life like that. The investigators say he died from head trauma." His eyes settled on mine. "Like the others."

My face went white. Mr. Crane's cheek twitched, and I swear he was holding back a smile. Thick, tarry blackness swooped off him and into the car, so dense with power and hatred that I nearly choked on it.

"Be very careful, Echo."

I hit the window button and the glass rose. Mr. Crane pressed down on the window until his knuckles grew white and jerked his fingers away before it closed on them. He walked back to his car.

My hands shook, and I tried to compare Mr. Crane's auric energy with what I'd felt at the library. Trying to do a match after so many weeks was impossible.

I'd sensed enough to suspect that he knew about my ability and that he might try to hurt me. The only evidence of this—his frightening aura—would never stand up in court. But if something happened to me, if I ever went missing, or worse, then I wanted Mr. Crane's name at the top of the suspect list.

The second I got home, I looked for Kimber. I wanted to tell her about my run-in with her psychiatrist friend and at least tell her about the encounter by the river and how I'd felt threatened.

I found Kimber curled on her bed with Tito, weeping. Mr. Crane had told her about Ryan. Why he continued to haunt her with these grisly murders was a mystery to me. The poor woman's emotions were fragile as china.

I lay with her, stroking her hair until she fell asleep. The more I thought about my accusations, the less fired up I was to tell her. What exactly did I expect her to do? Confront Mr. Crane? Keep it to herself and add to her emotional burden? The best thing would be to wait and talk to my dad the next time he came home.

"How'd you think you did?"

Becca and I had just finished a physics exam. Her question made me smile because I'd caught her copying my answers.

"I'm pretty sure we both got an A," I teased. Ever since the incident in the lab with Mr. Solomon, I'd been putting in extra study time to make up for the bad rubber ball experiment.

"Thanks for saving me. Lucas and I were supposed to study last night but..." She trailed off when she sensed someone coming up behind us.

"It's just Raquelle," I said.

"How do you do that? Know who it is without looking?"

"Mostly from the wicked stench."

Becca eyed me curiously. After failing to develop telekinetic ability, she'd come to the conclusion that something, or someone else, must be responsible for the odd things that used to happen. I say *used to* because I still kept my ability under lock and key. I hadn't let it slip in weeks.

We stopped at our lockers and as soon as Becca peeled off to join Lucas, Raquelle slithered in.

"What's this I hear about Connor dumping you?" she hissed.

The very mention of his name sent shards into my heart. I swung my locker door open, hard. It narrowly missed Raquelle's nose before banging against its neighbor.

"Temper, temper. You should be nicer to me, Echo. In fact, you should be treating me like your very best friend in the entire world."

I gave her my *back off* glare and busied myself exchanging books.

"Connor and I have a lot in common. Like, I just dumped Hunter Cassington. You know, that model from Riverdale High? We did everything together. And I mean *everything*." Her tongue flicked against her upper lip. "And then I got bored and now it's time to move on."

"So move." I slammed my locker and elbowed her to get by.

"Not so fast, Echo." She snatched my arm and shoved her phone in my face. "I need Connor's phone number."

"Well, I don't have it."

"Well, find it. Pretty please?" The girl was all saccharine. When we were friends, she'd pull this routine where she acted all chummy because she knew she was about to get her way. I yanked my arm free but eased up on the attitude.

"Why don't you just look it up?"

"If I found any listing for him, you think I'd be asking you?" She pressed a few buttons on her phone. "His address. Now."

"I told you, I don't have it."

"Are you sure? Are you absolutely, so positively sure, that you're willing to risk everybody knowing just how much of a freak you are?"

Her lips smiled but her aura flickered nervously. So did mine.

"I'm going to be late for class," I said.

The bell rang and I took the opportunity to break away.

"Have it your way. You'll see it soon enough on Instagram."

I stopped. She rocked her phone back and forth, taunting me with it.

"*See what?* Echo must surely be asking herself." Raquelle pressed another button and held the screen for me to see.

I was looking at Raquelle's private YouTube account. A video sat frozen on the screen. She pressed play. The video was taken in Trisha's kitchen, the night of the party. Whoever took it was hiding in the dark behind Trisha and McKyla. I stood in front of them in a fighting stance, eyes narrowed. The audio was soft, but clear.

I watched in horror as the entire, awful event played out: Trisha calling me names. My anger rising. My hand arcing through the air, sending the knife block slamming against the wall. My self-satisfied expression as my classmates tried to register what had happened. And then Raquelle's voice, low and mocking and close to the microphone: "Gotcha now, bee-otch."

The video ended. My vision swam. A mild buzzing on my brow warned me to hold myself together.

Think, Echo. THINK. "How much did it cost you?" I sputtered.

"Excuse me?"

I huffed a weak laugh. "Oh, please. All the special effects? That's pret-ty pathetic."

Every muscle in her neck clenched. "Nice try, Echo. I don't know what kind of witch you are, but if you don't get me Connor's address, *everybody* will see this video. Got that?"

It took every ounce of restraint not to zap her the way I had practiced. "If you post that video, I'll never give you his address. His family likes their privacy, and you'll never even find out what school he goes to." I felt a bump of hope at my fast thinking.

Raquelle hadn't considered that I might retaliate. Options flitted across her face. She weighed these against her hunger for Connor.

"You have until Thursday," she said, swaying out of sight.

The substitute teacher barely acknowledged my tardiness. I elbowed past rowdy guys and girls and sank into my seat, dazed. No doubt Raquelle was now coming up with a bigger way to threaten me, just in case the video wasn't enough to wrangle me into submission.

The video. She'd held onto it for over a month, patiently waiting until she needed the perfect blackmail tool. Raquelle would have sworn Trisha and McKyla to secrecy, too, so that she'd have full power over me.

The worst possible thought occurred to me then. Was it possible that Mr. Crane had seen the footage? Intuitively, it didn't seem right. I doubted she'd share this with her dad, but if it ever went public, everyone would know. Mr. Crane. Kimber. My dad.

I had to get into her account and delete the video, but how was I supposed to do that? Now I wished I'd told Connor about the incident at the party. He might have seen this coming. He might have been able to do something about it. Rage pooled in my stomach. Where was he when I really needed him?

Raquelle's password could be any combination in a million, and I had to figure it out by Thursday. The impossibility of my situation caused the fluorescent lights to blink erratically. Volcanic pressure surged up the back of my head. I staggered to the front of the room.

"Can I get a bathroom pass?"

The substitue teacher was typing on her laptop, long past caring what happened in the classroom. She handed me a slip and went back to work.

It was pouring outside so I jogged past the girls' bathroom and to the auditorium entrance. I slipped into the cool, dimly lit lobby and climbed the stairs to the dark balcony. My fists clenched against my pounding pulse.

I eased into a seat, afraid that a mere flinch would set my ability loose. Instead of releasing it the way I used to, I pulled it close and tightened my grip on it. The buildup was too much.

Little by little, threads of anger and confusion and heartache seeped into the auditorium. I pulled my legs to my chest and sank my teeth into my lip until I tasted blood. The seats around me rocked violently on their hinges. The curtains whipped and twisted as if caught in a hurricane wind. A stage light blinked on. Then, as if my power had been dialed to zero, all the disruption ended. My headache eased.

Down on the stage, a curtain still moved, ever so slightly. The pleats shifted, starting at the wing and moving toward the middle, as though someone were searching for the way through. The curtains parted in the center and Solomon stepped on stage. He raised his hand to cut the glare from the overhead light.

"Who's out there?" he called.

I slapped my hand over my mouth to hold in a screech.

He walked the length of the stage, peering into the darkness. Then he dropped into the seating area and began searching between rows. The chair next to me squeaked. Solomon's glare shot to the balcony.

"This area is off limits except during drama class," he shouted.

I ducked behind the chairs. The penalty for hanging out in the auditorium was probably minimal, but I had a feeling he'd seen the curtains whirling and snapping like they were possessed by demons. He marched toward the stairs, every stride coming closer to blocking my escape route. There'd be no dodging him once he got to the balcony.

I crept out of my seat and dropped down the steps two at a time. Then I darted through the exit and back to class, where I grabbed my books and excused myself. I got my backpack from my locker and ran for the parking lot.

I spent the rest of the day in my bedroom, trying to hack into Raquelle's account.

CHAPTER 35

My dad glanced at me from across the dinner table. Home for a visit, he was unprepared for the unsettling vision I had become. He wasn't sure how to react to the girl who so violently stabbed at her steak, the girl who had given him an aloof hug when he arrived. The girl who, just minutes ago, had accused Mr. Crane of harassment.

I'd wanted to lay out a constructive case for not allowing Mr. Crane into our home. Instead, I'd told a confusing, winding tale that made it sound like I was mad about being pushed to participate in the research study. I didn't blame my dad for not taking my concerns seriously.

My dad was supposedly between clients, but I knew Kimber had asked him to come home. She was worried about my odd behavior—the long absences at night that I refused to explain; my heightened anxiety caused by my rising, barely controllable energy; my dangerous driving, which was a total exaggeration. So what if I'd run a couple of stop signs and gotten a couple of tickets?

"Is there anything you want to talk about, Echo?" my dad asked.

"Nope." I tore the last of the meat off the bone with my teeth. What could I say? If I told him about the breakup, the table would surely flip on its side and send everyone sprawling. Denial was my safety net. As it was, the knife next to my plate jittered.

"We want to know where you're going at night," Kimber said.

"Nowhere."

"Is it to see that boy Connor?" she asked.

At the sound of his name, the scarred edges around my heart peeled back, exposing fresh, recently wounded flesh. I shot her such a vile look that her fork stopped in mid-air.

"Echo?" my dad pressed.

"I don't go anywhere. I sit on the portico until I go to bed."

"In the dark and the rain? It's freezing out there. And why don't you answer when I call you?" Kimber asked.

"Because I don't want to be bothered." My gritted teeth challenged her to ask another question, push another button.

"That's no way to talk to your stepmother," my dad snapped.

"Sorry. I just don't want to talk about it."

Kimber and my dad exchanged a glance, a signal that they'd take this up when I wasn't around. My dad launched into a story about one of his clients, and I retreated inward.

Why did Kimber have to mention *his* name tonight? It jarred the delicate balance I'd found when I'd settled on the real reason my life had deteriorated. It was because of *him* that my ability terrorized me daily. *His* irresponsible training made me cause a scene at the party. It was *his* fault that I lived an unbearable life.

I snuck a few pieces of steak to Tito and tuned into my dad's voice, waiting for him to finish so I could excuse myself from the table. I caught his last sentence, so innocently spoken.

"The contract was good," he said, "but they didn't give me any choice. So I severed the relationship."

My stomach lurched.

Severed. It's best if you sever your relationship with my son.

"Echo, are you okay?" My dad leaned to steady me.

The word rang in my head, shouted by my own voice. *Severed, severed, severed.*

The voice rose to a high pitch. My eardrums burned. Heat filled my throat and raced down my body's core until I was scorching from the inside out.

Severed.

"I need to be excused," I coughed.

"Honey, what—"

I was off my chair and out the door. Heat boiled in my stomach, and my dinner rose into my throat. I swallowed it down. Fire ignited beneath the layers of my muscle.

I burst into the freezing night. Sleet pelted my skin, stuck to my hair. I tilted my face skyward and inhaled. Flecks of ice stung my tongue and the inside of my mouth, but it didn't cool me. I kept running.

I lost my footing on the slick lawn and slammed onto the ice-covered grass. I bounded back up and into the street. My tennis shoes slapped against the wet pavement as I hit a full sprint.

At the bottom of the hill, I stopped, doubled over, gasping for air, my lungs coated with ice. Wind roared through the deserted intersection and into my bones. Still, the fever rose. I clutched at my bare skin, expecting it to peel away in great, blistering swaths. Bile churned in my throat. I couldn't hold it in any longer. I threw my head back to the sky.

"How could you do this to me?" I yelled from the bottom of my lungs.

Streetlamps along the boulevard flickered wildly. A sapling, already straining against the wind, snapped in two.

"You said I could go back! You said we'd be together! I trusted you!"

I spat out my rage. I bent over and put my hands on my knees, unable to breathe. The metal bracelets dug into my wrists. I yanked them off and flung them into the street. A second wave of energy surged through my body with such force that I convulsed.

"You abandoned me! I don't belong here, and you left me here!" I screamed at the clouds.

The streetlamps blazed white hot. A bulb shattered. Glass ripped into the night. A metallic groan cut through the wind as the lampposts nearest me began to bend, their black steel columns arcing away from me. The cold metal shrieked and folded in half. Another post quivered and snapped in two, its top half hurled into the middle of the intersection. Then, like a series of gunshots, the remaining bulbs in the lamps along the boulevard burst. Lights in houses on the hill flickered, and the neighborhood plunged into darkness.

My hand flew to my mouth. I stumbled backward in shock.

Was it possible… could I have done this? I froze, terrified that any movement would cause more damage. The internal fever was gone. I shivered uncontrollably, stumbled back up the hill through my dark neighborhood to our house. Once inside, I leaned against the door, panting and fighting a bristling fear.

"Echo?" my dad called from the darkness.

I dropped to the floor and pulled my knees to my chest. The truth was sinking in. My emotional explosion had caused tornado-scale damage.

"Echo, is that you?" His voice was insistent. I knew I should answer him, but I didn't know how. A simple "yes" didn't seem truthful. The Echo he knew didn't get traffic tickets, didn't travel through time with a secret boyfriend and plan to leave her family behind forever. His Echo didn't destroy steel objects with her fury.

My dad hurried into the entryway, led by soft candlelight. He knelt in front of me. "Honey, are you hurt?"

He reached for my face. I whimpered in warning, but my energy had diminished, and nothing horrible happened to him. My skin pricked beneath his touch.

"You're bleeding!"

Even in the pale light, I could see the red streaks on his fingers.

"Did someone hurt you?"

Kimber came in from the other room, carrying Tito and a flashlight.

"I'm taking you to the hospital," my dad said. He reached to pick me up.

"What on earth happened?" Kimber asked.

I pushed my dad's arms away, shook my head. I forced myself to speak, certain I wouldn't recognize the sound that came out. Nothing else about me felt familiar, why should my voice?

"The storm," I said.

"You got hurt in the storm?"

I nodded. My cheek stung from what felt like a hundred cuts. I touched my face and found it sticky with grit. I rolled the grit between my fingertips. Glass.

"One of the streetlights shattered," I explained.

Against my protests, we went to the emergency room. For two hours, the doctor picked glass fragments from my skin and sewed up one of the larger cuts. He sent me home with a bottle of painkillers.

On the ride home, my dad gave me uneasy, sidelong glances. Without his asking, I understood what I needed to tell him.

"Something Kimber said at dinner reminded me of Connor." I choked out his name. "And I lost it. I'm sorry I made you worry."

He nodded once. Deep lines still radiated from the corner of his eye.

"It won't happen again."

He nodded again, and his shoulders fell soft.

That night, I undressed in the dark even though the electricity was back on. It was hard enough to reconcile who I was with what had happened. Seeing my puffy, lacerated reflection in the mirror would only have sparked more doubt and confusion.

The episode on the street had served its purpose, though, and the crushing pain was gone. When I'd refused to use my ability, it was meant to be a kind of revenge against Connor leaving me. It had totally backfired.

A barb jabbed beneath my breastbone. I repeated his name. It still hurt, but a little less. I thought about how I had followed him to the warehouse that first day. How my power flourished. How I dove into Connor's world and fell for it. Fell for him. If I'd known how it would turn out, I would have stood fast against his smile, his green eyes. I would have walked away.

I said his name again, out loud this time, over and over until it no longer hurt.

Ladies and gentlemen, behold the mistress of darkness as she slices her hand through a solid wood desk! As her bed magically makes itself without touching it!

Be in awe as books flutter across the room like birds, empty shoes tap dance through the air, and a lip gloss wand writes on the mirror with a power all its own!

Applaud as the queen of outcasts levitates and changes a light bulb on the ceiling without a ladder!

I'd learned the hard way that I couldn't imprison my ability. So, before breakfast each day, I reluctantly turned my bedroom into a Harry Potter funhouse. I released as little energy as I thought I could get away with. No more, no less. I felt like I was feeding crumbs to an insatiable lion.

My dad let me stay home for a couple of days to let the swelling on my face go down. Even while I was loopy from painkillers, I tackled the mystery of Raquelle's password. I thought the drugs might open a gateway to higher inspiration. Mostly, they put me to sleep.

Thursday, my dad decided I wasn't going delinquent after all and caught a flight to Paris. I dragged myself to my car, drove to Becca's driveway, and honked the horn.

"Yikes. That's a lot of makeup," she said as she climbed in the car.

"It's really not that bad. It's covering up some cuts." I had only told her I was out sick.

"Should I even ask?"

"Please don't." At the bottom of the hill, I braked at the boulevard's intersection. A utility crew was removing the two posts that I'd bent and was replacing all the broken bulbs.

"Did you hear what happened to those posts?" Becca asked.

I nodded. The damage had been broadcast on the news, along with outlandish speculations about the cause. Most people found it hard to believe the storm theory.

"Aliens is what I think. You know, like the ones that make crop circles? Nobody can explain how they get there and yet *bam*, they show up overnight, just like this stuff did."

"Sure, why not," I answered, completely absorbed with the password problem. Raquelle's deadline was today. She hadn't said when exactly the axe would drop.

Becca gave me a woeful look, pitying the lackluster person that her off-again, on-again BFF had become. "I miss my smartass friend," she said.

"Well, I'm in crisis central."

"What's going on?"

"I need to break into Raquelle's YouTube account and I can't figure out the password. If you were her, what would your password be?"

Becca's eyes flit side-to-side. "Why would I know?"

"I'm not saying you do. I'm saying, what's your best guess?"

Becca turned up the volume on the radio. "Dunno," she said, a little too casually.

She seemed all too fascinated by the scenery outside her window. And just like that, I remembered why Becca had been so amazed that Lucas asked her out.

"You know," I said.

"I don't."

"You do. You know her password! You know because Lucas went out with Raquelle, and he knows, and you somehow found out."

Becca shook her head. "I can't tell you. If anything happens to her precious accounts, she'll blame Lucas first. And I won't be able to lie to him about it. And then he'll be mad at me."

Her refusal startled me. "*Becca.*"

"I *can't.*"

"I can't believe this. We're supposed to be friends."

"Then tell me why you need it."

"It's Raquelle, Becca. Do I really need to explain? She's evil incarnate. She's trying to ruin my life, and I have to know *today.*"

Caught between a rock and a harder rock, Becca threw up her hands. "Okay, here's a hint. Her user ID is her name, and the password is super easy. It's like, '*duh, how'd I miss that?*' You'll totally figure it out."

"I'll figure it out??" I smacked the steering wheel. "Geez, Becca."

"Don't do this to me, Echo. Lucas and I are really great

together." She fixed her attention on the cars funneling into the school parking lot.

If I wanted Becca to make a sacrifice, I had to be willing to give something in return. I'd have to tell her why I needed to get into Raquelle's account. I'd have to start from the beginning, tell her how my fall off the banister gave me paranormal powers, how I struggled daily, how I'd lost it at Trisha's house.

If I showed Becca one of my tricks and told her about the video, maybe she'd understand and give me what I needed. But I'd be selling my secret to Becca in order to delete the secret from Raquelle. Two steps forward, one step back.

"Thanks for the hint," I said.

Her voice was soft. "Yeah, sure."

CHAPTER 36

Solomon stood outside the classroom, whistling that same, eerie tune he did every day before the bell rang. Like most people, he stared at my swollen face.

"My goodness. Have you been in an accident?"

Showing any expression aggravated the cuts, so I simply nodded. "Broken glass."

"Hopefully, the stitches won't leave a scar." He lifted a finger to his pocked complexion.

A wave of compassion lifted my spirits. I'd gotten over the awkward incident in the lab and felt like a real jerk about the way I'd stared at his skin disorder. "The cuts will heal okay. It's really nice of you to ask, though." I gave him a broad smile, even though the scabs pulled.

Like the rest of my classes, I spent Physics head down, scribbling possible password combinations into my notebook. The list was long and none of the words were flattering. I wished I hadn't thrown my phone in the river. Now I'd have to wait until lunch to test the guesses in the computer lab.

Raquelle sat across the aisle, a departure from her usual spot behind me. From her constant smirk, I figured she wanted to add pressure to my growing panic. While the class worked on a problem set, she slid me a note. I unfolded it. My hands shook.

Time's up.

Her head was down, one cheek plumped by a hidden grin. She discreetly pecked into her phone.

Solomon cleared his throat and caught my eye. I moved my pencil to make like I was working on the problem set and scrambled for what to do next.

I'd told Kimber that Connor lived on the northeast side of town. I'd told Becca the same thing when she asked. Raquelle wouldn't know for sure whether the address I gave her was accurate until she checked it out herself. I jotted *1228 NE Hancock St.* on the note.

In the far row, Becca slipped something to Lucas just as Solomon walked by. Solomon turned to see what they were up to, and I shoved the slip of paper back to Raquelle. She smacked her gum when she read it and tucked it in the left cup of her push-up bra. Then she tilted the phone screen so I got a good look at what she was watching. It was the footage from the party.

"That address better be right," she mouthed, and she lay the phone face up on her desk.

A shadow fell over us.

"*Raquelle,*" I hissed. "*Raquelle!*"

Solomon hovered over Raquelle. He trained his gaze on the video. His eyebrows rose. He leaned closer and squinted.

"Raquelle." Our teacher's voice made us both jump. "Put your phone away and see me after class."

She shoved the phone into her purse. My veins went icy, wondering what was going through my teacher's head right then. It was impossible to tell if he recognized anyone on that tiny screen.

Tense minutes passed and the bell finally rang. I took my time gathering my books, keeping one ear tuned to the front of the room where Solomon lectured Raquelle. I couldn't make out their conversation.

"Guess who's got a hot date." Becca was next to me, wagging her hips.

"Um," I stalled, still trying to hear Solomon and Raquelle.

"It's not that hard a question," Becca said.

"Sorry. Where's he taking you?"

"Not sure, but someplace nice. He said to wear something sexy."

Raquelle's voice rose, but whatever she said was drowned out by the sound of kids heading for the door.

"So," Becca continued, "you want to come with me to the mall tonight?"

"What about all the dresses you already have?"

"Too Wiccan. I'm going for hot. Rocking, sizzling hot. Just this side of obscene."

Raquelle stomped out of the room, her complexion beet red. Solomon began wiping down the board. Relief practically bowled me over. He'd reprimanded Raquelle for using her phone in class, but if he had seen the video, he hadn't linked me to it.

"Sounds like fun," I said.

We were nearly out the door when my teacher said, "Echo, if you're looking for more extra credit, stop by after school."

"No thanks, Mr. Solomon. I'm behind in English."

"Say, your neighborhood had quite a power outage. Did they find out what caused it?"

A sense of unease passed through me, like when you hear a noise in your room in the middle of the night. "They said it was the wind?"

"Mm. Well, I'll have the room open late if you change your mind."

A subtle shift told me something happened between us, but I couldn't read exactly what. Sometimes, a smattering of someone's aura was more frustrating than none at all.

"Kiss-ass," Becca said when we reached the hall.

"Bite me, witch."

She threw her arm around my shoulder. "Finally, the Echo I know and love is back!"

Partychick

Queenbee

Cheercaptain

Hit list

Superslut

I stole a few precious minutes trying to hack into Raquelle's account before Becca and I headed to the mall. At that very moment, Raquelle was probably driving to the fake address I gave her. Any minute now, I expected an angry email from her, telling me that the video was about to go live. I wiped sweat from my cheek and kept trying.

Why was this so hard to figure out? Raquelle wasn't known for her high IQ. I mean really, someone who wore sweatpants with *Partychick* written across her butt wasn't a very complicated person.

Partychick wasn't the password, but what if…

On a whim, I typed "kcihcytrap", partychick backwards, into the password line. Voila, I was in Raquelle's account.

"Ohmigod. Oh. My. God! I did it!" I jumped out of my chair. I smacked the heel of my hand on my forehead. "Duh! Partychick in reverse! Duh!"

I scrolled to the video of me at Trisha's house and clicked the Remove button. The screen asked if I was sure.

"Heck yeah." I clicked the video into oblivion. Then, just for good measure, I deleted all her other content. That way, she'd be less likely to point blame at anyone in particular. Technical glitches happened online all the time, right?

And with the press of a button, all my anxiety lifted. The video was no longer an issue; since I'd returned from West Region, I'd seen no evidence that factions were a threat; though I still didn't know what to do about Mr. Crane, I felt in control now, confident in my safety as long as I kept my distance. If he said or did anything that made me the slightest bit uncomfortable, I would have a serious conversation with my dad.

A smile, one of the few in a month, spread ear to ear. I blasted music at full volume, dancing while I got ready to meet Becca.

Becca and I stepped into the warmth of Pioneer Mall. A slight adrenaline rush skipped through my belly when all the auras bounced into mine, but it quickly passed. I'd decided not to tell her what I'd done to Raquelle's YouTube videos. That way, she wouldn't have to lie to Lucas. Besides, we had more important business.

"You still haven't told Lucas you're Wiccan?"

"I was going to, but," she hedged. "I moved most of my business to the girl's bathroom. After what I did at the party, I decided to lay low, so he doesn't think I'm weird."

Seconds passed, and then I got the gist. "Becca, you didn't."

"It was no biggie. I just spilled a bit of potion on his hand."

I squelched the impulse to shake her. "You've got to stop this. You're messing with power you don't understand, and if it works, someone could get hurt."

"*If* it works?"

"I'm just saying, Becca, be careful what you wish for."

Becca frowned. "I really wanted him to like me."

"You're great, Becca. Of course he would like you. He just needed to get to know you."

"Yeah, but the competition is fierce. I needed to make sure he'd lock eyes with me all night."

"From what I hear, you locked more than eyes at that party."

"See how well the potion worked? It was hard enough keeping Raquelle away from him. You remember what it was like with Connor." Becca caught herself. "I didn't mean to bring him up."

A small place in my heart, too recently scarred over, throbbed. "It's all right."

We walked to the center of the circular atrium, surrounded by three stories of clothing boutiques. Becca would want to hit every one. It was going to be a long night.

By the time we got to the top floor, I'd offered advice on about a million different skirts and dresses.

"I think this the one," Becca said as she emerged from the changing room. She modeled a dress that had cutouts running down the side.

"Are you going for sexy chic?"

"Well, yeah."

"Then that's your dress," I said. The lights flicked off and on and for a second, I thought I was the source. Then an announcement came over the speakers telling us the mall would close in fifteen minutes. Becca hurried back into the changing room.

It felt good getting pulled into Becca's dating drama, helped steel me against the memories from the last time I was at the mall. The jewelry store where Connor bought my necklace, the corridors where we'd walked and joked, all these places still brought heartache. The AT&T store was right next door, and I hadn't anticipated the swell of emotion I felt as we walked by. Now, bits of conversation with him trickled back, ran loose in my head. I remembered the sound of his laugh, the soft cotton of his t-shirt, the glow that warmed my back when his hand wrapped around my hip.

Warmth tingled in my fingers and between my brows. No biggie, I thought calmly. There were plenty of ways to burn off my auric disturbance before it got out of hand. I moved to a table stacked with sweaters and casually glanced around as I picked one up. The store was empty except for the clerk and a customer at the register.

"Gray is so yesterday," I said and shook the sweater twice. On the second snap, it changed to peacock blue. A smile tugged at the corners of my mouth. I changed another one from black to green to yellow, and added a hood just to see if I could.

This felt so good. Why did I continue to fight my gift? I bet I could have shaved an hour off the shopping trip if I'd discreetly altered dresses that Becca liked but hadn't come in the right color. Or maybe I could have created a different one altogether, a perfect dress for my sweet friend.

I grabbed a nasty-looking dress with puffy sleeves and imagined making it wildly different—beaded straps and a slit up the skirt. I was about to give it a good snap when I sensed someone watching me.

I turned and my breath caught. "Oh. Mr. Solomon."

CHAPTER 37

Mr. Solomon smiled at me with a mouth full of crooked teeth. From the other side of the sweater display, he nodded at the dress in my hands. "No wonder you didn't want to come to the physics lab tonight."

"Um…"

"You look like you're having fun shopping."

"Yeah, I'm here with Becca." I adopted a bored tone and calmly returned the dress to the rack. If he had seen me playing with the sweaters, he wouldn't be chatting so casually. And I would have felt shock coming off him. Or would I? I rarely sensed his aura at all, even when we stood side by side.

"I'm sure you'll do well this semester without the extra work. Of all my students, you're the last one who needs more practice. You're showing a real gift."

He was being friendly, but the hairs on the back of my neck rose. Were we still talking about physics?

"Thank you. I appreciate the bonus questions." We stood there for an uncomfortable moment. The lights flickered.

"I guess they're about to close," I said.

Solomon craned his neck to look at the clerk. She was still taking care of a customer.

"I've been shopping all night, trying to find a gift for my wife. These look nice." He pointed to the stack of sweaters. "She likes blue, and I see they happen to have just the one."

His eyes locked onto mine, and his mouth lifted in a knowing smile. My veins cooled.

"Well, good luck finding something for her. I'll see you at school," I said.

"Wait, maybe you can help me with the size. Do you mind? I just don't have an eye for this sort of thing. It's her birthday. Tonight. And here I am without a gift."

"Uh, sure." If he'd caught part of my magic act, he wasn't in a hurry to confirm it. If I played it cool, maybe he'd brush away any suspicions he had. After all, he taught us the ground rules of our physical world: mass, gravity, acceleration. Physics theories did not allow for the supernatural.

"What size does she wear?" I asked.

"She's about the same as Mrs. Fullner, your trigonometry teacher. Do you think the blue one would fit?"

Before I could hand him the top, it rose from the pile on its own and unfolded itself. I inhaled two sharp breaths.

"She also likes red," he said. A red sweater floated into my teacher's hands. My eyes jumped from Solomon to the sweater.

"I didn't mean to frighten you, Echo. I just wanted you to know you're not alone. From the very first day, I knew there was something special about you," he grinned.

His statement jarred me. I thought back to when he started as a substitute teacher. Was it possible that, every day while I sat in physics class, a truly gifted person was literally right in front of me?

As I thought about this, Connor's warning about the factions surfaced and then, just as quickly, left. I'd only caught an occasional smattering of Solomon's aura over the past couple of months, and aside from our weird session in the physics lab, neediness seemed to be his ruling emotion. Compared to Mr. Crane, Solomon's energy was about as alarming as a Christmas elf's.

"If you knew about me, why didn't you say something?" I asked.

"It's not a safe world, is it? We like to take our time and make sure we're right about someone before we approach them. Once I observed your flair here in the store, that sealed it."

My ears clenched onto the word *we*. "There are others," I gasped.

"Lots of them. I'll see some of them tonight, in fact."

"Here? In Portland?"

"Does that surprise you?" Solomon rubbed his fingers together, like he did just before the bell rang. "Why don't you join us? We're meeting just around the corner. I'm on my way there now."

"Is it your wife's birthday party? I couldn't just crash it like that," I said, but only because it seemed the polite thing to say.

He paused, like he'd lost track of the conversation. "Not at all. We'd love for you to join us."

While I debated my decision, one battered emotion, long ignored and left for dead, surfaced: a sliver of hope.

Becca exited the dressing room with an armload of clothes. "Huge score! Did you know this dress is Valentino? Oh, hey, Mr. Solomon."

"Hello, Becca." His smile wavered.

She looked from him to me, sighed and rolled her eyes, sure I was sucking up to our teacher.

"I'm going to go pay." Becca left for the register.

"I've got to drive Becca home, but I can meet any other time. Pretty much whenever you want." Desperation practically oozed from my pores and I didn't care.

"How about tomorrow?"

"Yes!"

"We'll talk more after class, then." Solomon reached into his coat pocket and pulled out a stack of metal bracelets.

"I nearly forgot. I was out for a walk and found these at the bottom of your hill. Didn't you have bracelets like this? I thought they might have fallen out of your school bag."

"Yeah, those are mine." When I reached for them, he pulled back.

"Ah, we'll know they're yours if they fit," he teased.

A niggling voice in the back of my mind was trying to formulate a question. I ignored it, took the bracelets, and slid them onto my arms. Their weight was comfortable and familiar.

"See?" I laughed. "Told you so. Thanks."

"Anything for a gifted friend."

As Solomon considered the space between us—maybe he was going to give me a friendly hug—Becca breezed in front of him.

"Can I borrow your credit card? Mine's not going through," she asked.

"I only have cash, but yeah." And then, "I gotta go, Mr. Solomon. Tomorrow?"

"I look forward to it." He strolled out of the store.

"What was that all about?" Becca asked on our way to the register.

"Just school stuff."

What a day this had been! First I wiped out Raquelle's incriminating video of me and now I was on the verge of meeting my new tribe. Right here in my own city. I'd bet my life they knew about the factions, too. They might know whether or not Mr. Crane was dangerous. Or maybe they didn't know about him yet. Maybe I'd be giving them new information they could use to keep us safe. I basked in the great first impression I'd make. But not until tomorrow. I felt a pang of regret at passing up the opportunity to meet Solomon's friends that night. What was I waiting for?

While I dug out the cash for Becca, I scoured the outside of the store for our teacher. I fidgeted while the cashier bagged up the dress. Then Becca and I ducked beneath the half-closed security gate at the front of the store, and slipped onto the empty third floor. All the other stores were closed. Becca headed for the escalator.

"Becca, hold on a minute."

I peered over the railing at the main floor, three flights below. If I could spot Solomon and see where he exited, maybe I could still catch up with him. A handful of shoppers lingered. Solomon wasn't one of them.

"Shoot," I said.

"Are you looking for Solomon? 'Cause he's over there."

Directly across from us in the circular atrium, Solomon was looking in a store window. He didn't have a shopping bag. He must not have found a gift for his wife.

I held my car keys out to Becca. "Can you drive my car home? There's this birthday party for his wife and he said I might know some of the people. It's just around the corner."

"Seriously?"

"I know it's weird, but they're friends of Kimber's and I said I'd go down and say 'hi,'" I lied. "I'll get a ride home."

Becca narrowed her eyes and shook her head, perturbed. "One of these days, will you please tell me what's going on?"

I gave her a sheepish smile and dropped the keys into her hand. "Thanks."

"Yeah, yeah." She waved back at me and got on the escalator.

I jogged along the curve of the atrium railing to catch Solomon before I lost him again. Despite the giddiness rising in my chest, that niggling voice was back. It sifted through the conversation I'd just had with him. Hooked on a word he'd said. Then another. As I hurried toward him, the voice came through loud and clear. *How does he know where you live?*

There were plenty of good reasons. School records. Maybe he lived in my area. But none of them felt right.

"Mr. Solomon," I called out.

He turned, and I slowed to a walk. I smiled and waved. My eyes landed on his face, then his body. My smile dropped away.

Solomon's image was transparent. I could see right through him and into the store behind. A dense cloak of hatred, envy, and disgust slammed into me. Foul with viciousness, Solomon's malignant aura hit me with such force, I grew dizzy.

"Did you change your mind, Echo?" His yellow teeth bared into a grin. "Everyone will be delighted to finally meet you."

I stared at him in shock, struggling to reconcile the horrific energy coming off my kind teacher.

"Mr. Solomon?" my voice quaked.

Bruises stained his face and neck. The pocks on his cheeks were raw and crusted. Solomon glanced down at his transparent arm. He laughed, sharp and brittle.

"There's nothing to fear. Come, we don't want to miss the festivities." He took a step toward me. I turned and ran.

I made it ten feet before a vice-like pressure gripped my forehead. The intensity weakened my legs and forced me to stop. I cried out in pain. He took a few tentative strides toward me. His hand clenched the air in front of him, claw-like, as though he were squeezing the life out of a small animal. A spasm shot through my skull.

"Stay away from me." I tried to yell but could barely speak. Incredibly, the pain eased up.

He circled wide, his eyes traveling over my body as though appreciating me from every angle. "You blended in so well with your classmates," he said. "At first, I thought the gifted one might be Becca or even that deplorable Raquelle. It was you the whole time. I'm astounded that I missed it. I can feel you so clearly now."

Solomon waved my aura to him like he was taking in the smell of the ocean. He let out a lascivious moan. The transparent edges of his body sharpened and his bruised skin renewed itself. "So fresh and pure. So untainted."

The malicious desire coming off him sent terror through my limbs.

"I understand now why that McCabe boy was coming here. You must be incredibly powerful for him to travel all this way. All the better for us."

"Connor?" I whispered. How did he know about Connor?

"And the things he must have taught you. Tell me, what did he expect you to do with so much power? What could you, a mere girl, accomplish in this primitive world?"

My battered heart trembled. He was right. Connor didn't teach me how to thrive in my world. He'd only taught me how to survive, how to defend myself in a situation like this. Or he'd tried to. Flight was my best option now, but the pain searing into my head was overwhelming.

Solomon took a step closer, watching me carefully. "If he were smart, he would have taken you to West Region. But, your talent would have been wasted there, too. I think the boy knew that. He stopped training you, didn't he?"

I moved my mouth to speak but could only groan. Solomon read the flicker of anguish in my expression. "Ah, he did leave you here. Not a wise political decision, but in a time of war, we feast on our enemy's stupidity." His eyes gleamed. "You were born with power for a reason, my girl. You belong where your ability will reign supreme. We're going to a place where you will be treated like a queen."

He extended his hand.

I struggled to understand what he was talking about. "Stay away from me," my voice rattled.

He clawed at the air again, his grip tightening, and black dots danced across my vision. This was what happened to the murder victims, the psychics, the medium. And Ryan. When they refused to cooperate with Solomon, he'd psychically punched a hole in their skulls. But Solomon hadn't been looking for them. When he discovered that they were limited in their power, he'd killed them and left them on the street. In the river.

The whole time, Solomon had been searching for me. He intended to take me alive, to the faction leader, wherever that was.

"If I don't show up at home tonight, my parents will call the police. My dad will find me no matter where you take me," I croaked.

"Not where we're going. Your existence in this time will be nothing but a memory."

"This time?" My head swirled.

"East Region, my girl."

Panic crashed through me. "No," I whispered.

"Your ability is wasted in this century. Even the factions in your time are rudimentary compared to us."

"No… no." This couldn't be happening. I shook my head violently, despite the excruciating pain.

"You were meant for great things, and what greater way to leave a legacy than to reunite two regions into one country? And when the country is whole again, East Region will rule it.

It won't be that different from your world. Those who deserve power will have it. The rest of the people exist only to serve."

"You're going to use me to hurt West Region?"

"People only get hurt when they resist. Which someone always does," he grinned.

"You're disgusting. You liked hurting those girls and Ryan. You killed them, and you liked it."

"Don't look at me like that. You will never know your true power until you've met your dark side. When you do, your thirst will become insatiable. You'll find out for yourself. We're going to take that beautiful journey together, Echo."

Solomon eased closer, his hand still extended. "Take my hand. Everyone will be so thrilled to meet you."

As he eased closer, it all clicked into place. East Region must also have a portal. He needed to grab me so that we could transport together. I scrambled away.

"Tsk tsk. You're making this harder than it needs to be," he scolded.

He clawed the air again. An agonizing spike drove into the soft tissue of my brain. My mouth widened in a silent scream. My vision blurred and darkness closed in. I went blind.

CHAPTER 38

"**O**h my God! Oh my God! What happened? I can't see!" I was barely able to whisper my terror. I threw my arms up in defense, expecting Solomon's hand to clamp down on my shoulder any second. His aura seemed to come from every direction. I pricked my ears and picked up the squeak of his shoes edging closer, directly in front of me. But then I heard him closing in from the side. He was circling, testing, never approaching more than a few inches at a time.

Why was he being so cautious? The answer hit like a ton of bricks. He was afraid of me.

"Sshh. It will all be over soon, and you will start a glorious new life." His voice came from my left. Then, the sole of his shoe squeaked on my right.

"You'll give me anything I want if I go with you?" I whimpered.

"You'll have everything you dreamed of and more."

"You'll teach me," I wrenched out the words, "to be more powerful than anyone in West Region?"

"Yes, oh yes."

"Okay." My voice shook, nearly inaudible. "I'll go," I said, louder. "Just please, please stop hurting me."

"That's my girl."

Just as I'd hoped, the pressure relaxed on my forehead. The jagged pain eased. Keeping my hand close, I raised it in a gesture of peace. "I'll do whatever you want."

Victory flooded Solomon's aura and spilled over me from behind. That was my cue. I kicked myself around until I felt that sickening presence on my face. I thrust my palm between us, focused every remaining ounce of energy through my arm until my palm flared with heat. I heard a snap, and my hand crackled. Solomon bellowed, and I heard a dull thud. The vice grip released.

The blackness cleared instantly and my surroundings came into focus. I must have hit him square on because he was getting up off the floor, twenty feet away. His thin lips pulled back and he let out a primal sound. Fury rolled off him.

"That tactic will come in handy when you're convincing President McCabe to surrender. Perhaps we'll have you use it on his son first."

This time, when I raised my hand against him, I watched the hot white bullet leave my palm and nail him in the center of his chest. He wobbled but stood firm. My stomach fell. I'd ripped steel lampposts in half without even trying. Why wasn't I able to destroy Solomon?

He took a wary step toward me and I crab walked backwards. My bracelets clinked against the floor. The bracelets! I yanked two of them off while Solomon calculated the distance between us. Energy surged into my arms.

"We won't have any of that," he said. With a flick of his wrist, he sent me sprawling across the floor. I slammed into the atrium railing and heard my ribs snap. He closed in with long, fast strides. I struggled to my feet and threw a bolt of light at him. A loud *crack* echoed through the mall as Solomon deflected it. The shock wave hit us both. He grunted from the impact and his body was thrown toward the wall. I screamed as the shock wave threw me backward over the railing.

Time really does slow when death seems imminent. I flailed, airborne long enough to catch glimpses of my life: Becca, as she reached the bottom floor and searched for the source of the scream; the few remaining shoppers shrieking as they watched a girl about to plummet three stories to her death; Connor's face the last time he twirled me on the dance floor.

Gravity took over, and I fell. My arms thrashed, in search of something solid. By some miracle, my fingers latched onto the bottom rung of the railing. The rest of me yanked to a stop and the tendons in my arm snapped taut. Three stories above the atrium floor, my body swayed.

Panic stole my ability to blink, breathe, act.

"Echo!" Becca ran back up the escalator, her screams for help carrying through the atrium and rattling me back to life.

I knew all I needed to do was levitate, just enough to take me to safety before Solomon got to me, but the remaining bracelets sapped whatever power wasn't paralyzed by fear. If I let go, I'd drop like a rock.

Any moment now, he would grab my wrist and drag me through his portal. I'd never see my family again. East Region would try to force me to do horrendous things to innocent people. Even if I refused, what would I have to endure before they decided to kill me?

Above me, I heard a footstep, followed by a dragging sound. Solomon moaned. "Stupid child. You'll pay for this." Spit clogged his throat and he moaned again. He couldn't be more than a few feet away from the railing. Gruesome tentacles of energy reached over the ledge, played along my windpipe. I jerked my head in a futile effort to escape it.

"No," I scream-whispered. The movement made my body swing.

The tentacles settled on my throat. They squeezed my airway, and I was forced to hold still. Solomon wasn't taking any chances. He was going to subdue me until he could make contact with me. Then it would be all over.

There was only one way to avoid that ugly chain of events. I couldn't let him take me alive. I had to do whatever it took to get away from him, and there was only one direction to go. Down.

Blood pounded in my ears. Sheer terror kept my hand clamped to the ledge. My body ached.

Just let go, I urged. And then all I could think about was Connor. How he had tried so hard to protect me. The risks he'd taken. *You've already let him down,* I thought. *Just. Let. Go.*

Sweat dampened my fingers. My arm shook violently. A shadow passed over me and I heard a hoarse animal sound, part growl, part groan, too close to my ear.

"Please, no," I whimpered and closed my eyes. I let go of the railing. The grip on my throat released. I screamed.

My free-fall lasted all of two seconds, and then a hand clasped my wrist.

"Let me go!" I lashed out, prepared to fight to the death.

In one sweeping motion, I was lifted over the railing. I raised my palm and turned to attack my enemy. My hand was batted to the side, and I found myself face to face with Connor.

With one arm, he swept me behind him and pressed me protectively into his back. I caught a glimpse of his cold, merciless eyes before he turned to face our attacker.

Solomon was rising to his feet, leaning heavily on one leg. The other hung broken and mangled. His lip curled into pure hatred as he flung a light bolt at Connor's head. Connor dodged to the left but with me behind him, he couldn't go far. A fragment caught him in the forehead.

Solomon shot at us again. Connor retaliated with a bolt of blue light. The two bolts clashed in an explosion of fire and sparks that flattened my teacher.

Still, Solomon rose. Connor made a fist and energetically punched him backward into the marble wall. A chunk of marble broke away and smashed to the floor. Solomon crumpled on top of it. The back of his head was caved in from the impact. His legs tangled at an odd angle. A pool of blood spilled around him.

Connor's voice eased me out of my stupor. I didn't know what he said, but he was feeling my limbs and running his hands down my face and neck. I yelped when he prodded my broken ribs.

"Can you walk?" I heard him say.

I nodded. A red gash ran north from his eyebrow to his hairline. "You're bleeding," I said.

He wiped away the blood with his sleeve. The trickle started up again.

Becca sprinted toward us, a small group of shoppers close on her heels.

"Oh no." I glanced toward Solomon's body, wondering how we'd explain the bloody evidence of the fight, but he was gone. His blood was gone. The chunk of broken marble was the only clue that anything out of the ordinary had happened.

Connor's jaw clenched. "They pulled him back," he said.

Becca grabbed me in a hug. I let out a soft cry, and she let go. She saw my arm clutched against my ribs.

"It's just a bruise," I said in the most unconvincing role of my life.

The rest of the shoppers looked at us, puzzled. Becca summed it up for everyone. "What the hell just happened?"

"I guess I leaned over too far."

"You just *fell* over the railing?"

I nodded.

"Why didn't Mr. Solomon help you?"

"He must have left. He never even saw me." Becca's jaw dropped at the audacity of my thin story. Then she noticed Connor.

"When did you get here?" she asked, confusion adding to her disbelief.

He didn't answer. Instead, he pulled me into him and kissed my hair. The electricity beneath his skin, usually gentle, pulsed with such ferocity, it felt like nonstop static shock. I pulled away.

"Echo," he whispered. The strain in his expression was agonizing, but inside, I turned to stone. Not even the emotions colliding on his face–worry and relief and pleading—softened it. He'd saved my life—again—and that was enough compensation for ripping my heart to shreds. We were back at a clean slate, free of botched expectations and promises about things that we wanted to be possible, but never would be. Not in this lifetime.

Someone gave Connor a handkerchief to sop the blood that now ran down his temple and onto his cheek. Then, the onlookers who had come to my rescue left. Becca nodded toward the two security guards riding up the escalator.

"Mall cops to the rescue," she said. "Time to get out of here."

CHAPTER 39

To avoid mall security, Becca led us past the AT&T store and into the cavernous bowels of the building, a route she used to take when she worked at Rings N Things during the summer. Then she drove us home.

In the back seat, Connor wrapped me in a blanket and held me close. At first, I pulled away, but I was so exhausted, I reluctantly sank into him. A strained silence filled the car.

Outside the rain-streaked windows, the city was dark and ominous. Every shadow carried a new threat. Rain-soaked pedestrians made me want to curl into a ball as they ran toward, and then past, our car. I recoiled at a honking horn. Connor looped his arm around me so that I was cocooned in his heat. He breathed into my hair, planting kisses on the top of my head. I was afraid he'd start talking, would try to apologize for his absence and then line up excuses for why he stayed away. To his credit, he didn't utter a word.

Becca parked in our garage and gave me a long, troubled look before walking home. I knew my reluctance to share the truth with her had tested the bounds of our friendship, possibly for the last time.

The second Becca was out of earshot, Connor peppered me with questions so fast I had no chance to answer. I cut him off. "Solomon was going to take me to East Region," I sputtered. "He was going to—"

"I know what he was going to do," Connor growled. "He's one of the Imperators, one of the leaders that are trying to overtake West Region."

My jaw dropped. "Why didn't you tell me this could happen?" I demanded. "All you ever warned me about were the factions here."

"Because I didn't know they had the capability to get here and I still don't know how Solomon did," Connor snapped. "How did he know about your ability? Was he following you?"

"He's my Physics teacher."

Connor's tone was livid. "He's *what*? For how long?"

"Beginning of October?"

He pressed his eyes closed and spoke with forced calm. "Right after my first trip here."

I knew what he was thinking, that he had somehow led Solomon to me. The timing made sense. I searched my memory, intent on denying this possibility, but I couldn't. Connor's face went dark. He paced the garage. For the first time, I felt the full force of his aura, and its intensity frightened me.

"Solomon might have picked up on your energy trail, like I did. Once he got here, he would have tried homing in on you. He wouldn't have been very good at it. The Imperators don't have much power of their own. Which explains why he got it wrong and killed those other girls. They weren't the one he was looking for," he hissed.

I began to see, with frightening clarity, the way Solomon had tried to track me. The gifted women were killed near the warehouse where Connor and I practiced. I knew now that the mysterious person in the library was Solomon. He must have had a hunch and tried to check me out while my guard was down. He'd done it in class, too, but he hadn't gotten anywhere because I'd kept my aura clamped down.

I clutched my stomach. "Omigod. Ryan."

"What?"

"He was a boy from my school. I bumped into Ryan at the mall, and…and maybe my aura flooded all over him. He disappeared that same day, and they found his body in the river, with his forehead punched in. Can that happen? Did Solomon pick up my energy on him? Is he dead because of me?"

"Nobody died because of you!" Connor grabbed me by the shoulders. "Echo, look at me." I straightened until we were eye to eye. Connor jabbed his finger against his chest. "If anyone's to blame, it's me. Solomon was here the whole time and I should have been able to sense him. How did I miss this?"

"I saw him almost every day. I should have been able to read him."

"Don't be so hard on yourself. You're still learning, and he probably put all his energy into hiding from us. I doubt he adapted well, which is why it took him so long to identify you."

I braced myself against the door. "They can still come back for me, can't they?"

Connor gathered me in his arms before I could protest. I waited for him to tell me I was safe from the Imperators. Instead, we stood quietly while the rain battered the garage roof.

The door opened and Kimber rushed out. Her face was drawn.

"Echo, I didn't know you were back. Oh. Connor." She was trembling so hard the keys jangled in her hand. "Mr. Crane's in the hospital. That…that *maniac* who's been murdering people tried to kill him."

"How do they know? Does he have the same head injury as the women who died?" Connor asked.

"Yes," she stammered.

"Do you want me to come with you?" I asked Kimber. She didn't look together enough to drive to the hospital. Not that I was in any better shape.

"No, it's getting late. You've got school tomorrow." She hurried to her car and was gone.

Connor and I exchanged a dark look. "Solomon," he said.

"Why would Solomon hurt him?"

Connor considered this. "If Mr. Crane is a member of a local faction, and I still think he is, then he and Solomon would have both been trying to get at you."

My stomach soured. "And Solomon won."

Everything Connor said made sense, especially given my recent run-ins with Mr. Crane. My entire body shuddered, close to total shutdown. Every bone ached, every muscle pinched with exhaustion. The full impact of my brush with death was setting in.

Connor's touch should have offered comfort against the physical and emotional trauma, but it had the opposite effect. Any minute now, he would say he needed to leave, and I'd be here, lost in the crushing traces he left behind. The urge to pull away overruled any solace I found in his warmth. I brushed off his embrace.

Life had been hard for him the past few weeks. Dark circles smudged beneath his eyes told of countless sleepless nights. The blue flecks in his irises were dull. His hair stuck out, unkempt and overgrown. What I was about to do seemed cruel, but drawing this out was the equivalent of stretching a rubber band to its breaking point—the further you pulled, the harder the sting when it finally broke.

"Thank you for saving my life," I said. I walked inside the house and swung the door closed.

Connor barred the door with his arm. "I'm not leaving you alone tonight."

My eyebrows shot to my hairline. I'd been alone for weeks and that hadn't seemed to bother him. "Mr. Crane's in the hospital. Solomon's gone. I can take care of myself." This was frighteningly untrue.

"First of all, that's absurd. You're hurt and you can't defend yourself. And we need to talk."

"Talk? Now?"

"About why I wasn't here. You need to know what happened."

"You left me! That's what happened!"

For the second time that night, Connor's expression turned livid. "You think I would do that? After everything I've put you through?" He was yelling now. "The night of the dance, Carina and Jaxon were under my father's orders to take you home. I learned this when I got to his office. Then he forbade me to use the portal ever again. He instructed the Harden Center to bar me from the lab. I would have worked around that, but he would have sent me to the university early. I would have been hundreds of miles from the portal. I couldn't let that happen. It's the only link I have to you.

"But the second I sensed you were in danger tonight, I raced to the lab. There wasn't time to call Carina or Jaxon and beg for their help. I broke in and set the portal on autopilot. I had to make the jump myself."

"How did you know I was in trouble?"

"All the time we spent together made our connection stronger. I've felt everything since you left." His gaze dropped to the floor. "Your anger. Distrust. When Solomon attacked you, I felt your terror. I got to the portal and pictured you in my mind so that it would send me directly to you. When I materialized at the mall, I was going insane trying to figure out where you were. Then I saw you over the railing."

The blood drained from my face. While Connor was racing to my rescue, I was trying to fall to my death. I curled my fingers around his.

His eyes were wide, searching mine. "I never meant to hurt you."

"You're still banned from the portal. You'll go back and I'll never see you again," I said.

"I'm not going to let that happen."

"When your father finds out…" I shook my head. "I can't do this. Not again."

I tried to push the door closed, but I was weak against his force. Tears filled my eyes, threatening to pour.

"Please, at least let me look at your injuries," he said.

I dropped my head so he couldn't see the single tear escape and splatter on the tile.

"Echo. How are you going to explain the bruises?"

"What?"

I thought he was referring to the cuts on my face until I glimpsed my reflection in the entryway mirror. My forehead was swelling where Solomon had gripped me. The damage was just as real as if he'd hit my forehead with a hammer. Greenish marks were forming above my brows. The color bled into the hollows around my lids. Before the night was through, I'd have two black eyes. Defeated, I released the door and dragged myself upstairs. Connor followed quietly.

In my bedroom, he inspected my injuries with a feather-light touch. Each time he grazed my skin, I flinched.

"It's bad, huh?" he asked.

I cast my eyes anywhere but at him. The physical pain, I could handle. Even having him here in my room, where the memories welled up out of the floorboards and cloaked me like a funeral shawl, I could deal with that. What threw me off balance were the irrational thoughts creeping in, the returning illusions that he and I maybe had a future together, the series of *what ifs* racing through my head.

"Should we do this?" he asked.

Countless possibilities jetted through my mind before I realized he was talking about my injuries. "Right. Let's get started." I swallowed, remembering how Tito had yelped when Connor repaired his mangled legs. "Is it going to hurt?"

Connor squinted in empathy. "It could hurt quite a lot."

I clutched handfuls of my comforter and he placed his fingers over the marks. He closed his eyes, and his breathing slowed. His head nodded slowly, up and down.

Beneath his touch, I was sure my head would split wide open. "It hurts," I said.

Connor pressed his eyes tighter. "I'm sorry. Almost there."

Short sobs escaped between my gritted teeth. Blood seemed to flood my eyeballs, and they threatened to burst.

"Connor," I tried to yell. My hands flew to his and I tried to pry them off me. The compression eased and was replaced by a soothing coolness.

He opened his eyes and turned me to face the mirror. "Better?"

Miraculously, not a single bruise marred my fair skin.

"That was awful," I croaked.

Connor gave a weak smile. "Let me know when you're ready to do your ribs."

"Let's just get it over with. Will it hurt worse? Wait. I don't want to know. Just do it."

Connor lifted my shirt and looked at the green bruise forming over the swollen knot on my side. He tried to hide his reaction, but I could tell this was not going to be fun. I was right. Healing my ribs was ten times worse. I passed out from the pain.

CHAPTER 40

When I came to, my head was cradled in Connor's lap.

"There was more damage than I thought." He stroked my hair slowly, from the top of my head to where it flared across my back. "You've got amazing pain tolerance."

Carefully, I pressed against my ribcage. Then I sat up and gingerly bent to the side. I was as good as new.

"Unbelievable," I said. How had I ever thought Connor would do anything to hurt me? If what he said was true, that he'd been able to feel everything I was going through in the past weeks, then he'd felt my hatred and anger, my accusations of betrayal. Worst of all, he'd been powerless to convince me otherwise.

I was at a loss for what to say, so I turned to the cut over his eyebrow. The bleeding had stopped, but the wound looked deep. "Aren't you going to fix your cut?"

"Doesn't work that way. I need someone else to do it." Connor grabbed one of the pillows off my bed and moved to my desk chair. He pushed the chair against the wall, sat down, and rested the pillow between his head and the wall.

"What are you doing?"

"I'm staying here tonight. I don't want to take any chances now that East Region knows about you."

My hands flew up. "And then what? What about the next night, and the one after that? You can't protect me forever."

"Says who?"

"For starters, your dad."

"Nothing has been set in stone."

"I think it has," I said, remembering Manny's words. "This lifetime, we were never supposed to find each other. If we were, your dad would have welcomed me into West Region or allowed you to stay here. It couldn't be more obvious, Connor. We're not meant to be together. Not yet."

"That's what you want? For me to leave and hope we'll bump into each other in, what, another thousand years?"

"No! What I want is to leave with you right now and start my life in West Region. I want to not feel like a freak when I inadvertently make something fly across the room. I want to train with people like me and then maybe someday teach others, and be with you through all of it. But that's never going to happen, and it kills me to face that fact. And then you have the audacity to ask 'do I not want to see you for another thousand years,' and I wonder if you have *any clue* how much I love you?"

Connor crossed the room in two long strides and answered with the most passionate kiss of my life. He held my face in his hands and crashed his mouth onto mine as if he'd never get enough. His tongue parted my lips, and mine reached out to meet his. I slid across his teeth, and melted into his velvety warmth. The hand cupping my face trailed down my neck and back, leaving a delicious tingling where our skin met. His mouth moved over mine, hungrily, and I pressed into him harder.

An unfamiliar fire lit inside me, and my body began acting without any guidance from my brain. Driven by a desperation I'd never felt before, I pulled Connor's t-shirt over his head. Connor slid my shirt off and our kissing grew more heated. My palms dampened and when I touched him, the electric sensation buzzed through the tenderest parts of my body. Everything happened so fast, I lost the ability to think.

His fingers were fumbling with the button on my jeans when he abruptly stopped. He leaned back on his arms, his breaths coming short and forceful. He trained his eyes on the ceiling until the rising of his chest deepened and slowed, until the spell that overtook us was broken.

Connor looked at me with what I could only describe as apology. "I don't want to do this without knowing what happens next," he said. "I can't do that to you."

I nodded. Our sense of urgency had fogged my judgment, and I wasn't sure this was a good idea. I wanted him in that way, but not like this. Not as our final, farewell moment. That would kill me for sure.

"We can always wait until the next lifetime," I joked.

"God, I hope not."

We pulled our shirts on. I lay in his arms, basking in a peace that I hadn't felt in weeks.

Connor was the one to break the silence. "I don't want to leave you again."

"I've learned how to take care of myself."

"It's not about that. I don't need West Region. I don't need to rule over a million people."

"How can you say that? You'd be giving up everything."

"If I went back without you, I'd *lose* everything."

If it were possible, I collapsed deeper into his arms.

"I'll make a few short trips back to learn what I can about Solomon and how he got through the portal, but otherwise, I don't want to leave your side."

"Where are you going to live?"

"Think Kimber would rent me a room?" he asked half-jokingly.

"Doubtful," I said.

"I'll figure something out."

"What about your body holding up here?" My hand rode down his hard, flat stomach and curled onto the waistband of his jeans. My safety meant nothing if his body was going to fail.

"I acclimated just fine when I was coming here before. It just took a while. I can do it again."

"You'd have to enroll in my school," I said, loving and at the same time super cautious about the direction this was going.

"Good. Then I can check out the rest of your teachers."

"I don't think we need to worry about them. They've all been there since before I moved to Portland. And do you really want to take a physics class that's outdated by a century?"

"Are you trying to talk me out of this?" he asked.

"I should be, but no. None of this makes sense, but it's what I've always wanted." Second to living this same life in West Region, anyway.

Connor rolled onto one side. "I almost forgot." He reached into his front pocket and pulled out a device, smaller than a deck of cards.

"What's that?"

"My communication thingy," he teased. "I forgot to leave it in the lab."

He slid this into his back pocket and dug into the front one again. He opened his hand to reveal my coin necklace.

My face lit. "You had it the whole time." Now I remembered that he'd held onto it while I tried on Manny's dresses. Thank goodness, or this would have ended up in the river, too.

We curled into each other, our heads sharing the pillow. Connor fell asleep with his arm firmly around my waist. I lay awake, listening to his breath fall in and out and squeezing his hand when he let out a frightened moan. A nightmare stalked him in his sleep, causing him to kick and jerk his elbows and yell out. I felt useless, unable to protect him from whatever haunted him, the way he had protected me from so many of my demons.

In the dark of night, the coming day loomed with uncertainty. I allowed myself to think what we'd do when the sun rose, how we'd set up Connor's new life here. I refused to think any further ahead than that. Daylight would come too soon and with it, too many unanswered questions. I wanted to stay curved against him, suspended in this perfect vignette in time.

The sky changed from pitch to charcoal grey, telling me the sun had risen somewhere behind the thick cloud cover. Connor was still deep asleep and I was happily pinned under his arm.

In the hazy light of dawn, my room came into shape. I decided I was far more tired than I realized when my eyes could no longer focus on my surroundings. Not that far in front of me, the lines shaping my desk began to blur. I rubbed my eyes and propped them open again. I refused to sleep through one minute of the passing night.

A couple of hard blinks chased the sleep from my eyes, but the blurring intensified near my desk. The air around it wavered and shimmered into human form. Every cell in my body went on red alert. Solomon had been in a pool of his own blood just a few hours ago. How could he have recovered?

I moved to wake Connor when the form took an unexpected shape. Mr. McCabe fizzled to life. Even in the half-light, I recognized the panic in his expression, the kind a dad gets when his child has gone missing. When he saw Connor asleep next to me, his spine relaxed. He let out a long exhale. His chin jutted as he gathered his composure. His posture regained, Connor's dad was a formidable sight.

"Never in the history of our family has an outsider brought so much trouble," Mr. McCabe finally said.

I held fast under Connor's arm, less for protection than as a statement of determination. Connor wanted to be here. I wanted him here and unlike my failed clash against Solomon, I was prepared to fight this battle.

"Connor saved my life last night."

This didn't impress Mr. McCabe the way I'd intended. He scanned my room, tiny in comparison to even the smallest in his mansion, and then rested his sight on the world beyond my window.

"Wake up my son," he said quietly.

Connor was already stirring. When he saw his father, he sat bolt upright.

"West Region security has been looking for you," Mr. McCabe said.

"I've only been gone overnight."

"It's been a very long night." His dad stepped closer. Fatigue ringed his eyes.

"I'm sorry you were worried, but I'm fine," Connor said.

"I see that. I've left word with your school that you'll be out today. We have a series of security meetings, and I want you to attend all of them."

Connor swung his legs to the floor. "Please send my regrets to the Council. I won't be attending the meetings."

"And why not?"

Connor swallowed. "I'm resigning my future position as leader of West Region. I'm staying here. With Echo."

Mr. McCabe let out a weary laugh. "You are, are you? Well, far be it for me to interfere in your plans. I'll be sure to alert the Council that you're relocating. I suppose you think you can create a life in this barbaric environment?"

"That's the decision you've made."

"*My decision*?" Mr. McCabe spat.

"If you had any idea how powerful Echo is, you'd want her in West Region. With us."

I held back a smile at this unexpected declaration.

"We've had this conversation, Connor."

"That's why I've decided to stay."

Mr. McCabe's temper rose. "And when your body fails, I suppose you'll come running home?"

"I can move back and forth until I completely assimilate. It's been done before. I saw it in the portal records, that people have been able to stay long-term."

This was the first I'd heard of this. "For how long?" I asked.

Mr. McCabe ignored me. "You're right. It has worked in the past, but only because the portal remained open the entire time."

"What are you saying?" Connor's voice was surprisingly harsh.

"The portal has been compromised, Connor. East Region hacked into a branch of it. Solomon was here, wasn't he?" It was more a statement than a question. "Transported through a connection to our portal. The news we're getting from the East is that Solomon is dead, and you are responsible. East Region has put a bounty on you."

Connor paled. "He was after Echo."

"I know why he was here! And why you are here, and why the security of our region is at stake more than ever." Mr.

McCabe's eyes burned into me. "She is not worth the safety of an entire nation. Or my son's life. Which is why you are returning to West Region, *now*, and we are shutting down the portal permanently."

My head jerked between Connor and his dad. "Mr. McCabe…" I pleaded.

Connor scrambled to his feet. "But, sir…"

"You insisted on breaking every rule in the book by interfering in her time."

"Sir…"

"They could have assassinated you here!"

"I cannot leave her here!"

Mr. McCabe's voice lowered. "You can, and you will. You have thirty seconds." His form shimmered, faded and disappeared. I understood immediately what was happening.

"No!" Connor's eyes were wild. "He can't do this!"

Out of pure emotional self-defense, calm settled over me. I took Connor's hand. Precious seconds were ticking by.

"Don't. It's done," I said. "It's going to be okay. Everything is going to be okay." Tears clogged my throat.

Connor grabbed me in his arms and I clung to him. "If the portal is shut down, you'll be safe from East Region." His voice shook.

"Yes." I clenched my teeth against the building sobs.

"But never let your guard down," he said. "You have to fight for your life, Echo. Do you understand me?"

"Stop, please." I didn't want to hear anymore, not in the last few seconds of this lifetime together.

"Abilities like yours come once in a hundred years."

I nodded. My breaths became ragged.

The electric sensation that I had craved since I first touched Connor grew stronger. The portal locked onto him.

I dug my fingers into him. This couldn't be happening. We'd come so close.

Trembling, Connor released me and stepped back until only our fingertips touched.

"I'll always be waiting for you," he whispered.

"Me too."

His form glowed in a dazzling array of pale white light, and he began to fade. At the very last second, he withdrew his fingers from mine.

He was gone.

Continue reading for a

preview of the exciting sequel,

ECHO
INTO
DARKNESS

PROLOGUE

I felt like I was in a horror movie, the kind where I was locked in a room and the monsters kept multiplying until they surrounded me and my death was just a matter of time.

But it wasn't my life that was at stake. That, I could have accepted. It was your blood they shouted for. My beloved soulmate's. The most powerful person I had ever known.

When they turned on the light in your cell and I saw you through the one-way window, bruised and bleeding, it nearly broke me. I was thankful you couldn't see beyond the glass, couldn't see the fear building behind my eyes.

If you could, you would have watched me fight for your life with everything I had. You would have seen them laughing and cheering as if they were watching a sporting match, instead of a grisly duel where your life was the prize.

They were placing bets that I could not save you.

I was terrified they were right.

It was ironic that these monsters would test my strength, my ability to destroy beautiful things, when all the time they were tapping into the very depths of my love. That was the key to everything worth living for, wasn't it? The power of love to overcome the darkest of fears? It had to be.

While they shouted to see your blood spill, love was the one thing that pushed my paranormal gift beyond its boundaries. It was the key to keeping you alive.

If I lost this contest, then they would have to take my life, too. I'd push them so far they would have no choice. Then you and I would finally be free to live out our destiny, together.

CHAPTER 1

There's something about the week between Christmas and New Year's that I've always loved. Presents have been opened and school is still out for winter break. The whole neighborhood smells like Christmas trees. Holiday lights brighten up every block. It's one big joy-to-the-world fest while everyone rides high on eggnog and sugar cookies.

I blew warm air on my hands and thought maybe I could enjoy the crisp winter night if I dropped the sarcasm. This was my first trip out of the house since the start of holiday break, and let's face it, no way would I be walking through my neighborhood alone at night except my stepmom, Kimber, had handed me Tito's leash and ushered us both out the door.

Staying inside was safer, but Kimber didn't know how my life had dramatically changed during fall semester. She knew nothing about the incident at the mall, when Solomon, a man from Connor's time, had tried to kidnap me. She'd never found out about the night when I nearly fell three stories to my death.

If it were up to me, I would have forgotten that entire incident, including the part about Connor coming to my rescue. Would have pretended he hadn't left for good the next morning. Ignored the constant feeling of vulnerability, like a chill I couldn't shake even when I burrowed beneath the heaviest of blankets.

Connor could have put an end to that chill. I'd felt secure when he was with me, protecting me. Also, his body ran a little warmer than anyone else I'd hugged, and the electric stream beneath his skin, well, that made me warm in a very different way.

Now I hunkered into my fleece coat, on the lookout for some nondescript faction people who would seriously mess me up if they found me. Connor had known my life was in danger, but he hadn't been able to point the enemy out. He only knew that factions in my city were rounding up gifted people like me, and forcing them to use their abilities to commit violent crimes.

This faction was stationed somewhere in Portland. They lived in secrecy, running companies, raising families, blending into society. This was fertile ground for my recent nightmares. I didn't know where these guys lived, what their names were, or how to find them. All I knew for certain was that my gifts— the telekinesis, the levitation, the whole crazy lot of it—put me in serious danger. I was walking around with a target on my back.

I shuddered and forced my attention back to the cheery atmosphere. The red and green lights decorating Becca's house across the street blinked, faded, and came on again, forming a snowflake pattern. The decorative electric reindeer at the end of the street bobbed up and down like they were excited to see me. I actually waved at them. That's what happened when you spent your entire winter vacation in self-imposed solitary confinement—you got desperate for friendship.

A couple of hardcore joggers ran by and I immediately clicked into aura-reading mode. I felt the damp heat of their determination, the clarity of their focus. They sprinted up the hill, giving no indication they saw me. I almost relaxed, but then I picked up another faint vibration in the air—something tentative and leaden. Just as quickly, it was gone.

I wrapped Tito's leash around my gloved hand and waited while he peed on everything that didn't move. My side ached a little bit, and I pressed my arm against my coat. Connor had healed my ribs after Solomon broke them, but they still nagged me when the weather got cold. I didn't mind. It was a sweet reminder that my soulmate existed out there somewhere. He had been gone for weeks but the sting of our last few seconds together had never faded. They never would. You didn't just forget about a supernatural guy with tropical green eyes who taught you how to levitate and push your hand through solid objects.

At the West Vista Bridge, I gave Tito a backward tug. My toes were numb, and he was shivering beneath his red and white Santa coat.

Tito strained toward the bridge and barked.

"Quiet, Tito. Come on, let's go home."

The West Vista Bridge spanned a ravine and highway, connecting my neighborhood to downtown Portland. Constructed entirely of molded cement, it resembled a relic from Gothic times, especially when the majority of its lights were burned out.

Tito's oversized Chihuahua ears twitched. A whimper came from somewhere on the bridge. A chill ran down my back when I realized the sound was human, not animal.

Tito pulled us down the sidewalk. There it was again, a broken sob, so short and soft that the night air seemed to steal the life from it.

Where was it coming from? Ahead of me, the entire stretch of sidewalk was empty, and beyond the railing? Nothing but a hundred-foot drop.

A rubber sole scuffed against concrete and I looked up. A few feet above my head a slender figure stood on the bridge railing and clung to the rough stone column.

"Omigod. What are you doing?" I asked.

The girl's mouth formed a surprised *O*. Her hair stuck out from under a striped knit cap and a reddish smear soiled one side of her blue nylon coat. My sixth sense told me the stain was blood. Hers. Her cheek pressed into the column, delicate features mottled by pale moonlight.

"Leave me alone," she whispered.

She turned her tear-streaked face to the drop-off. When her weight shifted, her nylon coat scraped against the stone like a scream.

"Wait! You can't do this!" I reached for my phone to call 911. It wasn't in my pocket.

"I don't have a choice." Tears garbled her words. "You don't know what I'm going through."

"It's not as bad as you think," I answered. It sounded horribly cliché, but what do you say in these situations? I scrambled for the right words. "Come down and talk. Tell me what's wrong."

The girl laid her haunted eyes on mine. My skin went taut and I felt my aura bend outward. Her energy prodded it, testing its strength. The hair on the back of my neck rose.

"You're gifted," she said. "You can levitate and move things with your mind."

Only another gifted person would know about my abilities without me telling them. Once, a few months back, I longed to share my truth with another gifted person, to shake the never-ending loneliness.

This wasn't an ordinary gifted girl, though. I had tucked my aura in tight to keep my paranormal abilities secret. This girl had identified me anyway. She was hiding hers, too, like she had been schooled in the uncommon art of auric camouflage.

She let her aura loose and the air between us pulsed. A humid, chemical taste clogged the back of my throat. Alarm pinched my stomach. I scooped Tito and took three long steps backward.

"You're in the faction," I choked.

The girl blinked at me, her eyes as big as an owl's. Searing guilt drifted off her energy field and collected in my chest. What had this girl done to make her feel this way, to make her teeter on the edge of death?

Something Connor had said came back to me. When gifted people were enslaved, they were expected to follow orders, no matter how hideous the demands. If they refused, the faction forced them, using any method necessary, including torture. I wasn't sure exactly what this girl had been through, but I could not abandon her.

"Please come down," I said. "Come down and we can talk."

"They made me do it." She panted, unable to catch her breath. She clenched her eyes. "I can still hear the screaming."

I had no clue what she was talking about, but played along. "You're right; they made you do it. They're responsible for what happened. Now come on down."

The girl sensed my uncertainty. "You think I'm crazy." Her attention latched onto Tito. She levitated him out of my arms.

"What are you doing?" I strapped my dog to my chest. "Leave him alone. I believe you, all right?"

Tears rolled down her face. "The lightning strike. I made it hit those people outside the movie theater. They never even did anything to deserve it."

"Oh my God," I said. "You did that?"

During winter in the Pacific Northwest, it rained for months on end, but lightning was extremely rare. So it was beyond freaky when, on a clear day last week, a bolt struck and killed six people while they waited in line to buy movie tickets.

"If I didn't do it, they were going to hurt me again." She wiped her nose on the back of her coat sleeve. That, too, was wet with a red stain.

"Are you bleeding?" I asked. "Did they do that to you?"
She nodded.

"Who are they? Tell me who did it." If this ended badly—and please, please don't let that happen—I would at least have something to take to the police.

Her jaw trembled. An odd thought went through my mind. She couldn't have been more than seventeen. My age. She turned away and faced the gaping blackness beyond the bridge.

"Wait!" In one swift movement, I set Tito on the sidewalk and clutched the girl's coat in both my hands. The fabric was slick between my cotton gloves. If she jumped, she would slip right out of my grasp.

A glimmer of recognition swelled in her aura. "I've felt you before," she said in a dreamy voice. "I know who you are." She seemed to look right through me. "*They've* felt you, too. They can sense you're in the city. They'll figure out who you are and come after you. You have everything they want."

A tremor knocked through my legs. "Who? You have to tell me who runs the faction."

Her gaze was fixed on a distant point. "They'll never stop using me. This is the only way out for any of us."

Then, as though she had a sudden change of heart, the girl extended her hand. Yes, thank God, I was finally getting through to her. I took it, thrilled that she was coming down. Instead, she leaned away, her weight pulling me onto the ledge with her.

"Jump with me. Before they get to you. It's the only way out," she repeated.

I ripped my hand away. This girl was seriously sick. "I'm going for help. Please wait for me. *Don't jump.*"

No sooner had I gathered up Tito than the strangest thing happened. The girl became bathed in white light, as if by the simple act of intense wishing, she had become a celestial being. After a few seconds, the glow fell away, casting her in darkness again and drawing our eyes to the highway below.

A car had stopped on the shoulder, and someone aimed a spotlight at the bridge. It skimmed the abutment on our left, drew toward the center, slowing at each section. The harsh light drifted across the columns and spindles and settled once again on the girl. Her arm shot up to shield her face.

"They found me," she wailed. She dropped to the sidewalk, knocked me to the pavement, and sprinted down the hill toward town. Her blue jacket faded into the inky night.

The spotlight kept pace but then lost her. Instead of going dark, it arced and dove, retracing the girl's steps to the center of the bridge. When it glared between the railing spindles, cutting my body into vertical stripes of shadow and light, I grabbed Tito and ran.

Buy

ECHO INTO DARKNESS

today at all major book retailers!

Acknowledgements

A very special thank you to my core readers,
Rachel Bennett, Stefan Feuerherdt
and Dirk Ohling. I love your feedback almost as much as
I love our meet-ups.

Maggie Feuerherdt, you should get extra credit in your
English class for the contributions you've made to the
character development. And thanks for your
help with the cover!

Thank you, Susan Gottfried, for the editing.

And Val Brook, for your endless support, your vision,
and your courage facing the factions, thank you.

About the Author

Skye Genaro graduated college with a degree in microbiology and has a background in market research in the technology sector. She left that predictable and stable world behind and dove into a more adventurous life that includes rock climbing, whitewater rafting, foreign travel and writing fiction for a living. Skye lives in the Pacific Northwest with her husband.

You can visit her online at http://skyegenaro.com/.

www.ingramcontent.com/pod-product-compliance
Lightning Source LLC
Chambersburg PA
CBHW072200130726
47910CB00011B/1712